AF612710

Other Books by Jenn Matthews

Reasons to Heal
The Words Shimmer
Hooked on You

Sing for my Baby

Jenn Matthews

Acknowledgements

So many people helped me with this book! For the pregnancy info, I'd like to thank Katie, Claire, Emma, Nikki, Jae, and Kitty. Jen F also helped with a lot of the midwife information—much appreciated. Thank you to the fabulous Marie, my sensitivity reader. Thank you to Trudy as well, for checking the AA process and info, and to all the other amazing people I know in recovery, without whom this story would not have been written.

Dedication

I'd like this book to be dedicated to my best friend, excellent ex-housemate, and mother of our four brilliant God children, Justine. Mate, you've been there for me so much over the years, and I'm eternally grateful. I'm still waiting for you and Scott to get hitched so I can be a bridesmaid for the FIFTH time, and throw you a banging hen do!

Chapter 1

Rosie Tanner placed a clean piece of toilet paper over the white plastic stick and sat on the closed toilet lid. She started her phone's stopwatch. One whole minute. Time to wait. She bounced her knee. Balling a fist wasn't sensible; relaxation was the key. That and wiggling the tension out of her fingers.

She took slow, long breaths. She continued to bob her knee.

Her phone pinging nearly made her slip onto the lino. A text from Charlie, sending her love. Should she call her? Charlie would be able to see the pregnancy test through video chat, and Rosie could break the news to her then. After three weeks of visualising blatocysts and dividing cells, had it all been in vain once again?

Closing her eyes for a breath, Rosie then shook her head. There was no one there to see, but she did it anyway. Somehow, it gave her courage. It was something she could do herself. She needed to get used to it. That was the plan. Everything alone.

Fifteen seconds to go.

Her phone showed a fake second hand. Were those even seconds? They seemed more like hours or even days.

It was time. She wasn't ready.

Rosie pressed her fist into her thigh and set her jaw. *Get a grip, Miss Tanner.* That's what six-year-old Iris would say. Iris had just moved into Year Two and was already her own woman.

One last look at her phone. One last thought about calling her big sister.

Rosie removed the tissue with a trembling hand. She blinked.

Surely that wasn't *two* blue lines?

She'd have to do another. It couldn't be right.

Rosie fumbled with the second test in the packet, then repeated the process.

There were definitely two blue lines on this one too. When she'd chosen the test, she had turned her nose up at the ones that said "pregnant" or "not pregnant." She didn't need the actual words. Surely she could use the handy key on the box? One line or two.

Should have bought one with the words. Something flipped inside Rosie's belly, a panic she'd read it wrong. She studied the box again, turning it over and over, wondering whether it said something else. No, two lines meant she was pregnant.

She blinked again. Her vision was clear. There were two lines on both tests. Numb, she took a photo of them, then placed her phone beside the sink. She rested her elbows on her knees and breathed.

I'm pregnant. I did it.

Joy built inside her and made her skin flush and her heart bulge. Her hand shook for a different reason—not nerves this time—and she grabbed her phone.

"Did you do it yet?" Charlie's voice was a few tones higher than usual, like a mistuned violin.

"Yeah." Rosie sat with her mouth open before realising she should give more information. "It was positive."

Silence. Then two squeals threatened to burst Rosie's eardrums.

She put the phone on speaker. "Ow. My ears, you guys!"

"Auntie Rosie, that's, *well*, excellent."

Rosie hadn't realised Chelsea had been listening. Charlie must be on speaker too. "Thanks, mate."

More giggling. Chelsea started an "I'm gonna be a cousin!" mantra.

Rosie rolled her eyes. "So, Chelsea's happy."

"I am too." Charlie's voice was warm. "I know you've been waiting for this. I know how much it means."

"Yeah."

Rosie disposed of the urine. She considered keeping the tests but shrugged. The result wouldn't change if she binned them, and she had the photo on her phone.

"It's…" She took a deep breath and stopped tidying. "Fifth time lucky, huh?"

"Totally." Charlie made a kissing sound. "I love you even if you are a pleb."

"Tell that gorgeous niece of mine to think good thoughts." A tiny speck of sadness tugged at Rosie. The memory of an unmoving bundle in her arms hit her. She swallowed it away. "It's not confirmed yet. There're still bloods to take. And I'm not telling anyone until I get to twenty-eight weeks, okay? Not even Mum and Dad."

Charlie's whine turned into a happy hum. "They're going to find out. You'll be past showing by then, and you told Mum the donor was due three weeks ago."

Rosie laughed. "True."

"She'll be at home, waiting for the call. And if you don't ring her by Monday, she'll probably turn up unannounced at school."

"Oh, goodness." Rosie pressed her fingers to her eyes. "Yeah, okay. I'll tell them. But no one else."

"Damn good job Chelsea doesn't go to your school. She'll have it all round your colleagues in six seconds flat."

The squealing mantra continued in the background. Could the neighbours hear? "Anyway, I need to go sort out a few things. Text the donor. Let him know we created life."

"Madness." Charlie sighed. "I'm so pleased, Rosie."

"Got to go. Love you."

"Love you."

Chapter 2

THE COIN WAS WARM IN Amber Kingsley's palm. Its presence was powerful, a reminder of what she had achieved. The fluttering in her chest made her smile. *One whole year. I never thought I'd manage it.*

Various people gave her thumbs-up as they slipped out the door of the church hall. Friday night was always a good meeting—that was why she'd chosen it as her home group. A good variety of people: ages, genders, lengths of sobriety. Some meetings she had been to had been moan fests where nothing was really achieved or learned.

She hung around for a few minutes, waving to those who were leaving. The coin sat happily in her jacket pocket.

Jilly, her landlady and replacement aunt, was one of the last to leave. She gave Amber the biggest hug and rubbed her shoulder as she pulled away. "See you back at home?" Her clear alto made Amber smile.

"Of course. I'll walk Nico when I get back, if you like."

"Did it this morning. He's good until tomorrow." Jilly glanced at the sky. "Should be okay to walk home?"

"I'm just going to say goodbye to Harry. Want to arrange a stables meet-up." Amber patted the camera hung on its strap around her neck. "Take some more shots of that gorgeous horse of his."

Jilly chuckled. "I think you're in love."

"Might be." Amber shrugged. "Might walk along the seafront tonight and get some sunset shots too."

After kissing her cheek, Jilly strode away, her long blonde hair sweeping behind her. Jilly had her car, and she wasn't one to walk around much outside of her working hours. But Amber liked the walk home—it wasn't far, and September evenings meant it wasn't too dark.

When Harry stepped out, a grin lit up his entire face. "I'm so proud of you."

Amber pushed up her shoulders. "Thank you."

"Fancy doing step one together next week? Admit we're powerless to our affliction? Look at how unmanageable our lives used to be?" He made it sound like a fun activity.

"'Course. In exchange, I expect access to the woman in your life for some photos."

Harry frowned. "My mother?"

"Your beautiful horse, Florence, you daft thing." She poked his arm. "Reckon she's free next Saturday?"

"Reckon she is. Need to take her for a proper ride. Can't this week though." His eyebrows furrowed. "Matthew's taking me to the cinema."

"So nice you guys can still be romantic." Amber sent him an affectionate look at the mention of his boyfriend. "Florence will get jealous."

"She forgives me if I take her an apple or two."

Amber indicated her camera. "You go on. I'm going to catch the sunset."

"Should be a nice one tonight. Clear." A last hug and he left.

She leant against the wall next to the front door, checking for missed calls and messages on her mobile. A bit of social media, just for the few minutes she wanted to wait, to take note before the walk home.

Someone knocked into her, folders and papers flying all over the place.

Amber braced a hand against her camera, making sure it didn't swing around, as she stooped to help. "Gosh, you okay?"

"I'm so sorry!" A woman with brown hair, wearing a black leather jacket, crouched next to her. She swept up the folders she'd spilled onto the concrete.

Amber grabbed a few, then stood, neatening them into a pile. "You're in a hurry." Had she intended on coming to the meeting? She was over an hour late.

"Yeah. Choir starts in like three minutes." She stood but wobbled. Her eyes glazed over for a second.

Amber put a hand out. "You okay?"

The woman closed her eyes and took in a few deep breaths before giving Amber a dazzling smile. "'Course." She wiped a hand over her face. Her make-up was immaculate: dark smoky eyes with a touch of silver sparkle. Her hair was messy, but Amber reckoned she'd spent a while on it. "Tell me you're coming to join us? We're desperate for more sopranos this year. You sing soprano, right?"

Amber blinked. She almost put her right. But telling a complete stranger that she was an alcoholic gave her a dry mouth and a lump in her throat. She wanted to say she'd been socialising with friends, but what if this woman knew the AA meeting had just finished?

Words wouldn't come; she tried swallowing a few times. She was right there, hanging around at the beginning of, apparently, a choir rehearsal. She had no interest in singing, let alone any talent. She should have left as soon as she'd said goodbye to Harry.

Finally, her mouth came to life. "Sure. Of course." Amber had a vague knowledge of the different voices. Sopranos sang the high notes.

"We've had, like, half the buggers leave."

Amber gulped but yanked a smile onto her face. "Yeah. Was hoping to join, if that's okay?" Her gut twisted with guilt at the lie, but she figured it was worth it for the good of her home group.

It was also worth it to see the beam on the woman's face. "You're officially my hero. I'm tired of sitting with the warblers."

As the woman led her back into the hall, Amber made a pact with whatever deity or force was in charge. She'd make it right in some other way. She'd clean Jilly's bathroom as well as her own for a month. She'd donate to three different charities for a year. There was no way she would slip back into old habits—perpetual lying—if she could help it.

Instead of focusing on her still-twisting belly, she traipsed past the room they used for AA meetings into a larger room at the back. A piano sat in the corner and there was a small stage at the end. Everything was dark, varnished wood, and there was a smell like wax, old and musty.

The woman placed her folders onto the edge of the stage and beckoned Amber over. "Sorry, I'm Rosie."

"Amber." They shook hands and Amber nearly dropped her folders.

"Let me take those." Rosie grabbed them with a lopsided smile.

"So, um, yeah. The choir?" Amber bit her lip and searched for a backstory. "I've been thinking about doing something new for a while… and this seemed perfect. I'll get to meet people." She shrugged. That would have to do. She didn't want to oversell it.

"New term started last week, but that's okay. Presume you read music?"

Amber nodded but immediately regretted it. *Another lie? Stop it now.* A few people started to arrive. Amber inwardly cursed herself. *What am I doing?* "Are the songs hard?"

"You'll be fine." Rosie went to grab a chair. She seemed to hesitate before picking one up and walking slowly to the front, the right-hand side. She patted the back. "Stick with me. You'll be awesome."

Whilst Rosie got a chair for herself, Amber sat and got out her phone. The sunset would have to wait until a different evening. She didn't need to walk Jilly's dog. She'd had dinner before the meeting. Just a quick text to say she would be back a little later. She hoped Jilly wouldn't worry.

Rosie plonked herself onto a chair after she'd set it down next to Amber. "Nice camera."

Amber flushed. *Who turns up to a choir rehearsal with a camera?* "Thanks."

"Into photography?"

"Kind of a hobby, maybe an obsession." Coyness made her fidget. "Bought this thing a month ago. Saved up for ages."

"What d'you like to shoot?" Confidence radiated from Rosie, and the glint that had been in her eye since she'd bumped into Amber appeared to be a permanent fixture.

"Landscapes. Animals. My mate has a horse; she's the perfect model."

"Cool." Rosie took out a pen and wrote *Amber* above her own name, already in situ on the folder in her lap.

It felt final. The tension in Amber's belly coiled more tightly. She let out a breath, trying to settle the feeling, and smiled at Rosie. "I was going to shoot some sunsets later but reckon I might be too late."

"Rehearsal's for an hour and a half. You might just catch the last minute or so."

Amber stared at the floor. Her dejection must have been obvious because the next minute a comforting hand appeared on her arm.

"Hey, there'll be other sunsets, Amber." Rosie tilted her head, her gaze steady on Amber's own. "Oh, wow! You really have beautiful eyes." It might have sounded like a pickup line on anyone else's lips, but Rosie seemed sincere. With a wince, she looked away. "Sorry. Ignore me. Sometimes I say stuff without thinking it through."

"Oh, hey, it's fine." Amber chuckled. "I actually get that a lot." She gestured towards her face. "I get them from my mother." She gritted her teeth against a negative comment about her mum. She hadn't spoken to her in years. *No need to delve too deep after only five minutes of knowing her.* She considered Rosie. "You have very cool hair."

Rosie barked a laugh. "Needs a cut, but thanks." She softened, lowered her gaze, and opened the folder.

Amber got the feeling she was distracting them both toward a change of topic. Fair enough. "What are we singing, then?"

"A few of the usual. Songs from *Les Mis*. Some John Rutter. Nothing too complicated."

"Oh, good."

"And you need to pay Enid, so have two quid ready for when she—"

An older woman with thick-rimmed glasses and grey, wavy hair ascended the stairs to the stage and placed her briefcase on the floor. She opened it and took out a bulging folder fit to burst. When she lifted her head, she smiled at Rosie.

Rosie grinned and gave her a little wave. "That's Enid. She's the musical director."

"She looks stern."

"She is. In a good way though. Used to teach at the school I teach at now, back in the day. Head of music."

Enid put a large sandwich tub on the stage and a clipboard next to it. People started to go up and add money to the tub.

Amber fumbled with her purse, took out a couple of pound coins, and shuffled to the tub to pay.

Rosie did the same.

"You're a teacher?"

Rosie stuffed her wallet in her back pocket and crossed her legs. "Yup. Year Two. Top-year infants."

"Which school?" There were several infant schools which took children from four to six years old in the area.

"Worle Infants."

Amber folded her hands in her lap. "I admire teachers. I loved mine when I was little. I remember having the biggest crush on Mrs Sunderford when I was five."

The tiniest of eyebrow raises. "I started with the gay thing young too." Rosie's tone was low, but she didn't seem embarrassed by the fact.

A sort of understanding settled over them as more people filed in. *At least I might make a friend. Been a while since I met anyone. I'm pretty out of practise.*

Much chatter and scraping of chairs echoed around them as an orange glow filtered in through the high-up windows. Amber didn't mind—she was sitting next to someone she had something in common with and was guaranteed at least ninety minutes of their company. And all for two quid. Not a bad exchange, really.

Enid held up a hand once the doors were closed, and everyone went still. The men sat behind the women, on the left and right, separated by a gap. There were a few people in their thirties, but most people, as far as Amber could see, were past retirement. A slim, middle-aged man with round spectacles sat at the piano.

"Ladies and gentlemen, good evening. Hope you've all had a lovely week." Enid pushed her glasses up and regarded the room with a pinched smile. "I have an announcement. In addition to our usual Christmas concert on the third of December, we will be singing at the Colston Hall in Bristol next summer."

A few hushed murmurs. Excitement buzzed through the room.

"Something a little different, I know. That's why I need 100-percent attendance and 150-percent commitment. Once the Christmas season is over, I expect every single one of you to be at every single rehearsal. Not that you would ever want to miss one, hm?"

A titter from some of the women. One of the men snorted.

"We don't have anything good enough to perform at the Colston Hall," one of the women over on the other side piped up.

"Aha. Well, I've found us something new. A beautiful collection named *Lullaby of the Ocean*. I'll hand this out in the New Year. It's simply joyous."

Rosie's eyes narrowed. She sucked her bottom lip into her mouth. "I don't know of that." She leaned towards Amber so she could whisper to her. "But Enid has good taste. If she says it's good, it'll be excellent."

Panic rose inside Amber. It wouldn't be a few fun tunes she recognised. She'd have to learn an entire concert of new music with absolutely no expertise in the area. *I'll just have to leave after this week and never come back.* As pretty as Rosie was, Amber couldn't justify continuing with the choir, not all the way until next summer. She'd go home tonight, find the number on the website, if the choir had one, and phone to say she wouldn't attend any more. It'd save her two pounds a week if nothing else.

They began with some vocal warm-ups, which Enid led. She had an old-fashioned voice but pleasant. Amber wondered whether she had sung professionally in her youth. She could imagine Enid up on a stage in the sixties, a big band behind her and smoky tables with happy customers.

Rosie's voice carried over the rest of the choir—or maybe it was just because Amber sat so close to her. Surprise made Amber's jaw drop. Rosie sounded so—and there truly wasn't a better word for it—girly. Clear, like a young boy in a cathedral. Amber rectified her open-mouthed situation and echoed the scales quietly, hoping to fade into the background.

She didn't seem the sort to have that kind of voice. Amber's first impression had labelled Rosie as a butch with her black jeans, boots, and leather jacket. And her speaking voice was low—not as low as Jilly's but low enough for her not to sound like a prepubescent boy.

Amber shook the thought away. Who was she to have preconceptions of someone she'd known for only a few minutes?

"Good." A single nod from Enid. "Remember to keep those diaphragms strong. Drop your jaw as you go up to those top notes."

It all sounded terribly technical. Amber fingered her camera strap and tried not to worry too much.

The first song Rosie pulled from the folder reminded Amber of the *Blue Peter* theme song. It was lively and bouncy, and she could barely keep up with the lyrics. It was a bit jumbled, as if everyone was out of practise. Someone behind them seemed to think she should be in an opera. Her voice wobbled all over the place and grated on Amber's nerves.

Enid started with the sopranos—this was the part Amber should be singing. The pianist played the tune on the piano and they repeated it back.

The errors began to fade. Then the altos, the lower female voices. Then tenors and the basses, the two groups of men.

By the time they'd gone over each individual part, Amber was none the wiser.

Rosie caught her eye halfway through the fourth time they sung all the parts together. She gave her an encouraging smile and held the musical score towards her, one fingertip tracing the words.

The little blobs and sticks were an alien language to Amber. She mouthed the words but no sound came out. The desire to look away was strong, but Rosie was being so kind, giving her such supportive looks. She listened to Rosie and copied what she did.

By the end, everyone else seemed to have sorted out what notes they were supposed to sing. The harmonies made Amber's blood dance along. It was a joyous, comfortable song.

Rosie beamed, her face alight with pleasure when the song ended. This alone made some of Amber's worry fade. She really was pretty, and more so when she smiled like that.

Next came a slower song, one with less complication. It rang a bell for Amber—she'd heard it before somewhere. When she read the information on the first page, Amber realised it was one of the *Les Mis* songs Rosie had mentioned before. Confidence swelled in Amber, but she kept her voice quiet, still. It was nice to just listen to Rosie sing anyway rather than sully the experience with her own incompetence.

"A quick break now. Please utilise the water cooler at the back. Soothe those throats." And Enid stepped from her stage.

Chairs scraped again. Rosie stood and covered her mouth. She swallowed. "I'm just going to the…" She twisted her lips and pointed towards the door.

Amber assumed she meant the bathroom, so she nodded and took the folder from her. Whilst Rosie was gone, she studied the music. Balls and sticks with no apparent meaning but with words underneath. At least she could read those.

When Rosie returned, she had a cup of water in each hand. "Here. Drink up. She'll be starting again in a minute."

"Oh yeah. Better do as we're told."

"Good for your voice." Rosie sat next to her and wedged the cup between her knees before stretching both arms above her head. A small groan escaped her. "What do you do, then?"

"Hmm?"

"Work, job. I teach. What do you do?"

"Oh."

A sideways grin. "Mind if I try to guess?"

Amber folded her arms and gave her a curious look. "Go for it."

One of Rosie's eyes shuttered. "I reckon…you're a professional juggler."

Amber laughed. "Wrong."

"Really? Shame." Rosie took a sip of her water. "Consultant surgeon?"

"No."

"Lumberjack?"

"Clearly not." Amber indicated her skater skirt and ballet shoes.

"Right. Okay." She made a flippant gesture. "I give up."

"Remind me never to play I-Spy with you." Amber nudged their shoulders together.

Rosie nudged her back, her hair falling over one eye. "Spill."

"I work as a receptionist in a dental surgery."

Staring at her, Rosie lifted both eyebrows. "Oh. That's a—"

"Boring job? Yup."

"I wasn't going to say that."

"Right, everyone. Time to continue." Enid was back up on her stage.

"You so were," Amber hissed.

"I was not."

Amber chuckled but sat up straight and turned her attention back to the front.

The next song was another Amber had never heard before. Something about cats and rats and a very strange number of eyes for three animals to have collectively. It was another quick one. Amber copied Rosie again, finding if she sung under her breath she wasn't at risk of making a loud mistake.

A few more songs followed, each as obscure as the last. Amber tried not to think about Enid on the stage scrutinising the choir with such seriousness. She tried not to think about the other members of the choir either but did feel glad that, as they sat at the front, no one could hear her ineptitude. The pianist was focused on his own nimble fingers.

Mostly, she enjoyed the miniconcert Rosie was giving her, her voice angelic, sharp as a crystal. She'd never known anyone who could sing, certainly hadn't ever sat right next to someone who could give Aled Jones a run for his money.

Inside her pocket was something cold and round. The coin—her one-year medallion. A true follower of the twelve steps without fail for exactly 365 days. She relished the accomplishment but acknowledged she was lacking tonight. *I promised myself I would stop lying, and here I am, doing just that.* Would ringing Enid when she got home be cowardly? Yes. She'd have to come clean once the rehearsal was over—apologise to Rosie, and to Enid.

Enid clasped her knobbly fingers in front of her. "Good work. Same time next week. If you can, work on 'Five Eyes'; those parts are tricky. And remember to enunciate."

Rosie nodded once, stood, and carried her chair to the side to stack it with the rest.

Amber pulled her cardigan on, ready for the conversation she needed to have. She gathered her courage. Owning up to things as soon as she could was important—it was Step Ten. Her continued recovery relied on it.

Leather jacket back on, Rosie stood with her hands in her pockets, a curious smile on her face.

Holding her coin with sweaty fingers, Amber shot Rosie an apologetic look. "Rosie, listen…" She took a deep breath, her nerves wavering.

"I'm not stupid, you know." Rosie flicked her eyebrows. "I'm well aware you can't read music and have never sung before."

"Oh my gosh." Amber covered her eyes. "I thought I'd got away with it."

"I've been teaching for nearly fifteen years. I've been playing music since I was five. I can tell someone isn't a maestro after an hour of sharing a score."

"I'm sorry I lied."

"Oh, please." Rosie chuckled, and they walked out of the hall into the night. "I'll live. Anyway, I think you're cool enough to help you, if you'd like me to."

Amber blinked. "You…you want to help me?"

"Definitely."

What happened to coming clean? Amber gripped the coin until it cut into her palm. She released it and wiped her hand on her skirt. "That's really kind, but—"

"No 'but's,' dude. Like I said, I think you're cool, so I want to help you."

What were her options? She really didn't want Rosie knowing she had issues with alcohol. And she'd been honest about the whole not being musical issue. Her shoulders felt a tad lighter. And even if she hadn't meant to join the choir, she supposed there was no reason why she couldn't commit to it. It *had* been fun, and not just because Rosie had been there.

"Look," Rosie flipped her hand around, "I have a piano at home and far too much time on my hands in the evening. When I'm not marking spelling tests and simple maths, I'm just watching Netflix and eating digestive biscuits."

"So, I'd be doing you a service?" Amber looked Rosie up and down. She didn't need persuading away from any form of baked goods. But there was a hopeful look in her eyes. Amber wondered whether she was lonely too. "Fine."

"Excellent." Rosie beamed at her. "I live in Yatton. Do you drive?"

"Kind of." Amber had insurance on Jilly's car. "I can borrow my landlady's. She doesn't use it in the evenings."

"You rent?"

"Lodge, officially."

"I miss living with people. Being alone can get tiresome." Something undecipherable flickered across Rosie's eyes.

"Jilly's pretty cool. Bakes fresh bread at the weekend…and lets me share it."

"Kind of something between a friend and a cool auntie?"

Amber giggled. "Yeah."

"Give me your phone; I'll put my details in. We can arrange something then."

"Okay." Amber handed it over and peered as Rosie tapped away.

"No worries." Rosie gave her a lopsided smile and gave back the phone. She made a pistol motion with her forefinger and thumb. "Catch you later, okay?"

All Amber could do was nod. What had she agreed to? On the one hand, she'd get to spend some quality time with a very attractive woman at her house. She'd get to sit next to Rosie every week and hear her sing.

On the other hand, the knowledge that it had all started with a fib twisted inside her. Hope swelled though. *The fib can't escalate, can it? And Rosie barely minded I had lied. I'll just work really hard and prove I'm committed. It isn't like before; I came clean.*

Amber spent the entire walk home convincing herself of the fact.

Chapter 3

Something was making a noise.

Rosie rolled from her prone position and nearly fell off the sofa. She blinked and stared around. *What time is it?* One glance at the clock told her it was almost seven. Had she eaten yet? She didn't feel hungry, so she assumed she had. Where had the time gone?

Grumbling, she slid from the sofa and pulled her fingers through her hair. She'd been asleep. Week six of her pregnancy seemed to be sapping all her energy. She'd expected it—knew the baby would grow and therefore use her calories. But she couldn't remember the last time she'd fallen asleep before actually climbing into bed.

She rubbed the grit from her eyes and passed her palm over her belly. Nothing showed yet. Kind of as if it weren't real. There was the half expectation she would wake up one morning and find nothing there, like the weeks after little Ali had been stillborn. Her boobs hurt though, and they were getting bigger. *Good job they're not big in the first place.*

The noise was still going—a gentle knocking. Then it hit her: Amber was due at seven. And she'd been mulling over the size of her own boobs instead of answering the door. She shot into the hallway and jerked the door open. "Hi. Sorry."

Amber wore a red cardigan, a blue top, and a black skirt. She had thick black tights on underneath shiny black shoes, the type a schoolchild would wear. Rosie was hesitant to call them 'little-girly'; she always tried to stay gender-neutral even in her own mind.

"Hi." Amber narrowed her eyes. "Did you…um…just wake up?"

"Kind of." Rosie smothered a yawn with the back of her hand. "Sorry. Don't usually nap on a school night." She frowned. "Or any night."

"I can go, if you like." Amber looked at the blue Smart Car parked on the road.

"No, you're okay." Rosie stepped back, allowing Amber into her house. "Been a long day at school."

"Oh, 'course. Teaching, huh?"

"Yeah. New Year Twos: cute little monkeys." Rosie grinned. "Let me get those for you."

Amber handed over her scarf and handbag. "Want me to take my shoes off?"

"If you like. Got thick carpets, so…" Leaving Amber for a minute, Rosie went into the living room to check her make-up and hair in the mirror. *Not too scruffy, that's good.* Amber had made an effort with her outfit. She didn't look like she'd been curled on the sofa since dinner.

Soft footsteps told her Amber had padded in behind her in her tights. Rosie turned to find her with her eyes lowered and her hands clasped in front of her. "You have a beautiful home."

"Thanks. Would you like a drink?"

"Maybe just water."

I don't think I have any alcohol in the house anyway. Seems pointless when I can't drink it myself. "One water coming right up."

When Rosie brought two glasses back with her, Amber was sitting primly on the sofa. There was an expression akin to wonder on her face. "The grey really works in here."

"Thanks." Rosie handed her the drink. "My mum hates it."

"Well, she doesn't live here, does she?"

Rosie shook her head. "They don't live far though. Walkable distance."

"That's nice." Amber took a sip before considering her knees. "I'm really sorry I lied to you last week."

She tilted her head. "You really feel bad about it?"

"Yeah. I don't like to be dishonest."

Rosie sat at the other end of her three-seater sofa. "If it helps, I forgive you."

"Thank you." Amber laughed.

"I think being honest is a good personality trait. So many people talk rubbish."

"Me too."

"Right. Tell me about your history with music." Rosie leaned against the sofa back. "Did you have any lessons at school or…?"

"Well, yes. Sort of." Amber drank some more water and winced. "I had a few recorder lessons. Went to the recorder group everyone was required to attend."

Rosie chuckled, remembering the one she'd also been to when she was at school. *I had Grade One by the time I was in Year Four. I got so bored.*

"I never really got the hang of it. Always sat at the back and mimed mostly."

"Not unlike last week."

Pink tinged Amber cheeks. "Gosh, I really hoped I'd got away with that."

"Aw." Rosie touched her shoulder.

Amber didn't pull away.

"Like I said, I'm probably more aware than most. Teacher, from a musical family."

"You are?"

"Yup." She pulled her socked feet under her backside. "Mum teaches privately at home—singing and piano. Dad is a vicar."

"A vicar?" Amber's eyebrows lifted.

"Not the scary type. He's pretty liberal. He plays the guitar and sings Led Zeppelin."

"Legend." Amber grimaced. "I'm a bit jealous of people with nice families." Something darkened in her eyes. "I'm not in touch with my parents. Like, at all."

"That's more surprising than me having a rock-obsessed vicar as a dad." Rosie wanted to touch her again but resisted the urge. "Any reason? Or…"

Fidgeting with her glass, Amber pushed her shoulders up to her ears. "Lots of reasons." Apparently that was all she wanted to say.

That was fine with Rosie. "Anyway, so your entire experience with music was a school recorder group?"

"Yeah." Relief swept through Amber's features. "I'm basically a novice. No, less than a novice."

"Well, the choir isn't a professional group. It's a community choir. We're not expected to be Grade Eight standard." She wiggled her head and sat up proudly. "Even if some of us are."

"I'm guessing Grade Eight is good?"

"Highest you can get."

"Nice." Amber smiled over at Rosie's piano. "Your voice is lovely. You're clearly talented."

Modesty swirled in Rosie's belly. "Well. It was sort of expected." She stood, left her glass on the coffee table, and sat on the piano stool. "You got any siblings?"

"No. You?"

"One sister, Charlie. She's married with a kid. Plays cello, but not so much now. At school and the music centre when we were kids."

"Music centre?"

"Yeah, it used to be run by the local authority, but now it's kind of independent. Run by a load of music teachers in North Somerset. Usually happens Saturday mornings. They have a tuck shop." Memories of being allowed a quid for chocolate flowed through Rosie. Her mouth even watered a bit.

"Do you go?"

"I did when I first started teaching, but these days I have a lot more on, like after-school things. I like my weekends off though."

"Me too." Amber stood and came over to the piano. "So, um, you play?"

"Piano? Since I was five." She played a happy major chord with a bass note, ending it with a flourish.

"Such a cool skill."

Rosie wondered how many times Amber could compliment her. It was so alien to know someone that didn't have a musical upbringing. Not that she was naïve—Rosie was of course aware that people grew up differently to how she and Charlie had. It was just a shame. But Amber wouldn't have come along to the choir if she hadn't been interested.

"Let's go through the first one we did on Friday, okay?" Rosie glanced at Amber, who stood with her arms folded. "Okay, first of all: stand up nice and straight. Arms by your sides. Chin up."

Amber complied, a small smile tugging her lips.

"Weight on both your feet. And sing from your belly, rather than your ribs."

"Diaphragm, right?" Amber pressed a palm to the area below her ribcage.

"You got it." Rosie took the sheet music for the first song from the top of the piano and played the introduction. She sang the soprano part—the tune—clearly but not too loudly.

After a few bars, Amber sang along too, getting some notes wrong and some of the words muddled. She put a hand over her face and turned away.

Grabbing Amber's other hand, Rosie pulled her back round. "Hey. Come on. You're not going to get it perfect first time."

"Second time." Amber looked down at Rosie with large brown eyes. Her pale skin made her eyelashes look strikingly black.

She's very pretty. Rosie pushed that thought away, as amusing as it was. She was well aware that part of the reason why she'd offered her expertise to Amber was because she'd found her attractive. *Nothing wrong with looking and enjoying. I don't intend to do anything about it; relationships are not in my plan at the moment. My baby is my plan, and after failing miserably at finding someone who wants a baby with me, it has to be something I do alone.*

They went through the song several times. Each time, Amber got more and more of the tune and words correct. Her voice was soft, breathy. *Definitely a soprano. Probably a first soprano if we work on her upper range.* Rosie decided to give her some time before they tackled that.

"The song is about three cats, right?" Rosie pointed to the lyrics. "There's this guy and he owns this mill. And his cats are in charge of keeping the mice from eating the flour."

"So it's a story?"

"Sure."

"I hadn't even thought about what the words meant. I was just so worried about singing it right. Sounds kind of scary."

"Weird how the pace and key of the song can have that effect. The lyrics aren't actually that scary."

Amber stepped back, her mouth to one side. "I like it when songs do that. It doesn't matter what words are in them, but the tune and the rest… that really makes it."

"I expect "Stairway to Heaven" wouldn't have the same appeal if the tune was boring."

"And that guitar riff?"

"Not so cool when you've heard your dad play it repeatedly on an acoustic guitar."

They smothered giggles.

"Okay, focus." Rosie shot her a joke-stern look. "I do need to go to bed at some point." She barely held in a yawn.

"I'm sorry. Shouldn't be keeping you up, not when you've got to teach a load of screaming kiddies all day tomorrow."

A stone dropped in Rosie's belly. "You…you don't like kids?"

Amber shrugged. "I don't dislike them. I just…I suppose I'm impressed by those that work with them. Teaching must be stressful."

"It's rewarding though." *Does she not like kids? That'll be an issue in eight months' time.* "I do love it."

"I think it takes a special type of person to teach." Amber played with the bottom button of her cardigan.

Suppose I can hardly complain when she says something like that. Rosie smiled back. "It's lucky I enjoy things like times tables and reading out loud."

Amber gestured towards the music. "You're clearly good at the teaching thing. I'm almost getting this song."

"Let's finish on a high note, then, so to speak."

Amber nodded and went back to the sofa to drain her glass. "Thanks for this. I think I'll be okay now."

Rosie's chest ached. As weird and unintentional as it had been, she'd enjoyed teaching Amber. She didn't want it to be the last time they met up privately. Going to choir together was all very well, but sharing a snippet or two about their lives in a more private setting had been nice. *What am I doing? What happened to no dating for the foreseeable future?* "Don't think you're getting away with it so quickly." She spun on her stool to face Amber. "I fancy giving you a hand every week, so long as you keep coming to rehearsals."

"Really?"

"Let's call Mondays our day. Maybe next week we can have cake?"

"So long as you let me bring the cake." Amber's eyes were bright.

"Deal." Rosie made a clicking noise and gave her a wink.

To her joy, Amber blushed but maintained eye contact. "I like you."

"I like you too." She'd said the words before she'd even thought about doing so. Her jaw hung slack for a beat, but she finally closed her mouth and shrugged. "No reason why we can't be friends. Especially when there's cake involved." *That should save any misunderstanding.*

"So long as you don't only want me for the cake I bring." Amber's spirits seemed to have fallen a touch, but her smile renewed the longer they looked at one another.

"I'll try not to let that be the only factor." *Friends would be okay. Sensible move.*

Amber set her glass back on the coffee table and moved into the hall, then stooped to pull on her shoes. "Thanks for the help." She lifted her head again once her shoes were buckled. "And, in advance, for all your future help." She tugged her scarf around her neck.

"Pleasure."

With her bag on her shoulder, car keys in her hand, Amber opened the door and went outside. "I guess I'll see you on Friday."

"Don't be late. I can't guarantee some other pretty girl won't take your seat." She gave her a suave look. "I'm quite a catch, you know."

Lowering her head, Amber smiled. "I'll be there." As she walked down Rosie's path, she gave her a little wave.

Rosie waved back. *Should I stand at the door and watch her leave? I don't want to seem too keen, or keen at all, in fact. And what was all that about another girl stealing her seat if she wasn't on time? I really need to rein in my flirtatious streak.* She closed the door before Amber got into her car.

She sat at the piano for a while, playing some slow and calming arpeggios. Then she lowered the piano lid with a soft thump before tidying away their glasses. Nothing else needed doing—she'd made her lunch and packed the things she needed for tomorrow. She headed upstairs, brushed her teeth, and climbed into her pyjamas.

The full-length mirror called her. She stood sideways and pushed up her pyjama shirt. How long would it be before she had to tell people that weren't her family? Work would need to know at twelve weeks. But the choir?

Baby Ali appeared in her mind again. She'd been so excited with her last pregnancy, had strived to share her news with all and sundry. The women that sat behind her in choir, "The Warblers", as she called them inside her head, had scoffed and tutted. And she'd lost him, her baby boy. Her excitement had jinxed the whole affair.

When would she tell Amber? *Maybe when I properly start to show. She didn't seem too keen on kids during our conversation tonight. I don't want to put her off from being friends with me.*

Chapter 4

Wednesday morning was physical education, which meant running around and throwing balls at one another, which had been a fun activity eight weeks ago.

The room spun, and bile crept up Rosie's throat. *Damn morning sickness.* Her bra was too tight and her jogging bottoms pressed hard on her belly. It wasn't that she was bigger there, it just felt *so* constricted. It didn't help with her nausea.

Rosie stood as still as she could and tried to stay cheerful. She wanted to sit down.

A face peered into the gym. The door opened, and Claire—Miss Kondo—inched inside, her gaze fixed on Rosie.

Irritation gripped Rosie, along with a sense of foreboding. Of all the people Rosie needed to tell, Claire and their fellow teacher Vincent were high on her list. They were friends, not just colleagues, and knew about her baby plan. She had told them when she'd found a potential donor—Barry, a guy from Cornwall with a clean family history. She had told them when she'd met up with him and agreed he would be the one to donate. But she'd stopped there. She hadn't felt ready.

Claire was by her side in seconds. "You look peaky."

Who was looking after her own class? Probably her learning-support assistants. "I feel it." With no energy to fob her off with an fake excuse, Rosie pressed a hand to her chest, then her mouth. "Can you take over for just a minute?"

The staff bathroom was close enough for her to reach before she heaved into it. Not a huge amount came out, for which she was thankful. It wasn't lunchtime yet. Maybe that was the problem.

I should be snacking, but who has the time when you're teaching twenty-eight kids to aim a ball? She sucked in a breath, and another, eventually getting the retching under control. The closed lid of the toilet was perfect for sitting on. Breakfast biscuits: that was what she needed. She could sneak one periodically, even when she was teaching.

Her plan had been to wait until twelve weeks, just after her official scan, to tell the head teacher. She wanted to see that heartbeat, the thing that concreted the whole situation for her. But she felt too poorly to put it off.

Her stomach ached anew for not telling Claire and Vincent. They'd been really supportive whilst she'd been deciding what to do and how to go about it. And they'd been there after she'd lost Ali.

She washed her hands and rinsed her mouth. One last glance in the mirror secured her choice. *Okay, here goes.*

On return to the gym, she found her kids in four groups of seven, passing the foam footballs around. All terribly organised—Claire was good at that. Everyone loved Miss Kondo. She was a sweet but respected teacher and always had a colourful story to tell about her native city, Tokyo. She'd even taught her reception class some Japanese.

Rosie made her way through the groups of quiet children and reached Claire's side.

Claire put a hand on her back. "Have you been sick?"

Rosie nodded.

"You should go home."

She shook her head. "Keep it to yourself, but I'm pregnant." Rosie whispered it and wasn't sure Claire had heard until her eyes widened.

"Really?"

Rosie flapped a hand at her, a gesture she hoped displayed her desire for Claire to *shut up.*

"Sorry." Claire's mouth quivered as if she hid a massive grin. "Definitely talk at lunch."

"I've got playground duty."

"Oh my God, I'm going to have to keep this inside until the end of the day?"

Rosie looked at her watch. "Mate, you'll live. I currently feel like the world is moving about."

"My cousin said she had to eat snacks every hour when she was…" She thankfully left off the word. "Do you have anything?"

"Not on me." Rosie winced.

"I've got some cereal bars in my bag. Take over again here and I'll grab you one." Her dress shoes squeaked on the floor as she left.

Iris broke from her group and approached Rosie, an unsure look in her eyes. "Miss Tanner? Are you sicky-sick?" She didn't quite have a lisp. Her red pixie cut stuck up at the back.

"A little bit, but I'm okay." She smiled at Iris. "Thank you for being kind and asking."

"That's okay. When I'm sicky-sick, Mummy rubs my tummy and I have ice cream." She cocked her head, an exaggerated expression of thought. "Do you want me to rub your tummy? Have you got some ice cream for lunch?"

"I don't. Shame, huh?" Rosie let out a warm chuckle. "Thank you, sweetie."

"H'okay." Iris went back to her friends.

Rosie leant against the wall by the monkey bars. *I hope my own child is as sweet as Iris.*

The day dragged. Lunch was a buttered bread roll and a banana. Rosie couldn't quite face a filling, even something plain like cheese. Claire slipped something into her jacket pocket in the playground.

Rosie had trouble concentrating on the afternoon lessons, but her kids didn't seem bothered. The secret cereal bar, once she had remembered and investigated her jacket pocket, had gone down a treat—Rosie's sickness had retreated enough that she could finally function. If she snacked and focused on her breathing when a pang of nausea did threaten to take hold, she could cope.

The early autumn wind had picked up by the end of the day. The last child skipped off, gripping the side of the buggy his sister rode in.

The door from the corridor opened. "Hi." Claire's sleek hair dropped from her shoulder as she leaned in.

"Hi." Rosie perched on the edge of her desk. "Thanks for the cereal bar. I'm going to stock up on my way home." She clicked her fingers. "Just the ticket."

"You're welcome." Claire sat beside her. "When were you going to tell me?"

"Two weeks' time. Maybe three." She eyed Claire, cringing with apology. "It's just…I wasn't quite ready."

"That's fair enough. It must be hard for you, what with all that happened before. Losing your little boy so late into your pregnancy."

Rosie wrapped an arm around Claire's back, rested her head on her shoulder. They sighed as one. "That's why I don't want to tell too many people for a while. I told everyone last time and…I jinxed it."

"What's this about being sick in PE?" Vincent entered the room, his balding head catching the overhead light.

Claire made a high-pitched noise in her throat. "She's pregnant."

Rosie fake-punched her. "Hey. Dude. Not cool."

"You were going to tell him anyway." Claire shifted away from her.

Rosie narrowed her eyes but couldn't keep it up. "Fine. Yes. I am with child."

"*With child*, eh?" Vincent's Scouse accent rang across the room. "I didn't realise we were in the 1930s."

"I'll be getting my belly corset tomorrow."

Vincent gave her a one-armed hug. "Congrats."

"Thanks, dude."

"She's got morning sickness." Claire slid back to Rosie to give her a reassuring pat.

"Morning, afternoon, and evening, apparently." Rosie held up her hands.

"Sucks. You tried ginger?"

"Oh, suddenly everyone's an expert." Rosie glared between them. "Neither of you have children."

"But we both have family who have children." Vincent plonked onto one of the tables so he faced the both of them. "A menagerie of experience in the subject of mums-to-be."

"I have a sister who thinks she's done it all too." Rosie rested against Claire's side again, relishing the comfort she got from her. "If I need any advice, I'll ask, okay?"

Vincent lifted both hands in surrender.

"So, when's your first scan?" Claire nudged her.

"Week twelve. So, five weeks."

"Oh Lord, that's ages away." Claire's voice had taken on a whiny quality.

"I know." Rosie felt the same. It had seemed like forever since she'd waved off Barry, lain in bed with a few candles, and done the deed to the gentle, soothing tones of Eva Cassidy. "I still have flashbacks of going to A&E, seeing the scan last time. I just want to see that heartbeat, you know?"

Claire rubbed her back.

"When did you, you know...?" He made an upward motion with his index finger, accompanied by an ascending whistle.

"You're disgusting." Rosie angled an eyebrow at him.

He grinned.

"It was a sunny Tuesday six weeks ago."

"Excellent. Got to love the summer holidays."

"Well, I needed a couple of uninterrupted ovulations. I didn't fancy waiting until a weekend in term time. Far too much stress tracking my cervical fluid and sticking a thermometer in my ear."

Vincent's smile became blank. He nodded.

"Too much information?" Rosie laughed.

"Bit." His smile became strained.

"Okay. No more lady bits talk."

He let out a whoosh. "So, do you have a due date yet?"

"I could work it out myself, but I feel like if I did that, I'd jinx it. Don't want to piss off the powers that be, do I? I'll wait until my scan."

"And you, an atheist," Claire teased.

Chapter 5

Amber arrived early to the next choir rehearsal as the AA meeting finished with various people having to dash off. She took a chair and one for Rosie and placed them in the same place as the week before.

She studied her shiny Mary Jane shoes whilst she waited. She'd bought them three weeks ago. They had a barely-there heel, scalloping around the open part on the top and a thick band leading to a buckle. The moment she'd bought them, she'd been in love. Autumn meant they picked up a few flecks of mud, a tiny leaf or two. A quick wipe and they were good as new.

The large hall whispered as the wind tickled the eaves. It was eerie with no one else there.

She cast her mind back to last week. Jilly had been intrigued when she had returned, almost two hours late, despite the text she had sent her. She had pressed her lips together when Amber had admitted she'd joined a choir. It wasn't really her place to comment—Jilly wasn't her sponsor. She also wasn't one to pass on information to Fiona, whom Amber was seeing tomorrow evening.

Fiona lived in Clevedon—around ten miles away from Amber's—and they took it in turns to meet up at each other's house once a week. Fiona was there when she was needed. She didn't work, had retired early due to ill health—her lungs. She'd been sober over twenty years.

Amber's belly tingled when she realised she'd have to tell Fiona about Rosie and the choir. Fiona would ask so many questions, enquire about Amber's intentions and her motivations. At this evening's rehearsal, Amber would have to be a pillar of honesty and respect. It was what she strived to be anyway, so it wasn't as if it was too much effort for no reward. Amber wanted a positive story to tell, one that proved she'd changed.

People started to arrive. A large man with shirtsleeves rolled to his elbows smiled and came over. "Hi."

"Hello." Amber bit her lip and held out a hand. "I'm Amber."

"Gareth. You're new here?"

"Came last week, but yes."

"I saw you. Surprised to see a youngster." He cupped his hand by his mouth. "Makes a change." He seemed pleased she was there.

Amber pushed up her shoulders, unsure how to respond. She took a shuddering breath and forced herself to relax. "So, you…you sing tenor or bass?"

"Tenor. Well, baritone really. But we don't tend to get any five-part songs, so I stick with the tenors."

"Nice." *Honesty is key.* "I'm not very good. But I'm getting some lessons."

"From Rosie Tanner?"

She nodded.

"She's the best. Always takes the descant solos at our concerts. Glad about that." He cupped his mouth again. "Keeps some of our less-than-talented sopranos from singing them."

"Oh really?" She fiddled with her fingers. "Well, no worries. I won't be stealing anything from Rosie."

"Anyway, welcome." His attention was with a group of men detaching from a few women Amber presumed were their wives. "Catch you later."

Amber smiled at him. It made her nervous to sit and watch people—she always felt like she stared, which was rude—so she took her phone out, opened Facebook, and scrolled through her feed. A hand on her shoulder made her jump.

"Shit, sorry." Rosie slid into the chair next to Amber. "You looked engrossed."

"Just waiting for you." She checked her watch. "And here's me thinking you'd be on time."

"My bad." Rosie ran a hand through her hair before draping her jacket over the back of the chair. "Parking's a nightmare tonight. I ended up paying at Grove Park." She grinned, took their folder from her satchel, and turned to Amber. "So, how are you?"

They hadn't texted or anything since Monday, apart from Amber sending a thank-you text once she was home.

"Good." Amber took in the hazel eyes once again decorated with smoky eye shadow.

"Me too. Well, I was a bit poorly last week but…" Rosie blinked and pursed her lips. "I'm good now." A renewed smile. "You ready to sing your heart out?"

"Sure."

Confidence built. Amber had been singing the cat song all week in between walking Nico and doing housework. She'd even had to stop herself from humming the tune under her breath at work.

Enid arrived, a flustered aura surrounding her. But once she was on the stage, her music on the stand in front of her, she was the epitome of control. "Warm up first. Then 'Five Eyes', I think."

A warm, comfortable sound like a fluffy blanket surrounded Amber. Everyone was there for the same purpose: they loved music and wanted to create it together. A community choir in every respect. She was now part of something, something massive. It had nearly fifty members from different walks of life, and Amber was one of them.

At break time, she smiled across the room at Gareth, who gave her a sunny wave. She hung around Rosie's heels but gathered enough confidence to make eye contact with a few more people. *I didn't speak to anyone else last week.*

Several songs later, it was time to pack up. The time had gone by so quickly. Amber had spent a few moments listening to Rosie but otherwise had taken part. Maybe she was making up for her lack of candour last week—a contribution, a quality part of the whole.

Rosie looked at her with twinkling eyes and something akin to respect. "You've been practising without me."

"I find I keep singing when I'm doing something else. Like it's becoming a subconscious pastime."

"I'm impressed."

Amber hung her head. "Don't get too excited. Don't think I'm ready for *X Factor* yet."

Rosie wrinkled her nose. "Don't mention that pile of garbage in my presence." She smiled. "You're way better than that show."

"Some of those singers are excellent."

Rosie slotted their sheet music into her satchel. "Popular star machine churning out clones year after year." With a shake of her head, she placed a hand on Amber's shoulder.

When Amber looked up, she caught sight of dark circles under Rosie's eyes. Rosie's complexion seemed a little pale too. *Is she still unwell?* Concern rose within her, but she wasn't sure what to do with the feeling.

"You're an individual, with style and substance." Rosie cast her gaze up and down Amber's body. A coy sideways smile. "They'd put you in shitty sequinned dresses and make you sing stupid songs. You're brilliant just as you are."

Amber wasn't used to being complimented, especially by someone she'd only met three times. They'd talked a little about themselves, sure, but not so much that Rosie knew her darkest secrets. If she knew Amber's history, Amber reckoned she'd feel differently. The praise wouldn't come so freely.

Under Rosie's scrutiny, Amber's heart fluttered. She held her gaze though, wanting to give as good as she got. "What about you? Have you ever auditioned for it?"

"Once. I'm too gay, apparently." Rosie wiggled her index and middle fingers in the air. "It was a while ago. I was young and juvenile."

They made their way outside. Rosie jangled her keys and nodded down the road.

"I'm going this way."

"Me too."

"We can walk together a bit, if you like."

"Nothing would please me more." *Wow, confident much?* Amber rolled her eyes out of Rosie's vision and made sure to keep up with her brisk strides. "So, we doing Monday again?"

"Yeah. Seven o'clock again?"

"Sure." Amber stuffed her hands into her jacket pockets. "I'd return the gesture of hosting, but I don't have a piano."

"Shame. I'd like to see where you live."

"It's just a town house in Uphill. Kind of quiet—unless someone puts something through the letterbox; then Nico goes mad."

"Nico?"

"My landlady's dog. He's a Chihuahua. Very well trained, but can't quite let the postman do his job without a telling-off."

It was past eight-thirty and the sky was black. Not that it made much difference; the street lamps blazed a haze of orange. The light shone in Rosie's hair, making Amber think of rust on antique metalwork.

At the cross section where the road to the seafront met the road that led to the car park, Rosie stopped. She chucked her thumb. "This is me."

The desire to hug Rosie sparkled peripherally but still far enough away to be ignored. *Maybe I should be brave. Honest. I want to hug her, so maybe I should.*

She stepped forward and held out an arm, hoping intentions were clear. Just a friendly hug, nothing more intimate than that.

Rosie moved back and smiled. "Still feeling a bit sick, I must admit." Something akin to disappointment flashed in her eyes. She let out a big breath. "Be a shame if you got it too."

"Fair enough." A kind way of letting her down. "Hope you feel better soon."

"I hate feeling sick. It's one of the things…" Rosie twisted her lips. "It's one of my least favourite things."

"Me too." Amber tucked a lock of hair behind her ear. "See you on Monday."

"Look forward to it." Rosie clicked her tongue and winked at her. She strode away.

Fiona's house was up in the hillside of Clevedon, an area with neat front doors that more often than not were adorned with straw hearts or signs that held positive messages. Each front garden was meticulously primped, with autumn flowers in ceramic pots and wind chimes. Fiona had a brushed-chrome knocker instead of a doorbell.

Amber had spent Saturday morning doing housework and worrying about meeting her sponsor.

When she opened the door, Fiona wore her usual hand-crocheted cardigan and tie-dyed shirt. Her skirts swept about her feet as she ushered Amber inside. "I just made flapjacks. Want one?"

"Yes, please."

The grandmother in Fiona always shone when Amber visited. She wanted to feed, clothe, and pamper everyone. "They're linseed and pecan. Let me know what you think."

The living room was as warm as Fiona's personality. Decorations littered the mantelpiece: dried slices of orange, pine cones, ivy branches. A candle burned on the fireplace. Soft classical music played over the stereo.

How Fiona had carried two steaming mugs of coffee and a plate with two flapjacks, opened the door, and managed to set them onto the coffee table without spilling something was anyone's guess.

Amber enjoyed the way the mug warmed her skin. October was chilly, and Jilly's little car never heated up before she was on the motorway. "Thanks."

"No problem." Fiona beamed at her. "So how's your week been?"

The anxiety returned, but Amber pushed through it, taking a sip of scalding coffee to gather herself. "Okay, thanks. I did something a bit…" She placed her mug onto her coaster. "*Hasty* is probably an accurate word."

"By 'hasty' do you mean reckless?" Fiona's eyebrows lowered. She shifted in her chair.

"A bit. But not in a…" Amber stumbled. "It's been a good thing, I think."

"Have you written it in your—?"

Fiona hadn't even finished the sentence before Amber rummaged in her handbag. "Definitely." She found her notebook and opened it to the latest page. "It's a bit complicated."

"Start from the beginning."

Fiona's steady tone settled Amber's nerves a tad. Amber tapped a few times at the table she'd drawn in her notebook, the one she continued to fill in each time she had an issue. It was part of the deal with her sponsor: Step Ten. "Well, it was after the meeting week before last. I was hanging around outside the church hall and this woman bumped into me. Literally, actually. She was going to the choir that starts after our meeting and…she made this assumption I was joining too."

"Go on." Fiona sipped her coffee.

"I didn't know if she'd seen Harry or Jilly leave, or the others. I didn't want to say, 'No actually I'm just finishing up AA' because I didn't want her to realise all the others went. Anonymity and all that."

"Right. That's kind of you."

"Actually…" Amber twisted her mouth. "I got a bit tongue-tied. I didn't want her knowing I went to AA."

"Thank you for being honest with me."

Amber fiddled with the corner of her notebook. "So I ended up saying I was going to the choir. And I went, and…well, I can't exactly sing…I'm no expert. It was a bit weird."

"I bet." Fiona's eyebrows lowered again. "So the lie you told was that you'd turned up for the choir?"

Amber nodded.

"Why not say you were just walking past?"

Amber sat with her mouth open for a heartbeat. She looked at her knees. "She was nice-looking."

Fiona's smile held too much understanding.

"Okay, she was really fit. And she looked so hopeful that I was there to join. She made it sound like she needed me."

"What happened next?" No judgement for that.

"I went in. Ended up sitting with her. Truth be told, I think I was a bit overwhelmed with it all. She's got a beautiful voice."

"Has she?"

Amber resisted describing Rosie's voice any further. She didn't want Fiona to think she was smitten already; she'd thrown herself into relationships far too early before. "Turns out she's a teacher and a musician. Knew right away I couldn't sing. She challenged me about it at the end."

"Would you have told her the truth if she hadn't?"

Amber took a flapjack from the plate and nibbled. She made sure to give herself time to appreciate its delicious, buttery texture. "I went through a few back-and-forths. At first, I was just going to leave, saying I'd come again but then phone the director lady to cancel. That made me feel bad, so I decided I'd come clean, tell Rosie I was sorry I had lied, and say that I didn't think it was for me. Then she confronted me about it, and…" A smile tugged Amber's lips. "She asked if I'd let her help me. She wanted to teach me the songs, at her house. She has a piano and the skills. And she truly seemed to want to. Like it would make her happy."

"And you agreed?"

"Well..." Amber's cheeks burned. She snapped the notebook closed. "I hadn't disliked the rehearsal. I just felt out of my depth. I reckoned learning the songs would mean I'd have more fun."

"And you also made a friend?"

Amber nodded. She ate some more of her flapjack. "Kudos on the baked goods, by the way."

"Thank you, but you're deflecting."

Amber breathed out a laugh. "Sorry." She just about managed to not spray linseeds all over the carpet.

"Help me get it straight in my head."

Amber nodded and ate more of her flapjack. "I lied because I got tongue-tied, and then it felt too late to say I was in AA, and I didn't feel comfortable telling her anyway. But I followed through, did what I said I was going to do. Then I made the decision to come clean—well, as much as I could without outing myself—to tell Rosie it wasn't for me. Then I was given the opportunity to improve and therefore join a social group with a shared goal, something I might enjoy. And I decided to make a commitment."

"Okay." Fiona sat back. She tilted her head. "You made some good choices and not so great ones."

"I know."

"Did you identify which were which?"

Amber nodded and opened up her notebook once more. She checked her table before finding the right items. "Lying could have really upset Rosie if she'd found out." Amber stuck her hands under her legs and pushed up her shoulders, her notebook bouncing in her lap. "I took a gamble and, luckily, it paid off."

"Come on, more detail. Proper moral inventory, please."

"It was wrong of me to agree to do something I had no intention, initially, to carry forward."

Fiona's face crinkled into a smile.

"I was surprised at myself though." Amber toed the edge of the rug. "I almost immediately wanted to make it right. I think before..." She swallowed. "Before I stopped drinking, I would just have thought, 'Oh well. I'm not responsible if she gets upset.' You know, like, 'Lying is okay. I can do what I want and to hell with everyone else.'"

Fiona's smile broadened. "That's really insightful."

Amber didn't feel as though she was finished. "I really took stock of how it would affect Rosie. I cared about her feelings. And not just because she was attractive."

"It helped though, I bet."

A tease? It wasn't like Fiona to bring joviality into a conversation about Amber's shortcomings.

"It didn't hinder, certainly. I guess the fact that I might enjoy myself if I kept going, as well as the thought of making Rosie happy, influenced my decision."

"So that was two weeks ago. I assume you went again this week?"

"I went to her house on Monday so she could help me with some of the songs. And then yesterday, I went to choir again. It was easier."

"You both got something out of it?"

"Yeah, she seemed really happy. Like she enjoyed being around me, I guess."

Fiona's eyes gained a twinkling quality. "And you like being the focus of her attention?"

"I do." Amber looked up sharply. "It's not just that though. I realised yesterday that now that I'm a bit more confident, being in the choir is really fun. I feel like…I'm part of something."

"I know how you feel." Fiona relaxed into her armchair. "When I was playing in orchestras, I felt like that. Now I like going to the crochet group too. When we made that huge throw, all contributing little squares to it, it felt like I was part of something big."

"AA's like that too. Like, I'm one little cog in a big machine that runs on…on support and something good."

"That's right."

Amber let out a long breath. She drank some more of her coffee. "Do you think I'm okay, then? Like, I don't need to tell Rosie I'm an alcoholic and that was why I lied?"

"Would you feel comfortable doing that?"

"I don't feel ready."

"But you will at some point? If you guys become friends?"

Amber nodded.

"And what about asking her out, if you're attracted to her?"

"No." Amber's voice came out more forcefully than she had intended. She drank the remainder of her coffee and set her cup down. "That's absolutely not something I'm ready for. Not after last year." Memories of her previous relationship, of being strung along for weeks with promises of commitment and happiness, stung her mind.

Fiona leaned across the gap between the armchair and the sofa and rubbed Amber's arm. "I think that's very sensible."

"Thank you."

"Paramount in this situation is you *not* relapsing. I don't care what anyone says; *not* drinking is your primary goal. Nothing else will be worth it if you drink."

"I know."

Chapter 6

A couple of weeks of going through the songs with Amber had left Rosie looking forward to the end of the weekend. Mondays were their day now: a chance to learn more about each other and bond over the songs. As the last week of October approached, they were given their Christmas concert repertoire.

Amber, of course, knew many of the songs from the radio and TV, but a few of them were unknown to her. Enid liked to mix it up each year, with the regular "Away In A Manger" and "Silent Night" interspersed with some tunes from *Carols For Choirs* and arrangements of pop songs from the last few decades.

"O Holy Night" was back. It had been almost a given that Rosie would take the solo, but she tried not to make out it was automatic. "It needs a descant voice, not a vibrato-y older woman." She flipped a hand in the air. "Not that I'm young. Thirty-six is younger than most in the choir though."

"I actually really like that song." Amber tapped her mug of coffee. "It's usually a bloke that sings it though, isn't it? Like a tenor?"

"Enid prefers a higher range. Don't ask me why." Rosie's cheeks burned, and she let her hair hang over her eyes. "So, you want to go through it?"

"Considering all I know is the tune, I think it might be sensible." Amber chuckled. "Would…would you sing your part too?"

A wave of unexpected shyness nearly caused Rosie to decline, but the hope in Amber's eyes glittered. "Let's do it."

Rosie brushed her fingers across the piano keys and played the introduction. She played Amber's part over the top, some of which Amber remembered from last Friday's rehearsal. "You're getting so much better."

"Thank you."

Once Amber was more confident, they sang together. Again, Rosie kept her own part very quiet, even as the music swelled for the long top note. They completed the song together in reasonable harmony.

Amber stepped away and held her arms around herself. She squeezed her eyes closed and took in a deep breath.

"Wow." Rosie dropped her hands in her lap. "You really do like the song."

"I like singing it with you." Amber's eyes flew open. Her gaze flicked about the room, then settled on a spot somewhere over Rosie's shoulder. "Well, you know, it's nice to sing with a friend."

"It is." *Is it the music making her say things like that?* "Anyway, I reckon a little more practise in choir and you'll have that one down."

Amber looked at her watch. "Hey, um…" Her gaze shifted to settle outside the window. "Would you like to…I mean…how d'you feel about going for a drink?" A clear and huge swallow. "Somewhere nice, like, not loud or…" She moved away, went to sit on the sofa, and fiddled with her hands.

Is she asking me out? Disappointment roiled inside Rosie. That hadn't been the plan, had it?

"Just…just as friends."

"You're in luck. There's a pub just down the road. They play very cool music."

"A…a pub?" Amber cleared her throat.

"Funk mixed with folk. It's pretty cool."

Amber finally looked up. She twisted her mouth and ran a hand through her hair. "You really want to go for a drink?"

"Why not?"

"Now?"

"Grab your coat."

The Stag looked old-fashioned from the outside, and the deep mahogany and leather chairs kept the feeling going once you entered. But the atmosphere was contemporary, with modern lighting and a bright and clean smell. The music was funk, with a slithery fiddle thrown in at times. It was just quiet enough to be able to have a conversation, as many people were.

"Nice?" Rosie swaggered up to the bar and leant an elbow on it.

"Nice." Amber pressed her arm against Rosie's. "What do you want?"

Rosie had decided upon zero alcohol for the whole of her pregnancy. Research these days suggested the occasional drink didn't matter so much, but with her age and her determination to make everything as safe as possible, she didn't want to take a single chance. They'd spent a little more time together, but Amber was getting to know some of the choir now and Rosie didn't want anyone knowing her secret until she was ready. "I think if I have caffeine tonight, I won't sleep. Plus, work tomorrow."

"Good thinking." Amber averted her eyes. "Wine?"

Rosie tried not to grimace. "No. I'm not really one for alcohol on a school night."

Amber looked up in surprise. "Fruit juice?"

She looks happy about that. Strange. I suppose she is driving home though. "Orange?"

"Apple for me." Two pound coins tumbled on the bar from Amber's hand.

They took their glasses over to a table by an unlit open fireplace.

"I wonder if they light it in the winter." Amber swirled her straw so her ice cubes swam around.

"I love open fires. Reminds me of Christmas at my parents' house."

Although Amber smiled, a flicker of something dark crossed her eyes.

Rosie softened. She pulled her chair around the table so she sat next to Amber. "Okay?"

"Yeah." Amber stuffed her fingers under her thighs. "I wasn't brought up in a family like that."

"No?"

A group of people laughed behind them.

Rosie brought her attention back to Amber. "I guess there are all different types of families. It doesn't have to be Mum, Dad, two kids, and a dog. Or an open fire." She shot Amber a cocky grin before nudging her with her elbow.

Amber smiled. "I used to carry around this photo of this perfect family. They had a dog and a fire. It seemed so picturesque." She sighed. "I'd love to be able to take a photo like that, with such warmth."

"That's right, you like your photography." Rosie was pleased Amber had cheered up. No need to sink them into misery by boasting about her own family. She knew she was lucky.

"Yeah."

"But you usually shoot outside-type things, don't you?" Rosie wracked her brain back to their first conversation. Had it only been four weeks ago?

"Yeah. Landscapes, sunsets, animals, mainly." Amber reached into her jacket pocket. "I took this great photo of a swarm of starlings just as the sun was about to disappear." She took out her phone and swiped a few times before holding it out to Rosie.

Rosie squinted at the screen, took in the grey-blue of the sky, the pattern the birds made, stark and black against it. The burned-out pier, harsh lines that contrasted with the flowing flock—you could practically see them moving. "That's truly beautiful."

When she looked up, she found Amber blushing. "Thanks."

"Have you ever done portraits?"

"A couple. Nothing special. My landlady, before I lived with her. She transitioned about five years ago."

"Transitioned?"

"Male to female. Don't worry, she's happy with being outed as trans. Says she carries it like a badge of honour. Once she was happy in her skin, she asked me if I'd record it before things started to sag."

"Wow."

"She's forty-four and she won't let me tell her she looks great. I took a few pictures, left them unairbrushed. Treated her to some black-and-white too. I think she's stunning." Amber seemed to shiver with quiet joy.

"Do you have the photos?"

"No. They're on my old camera, and, to be fair, they're pretty personal. She wouldn't be happy for me to show them to you."

Rosie held up both hands. "Oh, sure." She fingered a droplet making its way down her glass. "I guess they would be kind of personal."

"She looks good for her age. I hope I get to look like her when I'm forty-four."

"How old are you?"

"I was thirty-one last month."

"Cute." Rosie bit her tongue. *Stop flirting.* "I'm a bit older, but we would have been in secondary school at the same time."

Amber took a sip of her juice. "Were you a good girl at school?"

"Didn't have a whole lot of choice." Rosie nodded towards her. "Vicar dad. Expectations to do well."

"I guess you didn't."

"Came out with twelve GCSEs, four A-levels. Straight into uni from sixth form."

"Me too, although I don't think anyone ever expected me to do that well."

Rosie sat back in her chair and crossed her legs. Her awareness flickered down to her belly. *Is it sticking out yet? Do I look pregnant?* Not wanting to draw attention to it if Amber had noticed, she left it a minute before sitting up straighter. "What did you do at uni?"

"English Lit."

"Enjoy it?"

"Yes, but it was never going anywhere. I just enjoyed reading. Didn't want to teach it or take it further." Amber shrugged. "Was just nice to have a degree."

"Well, obviously, my university course was teacher training. Did it at Bristol Uni, then straight into teaching."

"I went to Bath."

"Nice uni."

Amber shrugged again, an uneasy look in her eye. "It was okay."

Should she ask further about Amber's experience at Bath? Perhaps she should wait; that way if Amber wanted to embellish, she could without pressure.

Amber drank a third of her apple juice, her gaze downwards. When she looked up, she smiled. "So funk and folk?"

"You like it?"

"It's awesome." Amber waved towards the speaker above them.

Another song had come on—a lilting rhythm and another violin taking the tune. "Who would have thought the two styles would go together?" Rosie lifted her glass. "To funk and folk and the genius that mixed the two."

Amber grinned and clicked her glass with Rosie's. "And to many more drinks here."

"Ah, you want it to be a regular thing, then? Me and you meeting for a drink?"

"Only…" Amber started, her lip in her mouth, "if that's something you'd like?"

Rosie considered brushing it off, making a joke. Being seen as too keen wouldn't make anyone happy, especially if Amber was attracted to her. It did feel as if there was a spark between them, but she didn't want Amber to get the wrong impression. There was now someone else to consider; it wasn't just her alone anymore.

But it was nice hanging out with Amber. She was sweet, intelligent, and had a great sense of humour underneath her shy exterior. *I reckon I could be assertive if things went too far, let her down easily. It's not like I haven't done it before.*

"Yes, it is something I'd like."

Rosie enjoyed the walk home with Amber's shiny shoes treading the pavement next to her own boots. She had friends, of course, and she had her sister. But it was nice to have a friend she had something else in common with other than teaching and her parents.

And it had been nice that Amber had agreed to juice too. With both of them not drinking alcohol, Rosie hadn't felt so exposed. Seeing Amber's photos had been enlightening; Amber hadn't worn her camera around her neck since that first rehearsal.

Amber got into her landlady's car and drove away. Rosie had a strong urge to progress their acquaintance further—past simply teaching Amber how to sing and past going out for a glass of juice to a quirky pub with excellent music. She wanted to find out what made Amber tick. She wanted to find out what the heartbroken darkness in Amber's eyes had been about when they'd discussed Rosie's perfect family.

Chapter 7

November arrived. Leaves fell, and a hustling wind caught Rosie's coat as she skipped from her car to the hospital entrance. She'd put the last colouring pencils away and driven straight there. Drank about six glasses of water. Full bladder: check. Twelve weeks: also check. It seemed like an age since she'd had the blood test to confirm it all.

This was the next step: another cinder block in the construction of her becoming a mother. The word didn't sit comfortably with her—*mother* was far too formal and made her insides twist. She'd probably be *mum*, or perhaps *mummy* at first.

Chelsea and Charlie were already inside, the former swinging her legs on the too-tall chair in the waiting room of the radiology department. Unusually, she stayed seated rather than rushing over to Rosie to give her a hug, but she vibrated with excitement.

"Presume you've been a very good monkey?" Rosie winked at Chelsea.

"Yeah, totally. I've kept my room so clean just so I could come see the baby." She hissed the last two words.

Rosie glanced about her, anxious in case a choir member, with their ears wagging, might be in the hospital too. She didn't recognise anyone, however. Her insides relaxed and she managed a smile. "How lucky are you?"

"I've told her she has to keep her eyes closed until you've seen it first. Otherwise, it's not fair." Charlie cuddled Chelsea into her side.

"That's a nice idea. Thanks, dude."

Chelsea pressed her lips forward and nodded. She knotted her fingers together and swung her legs some more. Her shoes were shiny, like Amber's.

Rosie sighed and nearly laughed aloud. *On the pinnacle of seeing your child for the first time, you're thinking of a girl you met less than two months ago.* They'd spent a few more Monday evenings working on the Christmas numbers, as well as going out again for juice. It remained a friendship thing; they talked about day-to-day things rather than anything deeper. Once they lit the open fire at the pub, maybe Rosie would pluck up the courage to bring up Amber's family again.

She nearly jumped out of her plastic chair when her name was called. Her legs were numb as she walked down the corridor and into a small room with a bed. It smelled like antiseptic. The walls were too bright a white.

"My name's Lucinda. You've drunk plenty of water?" The sonographer was talking to her.

Rosie nodded and took a deep breath. "Yes. Sorry."

"It's okay."

A small, warm hand in her own. Chelsea's big blue eyes stared up at her. "Don't worry, Auntie Rosie. We're both here for you."

It wasn't every day eight-year-old Chelsea displayed so much understanding. Rosie hated to admit it, but Chelsea was somewhat *blonde*. She liked dresses and princesses and ponies. Charlie was similar with her golden hair, manicured nails, and sparkly make-up; she was the epitome of girliness. Not that Rosie minded—it was nice to have a sister who wasn't her mirror image.

"Thanks, monkey."

Chelsea beamed and sat primly on the chair to the side of the bed.

After climbing onto the bed, Rosie hesitated before pulling her booted feet up onto it. It was wipe-clean. No airs or graces needed.

Lucinda squirted the gel onto the ultrasound thingy and asked Rosie to lift her top. When she applied the cold end of it to her skin, Chelsea smacked her hands over her eyes. Charlie grinned and averted her gaze too.

Everything inside Rosie seemed like granite. Her jaw ached from where she was clenching it, and she pressed her fists into her thighs.

Lucinda laid a gentle hand on her knee. "Relax, Rosie."

Rosie swallowed. *How am I supposed to do that?* She tried to remember the mindfulness classes she'd done after the last couple of failed attempts to get pregnant. The idea had been to give her body the best chance at conceiving. It had made all the difference at the time so she tried it again now. Deep breaths in through her nose, out through her mouth. Taking note of the things around her, the delicate clouds in the sky out of the small window. The traffic she could barely hear, birdsong just on her periphery.

Rosie's bladder hurt, but that was insignificant. She turned her head on the paper sheet and gave Lucinda a tight smile.

"Oh my God, can I look yet?"

That made Rosie laugh, which in turn made her relax further. "I've not even seen yet, Chels. Give it a minute, yeah?"

Charlie snorted too, her attention still across the room.

Rosie rolled her eyes to the ceiling but remembered what was going to happen and turned back to the monitor.

A small, super-fuzzy, black-and-white kidney bean was just about visible. It had a head twice the size of the rest of it. It moved around a bit, or appeared to. Rosie squinted, incredulity rising up inside her. "Um…is that it?"

"Someone was easy to find." One of Lucinda's eyebrows rose to near her hairline.

"Probably an extrovert." She still wasn't sure what on earth she was actually looking at. She felt like she *should* know—who doesn't croon and sigh over their first scan?

"Most likely." Lucinda smiled. "I'd say your estimation was correct. We're just about twelve weeks. Due first of May." She shifted sideways to write that down, keeping the stick thing from the ultrasound in place.

A squealing noise sounded from across the room.

Rosie found two squirming blondes with their hands still covering their faces. "Okay, you can look."

Charlie and Chelsea crept over. Chelsea peered with a wrinkled nose at the screen.

"Here's baby's head, and arms, can you see?" Lucinda seemed more comfortable talking to Chelsea in such a way. It gave Rosie a chance to work it out too without her having to ask what the squiggly line was around the baby's backside. Apparently nothing, just some gunk inside her. *This is my baby. I can see my baby.*

Suddenly lightheaded, but also experiencing a surge of strength, Rosie tried to lean forward to see. She gripped the side of the bed and reached with her free hand to touch the screen where the radiographer told her the baby's head was.

"And here we have a strong heartbeat."

Thank goodness. Tears sprang to her eyes, and she startled and blinked. This wasn't her at all—she didn't cry, especially not at happy things. She might have shed a tear if someone she knew died—she had when Michaela, her best friend at sixth form, had—but this was the exact opposite of someone dying. This was someone she would know forever being confirmed as *alive.* And that was bigger than anything she had ever done.

Lucinda finished manoeuvring the wand across her belly, found the perfect picture, and printed it out for her. Rosie wiped the gunk with a paper towel before shuffling to sit on the bed between her sister and niece, the three of them craning to see the photo.

"Baby looks healthy. See you again in eight weeks?" Lucinda handed her a file.

Rosie wondered whether she was asking permission. Of *course* she'd attend all her appointments. Any chance to see her little kidney bean baby as he or she grew. *Kidney bean. That's a nice name for him or her before she or he comes out to meet me.* Rosie swallowed when she thought about the issue of gender. *A baby boy would be okay, but would he remind me too much of Ali?* Rosie's chest hurt as she remembered the too-small, too-sick bundle she'd cradled after the tragedy that had been his birth.

With a shake of her head, she banished the memory. *Boy or girl, I'll be happy.* Chelsea and Charlie had been given the privilege of taking the second and third glances at her baby—not including Lucinda, of course—but they didn't need to share in her residual grief too.

Once Rosie had relieved her aching bladder, they went across the road for a coffee. Rosie's mind still spun. She clutched her photo for a while before she realised what she was doing and smoothed it out, held it more carefully. Sitting on the squeaky leather sofa with Chelsea stuffing gingerbread down her gullet next to her, a joy crept up Rosie's body—from her toes to the top of her head.

I'm going to be a mum.

Chapter 8

Nico twirled on the spot, his curly tail waving. He placed his tiny bottom on the carpet, and his eyes seemed to grow even more round than usual. After a couple of seconds, he lifted both paws and stroked the air.

Amber relented and gave him his treat. He'd trotted by her side on his walk and hadn't tugged on his lead. He'd sniffed a few backsides, much to other owners' amusement, and although he was often far too short to reach, he had a good go anyway.

It only took a speedy roll of his ball across the floor to get him interested. He chased it a few feet before tackling it and lying down with the ball between his front paws. That would keep him occupied for a few minutes, time enough for Amber to make herself a drink

Steam rose from the spout of the kettle. One tea bag, one sugar, a little milk. The spoon tinkled against the mug as she mixed everything together, utilising the time to consider. She'd been to eight choir rehearsals. The songs were now implanted within her brain, their roots expanding more each time Rosie tutored her. Last week Amber had sung her part heartily, now ready for the Christmas concert in four weeks.

Amber checked her phone and saw she had a text from Rosie, asking how she was. Sunshine burst within her. It wasn't something they'd done yet despite having met up several times in the last few weeks. They didn't chat via text. Just a natter over fruit juice.

She replied, saying she was well, that she had done some training with Nico and had managed to snap some gorgeous pictures of him. Such a handsome boy all reclined on the armchair, his pointy ears to attention. His ginger coat shone in the light from the lamp.

Throwing caution to the wind, Amber sent Rosie one of the photos. She wasn't one to brag, but she was pleased with how that one in particular had turned out—his colouring, the green décor, and the orange glow; it was artistic.

She took her tea into the living room. Her phone buzzed with a reply. Positive comments from Rosie with a few emojis. The last one was a red heart. Amber tried not to allow her hopes to soar too wildly.

The front door opened and closed. Amber set her phone on the coffee table and pulled her feet underneath her.

Jilly pushed her way into the living room, the dog immediately at her heels. "All right, Nico. One minute." It made Amber smile—Nico was always keen to say hi to his mum before she'd even properly arrived home.

"Hey." Amber sipped her cup of tea, forgotten during her brief text conversation. "Good day?"

With one long leg holding open the door, Jilly slid her boot off the other and attempted to bat an excited Nico away with her free hand. Amber marvelled at her multitasking ability. "Not bad, thanks, hon. You?"

"Work was good. Usual stuff: much filing, directing people to the correct waiting room."

"You walked this crazy fool?"

Amber chuckled. "Yeah. He was a good boy."

Nico yapped once before sitting down, his tongue lolling out.

Finally able to pull her slippers on, Jilly scooped him up under one arm. "What you been up to, little man? Causing trouble in the neighbourhood?"

Kicking his miniscule feet, Nico wagged his tail and licked Jilly's cheek.

"Disgusting." She slumped into her usual armchair. Nico rolled onto his back in her lap, his belly exposed for her to tickle. "You clean your bits with that mouth of yours."

Amber smothered another laugh. "We did a bit of training. Then I took his picture."

"Aw, my little model."

"How was your day?"

"Okay. Mrs Brown wants more shrubs put in. I've told her once winter is over, I'll happily get all the plants she desires. Until then, she'll have to put up with me pruning the stuff she already has."

"Is that the old lady in the bungalow?"

"The same." Jilly stretched her legs. A rumble passed through her, deep and full of indulgence. "She doesn't seem to understand the seasons. Winter is cold, you know."

Amber's sweet tea sent warm tendrils into her belly. "I heard something about snow on the radio."

"Fine by me. Snow means a couple of days inside with the telly on." She turned her green eyes towards Amber. "Fancy a Chinese?"

"Could do." Amber's phone buzzed again. She pursed her lips and pulled the bottom one into her mouth, her gaze flicking down.

Jilly lifted her eyebrows. "Rosie?"

Amber nodded, then giggled. "She sent me a picture of a cat with a camera." She picked up her phone. "Oh. It's a moving picture."

"What is she sending you cat pictures for?"

"I sent her one of Nico looking all dapper. She said it was cool." Amber put a hand to her cheek as she checked the message properly. Once she'd replied to the text, she put her phone away.

"You meeting up again?" Jilly's tone was light, maybe too light.

"Yeah. Well, I expect so. We've been meeting up every Monday." She shrugged, scrunching her toes into the sofa. She flattened her skirt over her leggings before taking another sip of tea. "The pub near her house must be getting sick of us."

It was a while before Amber could look up. When she did, Jilly eyed her.

Amber tried not to shrink into the sofa cushions. "It's been fine. We've both had juice every time we've been." She shrugged. "I've felt okay with it."

A smile crinkled the corners of Jilly's eyes. "Good for you." She sighed, and the air in the room seemed less thick. "I remember when I first started going into pubs after I stopped drinking. It was weird at first with all that alcohol around you and people downing the stuff as if it were normal. I felt like such an outsider, an oddity. But I went with people I knew, so it didn't really matter."

Amber grinned at her. “Back in the day, right?”

Jilly was well past taking offence. “Back in the day.” She winked. “Hope Rosie was supportive.”

“She hasn’t been drinking either.” Amber furrowed her eyebrows and touched her chin. “I’m starting to wonder if she’s in recovery too.”

Nico squirmed in Jilly’s arms until she released him. He hopped onto the floor and went to chew his tennis ball again.

“Who knows? Not everyone shouts about it.”

“I guess that’s true.” Amber fingered the handle of her cup. “I don’t even remember who suggested we have juice. I think it was Rosie. She didn’t want to…didn’t want caffeine. Not so late.”

“Some people just don’t drink. They don’t have to be in AA.”

Amber nodded and checked her phone again. No reply. Well, that was okay. *I’m sure Rosie has better things to do on a Thursday night than text me.*

“I’m glad you’ve taken that step. Is Fi proud of you?”

“She is, yeah.” Amber pushed up her shoulders and wriggled. “She says I’m more self-aware than I was a year ago. More able to reflect.” She placed her phone screen-down onto the sofa. She shook herself and turned to Jilly. “Being in the pub, I was more concerned with Rosie not finding out I didn’t drink, or why I didn’t drink, than I was with the thought that I might relapse.”

“You didn’t feel the urge?”

“Nope. Far too much fun talking to Rosie.”

Jilly’s look was part impressed, part knowing.

Amber glared at her, jokingly. “No third degrees, yeah?”

Jilly raised her hands. “I wasn’t even going to give you a first degree, let alone a second or third. It’s your life.”

Still, Amber’s belly twisted into knots. She’d just have to get used to it, people knowing she went to a pub every week. Up until now, she’d avoided them as if they’d held the plague. Hopefully one day it would be so normal she wouldn’t have to worry about it.

Chapter 9

Rosie was in her car outside her parents' house when she felt it. A squirm, or a flutter, right in her abdomen. *Is that the baby?* She sat still for a while.

Nothing else happened. Maybe it had been a stray baked bean. Or her growing hunger. Luckily, the nausea had eased to the occasional twinge when she hadn't eaten breakfast yet. Good job—school was full of nativity rehearsals and kids too high on the expectation of Father Christmas for her to have time to snack. It wasn't even December yet.

She slid out of her car in a fashion just shy of awkward. The gravel crunched as she made her way up her parents' front path. Firelight glowed through the gaps of the curtains in the bay window.

After letting herself in, she caught a few notes on the piano—her mother most likely. Something classical, of course. Chelsea chattered over the top. The scent of bread and roasted chicken caught her appetite. A shift in her belly again, but this time it was definitely hunger.

Rosie pushed open the door to the music room, where much of the activity seemed to be located. Her mother, Kath, sat at the piano, trailing her fingers over the keys like anemone tentacles in a gentle current. Rosie's father, Nick, in his usual grey shirt, blue jeans, and dog collar, lounged in the armchair with a glass of wine. His eyes were closed and his head bobbed in time with the music. Charlie sat on the rug by Tom's feet, her cheek resting against his shin, a similar glass of wine cradled in her fingers. Her hair looked like a field of wheat in the firelight.

Chelsea saw her first, the only one who hadn't drifted off with the tune. She put an arm around Rosie's waist. "Hi, Auntie Rosie."

"Hey." Rosie leant down so she could whisper into her ear. "What's going on?"

"Grandma is playing *Inna Clinna Nact Music*. And Mummy is asleep on Daddy. And Granddad is drunk."

Nick peeked one eye open but closed it again, his lips wrinkling as he tried not to smile.

"And what are you doing?"

"I'm trying to decide what to call my new guinea pig."

"You got a guinea pig?"

"She's not getting one yet." Charlie stretched and stood from the floor.

"We're just in discussion." Chelsea made it sound very serious.

Rosie nodded. "Well, I hope you've got a time frame from them, monkey. Wouldn't be fair for them to leave you hanging indefinitely."

"Once a certain someone has proved and promised they can look after a guinea pig, a certain someone can have one."

"Oh well, you'll get one tomorrow, then, I expect." Rosie grinned at her.

With a squeal, Chelsea hopped across the room and jumped into her father's lap.

Tom appeared to wake with a jolt and grabbed Chelsea around the middle.

That was the end of *Eine Kleine Nachtmusik*. Dear Mozart must have turned in his grave.

After pushing the stool backwards, Kath rose as well, and she and Charlie took it in turns to hug Rosie. Rosie pressed her nose into her mother's shoulder, the cotton cardigan with the purple flowers. Lavender and rosemary tickled her nostrils. Coming home always smelled like her parents' herb garden.

"How are you feeling today?"

Typical. I'm just in the door and already she's dripping with concern. Rosie forced a kind smile. "I'm okay, thanks."

"You look well." The lines between her eyebrows suggested Kath wasn't convinced.

"Honestly, I'm good. My only complaint is that you're cooking chicken and for some reason it's not on a plate in front of me. K.B. wants chicken today."

"Kaaaay Beeee!" Chelsea clambered from Tom.

"You know what? Either K.B. moved in the car or I did a tiny fart." Rosie combed her fingers through Chelsea's golden locks. "What d'you think?"

More squealing, and Chelsea felt her midriff.

"At sixteen weeks? That's about right, isn't it, Charlie?" Kath still had that concerned expression, but Rosie chose to ignore it. She couldn't force her mother to relax when she didn't want to.

"About right, yeah." Charlie's gaze flicked down to Chelsea bouncing around them. "Did you want to go open that new bottle of squash we brought to keep here?"

Chelsea stopped her impression of a rubber ball. "Yes, please."

Charlie whistled and chucked her head towards the kitchen.

Once they were alone, with only adults within hearing distance, Charlie patted the sofa, and Tom moved up so they could all sit together. Kath perched again on the piano stool. Nick continued to enjoy his glass of wine.

"So, things are really okay?" No heavy concern from Charlie, just interest.

"Yeah not bad. Like I said, craving chicken like nobody's business. Otherwise, all good." She squirmed. "Trousers are getting a bit tight."

"I feel an imminent shopping excursion." Charlie winked at her. "Next weekend?"

"Don't think I'm quite ready to see what the great M&S has in stock for me yet." Rosie smoothed her palm over Charlie's hand. "I'm going to get some of those band things off the net. The ones that clip to your fly so you don't have to do your trousers up."

"Are your boobs getting bigger?"

Tom slapped his hands over his ears. Nick came to from his Mozart stupor enough to react in a similar fashion.

"Oh my God, like, not in front of the parentals, yeah?"

"Pfft." Charlie waved at her husband as if he didn't matter. "Tom doesn't give a crap, and Dad won't remember in the morning."

"*I* give a crap," Rosie argued. "I'm not discussing my breasts with my father or my brother-in-law."

Charlie looked at both men, then shot Rosie an expectant look. They both still had their hands over their ears.

Rosie rolled her eyes. "But yeah. Like two cup sizes."

"New bras too, then. M&S are so good for maternity bras."

"Are you kidding? Do I look like a maternity bra type of person?"

Kath shifted on the stool but rubbed her chin. "Darling, you'll need to get some kind of support if you're intent on breastfeeding."

"It's fine. I'll just..." She pulled at the neck of her T-shirt, then made as if to pop her boob out the top.

Charlie laughed. "I'm *so* coming with you the first time you try that trick in Waitrose."

Rosie's cheeks scorched. She gritted her teeth, looked from her mother to her sister, then, again, rolled her eyes. "Fine. New bras. But," she pointed at Charlie, "no flowers and shit, okay?"

"Language," Kath growled.

Rosie ignored her, her glare on Charlie real and strong.

"Oh no, totally. I know you: about as girly as Russell Crowe."

"Can I take my hands away yet? I'm getting bored." Tom sounded apologetic.

"Oh, we are so done with this conversation. Dad? Dad!"

Nick looked around him.

The door thwacked open, and Chelsea bounded in, her glass of squash slopping. Her expression went from happy to pure joy as she looked at Rosie. "Oh, wow. Look at your baby bump!"

Rosie frowned down at herself. *Am I showing? How did I not realise?* She wasn't one to look at herself in the mirror, not for longer than it took to apply her make-up. But, as she sat back on the sofa, squished between her sister and brother-in-law, she realised her tummy protruded.

"Oh. Would you look at that?" She directed a grin at Chelsea.

Chelsea knelt on the floor in front of her and cuddled her leg, her mess of curls resting against Rosie's bump. "Do you think K.B. will talk to me?"

"Not yet." Rosie patted her head. "But K.B. can hear voices, so you can talk if you like."

Chelsea looked as if she'd been given a thousand guinea pigs. Kath took the glass from her and placed it on a coaster on the piano whilst Chelsea shifted to get a better angle. She climbed onto the sofa in the end, the opposite side to her mother. "Hi, little K.B. Can you hear me? This is your favourite cousin, Chelsea."

Kath took Nick into the kitchen to help with dinner. Tom followed soon afterwards.

The three of them were alone. Charlie snuggled back next to Rosie and threw an arm around her shoulders. She was warm, and her cashmere jumper was soft against Rosie's cheek.

Chelsea continued her conversation with Kidney Bean, occasionally patting Rosie's bump and rocking her head from side to side.

"You all right though?" Charlie breathed.

"Sure. Tickety-boo."

"They only care. I know you know that."

"Yeah." Rosie let out a strangled but quiet moan. "I just… I know they think it's going to be difficult as I'm by myself. But it's also going to be brilliant. Like, I don't have to argue with someone else about whether my kid can have sugar or inoculations or a dummy. I get to be autonomous. Self-ruling, you know?"

"I'm not saying Tom and I agreed on every single thing, but it was easier having him around. Obviously, it still is." Charlie rubbed Rosie's arm. "I don't want you to struggle."

"I know." Rosie lifted her head from Charlie's shoulder. "And if I do struggle, you'll be the first to know and the one I come to."

"That's always been the agreement even before you decided to get up the duff by yourself."

Rosie stuck her tongue out at her, but it was short-lived. She snuck back under Charlie's chin and turned so she could wrap an arm over her belly. "Love you, mate."

"Love you too, you imbecile."

Chelsea's head popped up. "What's a *nimbecile*?"

"Don't ask." Charlie pulled Chelsea back against them both. "We're going to give Rosie lots of cuddles, aren't we, Chels?"

"Of course. Cuddles are the best things in the whole world." A pause. "Apart from guinea pigs, which I am totally having before Christmas."

Laughter bounced around the music room until they were all called in for dinner.

Chapter 10

Rosie smoothed the front of her maternity vest top and strode into the church hall. She glanced about, but the place was deserted.

A few people from the other room were just leaving. She gave a tight smile to a few of them, unsure what the group was. Seemed to be some sort of therapy or maybe a support group. It was nice struggling people had a place to go, especially so close to Christmas. She wondered whether they sung "Kum Ba Yah" and held hands. A flashback to her own primary school days.

She went into the choir room and took chairs for herself and Amber. She didn't want to be the kind of pregnant person who refused to lift anything ever again, but she knew the risks. All the sensible things: lifting with her knees and holding each chair close to her body. Even so, she worried she was pressing on her bump too much.

Had it grown in the last week? Finally looking at herself in the mirror in the nude, she'd considered the protuberance with interest. It was fun to smooth her hands over her naked belly and trace the dark line from her navel. She looked as if she'd had a very big meal…and as if she was pregnant.

Choir members started to arrive, and she sat down. The open man's shirt hung over her, covering her belly. It obscured the top of her jeans too, which were elastic. Another maternity thing she hadn't planned on getting. Admittedly, they were comfortable.

Amber trotted in—shiny shoes and black skater skirt—her camera around her neck. "Hi."

“Hey.” Rosie tensed as she waited for some kind of comment about her outfit.

“It’s horrible out there, isn’t it?” Amber combed a hand through her hair and tucked a strand behind her ear. It had a few curls, maybe due to the rain. “I’m just waiting for it to snow or something.” Her nose wrinkled.

Rosie took a breath. “Yeah. Really horrible.”

After settling in the chair beside her, Amber held her hand out. “Can I just look over that new Christmas one? The Rutter one?”

Rosie blinked. “Oh. Sure.” She rifled through their folder and handed Amber the piece she wanted.

For a little while, Amber poured over the music. She sucked her bottom lip and furrowed her eyebrows.

Maybe she hasn’t even noticed my outfit. She hasn’t commented on anything I’ve worn before. A surge of bitter reality coursed through her. Why would Amber notice Rosie’s clothes? And if she did, was she too polite to comment? She was here to sing, to take part in a choir, not to be Rosie’s fashion critic.

Everything loosened. Rosie wiggled her shoulders a bit to get rid of the last bit of tension.

Amber arched an eyebrow. “You all right?”

“Yeah. Excellent.” Rosie shot her a cocky smile, caught herself, and turned the volume down to pleasant. “You?”

Amber nodded. “Can’t believe it.”

A hard stone appeared in Rosie’s stomach. “Can’t believe what?”

“That it’s only two weeks until the concert.”

“Oh.” The stone dissolved. “It’s going to be great.” She nudged Amber with her elbow. “You’ll see.”

“You know what? I thought I’d be feeling nervous about it.” Amber pushed one shoulder up to her ear. “But I’m kind of not.” A deep and joyous look. “And I guess I ought to thank you, once again, for your help.”

Rosie flapped a hand at her. “Don’t be silly. Was nice to do some private teaching again. Been a year or two.” She chuckled.

Amber appeared to be about to say something else just as Enid clapped to get everyone’s attention.

After a very productive rehearsal, during which the warblers behind Rosie and Amber had been less warbly than usual, Rosie helped Amber clear their chairs.

Before she knew it, Amber was looking her up and down. "Oh. I like that shirt on you."

Maybe she does look at what I wear. Rosie tried to keep her cool. "Thanks."

"Is it new? I've not seen it before."

Rosie followed her out of the hall and into the chilly but dry night air. "Um, yeah." She shrugged. "Fancied something a bit looser. I wear a lot of tight clothes for work."

"Yeah, I mean I like your tight T-shirts and stuff," Amber's cheeks reddened, but it could have been the sudden change in temperature, "but I can imagine something looser would feel more comfortable." Her eyes shone under the streetlamp. "And I'm all for comfort." She swept her hand down her own outfit as if in indication. "Obviously."

"Yeah, you always look really comfortable." Rosie walked beside her, her leather jacket exchanged for a thick wool coat. It hid her figure and made her relax despite the cold. "I like what you wear." She hoped she didn't sound forward.

"Thanks." Amber shot her a confused look. "Are you walking me home as well as complimenting my style?"

Rosie laughed, her breath spiralling upwards. "I'm parked down by Beach Lawns. Nowhere to put my car this time of year, especially with all the late-night shopping."

"Bloody Christmas." Amber grinned. "Nice to have a little more time to chat though."

Rosie considered her options. They'd spent so much time together talking about this and that on their Monday evenings, but she hadn't scratched the surface with Amber—hadn't got to the bottom of that sadness in her eyes. But did she want to? Despite her decision to, on the one hand, *not* tell Amber about her pregnancy and, on the other, put her straight if Amber made a move, Rosie didn't want to lead her on. And talking about things like their miserable pasts would lead them in that direction.

It annoyed her that she'd met Amber now and not two years ago, or maybe even in two years' time. She'd have had an eighteen-month-old with the latter option and would be able to date occasionally, woo a woman. Plenty of time then to sort out her love life, if she even wanted one.

But that was life, she supposed—a wide collection of mishaps until sometime along the way you found a sort of happiness.

"Yeah really nice." She clocked Amber's camera. "Were you going to take some pictures?"

"Yeah. Night ones." Amber stopped, fingering her lens cap, her bottom lip in her mouth. "I can wait until you get to your car though."

"Don't mind me. Can you talk and shoot?"

A bright smile. "Yeah, I can."

"Multitasking. I like it." Rosie bit her tongue but tried not to let it show. *Stop it, you fool.*

A flicker of relief crossed Amber's face. She stepped up to the wall in front of the beach and clicked the cap from her camera. She stood for a while, turning knobs and flicking switches.

Rosie couldn't keep her gaze off her. The way Amber caressed each part of the camera, coaxing it to do her bidding, made her mouth water. She sat on the wall, the stone bumpy under her backside. She huddled up, the wind pulling her hair about, chilling her cheeks. At least she had enough layers that nothing else was cold.

Amber's exhaled breath misted around her, then disappeared as she peered into the screen on the back of the camera and nodded just once. "Brean Down gets lit up sometimes." She indicated the tall jut of land that stuck out beyond the pier. "I think it's beautiful."

A dark evening. Michaela calling, from too far away to reach, encouraging Rosie to follow her. Excitement at the prospect of reaching Brean Down on foot across the sand. Then fear. Then silence.

Trying to hide the twisting of her insides, Rosie kept her attention on Amber. "Is…is that what you're shooting?"

Another nod. "I'm going to capture the Grand Atlantic Hotel too when we get closer to it."

That was safer ground. At least Rosie could pretend Brean Down didn't exist if she focused on the hotel halfway along Weston seafront. "Let's get walking, then. I'm about to freeze my tits off."

Amber giggled, replaced the lens cap, and dropped into step beside her.

A few gulls circled the beach, and the string of lights that stretched along the promenade swung in the wind. Rosie didn't realise she'd moved closer until their arms brushed. She pulled back a tad, but Amber smiled and hooked her arm through Rosie's.

Amber's elbow was close to Rosie's side. The mad fear Amber would touch her waist and feel the baby bump, even through two layers of clothing and a thick coat, made Rosie ball her fist in her pocket. But Amber's hand on her upper arm was consistent and grounding. Rosie couldn't avoid taking pleasure from it.

"What are you doing for Christmas?" The question left Rosie's mouth before she'd decided it might not be the thing to ask.

Amber stiffened against her. "I'm staying in with Jilly and Nico."

"Not seeing your folks?"

Full lips became thin. Amber let go of Rosie's arm. "No."

Rosie came to a halt. "How come? That sucks."

"Yeah, well…" Amber sighed and lifted one shoulder. "I told you. I'm not in contact with them."

Rosie blinked. "What, not at all?"

Amber shook her head.

Oh. Her boot scuffing the concrete, Rosie stared somewhere across the promenade, into the night.

"It's no big deal." Amber fiddled with her fingers before stuffing her hands into her coat pockets. Her mouth twisted. Then she seemed to snap out of it and smiled again. "We're just very different."

"But what about the rest of your family? Aunts, uncles? Grandparents?"

"I only have one grandmother, and she isn't in touch with me either."

Sorrow pulled at Rosie, then guided her forwards. For a moment, she didn't care about her secret or about keeping it concealed. There was just the devastating desire to comfort Amber.

She slid her arms around her, rested her chin on Amber's shoulder. She was a couple of inches taller than Amber, something she'd never noticed before.

Amber responded in the same fashion. The embrace didn't last long, but Rosie inhaled every scent that clung to Amber's hair in the process. She didn't try to; it just happened.

When they pulled back, Amber looked happier. "It's okay, really. I have a great unit of friends." She held her hands out as if to show Rosie the size of the unit and how close it was. "My bestie, Harry, he and his boyfriend might come round too. Jilly keeps saying she'll make mince pies. I've not had them homemade before."

"You've never had…?" Rosie bit her tongue again. After taking a breath, she shook herself. "Sorry. That sounds lovely, actually."

"I'm guessing your family all get together, and you have turkey and all the trimmings."

They started to walk again, the air now a little brighter.

"We do. We even sing carols around the piano, if you can believe it."

"With your epic open fire and matching jumpers."

Rosie took the tease with good grace. After all, she was very lucky. But a Christmas with good friends sounded just as uplifting as one with good family. Who was she to judge?

That explains why she looked so upset the first time we talked. Rosie made the decision there and then to treat Amber with care. Whatever had happened between her and her parents—and the rest of her family, apparently—it didn't sound good. Or maybe they had, as Amber had hinted at, just become different people. But Amber was so lovely. Who wouldn't want to spend time with her?

They parted at Rosie's car, and she made sure to faff with things in the boot for a while so Amber didn't see her slide in with her hidden bump. She whacked up the heat and waited for her windscreen to clear, all the while trying to imagine a life without the loving family she was so very used to.

Chapter 11

The journey to The Range, a large store that sold everything from homewares to gardening things, was pleasant, with much giggling at the Christmas songs on the radio and Rosie's delightful impersonations of the singers. Amber wondered why she wasn't on the stage with her ability to copy such a range of artists, however exaggeratedly. She'd be a great comedian or impressionist. Such presence too; an energy that flowed farther than the walls of the car. Amber could imagine her class hung on her every word.

Rosie had phoned Amber that morning—the Saturday after their walk along the seafront—to request her assistance with buying a Christmas tree. As Amber had nothing more important to do, and at the promise of a hot drink in the store's café, Amber had agreed. The tingly feeling Amber experienced at the thought of spending time with Rosie also made it an easy decision.

They found the Christmas section—perhaps *wandered into* was more accurate as it was the first thing they saw when they entered—and stepped into an aisle.

"Jilly gets her tools from here." Amber took in the array of sparkling and flashing decorations. If she blocked out her peripheral vision, she could pretend she was immersed on all sides by the festivities. The glow coming from them was almost warm on her cheek.

When she turned her smile to Rosie, she found Rosie's expression half-curious, and half something she couldn't identify.

Amber's cheeks burned. "What?"

"Nothing. You just look really happy."

Amber smiled to herself and went to touch a glittery penguin. "Am I not allowed to be happy?"

"Of course you are." She could feel Rosie behind her, and when she looked, she found she was still watching her. "I just…you know…you were sad yesterday when we discussed Christmas and families and stuff." She blew out a breath as if searching for the right words. "It's nice, I suppose. I'd much rather you were happy."

Their gazes locked, and before Amber could stop it, a spark passed between them. She looked away. The feathery head of the penguin was soft under her fingertips.

They continued along the row of lights and ornaments until they arrived out the other side and at a large collection of Christmas trees.

"Aha, just what we've been looking for."

"Excellent." Rosie rubbed her hands together and paced through the selection, stopping at a few, touching her chin as she checked out the photos on the boxes.

Amber tried to shake off her own daze but found it stuck to her like superglue. Perhaps if she ignored it, it would leave. She approached a box that said it contained a seven-foot tree and scrutinised the picture. It looked almost real—fluffy and different shades of green. She glanced up to beckon Rosie over, but she was nowhere to be seen.

I could go look for her, but I could do with a moment more to myself. Half of her pulled her towards Rosie, laughing at her fear of getting close. The other half cowered but spoke with a stern voice. Just friends. Hadn't they decided that weeks ago?

A touch to her shoulder made her whip around.

"I found what I thought was the perfect tree, but I see yours is way better." Rosie smoothed the top of the box and tilted the whole thing backwards to read the description. "Epic. Perfect. I want this one."

Rosie stood close to Amber—so close, in fact, that Amber moved into her side. She snuck her hand under Rosie's arm as they stood there. It was so nice to be close, whatever Amber's fears told her.

Amber cleared her throat. "It's really pretty."

Something musical chimed from a few aisles away. Two young children laughed and thundered from left to right. Santa ho-ho-ho-ed, which clashed with the music over the sound system.

"Do you need ornaments or anything?"

"I have plenty." Rosie bent to grasp the box with both arms and made to lift it.

"Oh, I'll get it." Amber stooped too and held on in a similar fashion. She expected Rosie to argue, say she could get it herself.

"Actually, yeah, if you could? Makes getting my purse out and paying a lot easier."

Amber was content to carry the large box over to the counter so Rosie could pay for it and to lug the thing outside to the car.

After much manoeuvring and some light swearing, they got it in the boot with the back seats down. The image of it next to Rosie's piano, in pride of place in her living room, covered in lights and stylish baubles, flashed through Amber's mind.

"Thanks." Rosie locked the car and they returned inside the shop. The escalator clattered as they ascended to the café. "You deserve a coffee on me."

Amber tucked her hand into the crook of Rosie's elbow again. "Tea, actually. I've had my one coffee for the day."

"Fair enough."

They sat with their drinks near the glass barrier that looked out onto the lower level. Amber watched the shoppers, many with children causing general havoc, pushing buggies and filling trollies full of gifts. One little lad ran from his mother's arms and threw his own around a massive stuffed polar bear, refusing point-blank to relinquish his hold despite the mother's efforts.

"Cute kid." Amber gestured with the hand that didn't hold her teacup. "Bet it takes her an hour to convince him he doesn't need a six-foot bear though."

Rosie turned to look. "Yeah. The things these shops sell. Must be so difficult when your kid begs you to have something like that."

Amber snorted. "Maybe if you're a pushover parent. Spoiled kids that get what they want if they whine long enough, you know? I remember asking for months for this doll I wanted; one of the ones with eyes that open and close, you know? I never got it. Not that my parents were interested in buying me things. Or spending time with me." She glanced down at the kid again. "Hopefully, she's handling those puppy-dog eyes."

Rosie chewed her lip and took a sip of her coffee. "I teach a lot of kids that get everything they want. And I see the parents when they come to pick them up. It tends to be the ones that are at the end of their tether that give in, I think."

Amber shrugged. "I think if you don't have the energy, don't have kids. You need to be on the ball with it; otherwise, the little terrors will run rings around you."

Rosie gave her a long, penetrating look. She twisted her mouth to one side, stuck her nose back into her mug, and fell silent.

Did I offend her? She seems close to her niece; maybe she sees her like her own kid. Maybe she spoils her rotten. Amber deliberated her own cup for a while, hoping that when she looked back up, Rosie would have moved on.

The steam from her drink fogged her eyes briefly until Amber realised she was humming "O Holy Night" under her breath. She lifted her gaze.

Rosie gave her a wry smile. "Get you, humming one of the songs we're rehearsing."

Tingles flooded Amber's body. She wanted to reach out, to touch Rosie's hand or do something equally intimate, but refrained. The feeling she'd insulted Rosie's relationship with her niece loitered. "Yeah. I keep doing it at work."

"Aw, Amb."

No one had ever called her that before. It sounded very cool on Rosie's lips. Further quivers shot through her. "People are probably getting annoyed with it, actually." She slipped into self-deprecation so easily. "I should stop. Probably sound far too happy."

"No way. Never feel guilty about being happy, or showing that happiness." Rosie nudged Amber's forefinger with her own. "Anyway, it's catching. And this world is far too crap to limit the amount of happiness we can share."

A huge admission if ever Amber heard one. "It's not so crap for me at the moment." She flipped one hand into the air. "I have a great job, I joined a choir, and I'm hanging out with a very kind friend who buys me tea in exchange for lifting and moving services."

Rosie's face shone. "You're welcome."

They shared a long sigh and both broke into a chuckle.

Rosie lifted her mug to her lips before suddenly inhaling. She placed a hand on her belly.

Amber slanted her head to the side and pushed her eyebrows down. "You okay?" *I wonder if she's got that sickness bug again. I bet she picks up loads of illnesses from her kids at school.*

Her lips parting, Rosie seemed to look around them for a beat before removing her hand and wetting her lips. "Yeah." She tucked her hair behind her ear. "I had this delicious pastry knot thing for breakfast, but it was rather sugary and I think my gut is complaining."

"Well, if you have to rush off to the loo without explanation, I won't hold it against you."

Rosie laughed. "I'll bear that in mind."

On the way home, they turned up the music until it rattled the windows, shouting the words to the songs to express the extent of their joy. When the radio station cut out the rude words, they bellowed them. Amber worried Rosie would cause an accident, so exuberant was their combined mirth.

The car stopped beside Jilly's gate, her front garden sparse due to the time of year. Amber stared at her knees before smiling at Rosie. "I guess this is me, then."

"See you on Monday?" There was the echo of hope in Rosie's tone. It made Amber smile all the more.

"Of course." She patted Rosie's hand where it rested on the gear stick. "Where would my week be without Juice Night?"

"That what it is? Juice Night?" Rosie put air quotes round it. "And to think it only started out as a singing lesson."

"It's evolved. And you can drink what you like." Amber's breath hitched. This would be the perfect opportunity to come out, as it were. But they'd had such a perfect morning. Why spoil it? "Personally, I like the vitamin C."

"Me too."

Amber took a deep breath. "Okay. Better go. Lunch to be made."

A nod from Rosie. She tapped the steering wheel.

Realising she hadn't moved, Amber opened the car door. One last look back to Rosie, and she skipped up the garden path, back to the warmth of home.

Chapter 12

Rosie applied her eyeliner with a precise hand. The Christmas concert, which started in fifty-nine minutes, was being held at the church next to the hall where they had rehearsals. Just a few last-minute checks in her hallway mirror and a grin at her Christmas tree on the way past and she was out the door. She clutched her and Amber's folder to her chest, confident neither of them would need it tonight. It wasn't as if they were doing *The Messiah* or anything. Just a few carols at the local church.

She'd chosen a black vest—maternity, of course—and a red blouse to hide her bump. Black dress trousers. A pair of shoes she rarely wore other than at concerts and funerals. Silver eye shadow. Black eyeliner. A silver Celtic knot pendant.

Once the car had warmed up, K.B. took the opportunity to dance around a bit. *Can he or she feel my nerves? I'm never this nervous before a concert.* She placed a hand on her belly and turned her thoughts inwards. No music on, for once. Just her and her baby.

"Listen, none of that tonight, okay?" She pouted at her bump. "You nearly blew my cover last Saturday at the café, jumping around like that when I was with Amber. No fair, dude." She patted the soft cotton. "I guess you don't have a choice, do you? And you're not really the size of a kidney bean anymore, hmm?" She laughed at the fact she talked out loud to the kid. "More like an avocado. Such a middle-class child."

Then, as it had a few times since going out to buy the tree, anxiety caught her. Amber had expressed some pretty strong views about childrearing. On one hand, it annoyed Rosie. Amber didn't have children, she didn't have nieces or nephews, and she didn't teach. She didn't know what it was like.

On the other hand, it worried her. Amber had called them "little terrors". Perhaps she looked down on mothers who couldn't control their children, ones who gave their kids the things they wanted. The parents that spoiled their kids. Rosie didn't want to be that kind of parent, but who knew what kind of parent she'd be? Rosie had plans, had aspirations, but in the end, she would just be the best she could. And if that meant showering her child with love and affection every day, buying them the things they wanted, so be it.

But there was a concert to get to. She put the car into gear and pulled out of her drive. The journey to the church didn't take too long, and she made it with time to spare.

"Good evening." Enid was dressed in her usual suit, the collar of her blouse as frilly as a flamenco skirt. Her shoes were patent and pointy. Large opal rings adorned her fingers. Her perm was coiffed to perfection.

"Good evening." Rosie stepped into her quick embrace. "How are your family? Ready for Christmas?"

"Just about. Bobby maintains he has finished his shopping, but I expect he'll disappear on Christmas Eve, just to make sure."

"I expect."

Bobby was Enid's husband, and they knew Rosie's parents from way back.

"And how are things going with you?" Enid's eyes flicked down a couple of times, and she arched one grey eyebrow.

Rosie shrank inwardly, but there was no one close by, so she gave Enid a smile. "Good. No problems so far."

"Remind me of your due date again?"

"First week of May."

A long look from Enid. "Our summer concert will be a month from then."

Rosie blinked. "I still intend to be there."

"But..." Enid lowered her voice. "I assumed you'd be up for the solo. And I can't rely on you, can I, just in case something happens with the baby?"

Discomfort twisted Rosie's insides. "Oh, right." She grimaced. "I guess I can't really guarantee I'll be okay to do that."

"It's an important part of the piece. Without the soprano solo, we might as well not sing any of it."

Rosie shifted before drawing in a steadying breath. "Someone else can take it." She patted Enid's upper arm. "It'll be fine."

Enid closed her eyes and turned her face to the heavens. She smiled and nodded. "It will."

"Enid." Rosie glanced around her, anxious about those that entered the church overhearing. "I'm still not quite ready to tell people, okay?"

Enid swept her hand through the air. "People are going to start noticing soon."

"I know, I know. I will tell people. What happened before, losing Ali so late on…" She winced. "I know it's stupid, but I'm so scared of that happening again. I feel as if I jinxed it by being so open about it. I need to wait. At least until just after Christmas."

"We won't be back in rehearsals until the end of January anyway, lovely."

"Good. Yeah, I know. Thanks."

Enid squeezed Rosie's arm once more, before going off to speak with the pianist.

Rosie located the room off to one side they used to dump their stuff. She smiled at a few people already there and sat with the sheet music of "O Holy Night", needlessly reminding herself of her part. *Maybe I am nervous. Maybe this pregnancy has changed the things I'm afraid of.*

K.B. slopped about a little.

Amber padded over to sit next to her. She wore a red blouse with short sleeves, a black cardigan over the top, and her usual black skirt and tights. Shiny shoes.

With the clearing of her throat, Linda—Chief Warbler—made a motion with her head. "I think that's a little short, don't you?" She didn't direct her comment at Amber but at the warbler next to her.

"Is it?" Amber asked Rosie.

Linda gossiped with her choirmate, giving them snide glances as she did so.

An urge crept inside Rosie. She went with it and slid her arms around Amber's shoulders, but made sure her belly was nowhere near. "Ignore that cow. You look fine."

"Are you sure?"

"Hundred percent." Rosie glared at the warblers until they looked away. *How dare that bitch say such a harsh thing to Amber.* She turned her attention back to Amber. She had painted her nails and lips the same shade of red. "I'd even use the word *pretty*."

Some of the lines smoothed across Amber's features. "Thanks. So do you." They pulled back. Amber's knuckles were white as they gripped her handbag. "I didn't know whether this was what Enid meant when she said 'red and black' or whether I should have worn trousers or…" She pulled at the edge of her skirt, evidently wishing it covered her knees.

"You look perfect."

Amber smiled, her cheekbones pinking. "You're liking the shirt and vest top combination at the moment, aren't you?"

"Comfy and stylish." Rosie waggled her head and lowered her voice. "I think our friends over there could have benefitted from some advice when it came to comfortable shoes, don't you?"

Tottering about on high-heeled court shoes, the warblers always dressed as such for a concert. Enid didn't care so long as the colour scheme was adhered to; people could wear bikinis if they wished.

"At least they look smart." Amber bounced her foot. "I don't feel smart, not really."

Rosie took Amber's chin and lifted her gaze to her own. "Hey. I've been in this choir for years. If I say you look perfect, you look perfect."

Berry-coloured lips pinched, then widened into a smile. "Yeah, okay."

Clapping made them look up. Enid was in excellent military form. Before long, everyone was lined up, ready to enter the main part of the church.

Fifty pairs of feet sounded like thunder on the stone floor. The pews were full of friends, family, and locals. The choir used the two steps up to the altar as tiered standing room. Some of the men were shorter than the women, so this worked to their advantage.

Once everyone was gathered, Enid held up her hands to begin.

The occasional tremble shot through Amber, who stood next to Rosie. Rosie wanted to touch her hand, to reassure her, but they were standing right at the front and the entire church would see. *Better just send her positive thoughts.*

They went through the usual Christmas carols. Polite applause between each song, smiling faces all across the rows.

Amber's voice rang with vigour. She had improved so much in just a few short months. Pride made Rosie itch to shoot her a smile.

It came to the last song. In previous years, they had ended with "Once In Royal David's City", a song where Rosie had also taken the solo. But this would be a new one for the congregation and for the choir. Rosie stepped forwards.

Enid counted in the pianist. She gave Rosie a wink, stepping to one side so she was visible to the audience.

Rosie was very conscious of her belly. She held her hands still at her sides, as she'd always taught pupils to when they sang. The urge to cover her front was a strain.

And she sang. The tune carried well up into the rafters, pinging off the wooden beams and the walls and the long benches the audience sat on. Christmas spirit flooded every one of Rosie's senses. A gush of love and happiness. *I am doing the thing I have always wanted to do: be a mother. I am happy in my job and the choir. I have made a good friend whom I care for very deeply.* The song added to the joy she felt. She smiled, lifted her cheekbones, and the song resounded from her.

Once her solo was done, the choir swelled to sing the rest, and Rosie returned to her place in the front row.

A small, warm hand slid into her own for the briefest of heartbeats. Amber pressed her shoulder to Rosie's, and Rosie could hear the happiness in Amber's voice. She wanted to hug her again, baby bump be damned.

The song ended with a long top note that Rosie sang with the rest of the choir under her. Enid conducted the conclusion of the note. The church congregation erupted.

Rosie had experienced this so many times, from the first choir she'd been in as a child to the chamber choirs she'd sung in at college and uni then to the regular concerts during her adult years. But Amber had never sung in public before, and it was evident in the way she dropped her head and allowed her hair to hang over her face that she was unused to the applause.

As usual, Enid held a hand out to Rosie.

She took her bow with as much grace as she could muster.

A few kids from her school squealed their cheers.

She gave them a thumbs-up and a grin. The choir bowed together. More cheers and stamping of feet.

"Thank you, everyone, for coming to listen to us sing. And Merry Christmas." Enid dipped her head one last time and strode out.

The choir filed back out, one line at a time. The muffled noises of the audience gathering their things and getting to their feet rumbled through the building.

"Oh my goodness." It sounded is if Amber was trying to contain her glee. "That was so awesome."

"You did really well." Rosie threw all caution to the wind. She wrapped her arms around Amber's waist.

Amber jumped up and down a few times in Rosie's arms before pulling back, her gaze on something behind Rosie.

One of the warblers sucked air through her teeth at them.

Rosie ignored her. "I'm very proud of you."

"Are you kidding?" Amber still had her hands on Rosie's shoulders. "You were just…you were so amazing. You have such a beautiful voice."

Perhaps Amber's elation loosened her tongue. Not that Rosie didn't like being showered with praise by pretty women.

Rosie shrugged. "Ah, well, I've been singing all my life."

Their little party was interrupted by various people congratulating Rosie, and praising Amber too. Gareth hugged Amber with a loose arm, ending Rosie and Amber's embrace.

The loss was like a cold bucket of water over Rosie. *Get a grip.*

They gathered their things, the evening done. As they walked from the side room, back into the church, a tall woman with blonde hair and a piercing smile approached them. "Hi."

"Hi." Amber beamed at her.

"Kiddo, you did really well. I really enjoyed it."

"Thanks. I was basically wetting myself the entire time, but it was good."

Rosie poked her side. "You were not. You were brilliant."

"Oh, shut up."

The woman raised her eyebrows, and her gaze flicked from Rosie to Amber with an expectant air.

"Oh, sorry, you guys haven't actually been introduced." Amber held one hand out to Rosie. "Jilly, this is Rosie."

"Aha, finally. The woman who has turned my tenant into a superstar." Jilly shook Rosie's hand. "Nice to finally meet you."

"Likewise. Heard a lot about you."

They moved down the church and outside, slipping around those not willing to brave the cold just yet.

"You too." Jilly nodded with warmth in her eyes.

"I'm glad Amb had someone to support her." Rosie pulled her coat around her, the wind whipping it about her knees for a moment before she got it under control.

"It's a shame dogs aren't allowed in the church," Jilly replied. "Nico would have enjoyed singing along."

"Oh, you." Amber nudged Jilly.

Jilly grinned more. "Careful, miss, or I'll put your rent up."

Amber gave Jilly a glare, then smiled. "Anyway, I've got work early in the morning." She gestured towards the car park. "We should get home."

"And I've got to pop by Mrs Peterson's early to do something about a wayward rubber plant that needs a trim." Jilly held up one hand to Rosie. "See you."

"See you." Rosie hesitated. Their previous joy had dissipated, and now they were left with calm camaraderie. Did she want to cause potential awkwardness by giving Amber yet another hug, and in front of her landlady too?

Amber made the decision for her. She stepped into her arms and rested her cheek on Rosie's shoulder, snuggled a bit into her scarf.

Unable to resist reciprocating—and it would be rude not to, wouldn't it?—Rosie sunk into her with abandonment. Once she closed her eyes, she didn't care who saw, didn't care they were in full view of the tutting warblers. Amber was warm and smelled like flowers. Rosie held her close, their coats pressed together almost down to the swell at Rosie's middle.

This is so unfair. Why didn't I meet her last year? Rosie squeezed her eyes closed and wondered whether burying into Amber's embrace was wise. She didn't have much time to decide, however, let alone carry it through, because Amber pulled away.

Amber stroked Rosie's cheek. Then she was gone, across the concrete of the car park.

Rosie stood still, savouring Amber's touch and the little smile she'd sent her as Jilly drove them out onto the road.

I'm in deep. Fuck sake, Miss Tanner. Stop letting yourself get so close to her.

She pressed a hand to her belly once she was in the safety of her car. "Well, at least the concert went well, huh?"

Chapter 13

The smell of sweet hay and horses surrounded them. Amber lay on her back along a wooden bench with Harry in a similar position, their heads together, feet at opposite ends. Matthew sat on the floor, his back against Harry's middle. The kettle in the stable office had been put to much-appreciated use.

The tips of Amber's fingers poked out from her wrist warmers. A gift from Fiona, bright red and hand-crocheted. She'd worn them until May last year, and they'd been redonned for Halloween. They were as soft as kitten's fur and warmer than a hot water bottle. Her mug of tea was balanced on her belly.

Matthew sipped at his, blue eyes twinkling. "Best thing about coming to see your darling girl in the dead of winter?"

Amber and Harry both looked at him in question.

"The expensive teabags." Matthew smacked his lips. "Absolutely stellar. Even better than the brew we get at Ollie's."

"Don't let her hear you say that." Harry squeezed Matthew's shoulder.

Matthew threw his head back. "Would I? Anyway, she's far too loved up with Anna these days. Those two are as bad as Sarah and Christian."

Amber didn't go to the group at Ollie's craft shop, where Matthew and Harry learned to crochet. She didn't have much interest in crafts in general. Anyway, with the choir taking up two evenings a week—the actual rehearsal and then her lesson-cum-juice-night with Rosie—she didn't have time for anything else.

"What's new with you guys?" Her tea was too hot to drink just yet.

"Some stuff," Matthew replied. "We're looking at maybe buying a house soon."

"Just an idea so far." The bench squeaked as Harry shifted.

"That's awesome news." *It's high time they did something like that.* They'd been together nearly two years.

"I got some money recently, did I say?" Matthew blew his tea. "Some cousin of my mum's. No idea why she left me the money, but she doesn't have kids and I used to go see her in the holidays. Fond memories, you know."

"I've told you. I don't want the deposit to come from just you. Let me save up for a while, hmm? Contribute too."

"And I've told you," Matthew replied. "It's fine. I don't have anything else to spend it on. It's not like I intend on buying a horse or anything like that, is it?"

Silence, of the awkward kind. A few birds fluttered from the roof, scrabbling around in the dust, looking for bugs. A horse whinnied.

Amber sat up, neatly ending the move with a sip of her tea.

Apparently forgetting the tension, Matthews grinned and gave her a miniature clap for her skill.

"They do provide good tea here, as well as exceptional horse care facilities and outstanding photographic opportunities." Amber patted her camera, which was in its usual position around her neck.

"Once we have tea inside us, we shall go spruce her up." Harry took a little more time, as well as a lot more groaning, to haul himself into a sitting position.

Matthew carefully handed him his tea.

"Thank you." Harry dropped a kiss onto his head. "I hear the carol concert went well?" Harry had a look in his eye, one that suggested he was about to pry. "I'm sorry we couldn't be there. Bloody work Christmas do."

"That's okay." Amber tried not to sigh. "It went so well. A new experience for me, being in front of an audience. But it was really fun once I got over my nerves."

"You'll keep going, then? Now that the concert is finished?"

"I'll admit…" Amber sucked her bottom lip for a while. "I didn't intend on going much past that first rehearsal. I didn't think I'd enjoy it; I'm not exactly the most confident person. Never thought I'd manage performing like that, to be honest."

"But?"

Amber nodded once. "I like being in the choir. I like how it feels, to be part of a whole. It's a bit like AA, you know: a shared objective, a combined conscience. I don't know. And not everyone in the choir is perfectly nice." The warblers' words and reaction to the hug she and Rosie had shared had not left her. Memories of school, of her last job, the nasty manager that had bullied her and who'd picked up on every little thing she'd done wrong, tugged at her gut. She drank some tea to banish the thoughts. "But most are."

"Rosie, especially?" Matthew always managed to hit the nail on the head when it came to teasing her.

Harry placed a hand on Matthew's. "You've been complaining that I've been hogging all of Florence's time. Can I suggest you go start grooming her whilst we finish our teas?"

Excitement lit up Matthew's eyes, and he was on his feet in a flash. His hips wiggled as he walked out of the barn.

Harry turned to Amber. "Right. Now that he's off being busy, let's talk."

Amber buried her head in her hand. Some of her hair fell forwards.

A warm fingertip coaxed her to drop her hand. "I know you're struggling with this Rosie thing. I can tell."

Resigned to her fate and supposing she might as well go all in, Amber caught his gaze. "I don't think *struggling* is the right word."

"What word would you use?"

"Treading on thin ice? Tiptoeing around life? Drinking juice and not really talking about why?"

"Ah, yes. The great juice nights."

"They're fun. We mostly chat about the choir and people in it or about work. I tell her the atrocious amount of missing teeth I come into contact with each day." She snorted. "Not literally, of course. And she tells me about kids she's taught. Teachers she's known. Things like that."

"So you're still drinking juice and neglecting to tell her you don't drink alcohol?"

"She's never drunk alcohol in front of me either." She waved her hand. "Maybe she doesn't drink."

"Maybe." Harry was so like Fiona: calm, collected, waiting for her to make her own comments about the things she said.

"Maybe she's just being polite. Maybe *she's* not drinking because *I'm* not drinking. And she thinks I'm not drinking for the same reason." A large huff. "Or maybe, like she said, she just likes the vitamin C."

"It's not about not telling her you're in recovery." Harry slotted his fingers between hers. "It's about you not feeling good about not telling her the truth." He lifted his mug as if indicating her situation. "I know you've made a real effort to change how you were when you were drinking—all that lying. You've done really well. But I can see it eating you up now."

"I want to tell her." The words felt fluffy in her mouth, but warmth spread up her arm where he held her hand. "I feel like I've left it so long now though. Like, if I tell her now, she'll hate me."

No reply, just a continued gentle gaze onto her face.

"It's nearly Christmas. We're not seeing one another until January."

"No plans to meet up?"

"She's got loads of family things…parents and siblings, and her niece. As well as school concerts and stuff."

"That'll be nice for her."

Amber nodded. "I just feel like she's got it so perfect and I'm…" She caught his gaze. "I love you guys, and I love Jilly and Nico. But a real family? Like, with mums and dads and siblings? I don't have that."

Again, no reply.

Amber didn't want to hear she had it good—friends all around her, her alcoholism under control for over a year, a good job. She wasn't on medication anymore for her anxiety, and she had enough money to be comfortable, even if there were things she still wanted to achieve.

Harry squeezed her fingers. "I love you, darling."

"Love you too." She finished her tea and rested her cheek against the furry hood of his coat.

"I just… I don't want you to get so into this girl that you get hurt."

"Neither do I. Last time…"

More memories. Her last girlfriend, the whirlwind romance, all those blasted promises. Then she'd left when she couldn't handle the fact that Amber wasn't perfect.

The bottle of vodka Amber had bought on the way home. The wonderful, numb feeling she'd had when it was empty. The crash of emotions afterwards, the tears, the screaming.

Walking in the rain, wanting to be anywhere else but in her dingy flat with no girlfriend. The sea roaring and rolling against the sea walls. Salt in her eyes.

A large set of strong arms enclosing her, the familiar scent of compost and dog.

She shook her head. That wasn't for today. "I don't want to relapse."

"I don't want you to relapse."

She sucked her bottom lip again. "It's been just over a year. You don't think I'm ready?"

"I think you need to go into anything more than friendship with both eyes open."

Amber swallowed. "I think she's beautiful. She makes me laugh. She's kind to me but says what she thinks." Heat crept into her cheeks, despite the winter air. "She gave that woman in the choir such a look when she said my skirt was too short. Really put her in her place."

"She does sound nice."

"Yeah, she's special, I think." She prodded him, figuring now that he was on his own she could bring it up. "Anyway, so what's this about a house?"

Harry blew out a breath and looked away. "Matthew's got all that money and I… Well, I rescued Florence way back. I've spent more than I should have towards her upkeep, and I'll keep having to do so for the whole of her life."

"But you're practically married."

Harry wrinkled his nose. "A patriarchal invention to make women possessions for men."

"I'm aware of your views on the issue, and they're very honourable. But surely it doesn't matter who puts the money into the house so long as you can both enjoy it."

"I love Florence." He sighed. "But there are times I wish I hadn't taken that leap. It's a lot of money, and now I can't put anything towards a house because I can't save that much."

Of course she understood. She'd always wanted to be independent too, moving away from her parents. Having her own money and being able to contribute to meals out and coffee and food was important to her. "What does Matthew think?"

"He thinks be damned about the way I feel. He should provide the deposit, and then we can buy somewhere straight away."

"Don't regret Florence." She snuggled her cheek into his shoulder. "She's wonderful. The way your eyes light up when you see her..."

He chuckled. "She does make me pretty happy."

A last squeeze. With a look through the double doors, Amber squared her shoulders and stood. She held her hand out for Harry's mug. "Talking of your beautiful woman, Matthew will be brushing her bare. We should go get some good pictures before he renders her unphotographable."

"Is that even a word?" Harry laughed and followed her out of the barn into the crisp sunshine.

Chapter 14

Rosie had been surprised to get an appointment on Christmas Eve. Once again, here she was with her belly exposed and Lucinda squeezing jelly gunk on her skin. This time, however, she was on her own. And that was fine. She'd brought her sister and Chelsea with her the first time mostly for their benefit, but she wanted to do the twenty-week scan by herself.

"Did you want to know the sex?"

Rosie was yanked from her thoughts. She smiled and nodded.

"Have you heard about those big gender reveal things people do on social media?"

Rosie giggled, which shifted the ultrasound wand across her belly. "Yeah. I suppose it's a lovely thing to do. But I wouldn't choose to do that. I'm still emotionally bruised from losing my last baby so late into my pregnancy." Her cheeks warmed, and Rosie couldn't quite meet Lucinda's gaze.

Lucinda rested a hand against Rosie's shoulder.

"I feel as if I told too many people, jinxed it." Rosie shook herself. "Anyway, I feel like the gender of a kid is up to the kid once they're old enough to know what gender even means."

"But you still want to know."

Rosie peered at the mass of blobs and squiggles on the screen. Probably the large lunch she'd just had—she was sure she could see a noodle or two from her soup—and let out a hum. "Yeah."

"I do a lot of these." Lucinda honed in on one area of Rosie's belly and moved closer to the screen on her wheelie stool. "And I'm always interested to find out the reasons behind those that want to, or don't want to, know. Would you tell me?"

Rosie breathed slowly, trying to enjoy the attention without getting annoyed by the intrusion. "I suppose because I'm by myself it won't be this big surprise I can share with someone when I deliver. And I have another twenty or so weeks to bond with my baby. I'd like to do that with a bit more information about what kind of baby I'm bonding with." She bit her lip. "Even if it ends in tragedy again."

"You're not the only one to have said that."

The sense of being intruded upon lessened. The care and warmth increased.

"Aha. Here we go." Lucinda turned the screen round. She poked a squiggly area between baby's legs.

"Is that baby's willie?" It came out before Rosie had intended it to and resulted in them both snorting.

"Lack of."

"K.B. is a girl baby?"

"K.B. is a girl baby."

A mixture of relief and anxiety swam through Rosie before dwindling and dying away. *There will be no comparison between K.B. and Ali. K.B. will be a truly fresh start.* She wanted to get up and dance but lay still so Lucinda could get some good shots of Little Miss Kidney Bean.

"What were you expecting?"

"I wasn't expecting anything. I suppose, deep down, I was scared that if it was a boy my new baby would replace Ali."

Lucinda shook her head. "Nothing could replace him."

"My mum thought it was a boy, but she's old and a wife and has plenty of tales in her."

"Lots of people come in with 'oh, my mother thinks this or that', and sometimes they're right, sometimes, they're wrong." She handed Rosie some paper towels. "With only a fifty-fifty split between answers—unless we're talking intersex children, and we can't pick that up usually on a sonogram—it's difficult to tell how accurate what Mother says is."

"I can be so smug with my mum now. She was very sure."

"So she'll have two granddaughters?" Lucinda had a good memory.

"Yeah. Chelsea and K.B."

"No reason why you can't call the baby Kayleigh Beatrice."

Rosie blinked at her. "That's an immense idea. If I didn't already have a name picked out, I'd so go with that." *Sidney is a much more gender-neutral than Kayleigh, although I suppose it could be shortened to Leigh.*

Lucinda placed the wand back in the holder and bowed. "It's my superpower skill. Thinking up excellent names for babies I won't ever meet."

"You'll meet K.B. I'll bring her in." The pronoun made tingles flush through Rosie as if she'd been doused with sparkling water. "I can't believe I can finally say *she*. That's so weird."

Lucinda laughed as she filled in the appropriate boxes on Rosie's maternity file.

I'll definitely tell Amber now. I have to. My baby has a gender and a name other than Kidney Bean. It still scares me though—what if I lose Sidney too? I just need to remember what my consultant said about Ali—the chances of another stillbirth are small. Rosie's chest ached with the thought of 'coming out' as an expectant mother to Amber, as well as the lingering fear she would jinx it again, but it had been long enough. The choir would need to be aware of why she was stepping down as their usual soloist.

She's going to hate me. Amber's reaction was important and another reason for Rosie's hesitation. However, she clenched a fist and tried to draw her strength. Sidney was top of her priority list. *I'll invite Amber out for juice in the New Year. I can tell her then.*

Amber was pretty and kind and had a huge heart. Rosie knew she was a hair's breadth from falling so deep it'd be difficult for her to climb back out. But she needed to use her head, not her heart. She needed to be strong.

Chapter 15

Amber couldn't remember eating so much in a week. The New Year was upon them, and their visitors had evaporated back to their own homes. Jilly had bundled Nico into his carrier to visit her sister for New Year's Eve, so Amber was alone, trying to work out whether her new shimmery skater skirt would fit after all the festivities. Thank goodness for elastic waists.

Amber and her friends had drunk a number of varieties of fake alcohol, made mocktails together in some strange flavours, and pulled crackers containing rude jokes. She didn't need her biological family. She didn't even consider them family, not really. A group of people she'd known way back. Her history, but not her present or her future.

It was time for some TV. She found something worth watching but not too strenuous. Drifting into postfestive stupors on the sofa was allowed.

She'd had a text, late on Boxing Day, from Rosie, wishing her Happy Christmas. Amber had wondered whether Rosie would send something religious—her father was a vicar after all—but she'd been pleased to see no mention of Jesus or God. Not that she didn't respect those that had a religion, she just struggled with the concept of a deity that controlled everything—one that had a face and a personality.

The sound of her phone ringing cut through her sleepy haze. She blinked at the name. *Mum.*

Really? She was phoning on New Year's Eve when there had been radio silence over Christmas? *Whatever.* Amber considered not answering or even blocking the number. But maybe it was important.

Before she created something to feel guilty about, which would mean a long conversation with Fiona that she couldn't be bothered with, Amber answered the phone.

"Hello, Mum." Just keep it at that. No surprise, no warmth.

"Amber. Sorry to phone you just out of the blue…" Tears? Snuffling definitely. Perhaps her mother had a cold.

"Um…that's okay. How are you?" Being polite was taking the higher road. *I'm the bigger person here.*

"Not great, actually. Your grandma died."

"Oh."

"She's been unwell for a while. Cancer, you know."

"I didn't know, but okay." Amber tried to keep the bitterness from her voice. She wasn't sure she'd managed it. Numbness consumed her. A cavern opened up in her chest, full of nothingness.

"So the funeral is in ten days."

"You've already scheduled it?" Amber sat up and dug her fingers into her thigh. "When did she die?"

"Christmas Eve."

Anger surged, but she pressed her fingers into her flesh, hoping the pain would stall it. "A week ago?"

"Yes."

"You didn't think to ring me before now?"

"Well…" Some more sniffling.

Amber rolled her eyes.

"I didn't think you cared, if I'm honest."

I don't care. Amber chewed her lip. She hated strong emotions, wanted to do something to banish them from herself. She took a deep breath, let it out slowly. "Anyway, so the funeral is on the ninth?" She turned her phone to speaker, found her calendar app, opened up the correct day.

"Yes. At eleven."

"At Worle Crem?"

"Yes."

Amber typed it in. She stared at the words *Grandma's Funeral*—they didn't even look like real words. "I guess I'll be there."

"I have something for you. I'll post it to you."

"You don't want me to do a reading, do you?" Disgust mixed with anger, mixed with a growing sadness, churned in her belly.

"God, no."

And there it was: the cold, sharp hostility Amber expected.

"It's something Grandma wanted you to have."

She left me something in her will? "Fine."

Her mother cleared her throat. "How are you?"

What to say? How deep was she expected to go? She didn't want to give too much away. "Okay."

"Working?"

"Yes."

"Good."

Amber rolled her eyes again. "Sorry, Mum, I'm..." She looked around the empty living room, the muted TV calling her back. "Jilly's got company. I should go."

"Of course."

Some comedian gesticulated and strode up and down on the screen. Amber longed for his strength.

"See you on the ninth."

"See you." Amber turned the sound back on, and the audience's laughter filled the room.

If only her heart weren't so empty that the din of the TV could fill it at least halfway again. But the only feeling it seemed to create was sadness, and that was just silly. She hadn't spoken to her Grandma for three years.

Her parents had moved to Scotland in 2010, but Amber had wanted to stay in the south-west: cue a terrible row. They'd barely spoken after that, but she'd tried to make amends three years ago when they'd returned to the area. After that failed attempt, she'd visited her Grandma in the nursing home.

Grandma was mentally fit and well but used a wheelchair and needed nurses to help her do everything. Arthritis and diabetes.

The nursing home seemed nice, situated on the seafront in a town not far away. A sleepy place with a small pier and very few holiday goers. Grandma had smiled when Amber arrived and held Amber's hand with gnarled fingers. Liver spots had dappled her skin, but the gentle warmth had remained in her eyes.

Amber wasn't her only grandchild. She had a couple of cousins that visited Grandma a lot more regularly, with big jobs and suits and fancy cars.

Grandma had exchanged pleasantries with her before listing a host of things Amber had done wrong. Things she'd been told by Amber's parents, things she shouldn't have known. But she'd done it with such a caring tone. Amber wished she'd shouted at her, shown some kind of anger. Somehow, kindness just made it worse.

And Amber had recoiled, not yet ready to admit any of her own shortcomings, and especially not in front of her dear Grandma. She'd denied it all, lied through her teeth, as usual. Grandma was an elderly woman who didn't know any better.

Bile rose in Amber's throat. Spoiled little shit. She'd still been drinking at the time and hadn't wanted to admit anything. She'd been in a job she hated and on the edge of becoming very unwell. It hadn't all been her fault…but most of it had.

Tears dribbled down her cheeks, her nose, and into her lap. One splashed onto her phone, which she threw to the side. Amber held her knees and struggled to hold everything in. Crying would just make everything worse.

Grandma was gone now, so what did it matter? She couldn't make it up to her. Her family continued to not understand or support her. She wished her mother hadn't even rung to tell her.

She stomped into the kitchen. After a quick look through the cupboards and not finding any alcohol at all—of course there wouldn't be, Jilly was in recovery too—she sat on the lino and leaned against the fridge. A wet sigh escaped her. The anger receded.

Left with only sorrow—something she could identify. Illogical, maybe, but true. She *was* sad her grandma had died. She was sad she hadn't been a good granddaughter. She was sad she hadn't been able to say goodbye.

So what now?

Drinking was not an option. She'd come way too far to smash all her hard work with one drink just so she didn't feel sad. She'd be straight out of Jilly's and into a dry house, or maybe even hospital. Mentally punching the words *the most important thing is to not drink* into her brain, she decided a moment more on Jilly's kitchen floor would not be the end of the world, at least until her backside went numb.

She allowed tears to flow this time, leaving her cheeks wet. She scooped herself up and went to the sink to wash her hands and face. Out the kitchen window, birds fluttered from one feeder to another, the grass crisp with December frost.

Fiona. She retrieved her phone from the floor of the living room and sat on the sofa to call her sponsor. After explaining the situation, her heart felt less vacant.

"There are just a lot of feelings," she said, "which is stupid because I'd given them all the heave-ho a long time ago. I've barely thought about Grandma for years."

"Just because you want them to leave doesn't mean they do," Fiona's voice soothed. *Maybe that's how a mother is supposed to make you feel.*

"I understand that."

"How are you going to get through the next few hours?"

Amber glanced at the TV, visualising the box of chocolate biscuits still in the cupboard. "I have snacks and funny programmes to watch."

"Company? When is Jilly back?"

"Not until tomorrow." Amber sucked her bottom lip. "Are…are you coming back early?"

"I'm not back until the weekend, hon." A note of comprehension in Fiona's tone. "What about Harry?"

"He's with his folks."

"Anyone else you could phone? I expect sharing anything left over from a Christmas party at Jilly's would be quite the incentive."

Amber picked at a loose thread on her skirt. "Maybe. I could see what Rosie's doing."

"You could."

Amber steeled herself for a judgement.

"It *is* what friends do, Amber: rely on each other."

Should I phone Rosie? "Um…yeah. I guess it is."

"I'll let you decide, okay? I can't tell you what you should do." A chuckle. "Except the not drinking. That's kind of a given."

"Course." It was like she had a mother but without all the emotional entanglements one got from being tied to someone biologically. "Thanks."

"Always here."

Amber hung up in a quandary. She needed someone with her—that was a big thing for her to admit. In past moments of crisis, she'd turned to a bottle and the oblivion that would follow. Maybe she could tempt Rosie over with good quality chocolate and funny TV. She'd understand; she knew how distant Amber was with her family. She'd be good to talk to.

So long as she wasn't busy, of course.

Rosie laughed at her reflection in the full-length mirror. The long maternity jumper her mother had just *had* to buy for her hung close to her knees. It was deep green and stretched comfortably, and with room, over her bump. She passed her palms over her belly, enjoying how the knitted pattern felt. K.B. did a weird movement that half tickled, half jostled her innards.

I look so feminine. The Rosie in the mirror winced, then stuck out her tongue. She could look feminine, she supposed. It wasn't the way she felt inside—although her bigger boobs and wider hips did help—but she supposed it was just a thing that happened when one was pregnant. *I'm a woman carrying a child. Can't deny it.*

Turning to one side, she pouted in the way she'd seen the youngsters on Instagram do, with their three inches of make-up and painted-on eyebrows. That made her laugh again. She cradled her bump and swung her hips from side to side as she sang a few notes from a song her mother used to sing to the both of them. Rosie thought she'd caught Charlie singing it to Chelsea when she was small. Something passed down from mother to daughter to granddaughter. *And now, to a second granddaughter.*

Kath and Charlie had beamed when she'd told them she was having a girl, although Rosie reckoned they'd have been pleased either way. Her father's baritone had rumbled with affection as he'd uttered the words "another granddaughter." Not that it mattered who was pleased by the gender of her baby. Happy and healthy was all that was important.

Her phone made the text message noise, and she sat on the end of her bed to read it.

Hi Rosie. I have chocolate and biscuits and the TV for the afternoon and evening. Are you busy? Would you like to come round? Ax

Not busy on New Year's Eve? A small part of her blossomed with heat, and a tingling began somewhere near K.B. Amber wanted to spend time with her. A date? A meeting between friends? It didn't sound like she wanted to actually *do* anything: just company and assistance to consume snacks. K.B. lurched at the thought of food, and who was Rosie to deny her daughter something?

Hey, Amb! Chocolate and biscuits? I'm in. When d'you want me? Rx

Rosie wondered whether her flippant tone might come across as flirtatious. So what? Friends could flirt, couldn't they? Especially in such a direct medium as a text message. Anyhow, what harm was a little fun on New Year's Eve?

Anytime. Feel free to come round now, if you'd like to. Ax

Rosie could tell Amber about the baby in a safe and private place. She could leave if Amber got upset. And they could work it out before next week when they'd be required to sit next to one another and learn a new selection of songs in choir.

After sending a quick *on my way* text, Rosie smoothed the jumper over her maternity jeans and slid into her car.

It was a quick journey to Amber's; traffic was non-existent. Rosie was sure it would become busier later—New Year's Eve revellers travelling home or whatever. She'd have to check the traffic report before she left in case she was held up and her bladder complained.

She noted the pots with dark compost but no plants on either side of the front door. What would sprout in the spring? Jilly, a professional gardener, would have a colour-coordinated front garden. Did Amber have much say in it? She pulled her woolly cardigan around her, pleased it concealed her bump so she could tell Amber without her guessing first.

Amber answered the door, her eyes red-rimmed. She ducked her head so her hair hid her face.

Rosie put her hand out, her fingers millimetres from Amber's shoulder. "I was going to greet you with a Happy New Year type of thing, but clearly a more appropriate phrase would be *What on earth is the matter?*"

Amber pushed her hair behind her ear and gave Rosie a watery smile. "My grandma died."

They moved into the house, which smelled of spice and fruit. Rosie clocked a couple of bowls of toasted orange slices, sticks of cinnamon, and dried flowers. The tree was real and decorated in all different colours.

They went into the kitchen, and Amber went to the kettle. She flicked it on, then let out a shaky breath. "Sorry, should have asked whether you wanted a hot drink…or…" Her face crumpled a second before she covered it with her hands.

"Oh, darling." Rosie couldn't help placing a hand on her arm. She circled her thumb against the cotton of Amber's blouse. "I'm sorry."

Amber leant against the counter and took a few hiccupping breaths. "I'm being stupid. Just ignore me."

"Hey." Rosie touched the back of one of Amber's hands. "Amb." When she tugged the hand away from her face, Amber didn't resist. "You're not being stupid."

Amber squeezed her eyes closed. One tear trickled down her cheek.

The urge to wipe it away was strong, but Rosie held back. "You're not. No way, dude. It's a sad thing, isn't it?"

"Maybe for someone who has actually seen their grandma recently? I've not seen her for years. I've no right to be upset about her dying."

"Fuck off."

That made Amber look up. It also made one of her eyebrows hitch.

"Whatever kind of relationship you had, she was still your grandma. You are allowed to mourn her. And anyone who says otherwise, you send them to me. I'll put them right." She squeezed Amber's hand. "Let's have a cup of tea. Then we can sit down with a big blanket or whatever and talk properly."

The creases between Amber's eyebrows smoothed before she nodded.

Rosie dropped Amber's hand and wafted her away. "I'll do these." The mugs were in a glass-fronted cupboard, and the tea, coffee, and sugar were labelled. "You go make us a little nest on the sofa. I'll be through in a minute."

Without a word, Amber shuffled into the living room.

Rosie rolled her eyes. *Well, that scuppers that, then. There's no way I'm telling her about the baby when she's so upset. I'll just have to hide it for a little longer.*

Carrying the mugs through in one hand, Rosie gave Amber a cheery wave with the other. "You have just one sugar, don't you?"

"Yes, please." Amber seemed to have stopped crying now, but her tone was still thin. She was curled up at one end of the sofa, a gigantic throw over her legs.

"Excellent." Rosie placed the mugs on two coasters and slid underneath the throw as well. *At least it covers my bump more thoroughly.* She tried to push all thoughts of her own condition to the back of her mind. *I'm here for Amber. Today is all about her.*

"Thank you." Amber bent to collect her mug. A further softening of her features suggesting that the warmth of the tea comforted her.

"So, come on. Tell me about your grandma." Rosie toed her trainers off and backed up against the opposite arm of the chair.

Amber pushed her feet into the space between the sofa back and Rosie's hip. Her cheeks pinked at the contact, but she didn't relocate.

How much do I want to hold her properly right now? After shifting to give Amber a little more room, Rosie smiled across at her. "Come on. Talk."

"She was my mother's mother. She and my granddad lived in Worle until he died. He looked after her, you see, helped her get showered and dressed and stuff. She had arthritis, and it made things difficult."

Rosie nodded, her heart aching. It was good to hear Amber talk about her past.

"She had to go into a home. My parents didn't have time to look after her, and I wasn't very old." Her gaze slid away from Rosie's. "I mean, I was at uni. I wouldn't have known what to do to look after her." She took a drink of her tea.

Rosie's crossed legs tented the throw, and she rested her mug between them.

Toes wriggled next to Rosie's hip, as if Amber were trying to burrow into Rosie's warmth. "Anyway. She was a hundred percent there mentally. Quick-witted and funny. I had such fun with her when I used to visit." She swallowed, looked at the mug in her hands. "My parents moved to

Scotland; I didn't want to go with them. This was about ten years ago. We fought, and I kind of cut everyone out. I didn't want to deal with them; they were all the same to me."

"What did you fight about?"

Amber blinked, her gaze connecting with Rosie's once more. "They wanted me to go with them. Practically forced me. I found a flat and moved out. They called me some names; I called them some names. They left.

"Then, about three years ago, they moved back. Didn't like it up there or whatever. More opportunities down here with work and stuff."

"What do they do?"

"Dad's done a lot of corporate jobs. Managing director, stuff like that. Mum's a freelance accountant. They worked for the same firm back in the day. Neither of them were home much when they lived here, so I figured why did I need them?"

Rosie rested her cheek against the back of the sofa. She wanted to throw her arms around Amber, cuddle her close, tell her it was all okay.

"I tried to make it up, have some kind of relationship with them again when they came back. They didn't care. I'll be honest: neither did I. Afterwards, I got a phone call from the care home. Grandma wanted to see me. I assumed it was to have a go at me, and she sort of did, but..." Amber's bottom lip wobbled. "She wanted to make things better between me and my parents. Make me see what I was doing wrong with them. But I didn't want to listen."

Rosie couldn't imagine what Amber could have done to be treated in such a way by her own family. She couldn't imagine the sweet, kind young woman in front of her being nasty to anyone, especially an old woman in a care home.

After setting her mug onto its coaster, she reached out to Amber. When Amber stared at her, Rosie made a beckoning motion. "Come here."

"Are...are you sure?"

"You need a hug, and I need to give you one."

Amber put her own tea down before inching closer along the sofa.

Rosie took in a deep breath and held it, hoping the two layers of clothing and the thick throw would hide her secret.

With a sigh that rang of relief, Amber snuggled down against Rosie, her jaw against Rosie's collarbone. Rosie wrapped one arm around Amber's waist and carded the fingers of the other through her hair. Her whole body reacted, tingles shooting across her skin wherever Amber's body touched her own. *Stop it. You're comforting her, not getting jiggy with her.*

For a while, Amber was still, her forearm resting against Rosie's around her. Her thumb caressed Rosie's elbow. Then she turned her head into Rosie's jumper. Shaking wracked her body.

Rosie pressed her nose into Amber's hair, continuing to stroke the dark tresses in a soothing rhythm. *She's so full of pain. Life has been hard for her. I wish I could take some of that away.*

She squeezed her a few times, when Amber's sobs became audible, hoping to create some sense of stability for her. Remind her they were friends and that Rosie was there for her. Was Amber grieving just for her grandmother, or was she weeping for all the other things? Her parents; the cousins she'd mentioned that she never spoke to? Aunts and uncles, perhaps? Years missed with a grandmother that should have been full of love and learning?

As the jolts within Amber's body became less and less and her breathing eased, Rosie allowed her a little more space. She trailed a hand up and down Amber's back and loosened the embrace of her other arm. *She feels so good in my arms. Stop it!*

Amber sat up, her face red but her sobs gone. She sat back on her heels and wiped her face. "Sorry."

"Don't be." Rosie gazed up at her, a complete mess but absolutely beautiful. She tried to push that thought away, grab back some kind of sense of logic. They were friends, weren't they?

"I must look a fright." Amber moved to take a tissue from the box on the coffee table.

The loss of her warm body made Rosie's heart hurt but Amber clambered back next to her after a few nose blows. Her face was clean, at least.

Amber cuddled the throw around their waists again and leant near to Rosie's side.

"There's one thing I try to stick to. D'you want to know what it is?" Rosie asked.

A mute nod.

Rosie held her cup of tea aloft. "The past is the past. If you feel bad about something, make up for it in the future." She drank some of her tea, toasting her life promise. "I know she's gone, but it doesn't mean you can't make it up to the universe in other ways." *Something I need to remember. Ali is gone, but it doesn't mean I can't keep on living.*

A sort of light flickered, then shone steadily from Amber's eyes. "You know what? You're this bright, colourful part of my life I never expected to get."

Unsure whether Amber's grief had loosened her tongue, Rosie peered at her with trepidation.

"I have epic friends, a great job, and somewhere cosy to live, and I'm doing okay. But you..." Amber placed her hand on Rosie's knee through the throw. "You're amazing."

Electricity shot up Rosie's leg where Amber touched her. "You're amazing too." Something else had pushed to the forefront—a feeling of desperation, of wanting, that Rosie hadn't felt about anyone else in a long time.

Amber brushed Rosie's hair behind her ear. "I also think you're beautiful."

More tingles spread down Rosie's neck. *This was not the way it was supposed to go.*

Lips squishing into a pout, Amber pulled back. "I guess I was hoping for something back. But it's okay. We can just be friends."

"Wait." *Oh God, oh God, what am I doing?* "I just..."

Rosie wanted to tell her, she really did.

But Amber was grieving. She already had a full cup when it came to feelings. There was no way she could add to that.

She also didn't want Amber to think she was a lost cause by not admitting how she felt about her. "I think you're beautiful too. I don't just mean when you're dressed up for a concert either." She let out a breath and allowed her discomfort to show. "Even now, when you're covered in snot."

Amber covered her face. "Oh, damn. I'm not, am I?"

With a laugh, Rosie took both Amber's hands and held them. "It was just a figure of speech."

They sat for a moment or two, smiling at one another.

Amber took one of her hands back to tidy her hair. "There's a *but*...I can tell."

Rosie sighed. "Let me be here for you today. Give yourself some time. Maybe when it's not so fresh, we can talk about what this," she gestured between them, "means then." *Logical, Miss Tanner. And kind too.*

Amber stared at Rosie, then nodded. "You're right. Of course you are." She wagged a finger at Rosie. "You're very clever, you know."

Rosie pulled on her best smart-alec face and wiggled her head. "I do come highly recommended."

"Oh, fuck off." At least Amber laughed.

"Anyway," Rosie nodded towards the kitchen, "so far I haven't seen a single crumb of biscuit. I was promised snacks."

"True. I'll go grab some."

Before she could stand, Rosie touched her arm. "You're okay?"

Amber's dark gaze locked onto Rosie's, the corners of her eyes crinkling. "I'm good. Thanks."

"Cuddles in front of the TV with chocolate?" She was pleased she could stay on the sofa, covered up to her boobs with the blanket.

"Cuddles, hmm?" Amber's voice carried through from the kitchen. "I like the sound of that."

"Excellent," Rosie said to herself. Suddenly, the room was toasty, as if the spirit of Christmas and the New Year had filled it up. So she'd indulge in a little affection and physical contact. As long as Amber didn't get too close, didn't break the barrier the throw gave her, all would be fine. *It's for Amber. Amber needs it. She's grieving; she's all alone today.*

Amber returned soon afterwards with a box of chocolates, a bowl full of luxurious-looking biscuits, and a teapot dressed in a green cosy. She set everything onto the coffee table and turned on the TV. "Something funny?" Her face was less blotchy. There was a small glimmer in her eyes as if she'd discovered some kind of mischief whilst she'd gathered supplies.

"Sure. Something funny." Rosie patted the space Amber had vacated a few moments ago.

After pouring them fresh cups of tea and nestling the biscuit bowl between them, Amber sat close but without touching. That was fine with Rosie—maybe Amber needed a little space.

They found a sketch show, an old classic, and munched their way through the bowl.

Rosie wiped the sides of her mouth before grinning at Amber.

Amber responded in kind, then shifted towards her with a hopeful look.

Lifting an arm to rest on the back of the sofa, Rosie forced herself to relax.

The warmth of Amber's body was heavenly, as if Rosie had always longed for it. Amber rested a hand on Rosie's leg on top of the throw, her cheek against Rosie's shoulder. She blinked up at her and when she spoke, her voice was barely audible. "I really want to kiss you."

Rosie cupped Amber's cheek and pressed her lips to her temple. She guided her back against her shoulder. "It's all right."

She hoped that was all she needed to say. No need to say something untrue like they needed to wait, that one day they would kiss. As much as her heart tugged her to ask Amber out, to declare her attraction to her, Rosie's head screamed at her to stop.

An embrace. Just for today. Rosie pressed her nose into Amber's hair and inhaled, committing the flowery scent of her shampoo to memory.

The sun dipped and left them with only the moving light from the TV. Evening drew in. Amber's body became heavy.

Before Rosie could check whether she had fallen asleep, Amber inhaled and sat up. She squinted into the darkness. "How is it nearly ten?"

"Is it?" Rosie noticed the wooden clock on the wall. "Time does fly."

"When you're having fun." Amber stretched her arms above her head. "I've kept you long enough. You should go home."

Rosie stood, smoothing her clothes where they had become ruffled. She was on the pinnacle of offering to stay the night, but her head chastised her in time. "You haven't kept me. I'm glad I could be here for you."

With a renewed sadness, Amber tidied away their snack paraphernalia.

Rosie put on her trainers. She wandered into the hallway.

Amber joined her and put a hand on the door before Rosie even had her coat on.

Deep dark eyes Rosie could get lost in. And she wanted to. Ruby red lips; it wouldn't take much effort to just lean in and kiss Amber. Rosie had done it before: made the first move.

"I'm glad you came over." Amber's words jolted Rosie from her thoughts.

"Me too. You going to be okay?"

"Yes."

Rosie frowned.

"Honestly, I'll text you if I need you."

Rosie touched Amber's shoulder. "You don't have to need me to text me."

A nod. Amber broke the eye contact and opened the door. "I'll let you get home."

"Sleep well."

Rosie felt Amber's gaze on her back as she walked down the path, before the door closed, and then all she was left with was the street lamp and the lingering feeling of a kiss that never happened.

Chapter 16

The next few days were full of bouts of sadness that caught Amber unexpectedly. It was irritating. She'd managed to keep her head level for over a year, hadn't so much as thought about her grandma for even longer. Now it was all she could think about.

The crematorium was a grey, sallow place. The auditorium was drab and in need of a lick of paint. Amber and Harry tiptoed in and sat at the back.

She recognised the music as Elton John, but knew no more.

Harry's brown curly hair was neatly combed. He was always smartly dressed—Amber wasn't sure why she expected anything less than a clean and pressed black suit. Even when he looked after Florence, his boots were polished.

Matthew had had to work. Amber didn't mind spending time with him, but he wasn't in recovery and didn't understand the things she and Harry had in common. Not that Matthew was unsupportive, not at all—he was a brilliant boyfriend for Harry and they were a good match—but Alcoholics Anonymous was a fellowship, and those in it had a shared empathy.

She tried to draw strength from Harry's warm hand. His skin was soft and his nails were super-clean. She'd taken off her nail varnish for the funeral, hadn't felt it respectful somehow. Black tights, of course. Black skirt, black blouse, and a burgundy cardigan.

As the song ended, the woman in charge stepped up to the lectern. "Welcome, everyone, to the celebration of the life of Mrs Julia Chilton. She was born on the twenty-eighth of July 1927 and died on Christmas Eve last year. A long and satisfying life…"

Amber wanted to listen, she really did. She wanted to find out about her grandma's life, hear things she'd never been told. Wasn't that what you did at a funeral? But her parents were an ominous presence in the front row, her cousins just behind them. None of them had turned around to see if Amber was there.

What's going through their minds? Do they send me awful thoughts, willing me to break, or at the least leave? Do they hate me and everything I stand for? Is their blatant disregard making Harry uncomfortable?

It swirled inside her, a horrible ache and anger. She forced her breath in and out: steady and measured.

Her mum grieved the loss of her own mother.

No mental glances were cast her way. *They don't even care I'm here.*

She tried not to allow that last thought to bring her down further. *Just get through it. You are strong. You can cope.*

A few things caught in the edges of Amber's attention—her grandma had worked for the Samaritans helpline back in the day. She'd had cats all her life, including a huge fluffy one called Tiger that Amber remembered. She was in choirs during her youth—that, Amber hadn't known. *Maybe that's where I get it from.*

When it came to the hymn, there were lyrics in the programme and Amber knew the tune. Once she opened her mouth, a sense of featheriness overcame her. The melody squeezed her heart before letting it go. It was as if tiny leaves were carried away in a gust of wind, her grandma's soul amongst them.

A single tear slid down her face, but she smiled. Maybe it was love that caused it.

Shuffling noises sounded as everyone took their seats again. More talking. Her aunt read a poem. All the while, Amber trained her gaze on her shiny shoes, wiggling her toes to make the light dance across them. Something undetectable to others, but keeping her focus.

The machine whirred, and the coffin backed through the curtains. Amber sent her grandma a mental farewell. Grandma had done many things, most of them worthwhile and selfless like the Samaritans.

Amber's life paled in comparison. She vowed she'd make a list of things she wanted to achieve. There was no doubt about the choir—that was something she'd do for a long time, even if Rosie stopped going. Amber's mum had never been musical; maybe Grandma's affinity with singing had skipped a generation.

It was bright and crisp when she and Harry strode outside.

She pushed up her shoulders and slipped around a few people without her parents catching her. Today was not about them having a go or her trying to make it up.

They strolled around the gardens, stopping every so often at a bench or plaque dedicated to a passed loved one.

Harry gave her his arm. "You're glad you came?"

"Yeah." Amber caught sight of her mother's greying hair amidst fellow mourners. "I think I'd have regretted it if I hadn't come."

"I understand." He slid an arm around her waist. "And, for what it's worth, I think you're brave as shit."

It made Amber smile. "I surprised myself. I thought I'd be a total mess."

He squeezed her and they continued to walk. "She sounds like a really nice lady."

"She was." Amber swallowed. "I should have made more of an effort. It was almost completely my fault we fought."

"You were drinking." It was not a question because Harry knew her history.

"Yeah. Pretty heavily. It was right when that horrible ward manager started working—you know, that Barbara?"

"On the general ward, right? The one that bullied you?"

"I went off sick after that. Really wasn't well. And not using appropriate coping mechanisms."

They both smirked at her choice of language before stopping by a marble-coloured stone that read *Peter Collins, loved and lost.*

"Grandma just wanted me to know some home truths." Amber sighed. "I didn't want to hear them. Everything was everyone else's fault, of course, and I had nothing to be sorry about."

"Let's talk about happy things." He gestured to a large but gnarled apple tree where a few spherical sparrows gathered, ruffled against the cold. "Nature all around us in this beautiful place? Not so much to be sad about."

The word *beautiful* made Amber think of Rosie. She took a moment to watch the birds before inhaling slowly. "Let me see... A happy thing?"

He didn't answer.

"What about your ongoing saga with Matthew about his inheritance and buying a house?"

A tendon in Harry's neck hardened, but he didn't comment.

"No? Okay. I suppose we could talk about the fact that Rosie came over on New Year's Eve and we cuddled on the sofa."

To his credit, he didn't lift his voice or his eyebrows. "Is that so?"

She couldn't help smiling, just a tad. "She, um… I made a bit of a fool of myself. Kind of invited her for snacks and TV and then cried on her."

"Fair enough." He so did not mean that. She got the feeling he was holding back from further comment.

"And then I admitted I fancied her. Well, in so many words. I also told her I wanted to kiss her."

"You did not!" His eyes were like dinner plates.

"A little bit."

"How did she react?" He blinked. "I'm kind of assuming she said she was on the same page. You're still smiling."

Amber stopped walking and twisted her lips. "I'm not sure. She told me it was all right. But I'm not sure if she meant it was okay I'd said it or that it was okay because she felt the same or…" She shrugged. "I have literally no idea."

"I presume she didn't kiss you?"

"I got the feeling she wanted to. Maybe. But I was looking kind of gross, all snotty and stuff. So I wouldn't be surprised if she didn't want to kiss me just for, you know, germ reasons."

He let out a breathy chuckle. "Well, I suppose it would have been a bit crass to snog you when you're so vulnerable. I guess I can thank her for that." He nodded towards the car. "You ready to go or d'you want to stay a bit longer?"

"No, let's go. I've shown my face." She bit back a nasty comment about being ignored. "And, yeah, I hadn't thought of it like that. I was pretty upset, and she just kind of gave me comfort. Didn't take advantage."

"Good."

They got into his car, and Harry set the blowers to toasty.

Amber held her fingertips—the only parts of her hands exposed below her wrist warmers—by the heater and allowed the air to surround her skin. It hadn't been warm in the crematorium, and outside was wintery too.

"So, enough about your love life, Missus." Harry edged the car across the gravel. "Tell me more about your grandma."

Chapter 17

The first choir rehearsal after the Christmas holidays had been scheduled for the tenth of January, but Rosie had sent Amber a text to let her know it had been cancelled. Apparently, the majority of the choir had some virus bug, and Enid hadn't wanted anyone else to catch it.

Amber didn't feel great herself and had asked Rosie round for a film, but Rosie had suggested a rain check—something about being tired after the first week of teaching after the holidays.

Finally, as if having journeyed at a snail's pace, the following Friday arrived. Amber's cold had all but finished, just leaving her a little bunged up and headachy. The excitement of seeing Rosie plus the added anticipation of new music masked her symptoms anyway.

She waved goodbye to Harry and Jilly after the AA meeting, then helped clear away the chairs. It was then too late to be early—what if Rosie saw her coming out of the AA room before she was ready to tell her?—so Amber hung out in the AA room for a few more minutes.

Once she was sure she wouldn't meet anyone as she came out, she skipped into the choir room. She let out a breath as she realised everyone was already there. Enid had just stepped up to the front to address everyone.

Amber legged it around the front to sit with Rosie in as inconspicuous a way as she could. Most people turned with her, but she tried not to care. She sniffed a bit and wiped her nose.

The smile Rosie gave her was wide, but she didn't make to touch or hug her. When Amber leant to see the music in Rosie's hands, Rosie leant away but proffered the music at arm's length.

I guess she doesn't want to catch my cold. Amber scanned the title page with interest.

"Happy New Year, everyone, and welcome. As I said a few months ago, this year we are learning something new. A series of new pieces by a local composer. The collection is called *Lullaby of the Ocean* and contains six separate pieces. It tells the story, that of a mother taking her baby boy across the sea from her home island to live with the love of her life."

Amber flicked through the music book with its blue cover depicting a silhouette of a sailing boat and two passengers atop swirling waves. It seemed professionally printed, something Amber hadn't expected from a local composer.

"I'll be looking for a soloist for 'Lullaby', soprano please, and a tenor for the 'Sight of Land' section. All suggestions on a postcard." Enid gave the choir a grin. "Warm up first."

At first it was as if no one had sung a note since they'd broken up for Christmas. As time went on, however, the overall tone became cleaner and rounder.

Amber's throat was like sandpaper, so she eased off. The damn virus constricted her throat, limiting her range. She wanted to stamp her foot. *I had so wanted to sing well on our first day back.*

Rosie, as always, sounded heavenly. Amber wallowed in it, allowing every note she hit to fill her up. She'd missed hearing her.

Once Enid reckoned they were ready, they tackled the fourth piece—"Lullaby". Each part was played on the piano individually, and the choir sang along.

As she had done back in September, Rosie followed each word with her finger for Amber's benefit. Rosie sang the song almost as if she'd heard it before, each note near-perfect with the piano. Could Rosie sight-sing? Yet another string to her bow.

Another thing for me to love her for.

Amber's voice petered out and she startled for a bar or two, her thoughts halting. Was that true?

She side-eyed Rosie and took in her hazel eyes, the way her cheekbones lifted when she sang. Was she a bit puffy around the gills? Amber supposed it *had* been Christmas—she herself had gained a few kilos since ravishing turkey on Christmas Day…and the subsequent chocolate and biscuits.

Come to think of it, hadn't Rosie worn tight, skinny clothes when they'd first met, then changed her wardrobe? The loose shirts looked good on her, but maybe her weight gain had started before Christmas. Not that Rosie looked unattractive with a little more weight on her.

Amber yanked her gaze away, not wanting Rosie to guess she'd stared. Better get back to concentrating on the song.

It was a sweet melody, lilting and simple. The sopranos took a breather whilst the altos, tenors, and basses took their turns. Amber leaned in, intending on whispering a hello to Rosie.

Rosie moved away, a tight smile on her face.

Oh, of course. My germs. "Sorry."

A shake of her head and Rosie's interest moved back to Enid.

Amber sunk her nose into the sheet music, trying to commit the lyrics to memory. They spoke of a mother singing to her baby, cuddled close in a boat on the sea.

It was time to put the parts together. The first time they sang it as a company, it was far from perfect. But the parts intermingled beautifully, and by the time they got to the end, Rosie's teeth were visible in the most sparkly smile Amber had ever seen on her.

The sudden urge to photograph Rosie climbed inside her. Amber touched her sternum, where her camera usually hung.

They went over "Lullaby" a few more times, then Enid allowed them a break.

Rosie nipped off to the toilet.

All alone, Amber checked social media on her phone, that sort of thing. Then she threw hell to the wind and decided to mingle.

Gareth, the large tenor who had been kind at her second rehearsal, waved. He stood with several of his section plus a few of the warbler women Rosie was so fond of. "Hiya, Amber. Nice to see you."

"Nice to see you too." She gestured him away as he leaned in to give her a hug. "I'm full of cold."

"You and everyone else, hmm?" Gareth leant his sizeable behind on a table at the back of the hall. "Return-to-school lurgy."

Amber looked around. "Are a lot of the choir teachers, then?"

"Some." Gareth pointed to a few. "Some LSAs and teaching assistants. Admin, pastoral care, etcetera."

"Coincidence?"

He shrugged. "Who knows? Maybe it's Rosie's influence." His eyes shone. "She roped a few of us in from schools when she first started coming."

"That's nice of her." Amber hopped up onto the table beside him and swung her legs.

Linda sidled up to them, her lips pursed.

Trying not to shrink away, Amber chewed her lip and ceased the swinging of her feet. Was she about to get some kind of criticism?

"I'm impressed you're here, even though you still clearly have a cold."

Amber's gaze shot up, followed by her eyebrows. "Well, I like coming. Even if I can't give it my all, I'd rather be here and at least learn some of the songs than be stuck at home, feeling sorry for myself."

Linda's expression smoothed as if she was satisfied with Amber's response. "Just don't get too close to the rest of us."

"I'm not." Relief flooded Amber at the change in Linda's treatment of her. *It is so nice to hear friendly words from her for once.* "Rosie held the music away from her so I could read it."

"And so she should. In her condition." The pinched expression was back on Linda's face. She moved over to her handbag, away from earshot.

Amber frowned and tilted her head at Gareth. "What did she mean by that?"

"Oh, don't listen to Linda. She likes her gossip."

"Gossip?"

He pushed away from the table, shifted from foot to foot. "Rosie's controversial life choice." He patted his chest. "Me, I say, 'Live and let live.' She'll make a great mum."

"*Mum*?" Amber slid from the table and looked around her. "What do you mean?"

"Enid let it slip at the Women's Institute Christmas gathering. Few too many glasses of white, I think. Since then, it's spread like wildfire; you know how these things do. Rosie's—"

"Right, everyone. Sit back down, please," Enid called them.

Rosie emerged from the bathroom. She chucked her head towards their chairs, indicating they should return.

Amber's brain reeled. *Mum? She can't be. She's single. Isn't she?*

With a stolen glance at Rosie as they sat, Amber realised she *did* look big especially around her belly. And she *did* have a strange happy glow about her. *And she hasn't touched a drop of alcohol since I met her.*

But Rosie was single. At least, that was what she'd indicated to Amber. Had she ever even stated she was gay and not bisexual?

Maybe she had some secret boyfriend. Maybe she was married. But Amber had been to her house. She'd never got the feeling anyone else lived there.

How could she possibly be pregnant?

Shame and anger roiled within her. Bile threatened to hit her throat. Either she had been the epitome of stupidity and had ignored the signs of Rosie's condition or Rosie had hidden it well. Either way, Amber was a fool.

The remainder of the rehearsal went by in a blur. Amber went through the motions of singing along, but all she could think about was the way Rosie had betrayed her. And all she could focus on was keeping her tears at bay.

A million years later, it ended. Amber pulled her jacket on in no time and put her chair away before Rosie had even put the music back in the folder. After giving Rosie the briefest wave, she jogged from the hall. She just caught Gareth's concerned expression before the cold of outside hit her.

The rain had eased, but it had left behind a mist that clung to her eyelashes and fogged her breath. Struggling with her handbag, she attempted to hurry from the entrance of the church hall but was stopped by a hand on her shoulder.

"Hey, you okay, Amb?"

Amber took her time turning around. A sigh billowed from her, adding to the mist. "Fine."

"You're so not." Rosie's hand was firm.

Tears filled her eyes but she shook them away. Renewed anger built. "Where are you parked?" Her voice came out harsh but she didn't care.

"Down by the Grand Atlantic."

"I'll walk you." Amber relinquished her arm and strode away.

Once they were on the promenade, by the Grand Pier, Amber slowed. A gull rustled some packaging inside a bin before it grabbed a discarded chip and soared into the air with it. It perched atop the bus stop and gobbled it whole.

Amber pulled her jacket around her, stuffing her scarf into the front to keep out the chill. "Why didn't you tell me?"

"What?" Rosie looked confused, but there was a pinprick of horror in her eyes.

"That you're pregnant?" Amber folded her arms and glared at the pavement. She didn't want to look at Rosie.

Rosie let out a squeak. "Who fucking told you?" Her tone was gravelly, as if she had indeed caught a cold from Amber.

"Everyone knows. Enid told them."

"Amb, I…"

The gull cried into the sea air, almost as if it laughed at them.

Amber's heart ached. "I've been such a dumb shit." She dropped her arms and held them out. "Look at you." She finally glanced at Rosie, the front of her coat tented by her bump. "It's so obvious."

Rosie chewed her bottom lip, then took a step towards Amber. "I'm sorry."

"What for?" Amber gestured emphatically. "For not telling me or for leading me on?"

"Not telling you." Rosie moved closer. "And I've never led you on."

"What are you talking about?" A tear dribbled down Amber's cheek. She swiped at it. "I thought you were single."

"I am."

"You're fucking pregnant. How can you be single?" Amber's shouts echoed off the seawall and the glass sides of the bus stop. She threw up her hands. "What was it, then? A one-night stand with some bloke? An accident?"

"No." Rosie sounded stronger.

It made Amber stop short. "So what, then?"

Rosie winced. "Please, stop shouting. Come. Sit?" She walked to the bus stop and sat on the metal seat before patting the space next to her.

After glaring at the tiny seat, Amber gave in to the request. She made sure there was a good foot between them.

"I *am* single. I never lied to you about that."

Amber just looked at her, unwilling to believe.

"I've always wanted kids. Ever since I was little. I've been in a number of relationships, with women and not a single one has worked out the way

I needed it to. My last girlfriend said outright she didn't want kids. So I hit thirty-four and just thought, 'sod it. If I'm going to do it, I'll do it by myself.'"

"By yourself?"

"Mm-hmm. I found a donor, got him checked out—all the tests and everything. You can get the kit off the internet; it's not expensive."

Amber's gaze trailed down Rosie's body. "How…how many…?"

"Weeks?"

Amber nodded.

"Twenty-three."

"You're nearly six months pregnant and I didn't even notice?"

Rosie lifted a hand, palm up. "I guess I hid it well."

Another tear escaped Amber's eye. "Why did you do that?"

After dropping her hand, Rosie stared at her boots. "I wanted to tell you. But I didn't want anyone to know yet. I told everyone I knew about being pregnant the first time around, two years ago—I was so damn excited. And I lost my baby boy at twenty-eight weeks. He was called Ali."

Grief for Rosie's baby made it difficult for Amber to breathe. *How awful.*

Rosie grimaced. "It's stupid to believe in jinxes and that kind of thing. But it scared me so much that it would happen again. So I hid it."

"The entire choir knows. Apparently, Enid told everyone when she was drunk at some party over the holidays."

Rosie groaned and fingered the bridge of her nose. "Fuck. I didn't mean for that to happen, honestly. I wanted to tell everyone in my own time."

"But…" Amber racked her brains. "Wait. Were you pregnant when we first met?"

A pause. The smallest of nods.

Amber exhaled, her mouth gaping. Then she shook her head.

"I know. I'm shit." Rosie brushed her palm over the top of Amber's hand.

Amber pulled away.

"I was going to tell you at New Year's. But then your grandma died and…"

"Sure. Blame my grandma."

"I wasn't." Rosie sat back and tried to catch Amber's gaze. "I just didn't want to burden you with the information. You were grieving."

"So you lied to me." Amber scowled. "And I fell for all that 'I think you're beautiful' shit too."

"That wasn't a lie. Far from it." Rosie's bottom lip wobbled. She squirmed and placed a hand on her belly.

Amber's attention was on Rosie's hand. She took in the way her bump protruded, then the image of a tiny baby popped into her mind's eye, curled up and moving around. She hiccupped and wiped another tear away.

"That isn't something I'd lie about." Rosie reached for her hand again, and this time Amber allowed her touch. "I was scared of getting too close to you. And then of you freaking out, especially as I'd waited far too long really to tell you." She swallowed. "I suppose I was enjoying the time we had together before inevitably you wouldn't want to be around me because of this." She indicated her tummy.

"Why on earth would I stop being friends with you if you became a mum?"

"Friends?" Rosie's eyes sparkled with tears in the lights strung along the seafront. Her eyebrows pushed down in the middle.

"That's what we are though." Amber gave a shrug but turned her hand over so Rosie could scissor their fingers together.

"I kept telling myself that's all we could be." Rosie gazed out to the sea—miles away due to the low tide. "But I don't think I want that." She looked up. "My feelings are… I like you more than friends, I think."

"You think?"

"I know."

How could Rosie be so sure after the bombshell she'd just dropped? Amber sat on the freezing metal seat, her hand warm in Rosie's. Her mind spun, a tangled mess of wool. It was far too much for her to unpick. "I don't know."

Rosie nodded. "I understand."

"It's a lot for me to take in." She pushed her shoulders up. "I don't know what I want."

"Do you want me? Ignore the other stuff for a minute."

"How can I ignore it?" Amber contemplated their joined hands, Rosie's longer fingers and neat nails contrasted with her own red, varnished ones.

It struck her Rosie was close to her now, her fear of catching Amber's cold outweighed by the way she felt emotionally. "It a very big thing."

"I know. I wish I'd told you right at the beginning. But I'd only told my sister and my parents then."

"How did they react?" Amber looked up.

The corners of Rosie's eyes crinkled. "After much debate and convincing, they are behind me a hundred percent."

"That's good."

Rosie seemed to flop with relief. "Yeah. It would have been super-difficult without their support."

Another pause. The waves could just be heard from far away. The gull clattered his feet above them and took off into the air. A white ghost in the inky sky.

"So, what do we do now?" Amber swung one leg.

A huge sigh from Rosie. "I had this planned out so meticulously. Getting pregnant, buying all the baby stuff, ready for my due date. My birth plan, breastfeeding, how she'd be raised…"

"You're having a girl?"

Rosie's free hand caressed her belly. "The one thing I didn't count on was meeting someone I might like. I thought I'd get at least a couple of years to raise my kid before I would start dating again."

"Yeah. That must have been a bit of a shock." Amber nudged Rosie, more gently than she would have before the big reveal but still with a teasing air.

"One hell of a shock. You scuppered my excellent scheme."

Amber rolled her eyes and laughed despite herself.

"Now I don't know what to do." Rosie's tone held something akin to anxiety. The way a tendon stood out on her neck only added to the effect. "I don't want to make any promises."

"Me neither. I'm not sure how I feel about it either." She took Rosie's chin, made sure their gazes were locked. Shyness overtook her and she let go. "I think we should sleep on it, maybe. Meet next week for a coffee." She smirked. "Decaf, in your case."

"Actually, studies show that consuming four or less cups of regular coffee has little or no effect on baby." She sounded like a smug textbook.

"Oh, is that right?"

They shared a grin.

"Sunday? I think your local has a coffee machine as well as excellent music."

"They do tea as well. I've seen people drinking it."

Amber nodded. "It's a date." She took a deep breath. *I want to tell her my secret too, but have we shared too much for one day? What if I wake up tomorrow and feel I can't handle it all? What if I change my mind about wanting to be with her? Is it worth the potential vulnerability tonight?* She let the breath escape her, fly into the night, along with her intention to come clean. "See you at two thirty?"

Rosie pulled Amber to stand. She stood close, a couple of inches taller than Amber. She lifted her chin.

Being slowly drawn in, Amber stepped closer. Rosie's lips were extra soft-looking.

The gull screeched above them and they broke apart, chuckling.

Rosie turned her face upwards. "Do you mind? Trying to grab a moment down here."

"Tenderly put." Amber couldn't keep the smile from her face. They still held hands.

"Sorry." Rosie had the modesty to look awkward about her choice of phrase. "I even forgot for a moment you have a cold. Don't want to catch that. Anyway. Sunday."

"Yeah, I should get going. And I should let you get in the warm." A surge of affection and concern swept through Amber. It surprised her. After her outburst, she hadn't expected to forgive Rosie, let alone feel worried about her. *I suppose that comes with the territory when you like someone as much as I like Rosie.*

"I don't need mollycoddling." Rosie winked at her. "But your concern is appreciated."

Amber squeezed Rosie's fingers before letting go. "See you." She started to walk away towards the safety and stability of Jilly's house. Her home.

"Amb?"

Amber stopped and glanced back.

"I'm really sorry I didn't tell you."

Amber sighed. "I get it." It started to make sense. Amber had learned a lot about Rosie in the four months she'd known her. And almost all of what she knew she liked. She could at least respect her for wanting to keep that part of her life private, especially when she'd lost a baby so late on. "Talk on Sunday."

"Text me when you get home, yeah?"

Was Rosie concerned about her now? That made Amber smile. "You too."

Turning back, Amber started along the seafront again. Her heart thudded, and she felt lightheaded. Thoughts bounced like rubber balls against the inside of her skull. She needed a good long cry, if only to get out the stress of the evening. And a long sleep.

Chapter 18

Rosie woke on Saturday with the sense of a weight having lifted. She wasn't hiding anymore. Strength energised her spirit, and she was ready to tackle any problem, including the critical glances of the warblers.

She went with Charlie to the nearest department store for some meticulous pushchair research. Rosie had read copious online reviews and had narrowed it down to her favourite two models. She picked the cheapest as there wasn't much between them when it came to practicality or safety. It came home in a box in the back of her car after she insisted the salesperson show her how to put it up and down.

An afternoon of housework followed. Rests were taken frequently with the way her back and legs ached if she moved around for too long. After much exercise with the vacuum, she ran herself a warm bath that contained essential oils she liked the smell of. A candle or two later, her muscles loosened, the water lapping against her bump as if it was an island sticking out from the sea.

It made her think of the new music. A woman with her baby making the long journey across the ocean to her new home. Very apt, considering her present condition. She was almost disappointed she couldn't take the solo.

Sunday was bright and chilly. The stroll to the pub was brisk. Another weight lifted as she walked—Rosie realised she'd been holding her belly in, in case Amber noticed her bump. No need to do that anymore. Pride made her wiggle her hips as she walked, presenting her bump with joy to the world.

A quick check inside the pub revealed Amber had decided upon a different location for their coffee date: a leather sofa next to the bar with red throw cushions and well-loved edges.

Her heart climbed high at the smile Amber gave her. "Hi."

"I'll keep my distance. Still a bit bunged up."

"Thank you." Rosie flung her jacket over the back of the sofa and sat. "Have you been waiting long?"

"Nope. I ordered you a latte."

"Aren't you sweet?"

Amber snorted and pushed Rosie's leg. "I am, as it happens."

The barmaid brought their drinks over. Amber poured her own pot of tea.

Rosie watched her. K.B. made slopping movements against her ribs. She touched the top of her bump and waited for it to pass.

Once the pot was back on the mat, Amber's attention shifted to Rosie. "Oh. Is she moving?"

"Would you like to feel?" Rosie waited for K.B. to do another somersault then moved Amber's hand to where she felt it.

Amber's jaw dropped. With eyes alight, she lifted her head. "That's mad."

"Tell me about it. Weirdest thing that's ever happened to me."

With a chuckle, Amber pulled her hand away. "How are you?" She fidgeted with the hem of her skirt. "I mean, has it been okay?"

"My pregnancy?" It seemed odd to have never discussed it with Amber before. "Better than I expected, so far. A bit of nausea at the beginning." She sipped her coffee.

"I guess you have a lot to tell me. If you want to, that is?"

"Definitely." Rosie caught Amber's gaze. "Listen. I meant what I said. I want to be honest now. I don't want to omit anything."

Amber nodded, the corners of her mouth tugging upwards.

"Like I said, there were a few girlfriends, and either we never got far enough to talk about kids or they outright didn't want them. I could have waited a bit longer, but fertility goes down by like…a lot…"—she couldn't remember the percentage, although if she'd been asked a few months ago, she could have rattled them off—"…after thirty-five. And if I'd have needed extra help to get pregnant, it would have been more difficult. And way more expensive."

"That's a massive decision." Amber stirred a sugar into her cup of tea and added a drop of milk. "To go it alone."

"I didn't make it lightly." Rosie caressed her tummy, K.B. now quiet. "It wasn't my first choice, but the more I thought about it the better it sounded. Not having someone else to make decisions with, argue with about how to raise the kid. I started trying in 2017, didn't get pregnant at first. Then I lost a baby."

Amber touched her hand, the one not on her belly. Something akin to sadness had settled over her face.

"It's okay." Why she felt the need to console Amber, she wasn't sure. She just knew she didn't want her to feel sad. "Ali, that was his name, stopped moving one day at twenty-eight weeks. I left it a while but then went to A&E to get checked. No heartbeat. They gave me medications to induce labour."

"That's so sad." Amber's eyes were wet.

"No real reason for it, at least not one they could give me. I held him once they'd wrapped him up. Said my goodbyes. He was so tiny. I took some time out from trying but I made a promise to myself that if I did get pregnant again I wouldn't shout so much about it. I started again last year."

"So…" Amber left her hand on Rosie's.

Rosie didn't move to hold Amber's hand like she had on Friday. *Amber gets to have some control today. At least until I've finished telling her my story.*

"So you used a donor?"

Rosie nodded. "I thought about a clinic, but it's so expensive. I always felt as if a clinic was something you used when you had issues. I've had regular bloods taken, all my levels are normal, and I've never had any issues with anything, apart from Ali, and they told me that probably wouldn't happen again. All you really need is the stuff and a syringe." She lifted one shoulder. "There's this website. It's specifically for LGBT couples and single women. All the donors have family histories and you can see a picture of them. You meet up and get to know them, then work out if you want a donation. You set up a date for him to come do his thing in a cup. Some people use a hotel but I was okay with him coming to my house."

"Coming *in* your house?"

Rosie laughed. "Guess I walked into that one." At least Amber smiled too. She wasn't disgusted by the whole thing. "I paid for his train fare and gave him some dinner money. He went on his merry way and I did the deed with the stuff."

"Is he going to want to see the kid?"

"No. We were both on the same page on that. He gave me a few things to put in a box: photos and a letter to my daughter once she asks. And so long as you don't do the horizontal dance of *lurve*, he doesn't need to go on the birth certificate."

Amber moved away to drink some tea. Rather than a rebuff, Rosie got the feeling she was creating a bit of space to think.

Content to give her anything she required, Rosie lowered her nose into the steam from her latte. It warmed her whole face. The aroma relaxed her too. It reminded her of Sunday mornings at her parents' before Sunday Service. Fresh coffee in the pot, Radio Four blaring. Croissants and jam and sticky fingers.

People chatted around them. The usual bouncy music had been replaced with something slower, gentler. Spanish with a hint of the beach and sun lounging. Glasses clinked behind them. A cold draft as a couple entered the pub.

"When are you due?"

Pulled back to the present, Rosie smiled. "First week of May."

"A spring baby. Nice."

Rosie sighed. "I'm not really looking forward to being big and uncomfortable in the heat, but at least it isn't July."

"True." Amber bounced her foot for a while, then stopped. "Is there anything else you've not told me?"

"I think that's everything. Apart from birth plans and all the paraphernalia I've bought. All the stuff I've still got to buy."

"I can imagine your bank balance is complaining."

"Not too much." Rosie was pleased to see Amber's hand back on her own, fingertips tracing little circles. "I was prepared. But I refuse to be one of those mums that buys everything they see that they like. I'm going minimalist."

"Cot, buggy, nappies?"

"Exactly. And green or yellow baby clothes. No way am I dressing her up in pink frills like my sister did with Chelsea."

Laughter bubbled out of Amber. "You're more of a dungarees and dinosaurs kind of mummy."

"You properly get me, Amb."

They shared a smile.

Rosie's whole body warmed. Each time she looked into Amber's eyes, new tingles shot across her skin. The tickling patterns against her hand just heightened the feelings.

"I think you get me too. Which takes us to the next issue." Amber sucked her bottom lip for a moment. "Where does it leave *us*?"

"I don't know." Rosie threaded their fingers together and was pleased when Amber didn't protest. "Like I said, I never expected to meet someone I liked so much. I wanted to stay single whilst I was pregnant, and then whilst I was bringing up my little girl. She comes first."

"Of *course* she does. I understand." A twinkle of disappointment flickered in Amber's eyes.

"It doesn't mean I don't want to…" Rosie took a deep breath. "To be with you. I mean…" She looked around them, then turned back to Amber. "Do you want kids? Or at least, to be with someone who *has* kids?"

"I…"

Rosie's heart flew into her throat. *What if she doesn't?*

"I've never been in a position to think about it. I've never dated anyone with children, and I've never been with someone long enough that we've discussed it." Amber squirmed so much that the leather squeaked. "But I think I do want kids. And I definitely would date a woman who had children of her own."

All the breath Rosie held escaped in a half-humorous 'Ha!' She recollected herself, her cheeks scorching. *Thank goodness.*

"And to continue the honesty," Amber continued, "I'd much rather be in your life than out of it. Like I said, I think you're beautiful and I like you."

"Ditto." For a while, Rosie's mouth was scratchy. She took a few sips of coffee and the feeling eased. "You want to have a go at this, then?"

"I do." Amber's gaze slid away.

I knew there'd be a 'but'… Rosie's heart was in her mouth again.

"I have something I need to tell you too."

Amber held Rosie's hand between her own. Rosie's story had made her feel extra affection for her. *Poor thing, having to give birth to a baby who'd died. I can't imagine being strong enough to do that.* But it wasn't fair she knew all of Rosie's secrets; it was time to come clean about her own. "You're not the only one with a secret."

"I'm not?" A guarded element appeared in Rosie's expression.

"It's not a bad thing, at least, not really. It's just a thing. I hope." She swallowed.

"You going to tell me, or am I going to have to guess?" A pinnacle of amusement glimmered in Rosie's eyes.

It gave Amber courage. "I'm an alcoholic."

The entire pub went still, although Amber knew this was a ludicrous idea. No one listened to them.

"A what?" Rosie's voice was barely a whisper.

"Alcoholic. But I've been sober for more than a year." Amber closed her eyes to remember. "Seventeen months, I think."

Rosie pulled her hand from Amber's. "Oh." A hardness creased Rosie's features. "Is that right?"

"Um…yes." Amber stuffed her cold fingers under her thighs. "It's why I've not been drinking when we've been out. Obviously."

Rosie just sat there.

"I have a sponsor, Fiona. I attend AA each week. Actually, I was coming out from a meeting when I met you for the first time."

Rosie sat up, her shoulders tense. A shiver passed through her. "Right."

Amber gave a little shrug.

Jaw set, Rosie shoved from the sofa. She snatched her jacket from the back and yanked it on. She walked away as she did up the buttons.

Amber was on her feet as soon as her brain connected with her body. "Wait!" She gathered her own belongings and scampered to Rosie, a hand on her shoulder.

"No." Rosie whipped around, then ushered Amber outside. "Amber, what the fuck?"

"What?" Amber felt like a rabbit with an invisible predator lurking somewhere. "What's the matter?"

"You're…" Rosie's voice dropped to a hiss. "You're a fucking drunk."

"Alcoholic." Amber enunciated each syllable, her shields going up at the fire in Rosie's eyes.

"Sorry, but I can't have that anywhere near me or my kid." Rosie waved frantically, then let out a sob. "I can't deal with this. You…you let me become your friend, get me to think I want a relationship with you, and then you drop that on me? Like it's nothing?"

Why is it okay for her to keep a secret from me but not for me to keep a secret from her? What is it about my secret that's so terrible?

A few cars went past.

Rosie strode away so Amber followed her.

"It's under control. I've coped well recently with my grandma dying and all that, much better than I would have a year or two ago." She grabbed Rosie's arm again but Rosie shrugged her off. "I'm in recovery."

Rosie turned on her, her hands wide and nostrils flaring. "I'm sure you have it all worked out, but I can't be near that. People with addictions: it's damaging for others to be close to them. Believe me." She held up both her hands. "It's a deal-breaker for me."

Amber gaped at her. "You're kidding."

"I'm sorry."

"So that's it? You're not even going to consider going out with me because I'm an alcoholic?"

Rosie glared at her, then flicked her gaze around the street. "I want my baby to have the best life she can possibly have. And I refuse to allow it to be tainted by someone who's..." A million words echoed around Amber: *damaged; sick; pathetic.*

With that, Rosie walked away.

Amber's own tears ran unabashedly. She wrapped her arms around her middle and wished she'd never met Rosie Tanner.

Chapter 19

Rosie left school early on Monday, ready for her first antenatal class. The room she was shown to had a selection of mats spread around; a kind-faced midwife called Cynthia was sitting crossed-legged on the floor.

Rosie chose a mat and lowered herself onto it. This change in her centre of gravity was strange; getting up and down was so much more difficult these days. She sat to mirror Cynthia. *I feel like a Buddha, with my round belly and floppy boobs.*

She was the only one on her own. To her left sat a lesbian couple, poking one another and curling up the sides of their mat like a flying carpet. Three more pairs, all heterosexual, sat on the other three mats.

Memories of Amber's revealed secret had plagued her all day. Her class had done a stellar job of keeping her occupied, but now that she was away from them, her gut hurt once more. The way Amber had looked at her with such sorrow wouldn't leave her.

When Cynthia cleared her throat, the lesbian couple stopped playing and sat to attention.

"Shall we all introduce ourselves? Name and how many weeks you are and then any information you'd like to give us about your family and your birth plan." Cynthia held up both hands. "You're not obliged to say anything you don't want to. Sometimes it's just nice to share, if you feel comfortable. You're all in a similar boat, don't forget."

Rosie tried to smile. K.B. wiggled as if she wanted to comfort her mum.

"We are Janet and Olivia, and we got pregnant via a sperm donor." Janet, with her belly rounder than Rosie's, had pointed at herself and then her partner as she'd introduced them. "We're having a little boy and we plan on a home birth."

"We're having one of those." A younger woman leaned back into her partner's arms. "I'm Rachael and this is Terry. We're twenty-six weeks…and we desperately need some help with renting a pool." She grimaced. "The bath isn't big enough, and I really want to give birth in water."

Rosie pushed the thoughts of Amber away and raised her hand. "I'm Rosie, I got pregnant with a sperm donor too, but I've chosen to be a single parent." She checked the group's reaction and was pleased to see no raised eyebrows or looks of horror. "I think I want a home birth too, although I'm still undecided. Going to just see how it goes. I'd like to go natural too, no drugs, you know, but, again, I'm just going to see what happens." A lump appeared in her throat. She tried to swallow it down but discovered tears in her eyes instead.

Putting a hand to her face, she tried not to think about everyone staring at her. Something warm touched her arm. She looked up to see Olivia, sympathy in her eyes.

"I'm okay." Rosie sniffed and blinked hard. "I just had a stressful weekend."

Cynthia nodded. "We'll have a little chat at the end, okay? Is anyone else hoping to labour without medication?"

Three out of the four couples raised their hands.

An overweight, older woman shook her head. "Absolutely not. Had my first with no epidural because he came like a kid in a water flume."

Rosie managed to chuckle with the rest of the group.

"And my second was an absolute shitstorm: long labour, knackered mum, cord round his neck. So number three is definitely coming out in a relaxed and well-medicated atmosphere." She held up a hand in greeting. "I'm Cathy, an old hat, one might say. This is my lesser half Jonathan. He's the least annoying and most supportive birth partner ever, mainly because he does exactly what I say and stays awake, even if I'm not finished after thirty-eight hours."

Everyone gave Jonathan a clap. He mock-bowed and kissed his wife on the cheek. She returned his smile.

"That's part of the usefulness of the prenatal class, guys," Cynthia said. "Getting the advice from your midwifery team, but also getting lived experience from each other." She glanced at Rosie. "Not one of you is alone in this."

They'd been sent videos to watch: the different stages of labour and the science of what happened when one's body went through it.

"Any questions about the birthing videos?"

Janet shifted on her mat. "Waters. Are they supposed to break before you get contractions, or after?"

"It's different for every mother. Some lose their waters right at the beginning of labour; some don't lose them at all. Some babies are born inside the amniotic sac, and we give it a little poke and baby emerges." Cynthia clasped her hands in her lap. "All I can say is: if your waters break early on and there's no sign of baby coming, you'll need to come in. Once baby isn't protected by the amniotic fluid, there's a risk of infection."

Rosie tried to file each bit of information with all the rest she'd read over the years. She'd borrowed every book from Weston Library, even bought a few from Amazon. So much information about something she had thought must be natural. Birth plans and getting the perfect latch, skin-to-skin, and cosleeping. Not eating brie and how much coffee was okay. She'd gobbled it all up—except the brie, of course—in those weeks before she'd had the donor visit. Now she wasn't sure she'd be able to remember much of it.

Is that what they call baby brain*? Oh, for goodness sakes, I didn't think I'd be like that. I guess no one is immune.* The way Amber would react to that made her smile, then the sadness crept back in as she realised it wasn't something she'd tell her anytime soon.

Several more questions, including some Cathy was able to answer with humour and accuracy.

"Right, chaps." That got a laugh. "Time to learn some practical things. If you have a birth partner, this is the time to sit back in their arms and relax." She sent Rosie a smile. "Do you have someone to be with you, Rosie?"

Not anymore. Rosie chewed her lip. "I haven't decided." She looked around, her foot bouncing. "I kind of want to do it by myself. I mean, the midwives will be there and they're the experts, right?"

"All true." Cynthia leaned towards her. "But what about a familiar face? And what if you want a snack from the vending machine? Or something from home? A midwife won't be able to do that for you."

Twisting her lips to the side, Rosie nodded. “I’ll think about it.”

“There’s time to get a doula if you want one,” Cathy said.

“I’ve read about those.” Rosie picked at a thread on the knee of her maternity jeans. “I’m not sure.”

“You have time to figure it out.” Cynthia patted her hands together. “Today we’ll talk about having an active birth and what we can do to relax during those potentially long hours of contractions.”

“I’ve already bought a birthing ball. Damn, that thing is comfy!” Janet rocked from side to side in Olivia’s arms like a canoe on a river.

“Excellent. We have those you can borrow on the maternity unit if you wish, but they’re really cheap to buy and you can use it whilst you’re still pregnant for exercise.”

Rosie made a mental note to order one as soon as she got home. She sat through Cynthia’s explanation of why moving around and being upright during labour was important. The information about relaxation was interesting too. She took an active part in the breathing exercises.

“Some studies say the reason home births are less risky is because the mum is in a familiar environment. I strongly believe this to be true and in my professional opinion, if we could all have home births, there’d be a lot less caesareans and assisted deliveries. But we need to stick to those clinical guidelines: if you have a high risk pregnancy, you should have your baby in hospital or at least in the maternity suite.” She gave them all a stern look. “It is *your* choice, and we as healthcare providers should *not* pressure you into a different one. But you should listen to us and make your decision based on our recommendations.”

Rosie hugged her knees. Her determination to birth alone waned. Perhaps she should ask Charlie to be with her, for company if not emotional support and chief chocolate fetcher. She tried to imagine what her mother would be like. Would she be an annoyance, especially if Rosie was in pain? Or maybe it’d be nice to have her mum there.

Charlie had given birth to Chelsea without a hitch on the maternity unit. Rosie remembered visiting and Charlie making jokes about Tom nearly passing out when the cord was cut. He’d been supportive as far as she’d been able to tell. Perhaps a birth partner was a sensible idea.

After the class, Rosie lingered and Cynthia came over to sit in front of her on her mat. “How’re you doing?”

"A tough week." Rosie rested her chin on her knees—something she was only just able to do these days.

"Want to tell me about it?"

"Girl issues." Rosie shrugged.

"Girl as in girlfriend?"

A nod, a sigh.

"I'm sorry to hear that."

Rosie stared at her boots.

"I read your notes. You made it pretty clear to your GP that you were a solo parent." A flicker of an eyebrow and a gleam in Cynthia's eyes.

"It's just the way it turned out, I suppose. Got tired of waiting for someone to do it with."

"I'm guessing this girlfriend wasn't in your plan, then."

Rosie laughed bitterly. "A million miles away from my plan."

"Is there anything I can do to make things better for you?"

She's not asking for more information; that's kind of her. I guess she trusts me to know what I need. Rosie blinked. "Do you have a leaflet or something about that doula thing?"

"I do. And if you need anything, my team are just a phone call away." Cynthia heaved herself to her feet and went over to her desk.

Rosie stuffed the leaflet into her maternity file and nodded to Cynthia as she walked out into the sunshine.

Chapter 20

Amber snuggled on her side on her bed. The teddy she usually kept on the floor was tucked under one arm. The theme tune from *Holby City* played on her small TV.

Nico was fooling around on the floor with a tennis ball—his current best mate. A bow to it, followed by a pounce with both front paws. He yipped once before lying down to give the thing a ferocious chew.

At least he's full of the joys of spring. Not that it was spring quite yet. Jilly was always quick to correct her on that front: "Twenty-first of March and not a day before." It was barely February.

Amber's bedroom door opened an inch. "Ah, wondered where he'd got to." Jilly poked her head in. "You all right, kid?"

"Mmm." Amber wasn't even sure what she meant by the noise.

"Want to come watch that in the living room?"

"Aren't you watching that home-repair programme though?" Amber yawned and rolled onto her back.

"Can tape it. The joys of DVR."

Amber cuddled her teddy close. "Actually, would you mind if I just hung out in here tonight?" She grimaced at the way Jilly's face fell.

"So long as you're not moping."

"I'm not. I just feel like I want to be alone right now."

A stern look, with an undercurrent of concern. "You've spoken to Fiona?"

"I have. Phoned her on my lunch break."

"Do you need to phone her again?"

"I'm good." Amber indicated the screen, full of people in blue scrubs and that nice nurse with the bouncy hair and pretty teeth. "Just comfy and feeling safe." Nico half hopped, attempting her mattress. She caught him under the backside so he could clamber up. "I've got this dude, but I'll send him back in once *Holby*'s done."

After one last imploring look, Jilly backed out and pulled the door closed behind her.

Amber snuggled back into her pillow. Nico plonked onto her teddy's tummy and shoved his face under its neck before sighing and nestling against Amber's belly.

She considered Nico a nephew-type figure. Jilly was quite aunt-like, and Amber viewed the miniature dog as partly her responsibility. He was confident for a Chihuahua, but any loud noises and he cowered under their legs. Big dogs scared him too; he had to choose to greet them, not the other way around. He wasn't as indestructible as he believed and needed protecting sometimes.

Her thoughts drifted to Rosie. *Maybe that's what it's like to be pregnant. A curled-up fidgety being against your belly that you've got to look out for.* Rosie didn't need protecting, or so she'd thought. But there had been fear in Rosie's eyes when Amber had told her she was in AA. She'd got the feeling Rosie wanted to either fight or run away.

I hate myself. Things never go right for me. Anger swirled within her, tightening her chest and making her want to curl up. Rosie was right to hate her. She was a pathetic addict with no future and no hope of ever finding love.

Do I really blame myself? Did she have control over how Rosie felt about things? Surely, all she could do was be a good person, stand up for herself and anyone she felt needed it, and do well in life. It was hard to admit, but Rosie was responsible for her own happiness.

Her mobile phone rang. Nico flinched but just let out a rumbled purr before burrowing back into her tummy. *Harry.* Affection flooded her. It'd been a couple of weeks since she'd spoken to him, not including AA meetings. She turned the volume down on the TV and answered her phone.

"Hey."

"Hi missus. What you up to?"

Suspicions tugged. "Did Jilly text you or something?"

"Jilly? No."

She figured he told the truth. Harry was a crap liar anyway. "Sorry. Yeah things are okay. You?"

"Matthew bought me the most gorgeous flowers. Did you see on Instagram?"

"I did." She giggled. "He's a good boyfriend."

"I know. I'm terribly lucky."

"Anything more on this house of yours?"

A long sigh. "Feels like we keep having the same argument about it."

"You guys are so bad at communicating."

"We're not. He just doesn't get how I feel."

"He's at crochet this evening?"

"Yeah. Let him go out by himself and everything."

"Wow. Will he be okay?"

"He's got Sergeant Ollie to keep him in line, so I'm guessing so."

A pause whilst the mood quietened. Amber enjoyed the easy and flirtatious way she and Harry interacted. It was nonthreatening and the jokes fell so fluidly from her mouth.

"How you doing?" Slow concern dripped from his words.

"I feel sad." She stroked Nico's belly. "It's been such a nice few months getting to know Rosie, and now…" She groaned. "It just feels like someone's cut this big, fat silky ribbon and I'm not able to grab the ends to glue them back together."

"Great analogy."

"Your craftiness must be rubbing off on me."

Another pause.

"And what explanation did she give?"

"Just that she doesn't want to subject her child to someone who's got issues. Stupid, really, isn't it? Who hasn't got issues?"

"Some people think they haven't. Rosie clearly has. What do you think her problem is?"

Amber stretched and winced when her spine popped. She propped up her pillow so she could sit against the headboard. "I don't think it's just naivety. She's an intelligent woman. She'd ask questions if she wasn't sure about something."

"Maybe she had an ex who drank and hit her."

Amber covered her face. "That old story. I know it happens, but it's a brush we shouldn't all be tainted with."

Nico, disturbed by Amber's relocation, circled a few times before making himself at home in the nest of her crossed legs.

Amber tucked her skirt under his chin so he didn't have his head under it. "Her dad's a vicar. Maybe he preaches about temptation and sobriety and…I don't know."

"What about forgiveness and kindness?" There was a note to his voice, harsh and hard. "She's behaving like a horrible human being."

"She's not." Rosie's grin flickered into her mind's eye, and it made Amber smile despite everything. "She's generous and sweet and funny and…" Amber rubbed the back of her neck. "She's got to have her reasons. Something must have made her feel like that."

"Or she's just a bitch."

"Or that." Amber laughed. She never felt rubbish after talking to Harry. He was on her side. "I love you so much, H."

"Yeah, love you too, Twinkle."

That earned him a raspberry down the phone. "Friday's going to be weird."

"You're still going to go to that choir?"

"Yes. Definitely." She hadn't considered it until that moment. But giving up the choir would mean she was basing all her decisions on how her romantic relationships turned out. And that was never a good philosophy on life. "I like it. It's given me something I didn't have—and it was initially connected to Rosie, but now, I don't know, I enjoy it."

"Even if you have to sit with someone else?"

"Yes. I also made a commitment. It would be unfair for me to stop going just because Rosie doesn't want to be with me anymore."

A pause. She could practically hear the cogs whirring in his brain. "You're absolutely superb."

The compliment felt too big for her, but she shouldered it and bit back the self-deprecating retort. "Thanks. I try my best."

"You do." He snorted. "Rosie's an idiot. What a wonderful thing she's just throwing away, hmm?"

Amber beamed. *If Rosie can't handle it, that's her problem. I'll go to choir with my head held high and find another cool person to sit with. Or I'll just sit by myself. I'll learn the music by listening to the piano and the other members of the choir. I shouldn't rely on one person to help me anyway.*

Chapter 21

Amber wasn't sure what she expected when she walked into the hall on Friday. Anxiety tugged when she realised Rosie might have informed the entire choir about her alcoholism, but she forced herself to keep her chin up and her shoulders back. No point worrying about something she had no control over.

Today. Get through today and worry about tomorrow when it comes.

Rosie, it appeared, had already found a new singing mate. She sat with her head lowered—Amber reckoned no one else would have noticed, but Amber had spent so much time with her that little things like that were obvious—eyebrows down and shoulders hunched. Was she perusing the new music? She didn't look up when Amber walked to the front row and sat at the opposite end.

A mousey woman with freckles and a pointy face smiled as Amber approached. "Hi."

"Do you mind me sitting here?"

"Of course not. I'm Hayley."

"Amber." Amber shook Hayley's hand, noting her finely boned fingers. *She's tiny. Wonder if she even eats.* "Nice to meet you."

Hayley's smile crinkled her eyes. "Y-you too."

She's got a stutter. I wonder if she has anxiety. Amber pushed up her shoulders and shifted her chair closer to Hayley. "Tell me you've got music. I don't have my own copies."

"Yes. I usually sit by myself though."

Pain for the sparkle of sadness in Hayley's eyes appeared in Amber's chest. "Not today."

Hayley chuckled. "Okay."

"If it works out, who knows…?" Amber made a random gesture. "It might become a permanent thing." Her insides crumpled as the joke fell flat.

The smile Hayley gave her made it much better. "Oh. Okay." She opened the music book.

Out the corner of her eye, Amber noted Rosie staring out of the star-speckled window. She had a hand on her round belly and pulled her bottom lip into her mouth before letting out a huge sigh.

When Enid clapped to get everyone's attention, Rosie blinked and sat up straight again.

Hayley shuffled the music into a neat pile and sat to attention. Amber copied her, wanting to fit into her new friendship pod. The urge to make Hayley feel comfortable was strong.

This week they revisited "Lullaby" and then began the "Casting Off" segment, which was upbeat and hopeful. Amber was bouncing a bit in her seat until she noticed Hayley's wide eyes in her direction. She smiled to herself and, twisting her lips, stilled. Rosie would have joined in, at least in jest. *It's going to be weird being here with someone else.*

But Amber refused to let it ruin her enjoyment and continued to bounce along with the beat internally, scrunching her toes inside her shoes and tapping a finger against her leg. The joyous piece made her insides lift, her heart flutter, and her head clearer. It was as if she was the woman in the story, in the song, setting her boat to sail with her baby son, their whole lives in front of them.

At the end of rehearsal, Amber looked about for Rosie. *Should I go up to her, say hi?* She hoped she'd get an idea about what was okay if she made eye contact with her. But Rosie had left early. Amber hadn't even noticed her go.

I wonder whether she's still upset about everything. Or maybe her hormones are making everything feel crap at the moment. She helped Hayley pack away the music before approaching Enid. "Hi."

"Hello, dear."

"Would…?" Amber scanned the room one last time. "Could I have a copy of the music for myself? I'd like to take it home and learn the words."

One of Enid's grey eyebrows arched. She bent to rummage in a large plastic box. "I noticed you weren't sharing with Rosie anymore."

Amber swallowed to cover her discomfort. Rosie had known Enid a long time. *I hope Enid doesn't think harshly of me.* "That's right."

Once she found the music book, Enid caught Amber's eye. "Nice to see you're still here, whatever happens with Rosie."

"Yeah. I didn't want to let the choir down."

Enid looked at her a moment more, then gave her a nod.

Amber slipped the music into her handbag before stacking her chair.

Hayley had put on a hooded waterproof jacket in pale green. She wore skinny jeans with sports trainers and a shy smile. "Was nice to meet you."

"You too." They walked out together. "I've got my own music now, but I'll still sit with you if that's okay?"

Hayley nodded.

"Where do you live?"

"Worle." Hayley clutched the folder close. "I get the bus."

"I'm in Uphill. I like the walk home."

"Oh, I like to walk too." It was warmer, and the wind had dropped from the previous weeks. Hayley's brown ponytail swung from side to side as they walked. "I go to this walking group every week. They take you to different parts…different walks."

"That sounds nice." Amber wondered about another hobby; a walking group might be just the ticket. "Can anyone join?"

"Um…" Hayley stopped and toed the pavement. "It's sort of just for people with mental health problems." Her eyes flicked up once before settling back on the concrete.

"Damn. I got discharged a few months ago. Guess it's a *Carlton Centre* thing, hmm?"

Hayley's eyebrows rose along with her head. A small smile tugged her lips. "You were under them?"

"Yeah. Anxiety and depression. Other issues too, but…" Amber held up a hand.

Hayley nodded, strength seeping into her expression. "I have social anxiety. Struggle in crowds, you know?" She started to walk again, the bus stop within their sights.

"I'm an alcoholic." The words sounded so small, so insignificant. When Amber had spoken them before, they'd rung from the buildings, banged against doorframes and windows. She usually closed down after releasing them, so worried she'd get hurt by someone who didn't understand.

"I have friends that... I think they call it dual diagnosis. When you have mental health issues and problems with drugs and alcohol."

"Sounds familiar." Amber smiled at her.

Hayley smiled back. The freckles on her nose made her look young, but Amber estimated she was about her own age.

When they got to the bus stop on the seafront, Hayley rested against the seat and wrapped her arms around herself. A gull pattered about on the roof.

Amber sighed. Memories of Rosie—arguing and making up—plagued her. Rosie explaining how she got pregnant and why. The loss of her little boy. Her plans for a family. Emotions flooded her. "See you next week."

Hayley gave her a nervous wave.

Almost wishing it was stormy so the wind and rain could numb her as she walked, Amber made her way along the seafront. The weight of the music book patted with every step against her leg. She sang the upbeat song inside her head, then out loud, not caring who heard.

If only her brain would make its mind up—one moment she was strong and didn't care what Rosie did or thought, but the next she hoped she'd catch her eye.

A new friend though; that was good. Maybe Hayley would be happy to spend time with Amber outside of the choir. But she'd give it time. *No sense in throwing myself into another friendship with eyes closed.* It was a mistake she didn't want to make twice.

Chapter 22

"I NEED SOME EXERCISE." ROSIE's back ached, and the staff room chairs did nothing for her posture. She groaned as she stood and went over to the kettle to boil it.

The muffled noises of children playing at lunchtime drifted through the large windows.

Claire came over, a hand extended. "Want me to rub your back?"

Rosie pouted; the mere suggestion she needed anyone's help was an atrocity. She rolled her eyes. "Go on, then." *If I make out as if I'm letting her, rather than her doing me a favour, at least I keep my independence.*

The gentle circles soothed, even if they did nothing for her complaining muscles.

"You could go swimming? Don't they do antenatal swimming classes?"

A groan escaped her. "I do not need a pod of whales teaching me how to move." She poured them both a cup of tea. "I've been swimming since I was a toddler. I can just do laps by myself."

"Have you got a maternity costume?"

Another groan. "Oh, for goodness sake. Another thing I've got to buy and then get rid of in three months' time."

Claire made a noise like an excited mouse, coloured, and went back to her quasi-massage. "Three months. Not—"

"Long now. Yes. I'm well aware."

The loss of pressure at her back and the way Claire's face fell made Rosie's gut hurt.

"That's nice though." She indicated Claire's hand.

Renewed joy filled Claire's features.

"I tend to just wear a tankini anyway. I expect the top will stretch and the shorts will go sub-bump." She pulled at the elastic waistband of her trousers.

"Well, if you need any help choosing one, I'm an excellent personal shopper."

Her friend's unending offers of support were endearing, once you got over the irritation. "I'll let you know."

Drinks made, they took them over to the chairs again. Claire handed Rosie an extra cushion.

Smacking it into some kind of supportive shape, Rosie stuffed it behind her. *Much better. At least I can sit up now without slouching.*

The door opened and Vincent entered, already snorting with laughter. "You'd think they'd have stopped putting things up their noses by age five."

"How was it at A&E?" Rosie sipped her coffee.

"Not as busy as it could have been for a Monday." He flopped into one of the chairs that circled the coffee table and put a hand to his head. "They got it out with one of those sucky tubes. Bella thought it was the best thing ever." He rolled his eyes. "The nurse was in a mood, so she got a telling-off. I didn't have to be the bad guy."

"Oh, poor you." Claire used the voice she reserved for kids that had fallen over.

"So how have your mornings been?"

"Less hospital-based than yours." Rosie lifted her mug in a salute.

"At least the snot monsters have left the building." Claire shuddered. "Why do the reception classes always come back with it after Christmas?"

"We need a lesson on blowing noses and washing hands." Rosie made a big demonstration, slotting her fingers together and rubbing them in and out over an imaginary sink. "Soap and water. Put your tissue in the bin."

"I'll bring it up at the next staff meeting."

As they all tucked into their lunches, Claire and Vincent shared glances.

Rosie rolled her eyes. "What?"

A moment of tension in the room, then Vincent sighed. "We were wondering how things were going with Amber?"

An expletive threatened to escape her, but Rosie held it in. "Things aren't."

"What do you mean?" Claire sounded almost affronted.

There'd been a reason why Rosie had only told her sister about the situation with Amber. After prying for details, her critical gaze burrowing into Rosie, Charlie had given up and thrown an arm around her in sisterly solidarity. Rosie hadn't wanted a load of fuss from Vincent and Claire either. It was enjoyable talking to them about the baby, as annoying as they were sometimes, but relationships were a different matter.

"We… I broke it off."

Claire blinked, and lines appeared between her brows.

Vincent cocked his head and stared at her.

"What?" Rosie stuffed salad into her mouth.

"But you—you're in love with her."

"No, I'm not." Rosie shot Vincent a look of warning. "We were just friends."

He sat back, unconvinced.

"What happened, darling?" Claire asked.

Rosie placed her fork into her plastic tub. She wasn't that hungry suddenly. "I found something out that made it impossible for me to see her again."

"What?"

A look around her told Rosie there was no one else in the staff room. "She's an alcoholic."

Dead silence, except for the kids' laughter. A flock of starlings flicked by the window with a rustle. A car honked some way off.

"And that means you can't be with her?" Claire's voice was tentative.

"I can't be with someone like that, someone who's in danger of, you know, relapsing and needing my support. I'm going to be a mum in three months' time; I don't have the capacity for that."

"And you had no inkling she had these issues before?" Vincent peered at her.

"Of course not. I wouldn't have got so close to her if I'd have known."

"She hid it well."

"She didn't need to. Neither of us really needed to drink when we went out. I obviously wasn't drinking, and she just seemed to go along with it." Rosie shifted in her seat and rearranged the cushion until she was more comfortable. "We made a joke about it. Like drinking juice was our thing."

"That's nice," Claire said.

"So, what, she just drinks when she's at home or something?" Vincent folded his arms.

"No." Rosie swirled her coffee so it redissolved into the milk. "She told me she's been sober for over a year." She shrugged. "I suppose that's an achievement."

"It is." Claire's lips twitched as if she wanted to smile.

Rosie narrowed her eyes at Claire. "She seems pretty together actually, but it doesn't change the fact I really can't deal with someone like that. Not after what happened with Michaela."

"But you were young. It was a terrible accident..."

"Which would never have happened if she hadn't been drunk. Michaela got stuck in that sinking mud and died all because of the alcohol she'd consumed. And I couldn't help, because of the alcohol *I* had consumed."

Claire closed her mouth.

"It's a dangerous chemical, and I can't be around someone who has issues with it."

Vincent nodded, smoothing Rosie's arm. "Fair enough."

Rosie went back to her salad. The dressing was sweeter, more delicious now. K.B. wiggled, and Rosie had to giggle. *Yeah okay, little one. Mum's okay.*

Vincent demolished his sandwiches in about five minutes. Claire's soup took a little longer. She stirred it with an expression akin to someone who was trying to make a decision.

Other staff popped in and left. Vincent grabbed his bag, heading for the gym for PE with his class after lunch. Something about putting cones out into an amusing pattern. Rosie smirked as she imagined him making a phallic shape, the kids not noticing.

Claire inhaled. "Rosie, darling, don't you think you're being a bit judgemental?"

Rosie stared at her. "Why would you say that?"

"Look, I know what happened with Michaela was horrible, and it would never have happened if alcohol hadn't been involved, but really? Is that Amber's fault?"

"I can't have anyone in my life that drinks like that. I can't have someone that isn't a mature adult, not around me and certainly nowhere near my child. I've got to be one hundred percent focused on her, not dealing with someone who has issues."

"But you said you didn't even know Amber had issues with alcohol until she told you. It can't be that much of a problem for her if you were with her for four months and you didn't even know."

"I wasn't *with* her. We were just friends." Rosie smacked the wooden armrests of the chair and struggled to her feet. She grabbed her lunch box before taking it to the sink to rinse. "I want my kid to have the best life I can give her. And that means no people in it who aren't absolutely there for me. I'm certainly not going to date anyone with alcohol problems, okay?" She jammed the box into her bag, threw it over one shoulder, and pointed at Claire. "I didn't even want a relationship before the kid was older. Amber was just a fluke, someone that walked randomly into my life. She wouldn't have even done that if she hadn't been coming out from a bloody AA meeting when she met me."

"But I just think—"

Rosie was out the door before she could catch the rest. *Who is she to dictate what I do with my life? I've got to protect my child and myself. I can't be with someone who has issues. What if they leave me like Michaela did?*

Chapter 23

After a long day at work, Amber's AA meeting was uneventful. She almost walked into Hayley on the way out, her face blossoming into a grin as she caught her gaze. "Hi. Lovely to see you."

"Oh, um, okay." Hayley shifted about, her shoulders hunched.

"Sorry."

Rosie hurried past them, her attention on her feet.

Ignoring her, Amber walked into the choir room with Hayley. "I've had a long day. How has yours been?"

"Not too bad. Saw my community nurse; she gave me some more mindfulness activities to do." She shrugged. "Not sure they'll help, but I'll give them a go."

"It's all you can do; just try. Then if they don't work, at least you gave them your best shot."

"I'll try and stay hopeful." Hayley wrinkled her nose. "Weird. I don't think I'd have said that a few months ago."

Amber looked around her. "You know what I think?"

Hayley shook her head.

"I think the choir's a real confidence boost. It's certainly made me more confident."

"Oh." Hayley stared at her hands. "Yeah, I think you're right."

"Who'd have thought? That just going to a thing and singing some songs would help so much?"

"Who'd have thought?"

They grinned at each other, then chatted until Enid began the rehearsal.

Amber didn't see Rosie at all. She was far too impressed with Hayley's ability to remember what they had learned last week and with her own sureness of the lyrics. *I'd never have remembered all of this before, especially not with the added pressure of singing out loud in public. I never was good at multitasking.*

By the end, they both stood tall and sang with vigour. Amber marvelled at Hayley even though she'd only known her a couple of weeks. Maybe they buoyed one another up; egged each other on. Whatever it was, the mere presence of Hayley made Amber belt out the songs as if she'd been singing all her life.

Hayley left for the bus stop after tentatively giving Amber a hug. Amber's chest nearly burst. She got the feeling Hayley didn't hug people very often.

As Amber pulled on her coat, she noticed a single chair with a leather jacket on the back: Rosie's jacket. She looked around, but all she saw was Enid, who caught her eye and shrugged. Amber sighed. *Must be baby brain or something.* Enid's arms were already full of boxes and folders, so Amber picked up Rosie's jacket and decided to keep hold of it until next week. *Give her a chance to at least exchange a few words with me.*

She nipped to the toilet before she left, figuring her bladder wouldn't quite manage the long walk home. As she sat on the toilet, musing over her new friendship, a muffled sob sounded from the cubicle next to her. She frowned and knocked on the partition. "Um, you okay in there?"

Silence. Then another sob. Sounded familiar.

"R-Rosie?" Why had her courage disappeared?

A massive sniff.

Amber knocked again. "You okay?"

Maybe she's still upset about what happened between us. But she made that decision. She can hardly complain. "You want to talk about it?"

Actual crying now. Fitful, almost guttural. A big dollop of fear tainted the sound.

After finishing, Amber stood before the larger, disabled cubicle next to her own. "Come on, open the door. Are you finished?" She waited a few seconds, then knocked. "What's up, Rosie? I know it's you." She placed a hand on the door, hoping Rosie would feel the concern coming through the wood. "Open the door."

Nothing.

Nausea churned in her gut. Was Rosie unwell?

She went back into her own cubicle, having left her bag and Rosie's jacket on the side by the sinks, and climbed up onto the toilet. "I'm going to look over, okay? I'm worried about you."

She hung onto the top of the cubicle and pulled herself to stand. Peering over, she caught sight of Rosie sat on the toilet, her jeans and pants around her knees, a bright smear of red on the toilet paper in her hand.

"Hey." She gentled her tone, hoping not to scare her.

Rosie continued to stare straight ahead.

"Are you bleeding?"

A nod.

"Okay." Renewed courage spurred Amber into action. Rosie clearly wasn't able to open the door by herself. "I'm going to crawl underneath and help you, okay?"

Amber jumped down. She knelt, then slid on her tummy along the less-than-clean floor until she was clear.

Rosie's skin was clammy and her breathing was laboured. She flinched when Amber touched her shoulder, then seemed to come back to herself. Hazel eyes blinked at her, eyebrows coming together and a tear rolling down her cheek.

"You're bleeding."

A nod, a shaking inhalation from Rosie.

"Is that supposed to happen?"

Rosie's gaze shot to the bloody toilet paper.

"Let's put that in the loo, okay?" Amber supported Rosie to stand and drop the offending article into the bowl. "Do you need an ambulance?"

"No. Not an emergency." It sounded as if words were a trial.

"But you still need to go to hospital?"

A swallow. A nod.

She checked between Rosie's knees. "Do you need a pad? Do you have one?"

After pulling her bottom lip into her mouth, Rosie shook her head.

"I always have spares. Just…one minute."

Amber unlocked the door and rushed to her handbag. She yanked out a pad and handed it to Rosie. She backed out of the cubicle and pulled the door closed in front of her.

"Okay, you put it on and then we'll go."

She had little clue how they would get there. Rosie presumably had her car, but she was in no fit state to drive. Amber was still saving up for a car of her own—her time out of work had meant funds were limited.

Either way, she wasn't leaving Rosie alone.

The familiar noises of a pad being opened, rustling as the packaging was removed and pad applied, the *thunk* of the hygiene bin. More rustling, this time, clothes. A sniff.

"Okay?"

The door opened. Rosie's cheeks were tear-streaked and she walked on quivering legs. Her mascara had run all over her cheeks.

Amber put an arm around her shoulders. "Let's wash our hands and then we'll go."

"I've lost it. I've lost her. I know I have." Rosie's face crumpled and she sagged against Amber. "It's just like with Ali."

Not much I can say. I don't know what's going on in there. Amber led Rosie to the sink and helped her wash her hands. Once she'd collected their bags and coats, she resumed her position next to Rosie and they moved out of the hall. *Good job she wasn't much longer or Enid would have locked up.* Without deciding on a course of action, Amber led them both towards the car park where she assumed Rosie's car was.

Rosie's keys bleeped when Amber pressed the button to unlock. Catching Rosie's gaze, she lifted her eyebrows, hoping that would communicate her question. *Will you let me drive?*

Rosie's gaze flicked to the passenger seat before she nodded and allowed Amber to open the door for her.

The car was different to Jilly's, but that was insignificant. *Rosie could still be bleeding and her unborn baby could be dying.* Amber swallowed several times, trying to quell the panic, and focused on driving the unfamiliar car. She parked in a space close to the front entrance, got Rosie out, and led her inside.

The lady on the front desk of A&E wore round glasses and a gleaming smile.

"Hi," Amber said. "Um, Rosie's pregnant and she's bleeding."

"Fresh, red." Rosie shook beneath Amber's arm.

The receptionist went over Rosie's date of birth, symptoms, and checked her in. They were directed into a waiting area half full of people.

It wasn't long before they were seen by the triage nurse, and a few minutes later they were led into Minors by a junior doctor. "I'm Dr Metcalf. Come through here." They went into a semi-private area with a bed and two chairs.

Rosie climbed onto the bed. Her eyes were like saucers as she watched Amber sit in one of the chairs.

Without hesitation, Amber took Rosie's sweaty fingers in her own.

After a few shaky breaths, Rosie was able to speak. "I'm twenty-seven weeks. I noticed fresh and red blood when I went to the loo at about eight-thirty."

"Tonight?" Dr Metcalf wrote everything down.

Rosie nodded. "I'm losing my baby, aren't I? I had a stillbirth a couple of years ago."

"I'm sorry to hear that. It might not be that though." He smiled at her. "There are a number of reasons you could bleed in your third trimester." He went to the trolley at one side, took out a shoebox-sized package and a pair of gloves. "One of the ways I can find out is to do an internal exam. Is that okay?"

Rosie nodded, but her cheeks coloured as she looked at her knees.

Dr Metcalf handed Rosie a hospital gown. "Just take your bottom half off and pop this around your waist."

Images of Rosie having to remove a stained sanitary pad in front of the male doctor flashed before Amber. "She'll need some privacy for a minute." Amber squeezed Rosie's hand. "Do you want me to go whilst you get yourself sorted?"

Rosie shook her head.

"Okay. I'll stay."

Dr Metcalf disappeared through the curtain and pulled it across to maintain their privacy.

Amber rubbed the back of Rosie's hand. "That's good, isn't it? Everything might be okay."

Another shudder went through Rosie. She got down from the bed and put her hands to her waistband. "Turn around?"

With a smile, Amber spun on the spot and closed her eyes.

"Okay. Ugh, gross." That plastic-rustling sound. The bin opened.

Amber hoped the pad would stay out of Rosie's mind, but she doubted it.

Rosie had taken off her trousers and blood-stained pants and now sat on the bed with the gown hiding her body from the hips down. She had her knees drawn up, thick black socks poking out from the bottom of the gown—a lost child.

After calling Dr Metcalf back in, Amber sat by Rosie's head, Rosie's hand in hers. The tension in her stomach ached. The knowledge that Rosie's dream might have broken was a bitter smell in the clinically white room.

When Dr Metcalf lowered the speculum under the tent the hospital gown created, Rosie whimpered.

"Sorry. I know it sucks." His sympathetic gaze peeked over the top.

Rosie turned her head against the bed and locked her watery eyes with Amber's.

Amber held her gaze until Dr Metcalf emerged, snapping his gloves off.

"It's good news. I'll do an ultrasound to check on baby in a minute, but it looks like you have an ectropion. It's a small graze on your cervix. It's totally nothing to worry about."

"How the hell did I graze my frigging cervix?"

Amber had to hold in a giggle. Rosie sounded mortified.

"It's not usually from anything traumatic. When you're pregnant, blood volume increases down there, and your cervix is a pretty vascular area. It bleeds easily."

"Oh."

"It's not uncommon. But you were absolutely right coming in tonight." He smiled at Amber. "Your wife takes good care of you."

"Um, no." Amber's cheeks flamed. "We're not…"

"Sorry, girlfriend. Partner? Anyway, all is well." He pointed out of the room. "You can put your bottoms on again. I'll go get the ultrasound and we'll see how baby is doing."

As he left, Amber's initial need to laugh returned. She put a hand to her mouth. "Sorry."

"It's okay." Crinkles materialised in the corners of Rosie's eyes. Eventually, as if emerging from a cocoon, she smiled. "At least he didn't assume we were sisters."

"Yeah, that would've just been weird." Amber studied their still-joined hands. She let go, and Rosie tucked her hand back in her lap.

"Sorry about earlier. I, um…" Rosie made a gesture in the air, illustrating all that had happened in the bathroom at the church hall. Her face coloured. "Oh God, you saw me with my pants around my ankles."

"Yeah, you were in a bit of a state."

Their gazes locked again.

Rosie looked away. "I'm usually pretty together."

"It's fine."

Rosie swung her legs from the bed and clutched the gown around her waist.

Turning to hide from the view of Rosie redressing, Amber wrapped her cardigan around herself and took a few breaths. *I suppose that's it, then. Once she's had the scan, my job here will be done. I'll make some excuse that I need to be home for Jilly or Nico or something, then I'll walk home.* Good job the hospital was only a few minutes' walk from Jilly's house.

Rosie cleared her throat. "I don't suppose you have another…"

Amber rifled in her handbag and passed Rosie another sanitary pad. "Got a good supply."

"Thank you. I'll replace them."

"Don't worry about it."

Time passed. Monitors beeped from outside, people rushed around. The voice of a drunk man bellowed in the distance.

Dr Metcalf poked his head in, his eyebrows furrowed. "Apologies. The scanner is being used right now. It'll be a few minutes; just hang tight."

"No worries." Rosie settled on the bed, her head against the part that was lifted. She closed her eyes.

Amber fiddled with the hem of her skirt. She made the harsh lights bounce off her shiny shoes by wiggling her feet.

"How're you doing with the new songs?"

Amber blinked and looked over. "Yeah, okay, thanks."

"Good."

A couple of people shouted, scuffling noises. A groan. The drunk guy wasn't winning the argument, whatever it was.

"I like 'Lullaby'." Amber wasn't sure what to say but wanted to keep talking. *Distracting her is important if we're going to be here a while. And the silence makes my ears hurt.*

"Yeah, I was surprised." Rosie turned to her. "Usually with local composers the quality of the music can be a bit dodgy."

"I'm guessing you've gone through the rest of the songs at home?"

A glimmer of a smile. "Yeah. Figured I'd better be a teacher's pet with it. I might not make the last few rehearsals."

"Oh, that's right." Amber sat more comfortably in her chair. "Your due date is super-close to the concert, isn't it?"

"Epic fail on my part. I get the feeling Enid thinks I did it deliberately."

A nod and more fidgeting with her skirt. *Should I bring up the reason for this tension? Will it go away if I do that or get bigger?*

She tried to imagine what Fiona would suggest. *I need to be hard on myself but tolerant of those around me. I think I've done that by accepting Rosie has her own reasons for keeping away from me and by acknowledging it's not my fault.*

A little part of her belly still tugged, however. The part that whispered to her the words: "You should have been honest."

"I'm sorry." That was a good start. She didn't feel as if she'd said it properly before now.

Rosie frowned at her. "For…?"

"You know, not telling you I'm an alcoholic." Amber forced herself to maintain eye contact. It wasn't something she was ashamed of—if anything she was proud of the fact she'd been sober for so long. "I should have told you when we first met."

Thin-lipped, Rosie just stared at her. Then she nodded and looked at her socks. She made a big deal about smoothing one jean cuff, then the other over her ankles. The gown she'd removed went around her waist like a blanket, tucked under her knees and around her feet. "Amb, I don't know what to do."

"About what?"

A guttural sigh that hinted at tears. "I wanted it to be so perfect, and it *was* until…" She glanced over at Amber. "I had it planned out so brilliantly.

Kid would be two, maybe three before I started dating again. I've never been the kind of person who needs a girlfriend. I'm pretty sorted by myself."

"And then I came along and spoiled everything?" It was meant as a joke, but Amber's belly continued to tug. *I'm self-deprecating. That's not helpful.*

"Sort of. But also sort of…not?" Rosie huffed. "I'm not making much sense."

Giving her some room to think, Amber folded her hands in her lap and waited.

The intoxicated guy shouted, and the noise of metal hitting the floor shook the walls. They both winced.

"When I was sixteen, I had this friend. I guess I loved her like I would love a girlfriend if it was now. Anyway." Rosie shook her head. "We used to go out drinking. Places we could get into without getting ID'd, you know?"

Amber nodded.

"We got properly rat-arsed this one night. Cans of cheap cider in Ellenborough Park. Michaela was all over the place, basically falling over me and singing these songs we were performing the next week in sixth-form choir." Rosie winced.

It was an odd reaction. Amber was used to people laughing with affection at memories of their youth, especially humorous ones. Being drunk when you were sixteen had been a right laugh, as far as Amber could recall.

"Anyway, Michaela had this great idea of walking to Brean Down from Weston Beach."

Amber snorted, remembering the news articles and local blurbs of people trying to do the very same thing. Brean Down was a large headland that stuck out at one end of Weston Beach. The Bristol Estuary was full of mud and, with the second highest tide in the world, the mud was like quicksand.

"I tried to reason with her, but we were both so wasted. She wasn't in a listening mood, you know? Took her shoes and socks off and started out towards the sea. I followed her, at a distance. I wanted to be part of the great adventure, but there was also this thing in my brain saying, *Woah, hang on a minute, that's stupid.* And when the sand got a bit too sinky for my liking, I stopped and tried to call her back.

"She carried on, laughing and making these little hops along the sand. Her feet started to sink. I got scared then, started shouting at her, 'Come back, you dozy bitch!'"

Amber's mouth went dry. The images were vivid; Rosie had a way with descriptions. But she could tell where the story headed, and she wasn't sure she wanted to hear its conclusion.

"She just kept going and going." Rosie hit her thigh with her fist. She smoothed the roundness of her belly as if to apologise to the baby within. "The stupid bitch just kept going—singing the fucking song we were singing at fucking choir." A wracking sob fell from her lips. "I remember the tune and the words, and if I ever hear it on the radio or something, it makes my heart feel like it's being ripped out."

Amber pulled her chair to the bed, cringing at the scrape. She wanted to hold Rosie's hand again but didn't know how to ask if it was okay.

"And she stopped. Absolute silence for a full minute. Then she panicked." The look in Rosie's eyes was so pained.

"W-what happened then?"

"She was up to her knees in quicksand. She fell. She couldn't get herself back up. I was frozen to the spot. Then I got my wits back together and pulled my shitty brick mobile phone out of my pocket and I phoned 999." She pulled the gown flat over her knees, staring at her hands as if they didn't belong to her. "An ambulance came, but they couldn't get to her, so they called the coastguard. They sent the hovercraft out. By the time they got to her, she'd stopped breathing."

"Oh no." Amber's voice was barely a whisper. Dread crashed down all around her. Tears filled her eyes.

"They worked for ages. Tried loads of stuff on the boat as well as when they got back to shore. She'd got too cold and had passed out with her face in the fucking sand."

Amber grasped Rosie's hand, not caring if Rosie pulled away.

Rosie slid her fingers between Amber's and hung on. "I should have phoned earlier, I should have tried harder to stop her. I was so drunk… She was a fucking idiot, but I should have looked after her. That's what friends do." She wiped her eyes. "Being pissed was the main cause. They even put that on the fucking post-mortem report."

It all makes sense now. I knew there'd be a reason for her pushing me away. It didn't make it hurt any less, but at least Amber had an explanation. She passed her thumb over the back of Rosie's hand a few times, marvelling at her soft skin.

"Okay, fine, I admit it." Rosie rolled her eyes and pushed a hand through her hair. "I'm terrified. What happened to Michaela…I can't have that happen again. And not when I'm going to be a mum. She…" Rosie touched her belly, her whole being softening as if the mere thought of her baby was a comfort. "I want to protect my baby with everything I have."

As if on cue, Dr Metcalf backed into the cubicle, pulling a machine with him. "Hello." Breezy as ever.

Amber grimaced and pulled her hand out of Rosie's. The temperature change jarred every part of her.

In contrast, Rosie smiled at him and wiggled her backside on the bed. "Let's get this over with."

Dr Metcalf squirted some gloopy stuff onto Rosie's belly. "What's going on in there, hmm?" His words were aimed at Rosie's baby.

Rosie sat expectantly whilst he pushed the wand over her skin, then smiled when he stilled.

"Want to see?" Dr Metcalf was still under the impression Amber was somehow involved.

Amber didn't have the energy to explain. When he pushed the screen round, she took in the large head of something similar to the unborn babies she'd seen on TV. Her heart fluttered—this was Rosie's baby, Rosie's daughter, after all—but she didn't have the strength to react. She supposed a smile might be appropriate. "Aw." Did it sound genuine?

A moment of hesitation, then a renewed smile from the doctor. "All good. Nice strong heart sounds."

With a swift wipe of her belly, Rosie jumped down from the bed. "Great. I'll be off, then."

Amber stood too and pulled her coat on, her shoulders up. Various pleasantries and "if this happens, this is what you do" were exchanged between Rosie and Dr Metcalf before Amber followed Rosie out of the hospital. Blinking at the bright floodlights, Amber handed the car keys to Rosie. "I'll see you around."

Rosie jangled her keys for a breath, then caught Amber's gaze. "Listen, thanks for tonight." Her hair flew as she turned towards her car, but she turned back. Lips parted, but nothing came out.

I can't handle any more excuses or apologies. I just want to get home and into my warm bed. "Bye."

Rosie blinked. "Bye."

Amber managed to turn and walk away before any of her tears fell.

Chapter 24

Once Rosie was up and dressed on Saturday morning, she tapped her sister's name and held the phone to her ear.

"What d'you mean you went to A&E last night? What the hell, Rosie?"

As expected. Rosie lowered her head even though Charlie couldn't see her. "I'm sorry, all right? I wasn't in any fit state to phone you before I went and once I was home, I just wanted to sleep. Anyway, all is fine, so no need to get in a flap."

"Get in a flap?" Charlie growled. Then, a pause, as if she tried to calm down. "Fine. I'm glad you're okay."

"Thank you."

"We're still coming over this morning though?"

"If you like." Rosie glanced over at the infant cot she'd bought last week, ex-display but still with a bit of wrapping on it. "Chelsea still want to help with the cot?"

"She does. And don't you dare move it upstairs until Tom and I get there, you hear? You're not allowed to move anything, especially as you were in hospital yesterday."

"It was nothing."

"And you'll be telling all when we arrive. Make sure the kettle's boiled. We'll be there in half an hour."

Rosie hung up before snorting, half in frustration, half in affection at the way Charlie demanded she be treated in her present condition. She wasn't weak, and she'd pleaded with Charlie not to behave as if she was before she'd even conceived. *Oh well, I can't exactly blame her. I was the same when Charlie was pregnant.*

She thought back to those months, nine years ago, when Charlie's belly was spherical and her ankles were swollen. She'd been a bubbly, glowing pregnant woman in a sea of cake and love. Tom had doted on her, waited on her hand and foot, and had refused to let her lift a finger. Charlie had taken it all so calmly, as if the threat to her independence and assertive personality did not exist.

Rosie had never been one to accept help that was offered, not unless she absolutely needed it. She'd done everything on her own—teacher training in a tiny one-bedroom flat in the city, her first job in her first school with a cheap old banger and smart clothes bought with vouchers she'd got for her birthday. Then deciding on children, doing it by herself, finding a donor, doing the deed. Ali.

Her family had been a barrow full of emotional support around that time.

Walking around her house with a damp cloth to remove dust from any surface she could find, she hummed "Lullaby" from *Lullaby of the Ocean*, hoping it would calm her nerves. She didn't want Charlie to proclaim she needed someone by her side to look after her. She'd never needed that.

When the doorbell went, she dried her hands on a towel.

The minute she got the door open, little Chelsea marched inside, her hands on her hips. "And *what* are you doing on your feet?"

Rosie was too shocked to respond.

Charlie smirked. "Answering the door. You got a key, Chels?"

A blonde swish of hair and Chelsea stomped into the kitchen, her nose high. "I'll make the teas. You sit down, Auntie Rosie."

Blinking, Rosie stepped back to allow Charlie and Tom inside before closing the door against the bright February sunshine.

Tom followed Chelsea into the kitchen.

"He'll make sure she doesn't smash anything in her bid to make you put your feet up." Charlie shook her head. "Honestly, I did try to play it down, but I had to tell her. She'd only find out some other way—you know what she's like."

"I do. Smartest kid I know."

"Just like her mother."

Rosie made a noise as if she wasn't sure.

With a swift smack to Rosie's shoulder, Charlie bustled them both into the living room. "Come on: spill. What the hell happened?"

Rosie told her every detail, flushing hot when she came to the bit where Amber had found her in the toilet. "I don't know where my head was. I didn't seem able to think, Char. It was weird."

"That's what happens when you're pregnant and scared."

The memory of Michaela's death hit her before being covered by the image of Ali lying still in her arms. Rosie cleared her throat. "Anyway, she was very kind. Got me to hospital and then didn't leave until I knew it was all okay."

"Great girl to have around." The knowing glint in Charlie's eyes made Rosie want to hit her.

"Don't."

Tom's overly loud voice carried through. "That's it, hon, carry them through carefully."

Their cue to shut up about in-depth topics. *Phew.* As much as Charlie wanted to talk about Amber's heroism in her hour of need, Rosie really didn't. Emotions churned within her. She was grateful for Amber's help but uncomfortable and embarrassed to have been seen like that. It wasn't even the blood, or the lack of dignity, it was being so vulnerable and out of control that made Rosie cringe. On the other hand, she couldn't forget Amber had lied to her and about such a huge thing, so it was difficult to feel affection for her actions, as caring as they were. *So confusing.* All she wanted to do was relax with a warm drink and company that loved her.

Chelsea's eyes lit up like the Grand Pier when she saw Rosie on the sofa. "That's better, isn't it?" Chelsea copied the way her mother treated her when she was sick, or maybe a teacher. It was terribly grown-up and comical.

"It is. Thank you, monkey."

Chelsea beamed. "Here's your drink. Decaf, for the baby."

Rosie found the cheer to grin; even a little extra to click and point at her niece. "Decaf for Auntie Rosie, milk for the baby."

"Bones and hair and teeth and stuff, right?"

"That's right."

Chelsea stroked Rosie's belly once or twice, then moved away. Maybe she could accept just a bit of pampering. Somehow, it didn't feel as bad coming from Chelsea.

Luckily, the subject switched to the impending guinea pig acquirement. "I'm going to call her Ginger and she's going to have her hair done every day and I'm going to teach her tricks."

"Don't you have to get two girl guinea pigs?"

"Auntie Rosie," Charlie said through clenched teeth, "would it be okay if you *didn't* double the number of pets my daughter thinks she's getting?"

Chelsea's eyes were huge. "Are you having a laugh? Are you *actually* having a laugh?"

Someone's been watching too many sitcoms. "Well, they live in groups. The boys sometimes don't get on, but the girls get lonely if they're not with other girls."

A stifled laugh from Tom.

Charlie threw up her hands. "You'll be in charge of them *both*, you hear me?"

Squealing, Chelsea hugged her mum, then her dad. She picked up her cat soft toy and hugged that too.

Again, conversation moved on. Rosie took time to sit and laugh, watching Chelsea line up her throw cushions and make them domino-fall one by one, punctuated by several rounds of applause. She played with her cuddly toys for a while—some story about an adventure up a mountain. Apparently, the cat toy was the leader.

Once she was bored, Chelsea crawled up to her mother's knees. "Can I go watch iPlayer?"

Charlie got the family tablet out of her handbag. "Stick with CBBC, yeah?"

With a little squeal, Chelsea held the tablet to her chest as if it were a long-lost friend. "Always." She turned to Rosie. "Can I go in the baby's room?"

"Go for it."

She traipsed upstairs, probably to sit on the dinosaur-patterned beanbag, leaving the adults to their tea.

A glance at Charlie and Rosie's insides dropped. *Here we go, brace yourself.*

"So what was wrong with the baby?" Tom's voice was concerned.

Rosie relaxed. "I'll tell you, but you have to promise not to take the mickey." Rosie pointed at him, then, with more vigour, Charlie.

Charlie held both hands out in a *would I?* gesture.

Rosie rolled her eyes. "I had an ectropian. It's a small graze to the cervix." Somehow, it was easier to distance herself from the part of her anatomy that had caused so much worry by using *the* rather than *my*. "Apparently it's quite common."

"I'm not even going to ask what you were doing."

"Singing at the time." Rosie gave her a pointed look. "It doesn't have to come from anything strenuous."

Tom's gaze slid away, the corners of his lips tugging upwards.

Rosie was thankful she and Tom had known one another long enough that such things barely mattered. "Anyway, it happened, I got it sorted, and now I'm fine."

"Did the doctor say you needed to rest or anything?"

"No more than usual. I should keep an eye on it, but otherwise I can carry on as normal."

"Hmm." Charlie didn't look convinced.

"I *am* taking it easy, I promise." Rosie drew patterns in the brushed beige fabric of her sofa. "I'm doing everything I should be."

"Good job Amber was there."

Rosie made to stand up but caught herself. "Look, yeah, okay, I admit she was good to have around last night. But stop bringing her up, please. It's really getting on my wick."

Tom stared into his coffee cup.

Charlie eyed Rosie.

After taking a steadying breath, Rosie settled back. She ran a hand through her hair and took a sip of her coffee. "Claire was going on about her the other week. Why can't I just be more understanding? Why can't I just give her a chance?" She huffed. "You know why."

Tom looked from Charlie to Rosie. He stood with his drink. "I'm just going to check Chelsea's watching something appropriate for her age." He shot Rosie an apologetic grimace, then left.

After taking as long as she could to watch his retreating back, Rosie winced. Her heart sunk an inch or two. At least with Tom around, Charlie would have been less of a pain about it.

When she turned back to Charlie, Rosie discovered a tiny glimmer of triumph in her eye.

"Come on, babes. Talk to me."

Rosie blinked. "Thought you were going to have a go."

With a sigh, Charlie pushed her mouth to one side. "If I thought it'd have any impact on your decisions, I totally would. But I know you. You get all..." She balled both fists and held them to her chest. "You get all defensive when someone comes at you."

A couple of bubbles circled the rim of Rosie's mug, then bunched together, like peas in a pod. "I had a plan. Then Amber arrived. I decided the plan could change, just a bit, that maybe Amber could be part of my life. Then she told me the thing she told me and..." She swiped her arm out. "I wish I'd never met her. I'm so confused about it all."

"I thought it was pretty done and dusted? You can't be with her because of the alcoholism?"

Rosie shrugged. "So did I. Then last night she was so good, so level-headed. I always figured—like before when we were kind of dating—that I was the strong one. She's quiet, very understated. I liked that about her. She has way more of a kind heart than I've ever had." She sniffed, surprised at the lump in her throat. "Like you said, she was a good person to have around."

"So now you're unsure how you feel."

"Something like that." Rosie hoped her coffee would comfort her, but it tasted bitter.

Charlie rubbed her shoulder, then slipped her hand down her back. "I get it. Before last night you could imagine Amber was this...unsorted, silly, broken woman that couldn't take care of herself, let alone anyone else?" She arched an eyebrow.

Rosie nodded.

"And then last night she was brave and strong and good in an emergency."

Rosie allowed the first tear to fall. It was good to get it out, and Charlie was much more able to put the situation into actual words than Rosie.

Charlie pulled Rosie against her and wrapped an arm around her shoulders. She made the shushing noises she made when Chelsea was sad. Fingers combed through Rosie's hair a few times.

After managing not to spill her coffee, Rosie sat up and wiped her face. She tried to send Charlie an apology through her gaze.

Charlie shook her head.

"What should I do?" Rosie set her cup down and took Charlie's hand. She marvelled the pale pink nails and soft skin, then remembered Amber's nails—usually red or black.

"I suppose you need to ask yourself what you really want. And whether your opinions about Amber are reasonable."

She's being so unblonde today. Rosie's tears dried. "What d'you mean?"

"Are you discriminating against Amber because she's an alcoholic?"

Horror gripped Rosie. *Discrimination?* It was a sour word in her mouth, so much so that she couldn't let it past her lips. "I'm not like that."

"Usually I'd have to agree. But, like you said, you were seriously considering a relationship with Amber before you knew. And then you completely shut it down. You don't know what she's like or how long she's been dealing with it or how she copes. What does Dad always say? 'It's the things we battle that make us who we are, not the things we run away from.'"

"Are you saying I'm running away?"

"No. I'm saying you're not appreciating Amber for the things she's managed to overcome. And you're tainting her with the same brush you've tainted everyone since Michaela died."

The mention of her name made Rosie's chest hurt. K.B. flipped about, so she rested a hand over her belly, hoping she would feel the tenderness of her touch. "I'm scared." And it was as if a weight had been lifted from her. She could breathe again.

"It seems a shame to miss out on what could possibly be an amazing relationship just because you're scared of something that happened twenty years ago."

Sniffing, Rosie reached for her coffee again. She wanted something between her and Charlie to give her space to think.

A voice from upstairs: "Doctor Who? Chelsea, isn't that a bit…"

Charlie snorted and looked towards the ceiling. "Oh my gosh, she loves that programme. Doesn't get scared by it at all, but I know Tom used to watch it as a kid and he once hid behind the sofa."

They both cocked their heads to listen. Just the theme tune from Doctor Who—an apparent submission by Tom.

Charlie rubbed Rosie between the shoulder blades. "Listen, I'm not saying get back with her. Knowing you, I'm sure you didn't handle it very well when you broke up…"

"Not that we were ever together."

Charlie shrugged. "From what you've said, she'll be wary of you now. Kudos to her for staying with you in A&E—I don't think I would have."

"Yeah, that surprised me too." With it all out in the open, Rosie snuggled back into the sofa, her head dropping to Charlie's shoulder. "She's an asshole."

"Excuse me?" Amusement and a touch of confusion.

"For changing my mind about her."

A noise escaped Charlie, but she smiled. The only sounds were those of aliens and Jody Whittaker that punctuated the silence.

Was that Rosie's problem? Had she shoved Amber into a box labelled with some skewed version of what she thought an alcoholic was? Had Amber ever shown she was anything other than a responsible adult?

She supposed being pregnant had been a convenient way for Amber to hide her issue—if Rosie had invited her out for a drink and she hadn't been pregnant, perhaps it would have come out sooner. *What kind of life has Amber led to have been directed to drink?* Amber wasn't close to her parents, or any of her family, but she seemed to have a grounded family unit with Jilly and her other friends. *Are they in AA too? Is it one big happy family?*

And what must *they* think of Rosie? They didn't know her history—she hadn't told Amber about Michaela until last night. They probably just thought she was some posh bird that looked down her nose at the things she didn't understand. Rosie's stomach churned. *That's not a pretty image.*

Amber's beautiful face popped into her mind's eye. Dark eyes, perfectly applied eyeliner, lips the colour of cherries. She wondered what kind of relationship they would have had if she hadn't messed everything up. She wondered whether they still had a chance and how she could help Amber see she was truly sorry.

A grand gesture in front of a load of people will only embarrass her. Amber was shy and gentle and didn't like too much fuss to be made of her.

Rosie glanced over to her piano, the black lid down, the pedals shining chrome. With her bottom lip between her teeth, a plan began to form in her brain.

Chapter 25

The daffodils by the stables peeked buttery petals from leafy cocoons. Amber had booked a day of holiday to enjoy the first signs of spring, as had both Matthew and Harry. With her camera around her neck, Amber jumped into the car to join them in brushing and riding out with Florence.

Whilst Harry rode the horse around the paddock, Amber clicked and clicked, hoping to get some good shots for an album for Harry's birthday. He had minimal photos of himself; the flat he shared with Matthew mostly consisted of landscapes and artistic charcoals. *And he's such a photogenic bloke.*

His curls glimmered golden tones and his breath, as well as Florence's, hazed the air. The dew still rose from the grass; it was early, only just past nine. The sun hung low, dusting the fields with an ethereal glow.

Managing to get more shots than her memory card could take, Amber deleted a few rubbish ones before Harry rounded the field at a canter and brought Florence to a halt close by.

Matthew leaned an elbow on the fence, blue eyes shining with affection. "God, you're sexy."

Harry dipped his head to hide his blush, twirled Florence in a circle, and leaned forward. His boots thudded as he hit the grass.

Florence threw her head before quietening.

After swinging his leg over the fence, Matthew joined them both. He cupped Harry's cheek and planted a kiss under his jaw.

Amber snapped that image before either of them could complain. She looked forward to blowing that one up later on her laptop screen. Perhaps it would make a good canvas print.

They led Florence back to her stable, Matthew collecting the tack-cleaning equipment and brushes on the way.

"You look so confident when you ride her." Amber weaved around a pile of trodden-in manure.

"I feel it." Harry patted Florence's neck as they entered the stable.

Florence snorted and hung back a little, clearly not wanting to go back in just yet.

An apple appeared from Matthew's pocket.

She strode in as if that was the plan all along. Harry took out her bit and unbuckled her bridle, freeing her. Her thick lips took the apple and munching noises filled the stall.

Once Florence was relieved of her saddle, Matthew took that and the bridle outside to clean.

Harry handed Amber a comb, and she slid her hand along the horse's shoulder before making it her job to untangle her mane.

A large nose pushed itself into the crook of Amber's elbow, and she soothed the horse for a minute.

"I'm so glad I've got that gallop sorted. I nearly ended up in the mud so many times. It's the year of being confident, isn't it?" Harry swept the brush down Florence's front leg. "Me on my horse, you in the choir." There was a smudge of dust on his cheek.

"I guess so." Florence's nose was so silky, like stroking the inside of a catkin seed. Amber rested her cheek against the horse's forehead and breathed in her musty smell.

Florence nudged her, and Amber moved away, going back to combing.

"Have you heard from Rosie?"

Amber shrugged.

"It's been a week." Harry sounded annoyed and saddened.

"I'll see her tonight. Or maybe I won't." Amber pulled the loose hairs from the comb. "After last week, I figured maybe I'd get a text or something. I don't want to text *her*—she made her feelings abundantly clear." She sighed. "But we shared so much intimacy. I saw her in ways I'm sure no one else has seen her, apart from her doctors and stuff. It feels so strange to not even be friends again now."

Harry sent her a sympathetic look. "That sucks, darling."

Amber looked out the door to Matthew, who gave her a little wave. She waved back, then continued to comb.

"You're going to look so gorgeous when we're done," she told the horse.

Florence butted Amber's shoulder with her head and whinnied.

Harry and Amber both chuckled.

"That's right. See, even Florence knows when you're evading the subject."

Rolling her eyes, Amber gave the horse's mane a last brush, then dropped the comb into the bucket.

"I wish I hadn't told her."

"No, you don't."

"No." Amber swallowed. "I don't."

"If she can't love you for who you are, then she doesn't deserve to love you at all."

"You're right."

"I know I am."

"Anything suck in your life right now?" A mean part of her hoped he would say yes.

He stooped to clean a little mud from his boot with Florence's brush. "Ah, the house issue?"

"House-gate, yes."

A chuckle. "We talked. At length."

"Oh, thank goodness." She widened her eyes at him. "I was beginning to think I was going to have to lock you in a room together or something."

"I think we just needed a bit of time to think." At her raised eyebrow, he strode to Florence's back leg. "Yeah, okay. *I* needed time to think."

"And your conclusion?"

"That I'm an idiot and should just let Matthew use his inheritance to get us a house." A shrug before Harry blew out a breath. "I thought it might make him all smug and stuff, but, actually, he's just happy. Keeps lavishing compliments on me and doing sweet things like running me a bubble bath."

"A house *and* romance, hmm?" Amber ruffled Florence's ear. "I think I might be jealous." She patted Harry's shoulder before stepping into his arms.

Another pair of arms encircled them both: Matthew. Safety surrounded her like a duvet. She peeped out from underneath Matthew's arm to gaze out of the stable door. So much affection in every molecule of the air, every tweet of a bird. Even the daffodils, which sung for her to bask in their sunshine, reminded her of the wonders of life. Her camera pressed between her and Harry, and she had a sudden urge to photograph every pinnacle of spring she could.

Amber showered the minute she got home—smelling like horse always made Nico far too excited for his own good. If he ever met one of the giant beasts, he'd shit himself.

She sat on her bed in her towel and flicked through social media. Her phone pinged: a WhatsApp message. A jolt of surprise when she realised whom it was from. *Rosie?*

That was followed by sickness in her stomach. *I don't even want to open it.* A few gulps of air before she straightened her back and opened the message.

Put your headphones in before you play the video. Rx

Blinking, Amber scoured her bedroom for her headphones. *Has she sent me some informational video about AA? To show me she understands? Or maybe a video with a list of negatives about alcohol.* She huffed as she found her headphones, poked them into her ears, and stuck the cable into her phone.

After a momentary hesitation—*should I even give Rosie the time of day?*—she pressed the YouTube link in the message.

The video took its time to load, but once it did, Rosie's face came into view. She looked serious, as if she couldn't quite look into the camera. She put her phone down beside the piano.

Rosie placed both hands over the keys. She began to play.

Amber recognised the tune—it was “Lullaby”. A minimalistic version, however, a few notes from both hands.

Then Rosie started to sing. The lyrics were different from the version Amber knew:

I am sorry, Amber,
You’re oh so sweet,
Amber.

I was scared,
Wanted to run,
In my past,
Things went wrong.

I am sorry, Amber,
You’re oh so sweet,
Amber.

I am here,
If you want,
From now on,
I am yours.

I am sorry, Amber,
You’re oh so sweet,
Amber.”

She repeated the chorus twice more. Instead of a song about a mother that rocked her child to sleep on the ocean, it was now an apology.

Amber’s insides twisted—it was cheesier than a soap opera. But Rosie played and sung with such a sombre demeanour Amber soon glided through the meaning of the words.

As the song ended, Rosie looked into the camera lens. She pulled her bottom lip into her mouth, nodded once, then reached forward.

The video ended.

Uncertainty whirred within Amber's skull. A scratching at her closed bedroom door propelled her to her feet and towards the sound.

Nico hopped in, his tail wagging. He yapped at her and went to lick her legs, which were still damp from her shower.

She couldn't hold in her laugh at his antics. "Okay, little man. Less of the cleaning me: I'm clean."

He sat and looked at her with black bulging eyes.

"If you give me a minute. I'll take you for a walk."

He spun in a circle and raced out of the room.

Shaking her head, Amber dried her body, an echo of the video poking her, unwilling to let her forget. Not that she could—how could she? A woman had rewritten a beautiful song, one Amber loved, had filmed herself playing and singing it, and had posted it on YouTube.

Is it a public video? The thought made her want to curl in on herself. If other people saw it, she'd feel obliged to accept Rosie's apology. She checked the number of viewers—only two, and there was the symbol to indicate the video was unlisted. Rosie had probably played it herself before sending Amber the link.

Dressing, she stuffed her phone into her jacket pocket along with Nico's ball before snapping his little harness on him. "Come on, then. A bit of exercise might do me some good too."

Her day of holiday meant it was her turn to take him out anyway, although she'd planned to do it later. She walked him along the beach towards town.

Once he was off the lead, he stared up at her expectantly. Running back and forth for his ball was his favourite pastime.

The sun remained brilliant. There was a wisp of wind in the air. Amber was glad of her wrist warmers, especially with the amount of damp sand that stuck to Nico's ball.

Her head cleared the farther she strode. Maybe it was the sea air, or some hippie reason Fiona would come up with.

What does Rosie want from me? Obviously, forgiveness. But she also wanted Amber back, as more than a friend. *Has she come to her senses? What if the minute she finds out something else about me she doesn't like, she dumps me once more?*

Protecting herself from stress was important to her sobriety. She had no control over the actions of others: only herself. In the past, she'd put herself in harm's way just so she would feel nothing, but that wasn't healthy. It wasn't responsible or helpful to scupper your own journey towards happiness.

But the glint of hope of reconciliation with Rosie was bright. To have the things they'd had before, to have the things that had been promised if they'd taken things further—that made her stomach tingle and her spirits lift. She'd wanted Rosie for a very long time.

Taking out her phone, Amber gazed at the motionless thumbnail of the video. She popped her headphones back into her ears and listened to the video again, all the while with one eye on Nico.

Such a beautiful song. So much emotion. It must have taken so much for her to put her heart on her sleeve like that.

She came out of the YouTube app and phoned Fiona.

"Hey, Amber."

"Hi." Amber whistled for Nico, and they headed for home. "Hope I've not caught you when you're busy."

"Nope. Just putting my feet up and finishing the edging on this cardigan."

"Something for yourself?"

"And why not, eh? My grandkids don't want anything Nanny's crocheted them. One day, they will appreciate handmade things again and they'll come running back."

"I'm sure." The wind picked up so Amber covered the mouthpiece on her headphones. "Sorry. On the beach with the dog."

"You okay?"

"Yeah." She stopped walking and stared out towards the sea. The tide was out, and the sun glittered off the wet sand. "Well, I guess not. Or I wouldn't have phoned you."

"Come on, then. Tell all."

Amber explained what had happened, the video, and how she felt. She held her arms around herself as she watched Nico try to kill a strip of seaweed.

"I understand your confusion."

"What should I do?" Amber toed the sand.

"Come on, Amber. I can't tell you what to do. That's not my job."

"Okay." Amber held in a growl. "What would *you* do? Or what *have* you done in similar situations?" That was what the members of AA were best at: sharing experiences and suggesting healthy ways of behaving.

"I have absolutely no idea." A short chuckle from Fiona. "Look, sweetie, I'm not going to give you permission to throw everything away and go off with a girl that might hurt you again. I'm also not going to dissuade you from entering into possibly the most wonderful romance you could hope for. I don't know how your life will work out; I'm not psychic."

Amber sighed. "Yeah, I know."

"All I can say is sometimes people react to things without thinking. Knee-jerk, you know? And we're supposed to forgive people, aren't we? Hard on yourself, lenient with those around you."

"I know that too."

"Decide what you want and go for it. You have people that love you, and you'll always be supported by them if things take a turn for the worse."

"I want to be brave." Amber threw Nico's ball as hard as she could, empowered by the notion of possibility. "And I want to try."

"Then I think you have your answer. Just keep talking to me, okay?"

Amber nodded, then sniffed. "I will."

"Good girl. You're off to your meeting later?"

"Of course." Amber smiled at Nico as he deposited both his ball and a clump of chewed-up seaweed in front of her. "And choir too."

"Fab. Give me a call later if you want to."

"I'll see how it goes." She wafted away the dog, a thin string of seaweed still hanging from his mouth, and hung up.

Courage was needed and strength of character. With all she had accomplished in the last few months, she wondered whether she could manage it.

The footprints she made on her journey home were deeper than on her way out.

Rosie sat with Lorna in choir, trying not to look too much at Amber, trying to concentrate on the music. But for the first time in her life, beautiful music could not keep her focus.

It felt as if it had been weeks since she and Amber had been friends. She was twenty-nine weeks pregnant, which meant she and Amber had met twenty-five weeks ago. *Mad, really, when you think about it. It feels as if I've known her years.*

Lorna gave Rosie weird looks. Rosie didn't blame her—her usual cocky attitude had fizzled out. Since seeing the two green ticks beside the message she'd sent to Amber, Rosie had been on tenterhooks. So far no reply.

And that was okay, Rosie told herself. Amber needed time, of course she did. Rosie had been awful to her. Diabolical, one might say. The thought made her feel sicker than she had at the beginning of her pregnancy. K.B. made a lot of fuss as well, squirming and sloshing about. Rosie sent her a silent apology. *I'll sort it, baby. I promise. We just need to be patient.*

At break time, Amber hung by the water machine with Hayley, the shy girl that had been coming to choir for a couple of years. She didn't look over and seemed deep in conversation.

Rosie left them to it. Who was she to interrupt a blossoming new friendship? Tears sprang to her eyes, and she went to the toilet as an opportunity to allow a few to fall.

She hates the video. It wasn't enough. Rosie failed to push the thoughts away. Singing didn't even interest her—another occurrence she was unfamiliar with. She wanted to hide away in her bed and cry herself to sleep.

When the rehearsal ended, Rosie's whole body softened. At least now, she could escape being silently condemned by someone who wouldn't even talk to her.

Rosie damned her large belly and inability to move at a quick pace. She struggled to get her handbag over her head and dropped her music folder, a splat of papers on the floor. Cursing under her breath, she knelt down, under the definite understanding that getting up again was going to be a trial.

A body beside her: probably Lorna. At least she had one friend in the world. But when she pushed past her embarrassment to look up, surprise shot through her.

"Couldn't very well leave you to pick your stuff up by yourself, could I?" Amber's dark gaze rested on Rosie's. "Not when you're a bowling ball with legs."

Indignation roiled through Rosie. Then their first meeting, when Amber had bumped into her, flashed through her mind. "Thank you."

"You're welcome." Amber helped Rosie get the music back into her folder. She sat back on her heels and regarded Rosie with something akin to deep thought. "Want to go for a drink?"

Rosie blinked. "A…a drink?"

"Yeah, you know." Amber's lips twitched. "Liquidy thing. Usually goes in a glass or a mug?"

She couldn't let that one go. Rosie shot her a glare.

Amber let out the faintest of amused snorts.

Relieved, Rosie hauled herself to her feet. "All right."

Rosie hung back as Amber said goodbye to Hayley. Hayley bowed her head when Rosie went by, and Rosie gave her a kind smile. *I wonder whether Amber would have kept coming if it hadn't been for Hayley. Maybe I should be thankful.*

Shiny shoes catching the street lamps, Amber strode along the road before stopping at a greasy spoon café, open late. The scent of fried food and mediocre coffee hit Rosie as she followed her in. It was kitted out in red and white, with plastic tables and chairs.

Rosie peered into one of the glass domes on the counter. "Would you let me buy you a slice of cake?"

Her mouth to one side in thought, Amber cast her gaze over the options. "Chocolate. I think a day like today needs chocolate."

Nodding, Rosie ordered them both an apple juice, with a single slice of chocolate cake for Amber. "So, um…" Rosie cleared her throat as they sat at one of the tables. She rested her elbows on the glossy surface and watched a droplet of condensation travel down her glass. "How are you?"

Amber was silent until Rosie looked up. She smiled. "The video was wonderful."

"It was?" Rosie's throat was like a desert. She took a sip of her juice, but it made no difference. "I'm…I'm glad you think so."

"You obviously spent time changing the words and…did you work out a different piano part too? It didn't sound like the one our accompanist plays."

Rosie nodded. "I can play by ear. I use chords to make stuff up, like you do on a guitar?"

A small exhale and shrug suggested Amber didn't know about that. Hopefully it didn't matter.

"Anyway, I wanted to do something to show you how sorry I was. How much I knew I'd messed up." The tears, kept at bay during rehearsal, gathered once more. "Sorry."

Amber touched the back of Rosie's hand.

Rosie nearly broke apart, overwhelmed and relieved at the contact.

"It's nice to see a bit of weakness." Amber smoothed her palm against Rosie's knuckles. "You've always seemed so stoic and hard, you know? I like this side of you."

"Probably hormones." Rosie wasn't sure whether she liked the excuse or not. *I don't want to be controlled by my hormones. I'm not some blithering, pregnant wreck.* She grabbed a napkin from the caddy on the table and mopped her eyes. "I've done a lot of thinking since being in hospital."

"Me too. Are you ready to talk properly now?"

Rosie nodded. She took a few long breaths, calming her insides so they didn't churn so much. A sip of juice gave her courage to begin. "What happened with Michaela, it broke me. It's been twenty years, and I still have nightmares about it."

Amber's fork sat forgotten beside her plate, which she pushed out of the way. She inched her other hand forward, to hold Rosie's hand between both of hers.

"But it was foolish of me to use that as an excuse for not being with you. I absolutely love you, and no excuse will ever make that go away."

Amber blinked at her.

"I accept my reaction was fuelled by fear and completely illogical. I also accept it was mean, and I understand if you never want to forgive me for the things I said." She tongued her bottom lip. "But I wanted to try and make it right; that's why I did the video. If there's anything more I can do to prove to you I want this and that I'll never make the same mistake again, please tell me. I'll happily jump into shark-infested waters right now if it will make you happy."

Amber laughed. "No, I think that would be pretty stupid, don't you?"

Rosie's cheeks burned but she couldn't help smiling. "Yeah. Suppose so."

"There's nothing else you need to do. It's up to me, I suppose." Amber took one hand away to drink her juice. The skin by her eyes creased as she rolled the taste around in her mouth. "Like old times, hmm?"

"Yeah." Rosie wasn't sure whether to laugh or cry. *We're talking, actually talking. And she's smiling at me.*

"I've done some soul searching too. In particular, I've mulled over whether I'm strong enough to risk you doing something silly again."

Rosie made a reflex move towards her, but Amber held up a hand.

"No, it's okay. No one can promise a thing like that. I can't promise you I'm not going to relapse, just as much as you can't promise you'll never act like an asshole again."

Rosie recoiled, but nodded.

"I'm scared too. Last time a girl broke up with me, I started drinking again."

"Did you…did you this time?"

"No." It was as if all the pride Amber felt shone from her. "I have a really good support network now. Back then, I didn't have that. I've never had much of one."

"That sucks."

"Yeah. I actually wanted to tell you my story. If that's okay."

I told her mine. There's no way on earth I'd stop her from doing the same.

"I started drinking when I was a teenager because I was bullied at school and didn't have many friends."

It was Rosie's turn to stay quiet. She had some more juice, then brought both hands to Amber's.

Amber took a large breath. "I did okay at school, got okay grades. But I always felt there was something different about me. And I mean other than being gay. When I went to uni, I discovered if I was drunk I became really confident. So that's when it all started, I suppose. I drank, got all these great friends, did wacky stuff, and had a good old laugh. I struggled a few times to get my assignments in on time, but otherwise, life was good.

"Once I finished uni, I missed the lifestyle. All my uni friends were off doing awesome stuff overseas or in brilliant jobs. None of them lived nearby. I moved back home, and my parents just didn't get it. I was this new person, I suppose, and they weren't interested in who I had become. All I got from them was nagging—I shouldn't drink so much, I should go out, I should make friends. I did a few admin temp jobs with an agency. Drank in my bedroom every evening, watching TV by myself."

Passing her thumb over the back of Amber's knuckles, Rosie sunk into the warmth of her skin.

"Anyway, Mum and Dad decided they wanted to move to Scotland. New jobs, great opportunities for them. I guess they thought I wasn't great by myself because they tried to force me to come with them. But I was comfortable in my loner lifestyle, flitting from job to job, drinking myself stupid. It worked for me at the time. I argued, wanted to stay where I was. They said they didn't want to watch me ruin my life anymore. They disowned me." Amber let out a wretched sigh. "I got my own flat. Finally, I had some freedom. My money went on cheap wine and a Sky subscription. I didn't feel as bad, so the drinking eased up a bit. I didn't have someone on my back constantly. And I got my first permanent job on a hospital ward.

"I was terrified my first day there, but the nursing team were so nice and made me feel welcome. I went out, drinking of course, with my ward colleagues, a few times. I think I became known as a bit of a wild child—I did some pretty mad things whilst we were out, but I guess that was just what I did when I was drinking.

"Then we got this new ward manager, Debbie. She was strict and negative about everything. It wasn't just me; she was stern with everyone. I had this whole way of organising the medical notes and stuff. But she wasn't happy with that—oh no. Wanted everything done her way and her way only. I tried to rationalise with her, say to her, 'Look my way works too, and I'm used to it now', but she wasn't having it. Then I made one mistake, lost a discharge letter somehow. After that, Debbie started picking up on every little thing I did.

"I started hating the job I used to love. I started looking forward to weekends—no work and I could just fall into oblivion. I stopped going out with the ward because Debbie sometimes came, and she just wasn't nice to me. I started to make more and more mistakes at work, drinking every evening, which was not something I was doing before. I just wanted to forget."

Rosie squeezed Amber's fingers to convey sympathy, care, and love.

"Then there was this massive incident where a patient had been given the wrong meds and…it could have been me that recorded something wrong or the medical team or the nurses. No one ever found out. Anyway, Debbie accused me of negligence; she smelt alcohol on my breath and shouted at me that I was drunk in front of the whole ward. I wasn't—I really, really wasn't—but there was no convincing her. It was like being back at school with the kids being horrible to me then. I was so anxious, I couldn't speak.

"I went off sick with anxiety and depression. Went on some meds, which didn't do much. I just holed up in my shitty flat and drank away the pain. It was the only thing that worked at the time."

"I'm sorry that happened to you." Rosie's voice was hoarse. "I want to take that Debbie woman and…" She shrugged. "Fuck knows. I just want her to hurt."

A smile and a nod of appreciation. "It's kind of you to say." Amber smirked. "I suppose you could sit on her."

"Give it a few more months. Get the full effect of my girth."

"Anyway…" Amber squeezed her fingers. "A few months later, I went to a bar. I got rip-roaring pissed, and guess who picked me up out of a hedge on the way home whilst she was walking her dog?"

Rosie frowned in thought. Then an idea came to her. "Jilly?"

"Yep. Nico pulled her over, and Jilly just bent down and dragged me out. I was in a pretty bad way. Black eye, covered in scratches from the brambles. I don't remember. Freaked the hell out of me when I woke up in her guest bed, having been put in a size-eighteen nightie and had the vomit washed from my face. Apparently, paramedics had assessed me and Jilly had promised she'd look after me, so they'd let her."

"Wow, What a woman."

"Indeed." Amber smiled off into the distance. "She took me to my first AA meeting. And I moved in with her just over a year ago. She's been so good, told me a few home truths and whipped me back into shape. Whilst I was too poorly to work, I helped her out in her garden."

A whirring dishwasher behind the counter was accompanied by the tinkling of ceramics. Rosie was glad the café was empty. It was warm and the juice wasn't from concentrate.

"I'd got the feeling your past hadn't been great." The lull had motivated Rosie to pipe up. "But knowing the real story, I suppose I understand better now."

Amber nodded. "Knowing all of that, does it make a difference to how you feel about me?"

"No." Nothing had ever come more easily. Rosie caught Amber's gaze and held it. "If it's possible, I love you even more because I know you better."

"I get why you were scared. What happened when you were young—I can't imagine how difficult that must have been." Amber chewed her lip. "I suppose now we have to come up with some sort of solution." Her eyes flicked downwards. "And that's not even considering your current pre-baby state. You wanted to do this by yourself, be a mum. Does that mean we can't be together?"

"I thought it might." Rosie stroked Amber's skin again with her thumbs. "I suppose I need to decide what to do, what role I want you to play." She ran her fingers through her hair. "I'm not sure what to do about that. It's a bit of a minefield." A huff later and her gaze implored Amber. "Do you want to be a mum?"

"My focus the last year or two has been: find a job I can handle, don't drink, and stay safe." A nudge to Rosie's knuckles. "It doesn't have to be something you decide now though. Why don't we just, like, *date*?"

"Date?" The word seemed alien on Rosie's tongue. *Haven't we been doing that all along?*

"Yeah, you know. Go out together with the intention that it's for fun and romance?" Another nudge. "Not just as singing or juice-drinking buddies."

Rosie pushed her mouth to the side. "That's actually a great idea." A new feeling rose in her, one that sparked possibility and excitement.

"I need to take things slowly anyway. And you definitely do." Amber grinned.

Rosie pulled her chair round to sit next to Amber. She took Amber's hands again. "Want to start now?"

"We have juice and cake." Amber's cheeks pinked, and she lowered her head, perhaps at the sudden proximity.

Rosie could smell her flowery perfume, could see each stroke of her eyeliner. Amber's pillar box lips enticed Rosie, and her mouth watered. "Which you haven't even touched." She narrowed her eyes in jest and indicated the cake.

A chuckle, one that tickled Rosie deep in her belly. "Mmm." Amber leant forward. "Can I just…?"

Rosie stayed still, half turned towards Amber. A different tickle slipped down her, one of anticipation.

Amber's lips parted. She moved closer.

In all her previous relationships, Rosie had been the one to instigate everything—first date, first hand-hold, first kiss. But there she was in stunned inaction whilst Amber moved to press her lips to hers.

The first touch was like a blackbird song. It peeled out over rolling hills and through sunny air, joyous for spring. Flowers blossomed around them, colours sharp as pop art. Amber was so *soft*. How was it possible? Rosie could barely breathe. Gentle fingers that cupped her face tilted her chin back.

Again, Rosie didn't do all the things she was so used to doing. She didn't stand and grab Amber, pull her away to privacy for some heavy petting or the like. She didn't drag her into her own lap, thread her fingers through Amber's hair, control the kiss to make Amber gasp.

It was for Amber to decide how fast to take it, so Rosie sank into the kiss. She filled her lungs with Amber's scent, but kept her hands folded in front of her bump.

The hand at her chin slipped to the back of her head, and Amber parted her lips to deepen the kiss. It was over far too soon.

Grinning like a fool, Rosie sat back in her chair. She had to look away, at the other tables, out of the window, anywhere that would give her a moment to take it all in.

"That was a long time coming." Unease tinged Amber's tone.

Rosie locked her gaze with Amber's, feeling guilty for looking away. "Yeah." She cleared her throat. "Really long."

Amber smiled, relief smoothing her brow. "It's a shame, but I think we should eat this cake and leave."

To her bedroom? To mine? To separate places? Does she want the evening to end? A rapid series of blinks put the brakes on.

Rosie reached over the table to set the cake back in front of Amber. "Cake is way better than kissing me, huh?" *Where did that come from?*

"I've no idea. I haven't tasted the cake yet." The gleam in Amber's eye was sure and teasing.

Rosie sat back and watched Amber devour the cake. When Amber's tongue came out to swipe a crumb of chocolate from the edge of her mouth, Rosie thought she might faint. *Have I really be staring at her and wanting her for twenty-five weeks?*

Once a single mouthful of cake was left, Amber pressed her shoulder to Rosie's. "Come on, you need to try this." She offered the fork.

Rosie was sure Amber's gaze dropped to her lips as she took the piece into her mouth. She was also pretty sure Amber's pupils dilated as she watched. With a renewed confidence, and also relief that—just maybe—Amber still felt as attracted to her as she felt to Amber, Rosie relished the sweetness of the cake, the buttercream filling, and the slightly bitter ganache. It reminded her of her mother's baking—of home.

Once the mouthful was gone, Rosie threw herself into the deep end and kissed Amber again. Their mingled taste was all chocolate. Amber giggled as Rosie sank her hand into Amber's hair. It was soft too, and thick. She moved her other hand to Amber's waist.

Amber slipped her hand around Rosie's waist with hesitation. She broke the kiss and looked down. "Sorry."

"What for?"

"I don't want to be presumptuous. I know it's not good etiquette to feel up pregnant women as a rule."

"Fuck that." Rosie spoke quietly, aware the waitress was within earshot. She placed Amber's hand on her belly. Perhaps it would be like in the films—K.B. would know Amber's touch was special and make some kind of huge gesture.

But for once, baby dearest remained unmoving.

Amber's expression glittered with wonder. Her jaw dropped and her gaze seemed fixed to Rosie's midriff. She inched her hand over Rosie's top, over where her navel had popped out a few weeks ago, and up to just shy of her breasts. "I know it's a natural and normal thing, but I think it's amazing."

"What?"

"You being pregnant. This…" She indicated Rosie's belly. "A baby being inside you."

Unsure what to say, Rosie settled on a shrug and a lopsided grin.

A loud cough sounded behind them. The waitress had her arms folded, but she smiled. “Sorry, ladies. Time for me to lock the doors.”

“No problem.” Rosie tidied up their glasses and plate before carrying them to the front counter.

She held Amber’s hand all the way back to her car.

Chapter 26

Rosie was on the doorstep of her eighth month. Heartburn and backache were now part of her daily routine, as were the remedies for the symptoms. She'd found a couple of simple yoga exercises on YouTube. She wasn't sure if they were of any long-term benefit to her, but she enjoyed limbering her muscles. And it meant she was used to sitting on an exercise mat.

"How are we all doing?" Cynthia asked the antenatal group.

"Great. Excellent." Cathy huffed and puffed to get onto the floor with much help from Jonathan. "Same as every other pregnancy. Except now my joints are a bit creakier and my home life's a bit noisier."

Sympathetic murmurs from the group.

"But I do go swimming twice a week, which I find astronomically helpful, and I make sure I've got Keith next to me every night."

"And Keith is?" Janet asked.

"Oh." Cathy laughed and kissed Jonathan on the cheek. "He's our nighttime companion."

"Pregnancy pillow," Jonathan said.

Cathy leant her head on his shoulder. "This one's far too bony these days to participate in a full-bodied cuddle."

Any cuddle from Cathy would be full-bodied, regardless of whom she cuddled. Rosie held back giggles. Sometimes she reckoned she'd benefit herself from one of Cathy's hugs, that much love and all-encompassing squish.

Amber's scent filled her memory. The lingering goodbye hug they'd shared last Friday made her shiver with delight. Rosie hadn't wanted to leave her arms, but it had been pushing for eleven o'clock and she'd been dead on her feet. *Gone are the days when I'd stay up into the early hours.*

Janet poked Rosie on the shoulder. "You look more upbeat."

Rosie tried to tone down her smile. "The girl problems I had a few weeks ago? They've been resolved."

"So you're no longer a one-will-become-two family unit? Are you a two-will-become-three?"

Rosie sucked on her bottom lip. "We've not got that far yet. But it's safe to say I'm hopeful. We're going on a date next weekend."

"Oooh, do we get to hear where you're going?"

"Chaps." The crinkles evident in the corners of Cynthia's eyes conflicted with her lowered tone. "We need to get on with the pregnancy stuff. I have a clinic in an hour."

"Sorry." Janet winked at Rosie. "Want a cuppa at the community café later?"

"Go on, then."

The class was a question-and-answer session, with a bit of biology and what-might-happen-ifs thrown in for good measure. Rosie was left inspired and invigorated by the knowledge that in nine-ish weeks she'd confidently introduce her baby to the world.

"I should have brought my sister." Rosie followed Janet and Olivia across the car park to the café. "She said she'd be there if I wanted her to be when I go into labour."

"I've got my mum on hand." Janet's belly was so large, even her maternity top had trouble containing it. "Livvi will need some support too. She's not good when I'm in pain."

"Jan had a miscarriage a few years ago." They exchanged a soft look.

Rosie's heart ached. "Sounds like our journeys are pretty similar. My first baby was stillborn."

"Yours will be a rainbow baby too?"

"What's that?" Rosie snuck under Olivia's arm when she held the door open for them.

"Not a gay thing, although part of me wants to wrench the rainbow thing back. It's the name some people use for a baby that comes after a loss." Janet shrugged. "Like, after the storm, I guess."

Olivia allowed the door to swing closed. "Was that difficult to deal with on your own?"

Janet shot Olivia a dangerous look.

Rosie shook her head—she wanted to talk about it. "My parents and my sister were excellent. Good support system."

"Ours too." Janet rubbed Olivia's back as they sat.

Was Olivia more affected by the miscarriage than Janet? Of the two, she was the one with the darkest eyes. Janet seemed to only want to project light onto her wife.

The waitress took their orders and left.

"I do worry my sister might be a bit of a flapper." Rosie pushed her handbag under her chair with her feet. "But I guess I can always banish her from the room if she gets too annoying."

"Ah, yes. Birthing mum gets the final say." Janet grinned at Olivia.

"Yes, she does."

"So, anyway, come on, miss. Tell us all about the new love of your life."

Whilst they waited for their drinks, Rosie brought them up to date. She wasn't sure what the rule was for outing someone in AA, so she didn't specify what Amber's issue was, just that she had one. Neither Janet nor Olivia asked.

"I suppose it must be difficult when you've got it all worked out and then..." Olivia flipped her hand. "...someone arrives into your life like that. Especially if they have problems you're not familiar with."

Does she think it's an illness Amber has? I suppose it is. Rosie hadn't seen it that way, and it was refreshing to talk to someone who didn't know her that well. "I still feel a bit shit about how I reacted, but I'm hoping I have time to make it up to her."

"I'm sure you do. And this song you wrote for her must have had some impact." Olivia's eyes flicked to Janet, a sudden look of discomfort creasing her brow. "When we first got together, I made a mistake like that."

Is that too personal to ask about? Rosie kept her mouth closed but attempted a look of curiosity.

"I...um." Olivia rubbed the back of her neck.

Janet threaded her fingers with Olivia's.

That seemed to give Olivia confidence. "I had breast cancer back in my thirties. I had a single mastectomy, but the reconstruction went wrong and I got an infection." She made a sweeping gesture towards her own bosom. "Clearly, I'm now as symmetrical as I ever was. But when we met," she smiled at Janet, "I was wearing his thing in my bra that looked like a piece of chicken and, I'll be honest, I really didn't want anyone to see what was underneath."

"She didn't tell me until we were almost naked."

Olivia rolled her eyes. "Yeah, you found it funny. I was mortified."

"*Someone* should have told me they had a Cabbage Patch Doll's face where their boob should be." Janet shrugged. "Seriously, when you're getting down to it and suddenly the woman you're attracted to starts blubbering about how sorry she is and she should have told you this thing… I could do nothing but laugh."

Pretty similar to what I did to Amber. The assertive and more logical side of her brain reminded her of the secret Amber had kept from her too. *It wasn't all me.*

"So, what?" Rosie died to know more. "You had no idea?"

"Nope. Nada." Janet kissed the backs of Olivia's fingers. "But that just means we're both idiots in an idiotic world, I guess."

A lot like Amber and I. A few beads of the tension Rosie carried fizzled out. *No one's perfect. And we were honest in the end. At least I didn't tell her as I was going into labour.*

"People do stuff, and most of the time it's pretty stupid." Olivia's face smoothed and she gazed at Janet as if she was the only brightness in a dim room.

Their drinks arrived, and they shared stories of inseminations and tests and side effects. Rosie found herself part of a group, no longer alone, no longer the only lesbian doing it a certain way. There were two of them, sure, but they'd got pregnant the same way, and they'd gone through some of the same heartache too.

When she left, Rosie was cosy with gratitude. *I hope we stay friends. I hope our kids know one another.* Driving home with their numbers in her mobile phone, she couldn't wait to tell Amber about her new friends.

Chapter 27

After their overwhelming reconciliation and her subsequent joy, not seeing Rosie felt so strange to Amber. A family gathering in Cambridge had caused Rosie to be away two weekends ago, and then she'd had a hen party with some university friends last weekend. Amber had been sent various photos of a gaggle clustered around a half-naked male stripper. It had not been difficult to see the discomfort in Rosie's eyes.

Choir had been simple in the end—Amber didn't want to leave Hayley by herself, not when Hayley had been so kind to her and had obviously gained so much from their friendship. Rosie seemed to understand that she and Amber wouldn't sit together. *We'd get distracted by one another anyway and get derisive looks from the warblers.*

Amber longed to take Rosie somewhere secluded and kiss her at the end of each rehearsal, or even just exchange some words of affection away from everyone else. They'd shared looks and smiles, and last week Amber had risked touching Rosie's fingers.

From the way Rosie's gaze followed her out, Amber guessed she probably felt the same.

Amber was surprised now to find a pinnacle of worry sitting stone-like in her belly. *What if she doesn't fancy me anymore because we've kept our distance? What if she's changed her mind about me being part of her life?* Reason battled with her usual anxiety, but she wanted to believe things would be okay. So there was that.

The walk into town, which bypassed the Saturday traffic, let some of her worry disappear. The fresh exercise also made her feel better, even if a spattering of unease still tugged her towards home.

Humming the "Sight of Land" movement, she pushed open the door of the café down one of the backstreets in the centre of town. Signs outside proclaimed they only served vegan produce and that many of their cakes were gluten-free too. Amber ate meat, dairy, and wheat—however she relished sampling new things. Variety really was the spice of life. She was desperate to try a cake with no wheat or dairy, if only to see how it managed to be palatable.

The smell of cake and cinnamon swam around her, easing her further into comfort. Her heart pattered anew when she took in Rosie. She wore a black top that gathered at one side and a red hoodie—one Amber reckoned she couldn't zip up.

Has her belly grown even more? Rosie had sent her a Welcome to Month Eight image, from the app she used on her phone to track her pregnancy, a day or two before. It was odd to think she'd be a mother in just a few weeks.

As Amber approached the sofa at the front of the café, Rosie started to stand. She wanted to tell her to stay seated but knew Rosie didn't like people mollycoddling her, so smiled back instead.

"Hi." Rosie stepped into Amber's arms, and it was as natural as if they had done it for years.

Resting her chin on Rosie's shoulder, Amber giggled at the bump that pressed into her lower ribs. She placed both hands either side of Rosie's waist and moved back. Then she gave Rosie a peck on the lips.

This time, it was new. They'd kissed nearly three weeks ago with gusto and sexual promise. But pecking Rosie on the lips was almost more intimate—the gesture of someone greeting someone they loved, not someone they simply fancied. *I wish I'd taken her somewhere private after the rehearsal—how did I ever manage three weeks without kissing her?*

The cheer that shone from Rosie warmed the whole café.

"Oh. Hi." A verbal reply hadn't seemed important compared to feeling Rosie's body against hers. "I swear you grew like…" She pushed one shoulder up, her cheeks burning.

"I did, actually. Little K.B. is sapping all my energy in her bid to be the biggest baby ever."

"Aw."

They went up to the counter together. Their hands gravitated towards one another. Amber's skin tingled where Rosie's touched her, the feeling travelling all up her arm.

"What's your carrot cake like?" Rosie's eyebrows furrowed as she read the menu.

The guy behind the counter clipped the jug back onto the blender and turned to them. "Delicious. Are you vegan?"

Rosie looked at her boots. "Um. No." She glanced around. "Is that okay?"

"Everyone's welcome; you don't have to bring your membership card or anything." The guy was a good decade younger than both of them. He had black hair and a spacer in his ear. A tribal tattoo emerged from his elbow-length shirtsleeve.

"You have membership cards?" Rosie asked.

"Joke." He gave them a lopsided smile. "We do have loyalty cards though. Buy four slices, get one free. I just asked because most people who don't eat vegan food are surprised by how good the cakes are here. We make them fresh every day, and they're always gone by dinnertime."

Amber peered at the menu. "We should choose two and share them."

With slices of carrot cake and coffee cake and two juice smoothies on their tray, they settled back on the sofa.

The hem of Amber's skater skirt brushed the knee of Rosie's jeans. "You look good though, as well as massive."

Rosie smoothed a palm over her bump. "Getting some of those cliché symptoms now, which is kind of annoying actually."

"Why?"

"I always promised myself I would just carry on as normal. I never wanted being pregnant to define me."

"But you don't have much control over the symptoms, do you?" Amber slotted their fingers together, aching at the sad look in Rosie's eyes.

"I guess not. Still pisses me off though."

Amber grabbed her smoothie and sipped through the paper straw. Strawberry and raspberry hit her tongue, followed by the vanilla essence she'd watched the guy drip in. A noise of enjoyment rumbled through her and she pointed to Rosie's glass.

Rather than pink, Rosie's drink was lilac-coloured with flecks of black. Her response to a mouthful was just as enthusiastic. "At least four of my five a day." Rosie squeezed Amber's fingers.

"I've missed you." It came out before Amber had thought it through. She held Rosie's gaze, determined to gauge her reaction.

"That's my fault. So much on." Rosie set her smoothie back onto the table. "Hen parties and family gatherings, to say nothing of GP appointments and antenatal classes and a guided tour around the maternity suite."

"Is that where you're going to give birth?"

"Probably. I'd love to have a home birth, but it scares me. Just having your two midwives and no backup other than an ambulance taking you in."

"What's the suite like? Is it in hospital?"

"Yeah. But midwife-led, which I think is important. They have a pool you can use and balls and stuff. Meds, if you need them."

"Do you have a plan for giving birth?"

"Yeah, although it's pretty fluid." Rosie combed a hand through her hair. "I want to be relaxed and do it as naturally as possible. Women have done it without meds and stuff for years. I've taken some online relaxation classes and the ones you get taught at antenatal. I've read lots of books, and it feels like that's key. Mothers that give birth when they're relaxed have a lower chance of needing assisted delivery."

"Like what? Caesarean?"

"That. Forceps, and the sink plunger thing—a ventouse. Labour tends to be shorter too because the human body reacts to stress like it's in danger. And no one wants to have a screaming baby pop out of them when there's a tiger on your trail."

"That makes sense."

"So me, a ball, and maybe the pool. Low lighting, nice music. Charlie will be there, but she knows if I find that too much I'll tell her to go grab a coffee."

Amber squeezed Rosie's hand. "I wondered whether you'd want to do it by yourself."

"Initially I did. But I've changed my mind." Rosie pushed up her shoulders and shuddered. "It's just a bit too scary, I think. Too big a thing to do without someone I know there."

Amber had a great urge to ask if she could be there, if she could help. But it wasn't her place to ask.

"Do you have a name yet?"

Rosie pursed her lips around a smile. "I do."

"Is it a secret?"

A look of guilt flickered over Rosie's face before she looked away.

Similar feelings churned within Amber. She set her jaw. "That's a secret I don't need to know if you don't want to tell me."

"I want to keep it to myself until she arrives. Is that okay?"

"Of course." Amber tucked a piece of hair behind Rosie's ear. She was pleased at the reaction—Rosie closed her eyes and leaned into her hand. "It'll be a nice surprise."

"I've gone classically gender-neutral. I bet *that* isn't a surprise."

"You can call your kid what you like, but I like the idea of a baby having a gender-neural name. It's cute and gives them more options when they grow up."

"Exactly." Rosie smiled as Amber tickled the side of her neck. "I met some cool women too at antenatal, a gay couple. They're a couple of weeks ahead of me, but we have a lot in common."

"Cool."

"They had…" Rosie cleared her throat. She lowered her voice. "They had a miscarriage. Apparently if you have a baby after a loss, it's called a rainbow baby."

"That's lovely."

Amber enjoyed a comfortable lull in the conversation. *It's nice Rosie has a couple to be friends with that have something in common with her.*

"What's your smoothie again?"

A sparkle of mischief appeared in Rosie's eyes. "You could always kiss me and find out."

Amber didn't need any encouragement. Rosie tasted like blueberries and ginger, a spicy and fruit-filled combination. When she parted her lips and allowed Rosie's tongue between them, Amber gasped. Amber passed her hand back up Rosie's neck, relishing the way Rosie's hairs stood on end at her touch.

When they broke apart, they both breathed heavily. "So?"

"Hmm?" Amber's thoughts flew around.

"The smoothie? You like?"

Rather than fumbling with words, Amber nodded. Was her grin as wide as Rosie's?

To give her brain time to gather itself, Amber cut both their cake slices in half, manoeuvring one half of each onto the other's plate so they had a piece of each. "I wonder whether cake is just as good with no real butter or wheat in it."

"The proof will be in the…" Rosie pointed to Amber with her fork. "Let's hope your choice of café pays off."

"Already has." The carrot cake, like the look in Rosie's eyes, was delicious in all kinds of ways. Next, she tried the coffee cake. *Wonderful.* A decent choice of venue by far, made better by the company.

They ate in a silence that flowed. The air was easy to breathe, and the soft music from the sound system added to the tranquillity.

A mother with an oversized buggy came in, a look of relief glinting her eyes. "Hi, Greg."

"Hey, lovely. Hi, boys."

One podgy hand came from the back seat of the two-seater buggy. There was a blue wheelchair sign on it. The boy in the front seat, who looked about five, hid his face.

"Good day at school, Tyler?"

The mum parked the buggy beside Rosie and Amber and angled it so it faced the middle of the café. Five-year-old Tyler nodded, hiding his face with his hands a moment later. The mum unclipped the toddler in the back seat, and he climbed out. She hauled him onto the chair next to her. "There you are. Want a brownie?"

When Amber turned to Rosie, she caught her glassy-eyed and wistful. Amber touched her shoulder.

Rosie's cheeks pinked.

The toddler sat nicely in his chair.

Tyler swung his legs for a while, then quietened when his mother brought them a slice of brownie each.

Amber giggled when they both ended up covered in chocolate.

With a heavy sigh, the mum lifted her tea to her lips and closed her eyes. Her hair looked lank—not dirty exactly, but unloved. A messy bun kept it away from her face, but tendrils brushed her shoulders. She replaced the cup onto the saucer and smiled over at them. "Tyler can't have lactose and James can't have wheat. And Tyler has sensory issues, so he can't manage busy or noisy places."

"Perfect café for you guys, then." Amber's straw made a bubbly noise as she got to the end of her smoothie.

James's giggle pealed through the café.

Amber winked at him.

"It's heaven. Everything I need for after school." Mum looked from Rosie to Amber. "You guys been here before?"

"No." Rosie's gaze drifted down to their joined hands. "First time."

"Get yourself a loyalty card." She nodded at Rosie. "Once your little one's here, you'll find a lot of cafés don't fit a pram."

"That's something I haven't thought about." Rosie grimaced.

"I can get Tyler's special buggy in here; that's what's so great about it. That and the lack of things that can make my boys poorly." She lifted her cup. "And the excellent range of tea." Again, she looked between them, her eyes narrowing just a tad. "You guys on a date?"

"Is it so obvious?" Rosie laughed.

"No. But I seem to have gaydar where it's not warranted. My best friend's gay. My brother's gay. Everyone's gay except me, I think." She chuckled. "Don't bother me. Live and let live, I say." She moved her attention back to James, who was drawing chocolatey lines over the table. A napkin swiped his artwork away.

Rosie sat back into the cushions, her focus back on Amber. "How has your week been?"

"Busy as always. Had to take my colleague Gemma aside and remind her to keep her cleavage covered."

Rosie passed her thumb over the back of Amber's hand. "I fully expect you did that with kindness."

"How do you know?"

"Because that's how you are. Standing up to someone is hard, especially when you don't want to upset them. I'd have just made her cry by giving her a good old-fashioned bollocking." Rosie bit her lip and sent the mum behind them an apologetic look for her language.

The mum brushed it off with a gesture.

Rosie grimaced. "I need to stick my teacher hat on. I don't have an issue not swearing when I'm at school."

Amber giggled. "You'll have lots of practise, I think. Babies don't know what you're saying for ages."

They both looked down at Rosie's bump. Amber tilted her head and lifted her free hand, holding it an inch away from Rosie's belly.

Rosie nodded.

Her hand warmed the minute she touched Rosie. Would anything happen? "Does she kick a lot?"

"Off and on. I can tell when she's sleeping—that's weird. She does these little fluttery movements."

"What does it feel like?"

"Kind of…" Rosie pulled her mouth to one side. "Like butterflies. And then, when she's awake, it's like 'Oh, okay, I'll just punch and kick your internal organs now.'"

Amber leant against the back of the sofa. "Is it uncomfortable?"

"Sometimes. Mostly when I need a wee."

"Ah."

Rosie placed her hand over Amber's, shifted her to a higher-up area. "Oh, yowch. Okay, girl."

Underneath Amber's fingers, a kind of rocking motion. Part of Rosie's belly poked up slightly. Then it went away. Then it poked up again.

"What's that?" Amber's voice became a whisper. Would the baby get scared and run away if she spoke anymore loudly?

"No idea. Maybe a knee. Or an elbow. She's pretty tucked up in there."

"Wow." Amber hadn't foreseen she'd be anything like as overwhelmed as she was, feeling Rosie's baby kick for the first time. *I'm being acknowledged. The baby wants me to know she knows I'm here. Maybe that I'm important to her mother. Maybe that it's okay I'm part of their lives.*

I'll be a part of a baby's life. That's huge. She swallowed. When she looked up, her vision was blurry. Swiping away tears, she turned away, looking for a napkin so her make-up wouldn't smudge.

A warm hand touched her shoulder. "Hey." Rosie's tone was gentle. "Come here."

Amber allowed herself to be embraced. The space between Rosie's neck and shoulder smelled like a different sort of spice to her smoothie.

Rosie passed her fingertips up and down Amber's back. "Talk to me."

"I just…" Amber sniffed and shook her head against Rosie's skin. "I suppose it's just massive, isn't it? You're having a baby. And it's something I want to be part of." Amber half-sobbed, half-laughed her way back into a sitting position.

Rosie smoothed Amber's hair behind her ear. "You're right." She chucked Amber's chin, a lopsided smile tugging her lips. "I don't want you to be scared." She indicated her belly. "K.B. is on her way, but it doesn't mean we need to rush. We need to find our feet with this, and that will take time."

Amber blew out a breath and nodded. "Okay."

"I got my first Braxton Hicks today."

Amber wiped underneath her eyes. "You did?"

"Yeah."

"What was that like?" Amber felt a little better when Rosie grinned.

"Like period pain. Kind of jabbing, like K.B.'s battling to get out."

"Like your body's getting ready."

A nod. "She's as big as a pineapple."

Amber snorted. "Weird."

"Tell me about it."

This time, Amber took up position against Rosie's shoulder without the need for comfort. She wanted to be close, to smell her, and to put her hand back on her bump.

Rosie enclosed her with an arm and made circles against Amber's shoulder. "And I've been having really odd cravings. The other day I wanted chicken nuggets and chocolate."

"Not so unusual."

"In the same sodding bowl? Mixed together?"

That made Amber laugh. She rubbed the place where K.B. had kicked her. "Did you go out and get some?"

"Had to cook the chicken nuggets myself, but yeah. Chucked a load of chocolate buttons on top and I was good to go."

"Anything you're not liking?"

"Hmm." Rosie rubbed her chin. "I had an aversion to potatoes the other day. No idea why."

"Weird."

"Yeah."

With happy dancing inside her, Amber wrapped her arm around Rosie's belly and pressed a kiss to her clothed shoulder. "I won't make you potatoes, then."

"When?"

"Next week. When I invite you for dinner."

Rosie smiled down at her. "We're doing a serious role reversal here, you know that?"

"Aha. I knew you were one of those women that likes to take charge."

"Well, since you picked me up off the toilet, I've been feeling awfully docile."

Amber poked her in the side, which made her squeak. "I didn't pick you up. You got up perfectly well on your own."

Rosie trailed her hand into her hair.

Behind them, James was placed back into the mobility buggy, and he, Tyler, and their mum left the café with a wave.

Amber waved back from the safety of Rosie's arms.

Chapter 28

Rosie strode into the leisure centre with a rucksack on her back, which contained a beach towel and some toiletries.

Chelsea and Charlie hopped from their seats in reception the minute they saw her.

"Hiya, Auntie Rosie." Chelsea turned to K.B. "Hi, cousin baby."

"Cousin baby?" Rosie took in Chelsea's tight plait and the pink goggles already on her head.

"New name for K.B." Charlie gave Rosie a one-armed hug. Her own sports bag was slung over her shoulder. "Did you try the stuff on?"

They paid for their session before walking towards the changing rooms.

"Yeah." Rosie winced. "Shorts are fine. Tankini, not so much. Screw it. I'll just have to deal. Not much longer now."

"Seven weeks." Chelsea threw her head back, a superior look on her face.

"Someone's maths is improving." Rosie flicked her eyebrows up twice.

Charlie needed to go into a cubical to change, so Rosie and Chelsea, who had their swimsuits on under their clothes, hung out on a bench.

Memories of being at secondary school washed over Rosie. It wasn't too much of a discomfort to undress in front of Chelsea, although Rosie wished she wouldn't stare quite so much.

The elastic waist of her board shorts just about tucked under her bump, but her tankini didn't fit anymore, so she'd chosen an old bikini top and a large T-shirt. So much for looking fit at the pool.

"So how're things going, guinea-pig-wise?" Rosie used hushed tones.

"We're going next weekend to pick two."

"Two?"

"Yes. Ginger and Tallulah." Chelsea rubbed her hands together. "Mummy says we've got to make doubly sure they're two girls; otherwise, they might have baby guinea pigs."

"Yeah, you wouldn't want that, would you?"

A shrug. "What if the two girl guinea pigs want babies?" She held her hands out to each side, as if she carried milk urns. "I don't know, Auntie Rosie. I don't want to stop them having a family."

Rosie chuckled. "I'm sure they'll be happy without babies if they've got you to look after them."

"Mmm." Chelsea slanted her head one way, then the other, her gaze back on Rosie's bump. "When you have *your* baby, will your belly go down again?"

"Yeah, but it's not instant. It isn't like letting the air out of a balloon."

"So the air stays in there? The air the baby breathes?"

Oh, hell. I wasn't sure I'd have to have this conversation until my own kid was old enough. Rosie glanced towards Charlie's cubicle. "Um…"

"Just tell her," Charlie shouted. "Saves me doing it."

Large blue eyes stared up at her.

"Right. You know what a uterus is?"

"Yeah, it's the inside house for the baby."

"That's right. And the uterus has a big sac with the baby and the fluid that protects the baby in it." She smoothed a hand over her belly. "And the baby doesn't breathe air yet; she's using a special thing called a placenta to get all her oxygen and food and water. The uterus has muscle walls which stretch with the baby as she grows. But then when the baby comes out, the walls take a while to relax back into shape."

"Oh." Chelsea chewed the end of her plait. "Is there a pill you can take to make it happen quicker?"

"Um…" Rosie wasn't sure going into breast feeding and oxytocin was something Chelsea would understand. "No." She nudged Chelsea with her shoulder. "My skin will be all wrinkly though on my belly whilst it's going down."

"Ew." Chelsea pulled a face. "Aw, don't worry, Auntie Rosie." She threw an arm around her back. "I'll still think you're pretty when you have a wrinkly tummy."

I never considered I might look ugly after giving birth. Even before giving birth, I'm not exactly a prize specimen. Dread clutched Rosie, a rubber band across her chest. She swallowed. *My usual trick is to date a girl for a bit, then take her to bed. I guess I'll have to do something different.*

But if I don't take Amber to bed, will she think I don't fancy her? What if we do *go to bed and she isn't turned on by the hippo I've become?*

These thoughts played on her mind for the entire swim session.

The water didn't do its usual thing of calming her down. She enjoyed the way her body was so buoyant, but she couldn't help stressing over this new worry. *And just after we'd sorted everything else out.* On the one hand, Amber might get bored if her sexual needs weren't fulfilled. On the other, she wouldn't be attracted to Rosie's body as it was now or as it would become post-pushing-a-baby-out.

She managed to put on a brave face for Chelsea. No point in worrying Charlie either yet again. It wasn't really a conversation to have with her sister, and especially not in front of her eight-year-old niece. They splashed and swam and played Tickle the Jellyfish, a game their father had played with them as children, and one Rosie intended to play with her baby.

Alone again in her car with hair damp, she bit her lip until she tasted blood on the way home.

Amber had wanted to cook dinner for her, but Jilly was hosting some sort of poker night at their house, so Amber was bringing something she had made to Rosie's. It made things simpler anyway—they had more privacy at Rosie's, and in the infancy of their relationship, time alone together was paramount.

Rosie stood before her full-length mirror in her knickers. She dried her hair, chlorine still hitting her nose despite the specialised shampoo she'd used. Her belly hung a little, the dark line running from her navel down into her underwear. Her breasts, previously small, rested atop her bump. She tried to make them rounder, held her flesh in either hand and lifted. Wrinkles appeared either side.

She'd put on weight too. Her thighs were thicker, and if she bent her head, a double chin appeared. *What happened to me? I knew my body would change, but I didn't think it would change so much.*

She checked where she'd chewed her lip in the mirror. *Such a state, and on the evening of being wined and dined.* A sigh escaped her before she turned to fumble into an outfit.

Right on time, Amber rang the doorbell. When Rosie went to answer it, she had to smile.

A black skirt, one with a slight sparkle, and a deep red shirt with a black cherry pattern. Her usual shiny shoes. Black tights. A black cardigan in a waterfall cut, which flowed over the skirt from underneath her jacket. Red cherry studs in her ears. Dark make-up.

If Rosie had wondered about her libido lessening due to pregnancy, those worries were dashed. She wanted to grab Amber, pull her inside, and have her up against her white goods. It was a few moments before she managed to step aside and let Amber in.

"Evening." Amber's voice was tentative.

"Oh yeah. Sorry." Was honesty the best policy? Perhaps a joke to lessen the effect. "You look amazing. Hence my inability to articulate."

A giggle. "Well, good because I spent a while on this outfit."

"I'm not saying you don't look sexy as hell most days, Amb, but, seriously, you'll put me into early labour." *Is that my first pregnancy-related joke?*

"Does that happen?" Amber looked more amused than bothered.

"I've no idea. They do say if you're past your due date, getting squelchy might hurry things along a bit."

"That and…" Amber lifted the plastic bag that contained a rectangular dish. "…curry."

"Spicy?"

"Yes, but not hot. Should only take a few minutes, it's already cooked."

Rosie led Amber into the kitchen, and they got the dish in the oven to warm. "Great."

Amber set a timer on her mobile phone, then leaned against the counter, her shoulders up.

A drink. That was what they needed. Shame neither of them could have a whisky. "I got some bits out." Rosie swept her hand across the array of bottles on her counter. "Thought we could make mocktails."

An affectionate smile blossomed onto Amber's face. "I'd like that."

Delicious scents filled the kitchen as they mixed a variety of juices, fruit pieces, and fizzy water into Rosie's blender. They giggled as everything whizzed, then poured the bright-orange concoction into two glasses.

The first taste was sharp and a little too sour. Rosie squeezed a little honey into each.

A lift of her glass suggested Amber was pleased with the final result. "I don't drink mocktails much at home. We usually have Diet Coke and squash or just water with dinner." She sipped. "But this is scrummy."

"I've consumed so much juice in the last few months. I'm surprised I haven't gone tangerine."

Amber laughed.

With the sudden realisation she hadn't kissed her yet, Rosie took the glass from Amber's fingers to set on the counter. She made a gesture with her chin, a question.

Amber slid her hands around Rosie's waist.

A version of Rosie's initial daydream. She had her up against the counter and they were kissing. Amber tasted of cool sweetness. Rosie slipped her hands into her hair, their lips joining over and over, heads tilting and tongues touching.

She tried to push her knee between Amber's, but their hips didn't meet. *Bloody bump's in the way.* Another casualty of her pregnant state. With a deep inhale, Rosie pulled away. Her anxiety returned full force.

Amber caught one of her hands. "You okay?"

"Sure." Rosie pushed her shoulders back as if she had not a care in the world.

Those dark eyes continued to squint at her.

Being scrutinised made Rosie shrink into herself. *I've had far too much of that today.* She was in danger of reopening her lip.

"Hey, come on." Amber moved away from the counter to touch Rosie's shoulder. "One minute you're snogging my brains out and the next you're miles away."

"I'm fine." Rosie swallowed. She waved her hand in the air, palm up. "I went swimming today with my sister." She cleared her throat. "Maybe I'm a bit tired."

Amber caressed the side of her neck. "Okay, we can chill tonight. I don't have anywhere to be." She pursed her lips and her gaze trailed down. "We can cuddle up in front of that film you promised me."

It wasn't a complete lie. Rosie figured she'd need to talk to Amber about it at some point but hopefully not tonight. *It's a second date, isn't it? Or is it a third? This is the kind of thing I'm usually good at remembering.*

The timer went off, and they dished the steaming *bhuna* into two bowls. Amber remembered Rosie's aversion to potatoesand so had brought crusty rolls to go with it.

"Sorry they're not naans." Amber pulled her chair in and smoothed her skirt over her thighs.

"No problem. Wow." The scent of onions, coriander, and tomatoes wafted up from her bowl. "And chicken with a brown-ish sauce. Practically my favourite craving."

"Well, I have a surprise for afterwards, if you can wait that long." Amber's shirt was unbuttoned. A pale cleavage peaked through.

Rosie's mouth watered for more than the curry. She turned her attention back to her food. *I've changed so much—I was more than happy to stare at a woman's cleavage a few months ago. But now, it just doesn't feel right.* The breastfeeding classes had made her think of her own breasts differently—something other than a sexual area. Or maybe her priorities had changed. She was more interested in spending time with Amber, getting to know her, than she was in getting her into bed. If only her body would agree.

"I finish at work next week." Rosie was keen to get the topic of conversation onto something less romantic.

"That'll be nice." Amber's gaze caught on the baby bouncer and the box of soft toys beside the sofa. "Are you all ready?"

"Yeah. Got everything now." She looked up. "I've not shown you the baby's room."

"Oh." Amber grinned. "I'd love to see it once we've finished dinner." A droplet of sauce trickled down her chin and she snorted, grabbing a napkin to clean it off.

"Hey, half this household will be covered in food in about six months' time, so I wouldn't worry."

Amber continued to laugh, her napkin the only barrier between her and Rosie's tablecloth.

"What?"

Finally able to contain her mirth, Amber removed the napkin. "I love that you think you'll be totally not covered in food too when your little one starts eating."

"Good point." Rosie pointed at her, winking. "I'll get some of those plastic overalls they make for painting."

"Maybe just feed her naked. It'll be easier." She swept a hand down her front. "Humans are wipe-clean."

Their chuckles punctuated the otherwise quiet consumption of their meal. Once their bread rolls had been used to wipe the last of the sauce from their bowls, Rosie pushed back her chair. She held her hand out for Amber's bowl.

"Nope. I get to wait on you tonight."

With an eye-roll, Rosie waited for whatever the postdinner surprise was. *Gosh, I hope it isn't some sexy outfit she's brought to seduce me.* Her apprehension increased tenfold, pulse quickening and palms sweating.

The ping of a microwave. The scrape of glass against ceramic.

Amber came back in with a small plate in each hand. She slid one in front of Rosie.

On the plate lay a small glass ramekin which contained a brown and white substance. Chocolate scents drifted up.

It was some kind of sexual potency drug. The velvety chocolate pudding was half mousse, half molten chocolate, with dark, milk, and white in perfect quantities. The minute it touched her tongue, Rosie squirmed in her seat. No amount of sexy lingerie would have been more effective.

To her credit, Amber ate the pudding daintily and with shyness in her eyes. "Is…is it okay?"

"Are you kidding?" Rosie's voice was a lot lower than she had meant it to be. "Amb, this is the most delicious thing I've ever had in my mouth." Her cheeks burned. "You know what I mean."

Amber motioned towards her with her spoon. "Wanted to treat you."

"The curry was fantastic; the pudding is like some kind of liquid ecstasy." She tapped her spoon against Amber's in a weird kind of high-five. "Kudos, gorgeous girl."

Amber smiled and went back to her pudding.

I don't even think she's doing it on purpose. Rosie pressed her thighs together to tame the ache between them. *I haven't been this horny in ages.*

Rosie insisted on helping to clear away. Once everything was done, they took two fresh glasses of mocktail into the living room. Rosie indicated upstairs.

"Oh yes, please. Let's see this baby paradise you've created."

"It's not *Grand Designs*, or anything." *What if she thinks it's stupid? Oh goodness, why didn't I consider other people might see this room?*

The door opened and Amber stepped inside.

Rosie's gaze flicked back and forth between Amber's face and the floor, wanting to see her reaction.

The slowest but most beautiful smile blossomed over Amber's face. She took Rosie's hand.

Tentative relief guided Rosie around the room. "It's a jungle theme. I like animals, and most kids do too, don't they?"

"I guess so. I always wanted to be a leopard in the jungle."

"Do leopards live in the jungle?" Rosie ran her hand over the oak rail of the cot.

"I've no idea."

"I always wanted to be a monkey. You know, mischievous and swinging through the trees."

Amber ruffled the head of a stuffed gorilla, then faced Rosie.

Sliding her hands either side of Amber's waist, Rosie tried to take the room in with fresh eyes. Green painted walls with various animal stickers created a border half way up. Cream curtains with dark green tiebacks. A rocking chair her mother had passed down to her after Charlie had used it with Chelsea. A dinosaur beanbag. Oak changing table and wardrobe, already hung with a few outfits, mostly yellow and green. *No forced stereotypes in this house.*

The rug was her favourite thing, although she knew there'd be a day not so far away when K.B. would deposit some kind of bodily fluid onto it. It was a large lion's head, a smile without scary teeth. Rosie often indulged in daydreams: sitting on the rug with a sixth-month-old, playing Pat-a-Cake or whatever.

It appeared as though Amber was still taking it all in. She played with the ends of Rosie's hair for a while, resting against Rosie's front, no longer shy about leaning into the protuberance between them. "Such a lucky kid."

"Reckon?"

Shared, slow breathing. The shade on the overhead light cast star-shaped patterns across the walls. It seemed, for the moment, that Rosie's libido had quietened.

They traipsed back downstairs. Lights needed dimming and curtains needed closing. Rosie's slippers scuffed the carpet as she moved to each.

When all was ready, she turned to find Amber curled up on her sofa. "Hi."

"Hi." Was she still blissed out from seeing the baby's room?

Rosie handed two DVDs to Amber before she plonked next to her. "You choose. I've seen both of them."

Amber hummed as she scanned both covers. "What do you think, K.B.?" She lowered her head to Rosie's belly. "One about two youngsters from different worlds who become unlikely friends, or a potential child-abduction mystery with action and a piss-take of AA?"

"Interesting descriptions of Disney films."

Amber shrugged. She moved closer to K.B. and, in a gentle tone, began to read the whole blurb for the first film. She stroked Rosie's belly with the back of her hand. Her voice lilted as if she read directly to the baby.

K.B. wiggled, then shifted, which made Rosie wince.

In a flash, Amber sat up. "All right?"

"She likes your voice, I think."

One thin eyebrow arched. The side of Amber's mouth quirked. "I guess *Finding Nemo* it is."

Rosie went to put the DVD on. "You don't mind?"

"I like the ocean bits; they make me sleepy." She laughed. "In a good way. I'm not going to snore on you or anything."

On return to the sofa, Rosie grabbed the throw off the back and tucked it around them. She pressed *play* on the remote.

Rosie rested her arm along the back of the sofa, around Amber's shoulders. Dark hair tickled her nose when Amber snuggled against her side, her knees bent against Rosie's thighs.

Much manoeuvring took place during the film. In the end, they lay down with Amber on her side, her back against the back of the sofa and her arm slung around Rosie's middle. Rosie half sat, half lay against the arm rest, and all the cushions she owned supported her spine.

K.B. settled but continued her fluttery movements. A couple of times, Amber pressed her palm to where the movements had been before softening. Soon, she trailed lazy circles atop the blanket over any place K.B. moved.

Unfortunately, this almost platonic caress reignited Rosie's arousal. She wanted to groan, to guide Amber's hand downwards; she didn't even care it might be through her jeans. She wanted to rock her hips and arch her back, anything to ease the ache between her legs. Even her breasts cried out for attention.

I want her to go home. But I don't want her to go home. We're having an excellent time, but I don't think I can last much longer. Her earlier nerves about being naked in front of Amber resurfaced.

When she couldn't stand it anymore, and way before the film was due to finish, she moved Amber's hand away.

"Sorry." Amber lifted her head and furrowed her brow.

"It's fine." Rosie wasn't sure her smile reached her eyes.

Amber rose and paused the film. The blue fish on the screen stilled, mid-whale-impression. Amber gave Rosie a look that could only mean, "Start talking."

"It's not really something I'm comfortable talking to *you* about."

"Why not?" Lowered eyelashes and pink cheekbones.

Rosie stood and folded her arms. "It's a personal thing." She fidgeted with her fingers and walked over to the TV. Was Dory judging her for her inability to contain her libido?

"Is there anything I can do?"

Rosie's strangled chuckle sounded loud in the quiet room. "Stop touching me."

"What?" Amber sat round on the sofa, her stocking feet dropping to the carpet.

"Just…keep your hands to yourself, yeah?" What was this anger that rose within her?

"I thought we were… I thought that was okay?" Amber's eyes sparkled.

It made Rosie's anger grow.

She threw up her hands and marched around the room. "You're just… you're sitting there, and I'm, like, this massive bowling ball, and you just… Your hands are all over me."

"I was touching the baby."

"Yeah, well, it's my skin, not K.B.'s you're feeling up. Just stop it."

"I wasn't feeling you up."

Rosie stomped into the kitchen.

She opened the fridge, just for something to do. Surely, she could check her milk was out of date or something?

She needs to stop touching me before I go insane. The heaviness between her legs was uncomfortable. Relief was nowhere in sight, and that just made her more irritated.

She kicked the bottom of the fridge hard enough to make a noise. She put her hands over her face and slumped against it.

Footsteps into the kitchen, then a soft-as-rose-petals hand pulled her fingers from her face. Amber's eyes were so full of concern, so appeasing.

Rosie let out a breath before she held Amber's hand between them. "Sorry."

"I'm sorry. I didn't mean to feel you up."

All her anger fled. "You didn't."

"Do you want to talk about it now?"

Amber led Rosie back into the living room and turned the TV off on their way past. Then she sat on the sofa, knees together and body turned towards Rosie. She lifted Rosie's hand and pressed gentle kisses to her knuckles.

I'm an idiot. Rosie took some time to stare at their joined hands and was relieved when Amber allowed her to do so. Words swam past, tiny flickering fish in an ocean as wide as her mind. It echoed in there with so much uncertainty. "Okay."

Again, Amber's lips remained closed.

"I've been worrying. About…taking you to bed."

"Taking me to…oh." A mixture of realisation and further confusion solidified across Amber's features.

"Oh, indeed." Rosie took a deep breath. "I'm, clearly, a massive blimp right now. And it scares me you might…if we did…go to bed…" She cleared her throat. "Maybe you wouldn't like what you saw."

Amber squeezed her hands.

"And then, if I didn't want to go to bed with you…if I thought maybe we should wait until I'm back with a pre-baby body or whatever the expression is, maybe you would lose interest. Because it would be months probably. Maybe that's like a deal-breaker for you. No sex." She forced herself not to chew on her lip, instead tried to focus on the way Amber's hand felt in her own.

"You think I wouldn't fancy you? If I saw you naked?"

Rosie pushed up one shoulder.

"And if we didn't have sex, I would get bored of you and look somewhere else for it?"

Why can she say the words without stuttering but I can't? I'm supposed to be the confident one here. But things had definitely changed in that respect. Amber had become so much braver in the few months they'd known one another.

"Something like that."

"Hmm." Amber shook her head. "I'm well aware of your pregnant status, in case you haven't noticed. I think you're beautiful."

"You might change your mind when you see me without my clothes on."

"But that's the same for everyone, not just people who are pregnant." Amber's lips pulled upwards. "What if you don't fancy me when I'm naked?"

"What?" Rosie snorted. "Well, I never thought of it like that."

"Have you never been self-conscious when you've first taken a girl to bed?"

"Meh." She shrugged again. "I suppose it's usually about giving the girl a good time. I guess I just assumed if she wants to get naked with me, she already fancies me."

"Okay, so why is it different now?"

Why is *it different now?* Rosie couldn't come up with a logical reason. "I suppose it's not."

"Well, then."

"Yeah, but when I've had the baby, and I'm all postpregnancy and gross, you won't fancy me then."

"I think I will."

"What like...pregnancy is some kind of fetish for you?"

Luckily, Amber laughed. "Fuck off. I fancied you before I knew you were pregnant, I fancied you when I thought maybe you'd put on a bit of weight, I fancy you now, pregnant or not pregnant. Post- or pre-baby. I like your body, but it's not just about that." She nudged Rosie. "Surely you've heard the phrase 'beautiful inside and out'?"

"Bit cheesy." Rosie nudged her back.

In response, Amber smoothed her hands either side of Rosie's neck and pulled her in for a kiss. "I love you and I fancy you. You make me laugh, you make me think, and I reckon you've helped me become a better person."

"Really?"

"Well, I don't think I'd have joined the choir if I hadn't been attracted to you." Amber grinned. "Just don't let it go to your head."

"I'll try not to." Rosie shook her head, attempting to take it all in. *So I worried for nothing, yet again. Maybe I don't give Amber enough credit. That's not the first thing I've kept from her that she turned out to be cool with.*

"So, when I touched you, did it make you uncomfortable?"

"A little bit." Rosie looked away, but Amber caught her chin.

"Why? Don't you want me to touch you?"

"No, I do. I promise I do." She shifted to take both of Amber's hands. "But, I guess, for some reason..." She grimaced. "You were sort of turning me on."

Amber's eyebrows shot up. Her mouth twitched as if she tried to hold in a smile.

"Yeah, okay. Don't let *that* go to your head, okay?"

"I saw on a TV show—don't know which one—that some women get horny when they're pregnant. For a bit of it, anyway."

"Really?" Rosie rolled her eyes. "I just thought it was me being a stud."

"Maybe it's your hormones." At Rosie's look of disgust, Amber chuckled. "Or maybe I'm just really, really sexy." An impish grin.

"The latter is certainly true. And that's not my hormones talking."

"Okay."

"Okay." Rosie smiled at her, locked their gazes together.

Long eyelashes lowered, then something passed over Amber's face, something akin to sadness, maybe part irritation.

"What's the matter?" *Maybe she's having second thoughts. I'm a horny pregnant woman, and she's really not into that.*

"Ah, well, you see, ordinarily I'd be terribly chivalrous and alleviate any discomfort you're experiencing."

"Would you?"

"Would only be good duty of care."

Rosie snorted.

"But, unfortunately, your hormones have terrible timing."

"You mean in ways other than when you're trying to be nice to my unborn baby?"

Amber tucked a piece of Rosie's hair around her ear, then trailed her fingertips down her neck. "I have my period."

Rosie almost pushed her bottom lip out. Instead, she gave Amber a sympathetic smile. "I didn't think you staying over so soon would be a good idea anyway."

"Didn't you?"

"Okay, the rational part of my brain didn't." She closed her eyes for a moment against Amber's hand. The tickles against her skin only made her tingle rather than cranking up her arousal.

"I was kind of hoping I *could* stay. Maybe." Briefly, Amber looked down, the sad expression on her face again.

"Maybe just, like, with actual sleeping?"

"If that's okay." A squirmy wiggle. "I don't want to impose—"

Rosie cut her off with a kiss, something between bruising and desire-filled. She laughed too when Amber giggled against her mouth.

Once they were settled back on the sofa, Amber had the time to think about it all. *We're definitely communicating better. And Rosie seems a lot more relaxed now that I'm not adding to her arousal.* That made her giggle inside—that she had such a dramatic effect on Rosie. Her hands would have to remain still until they were at a place they could follow things through.

She'd imagined sex with Rosie—she wasn't a fool and had an active imagination. It was usually a hindrance to her well-being, making her envisage worst-case scenarios, but lately it had been fantasies, visions of what it might be like.

A quick search of the internet had brought up a stack of photos of women in their third trimester, just so she was prepared. It wasn't difficult to imagine Rosie without clothes on—the bits of her that were different now were obvious even when she was fully dressed. Big belly, big boobs, and she'd have to be gentle, talk to her about what was okay to do. She didn't want to cause any more stress and, even though Rosie had assured her she didn't need to change any of her behaviour after her visit to the hospital, there was no way Amber wanted to do anything that would put Rosie at risk.

They adopted their original positions on the sofa, although Rosie was more on her side now, facing away from Amber. Amber was the big spoon, their hips aligned, their feet touching. Rosie smelled like a whole mixture of things: chocolate, spices, and a scent that was all Rosie.

Amber rested a hand against Rosie's hip, and she had to make a conscious effort to not move it. The ocean scenes in the film relaxed her. The body in front of her softened with each passing minute too.

Bliss was this: holding the woman she loved close and just being with each other. No choir as a common focus, no public places where they needed to worry about being watched, and no secrets. Amber wasn't naïve; she knew there'd be bumps in the road, but right this minute life was heaven.

The end credits rolled. Rosie's hips rocked forward and back.

Amber moved so she wasn't touching her. "Sorry."

But Rosie was dancing to the music, which was impressive in her position. A low chuckle rumbled from her before she sat up. She turned to smile at Amber, and when her gaze rested on her, the humour fled her expression. What was left glowed care and affection.

Under scrutiny, Amber's cheeks became hot. She pulled Rosie's hand to her lips. "Nice evening." She checked the clock by the fireplace. "It's only eight o'clock."

Lines flickered like candle flames between Rosie's eyebrows.

"Oh." Amber put her feet onto the floor and sat up too. "I'm guessing you go to bed fairly early these days."

A single nod. "I don't want to throw you out though."

"You wouldn't be." Amber yanked a smile onto her face. "But it's okay if you want to be alone tonight."

"I really don't." Rosie snorted. "I would like you to stay. Are you okay with keeping your hands to yourself?"

"I don't think it's going to be me that has the issue." Amber poked Rosie's side.

Rosie rubbed Amber's lower back. "True. I mean, are you okay to stay? You've got enough…stuff?" She chewed her lip.

"Always do. You've been on the receiving end of that little perk."

With a groan, Rosie stood.

The instinct to help her was strong, but Amber made sure she kept it under wraps. "Okay. So long as you have a set of pyjamas I can borrow."

"Several." She collected their glasses, which still had remnants of their mocktail antics in the bottoms, and went to switch off the TV and DVD player on the way to the kitchen.

Rosie pottered about downstairs, sorting out various things before she led Amber up. Flippant gestures indicated the bathroom. She found a brand new toothbrush in her bathroom cabinet and unwrapped it. "If you, um, want to leave it here, that's totally okay."

"That'd be nice."

More oak furniture was in the master bedroom; a pale duvet set with a large grey blanket on the end. A long pregnancy pillow lay lengthways on the left side of the bed. Small pieces of artwork, mostly cross-stitches of inspirational messages. Amber was surprised to only see one frame that contained something religious.

Rosie pointed towards the frame. "My mum does them. That's the oldest—I think she made that one when I went to uni. I suggested it would be nice if she did ones that didn't contain references to God."

"Do you believe in God?"

Rosie shrugged. "I guess I believe in something. Not the one my dad does—with his job it's kind of a prerequisite, but he never forced it on either of us. I guess that's a blessing in itself."

"I believe in something too. With AA, you have to relinquish yourself to a higher power, whatever that might be. I think for me, it's the universe. Or nature. Something big, but not with a human face."

A hum suggested Rosie understood. "Anyway, pyjamas?" She went to her chest of drawers and pulled out a T-shirt and some trousers. "These okay?" After handing the pyjamas to her, Rosie went out to use the bathroom.

They were dark blue and flowed like liquid but had a stretchy waistband. Once Rosie returned, Amber took them into the bathroom and got ready for bed. She squinted into the mirror above the sink and damned herself for not packing make-up remover.

When she re-entered the bedroom with her clothes over her arm, Rosie was already in bed, the duvet up over her bump.

"Do you have any wipes or anything? If I don't take my make-up off, I'll look a complete state tomorrow."

Rosie reached into her bedside unit and pulled out a pack. "Use as many as you like."

"Thank you." Stooping at the mirror on Rosie's dressing table, Amber rid herself of a potential panda-eyes occurrence in the morning. Her stomach tensed as she took in her own acne scars, which littered her cheeks and chin as if she'd been into battle. A deep breath sorted out her nerves; after all, she'd assured Rosie it didn't matter what she looked like, so she was certain Rosie would say the same about her skin. "I don't think you've seen me without make-up."

"Or you, me."

On inspection, Rosie's lack of make-up revealed a nose dusted with freckles. She wore a huge T-shirt with a dinosaur on the front. Amber threw the used wipes into the bin and slid into bed on the other side.

Almost on autopilot—how had that happened?—Amber placed her hand on the top swell of Rosie's belly. "She asleep or giving you grief?"

"She's good right now." Rosie's gaze dropped to Amber's lips.

Amber didn't want to ask; it felt far too contrived. Did Rosie want to kiss her? Would it make her too uncomfortable? She leant in, intending on simply a peck.

Rosie tasted like mint, all fresh. She held Amber close and steady. What would have been a chaste brush of lips became something a lot deeper.

When she broke away, Rosie's jaw was clenched. "Sorry."

Amber shook her head. "I like to kiss you. It doesn't make me uncomfortable. I'm on day four."

"Aha, the dreaded counting of days." Rosie closed her eyes. "Checking my cycle every five minutes so the donor could pop round on his way home from work when I was ovulating."

"I guess there must be lots of prep for that kind of thing."

"There is. Bloody straight couples have it so easy." Rosie shifted to lie with her head on her pillow. "Very much worth the extra maths though."

"I'll bet." Amber's pillow was cottony against her cheek.

"Have to sleep on my side these days." Rosie patted the pregnancy pillow. Disappointment shone in her eyes, but it was cut short by a wide yawn.

"We can cuddle like that, if you like?"

With a smile, Rosie turned to bend her knee over the pillow, her back yet again to Amber.

Such an invitation. Amber shifted her pillow closer to Rosie's and curled up behind her. She moved a hand around Rosie's waist before kissing the back of her neck. "Love your T-shirt, by the way."

The bump hitched a few times. "Yeah. Men's XXL. Only thing I can get on that isn't a cutesy nightgown."

"Suits you."

Another yawn. Some shifting around—something she would undoubtedly do until K.B. came into the world—and then Rosie lay still. Ribs expanded, and when she exhaled Rosie sounded as if she were sinking into a bed made of cloud.

"How you doing? Still horny?"

"A bit. I'll live though."

"I'll try not to make it any worse."

"Thank you."

"I hope you sleep well."

"You too." Rosie cupped the back of Amber's hand, her palm warm. She wiggled her hips back against Amber's. "Sorry."

"Stop it. It's fine." Amber squeezed her and closed her eyes.

Something about being there, snuggling, so much warmth and safety, meant that Amber drifted off with no hesitation.

Chapter 29

It had been difficult extricating herself from Amber's arms to use the toilet in the night. Amber barely stirred, just folded herself back around Rosie on her return.

The sunshine through the curtains suggested a beautiful Sunday morning. Rosie rolled onto her back and stretched. Her bladder complained yet again, but the rest of her was so comfortable. With regret, she slid out and padded to the bathroom.

Seven more weeks to go. Apart from a few packs of newborn nappies and choosing an outfit for her to labour in, Rosie was sorted. She'd always been the kind of person to prepare well and this was no exception. Her bag was packed, and Charlie was on standby to come get her and stay with her throughout.

Rather than turn on the light and wake Amber once she was done, she tiptoed back to bed in the dim light and climbed back in.

Immediately, Amber inhaled and shifted against her pillow. "Hi." Sleep-dusted eyes and a croaky voice—not unsexy at all. The fact she'd slept over, in Rosie's bed, diminished any effect her hair's disarray had on Rosie's opinion of her.

She couldn't help it. "Awesome bed hair. You look like Animal from The Muppets."

Amber's smile brightened. "Yeah, that happens." She shrugged before wrapping her arm around Rosie's bump and snuggling into her hair. "Did you sleep okay?"

"I slept fine. Took me a while to get to sleep because, you know, I'm not used to sharing my bed with anyone."

"Me neither. Except for the occasional night with Nico on my feet. He's such a duvet-hogger."

"Is he?"

"Don't be fooled by his cutesy demeanour. He's a selfish little devil deep down."

Rosie turned her head to nuzzle Amber's nose. "You got anything to do today?"

"Housework, the usual stuff. And then a walk on the seafront with Nico and the boys."

"Harry and…Matthew, right?"

"That's right."

A pause. Rosie got the feeling Amber was thinking by the sideways slide of her eyes.

"Would you like to come too?"

Her lip in her teeth, Rosie winced. "Would I be welcome?"

Amber kissed her jaw. "I've invited you. So, yes."

"They don't…" She gazed into Amber's dark eyes, noting the white flecks that dotted the skin of her cheeks. *Someone had acne as a teenager.* "They don't hate me for the stuff I've put you through?"

"Matthew might, but he's prone to grudges." At Rosie's pout, Amber smiled. "But the minute he meets you, I expect he'll love you. And Harry's my best friend. I'd like you to meet him."

She took a big breath before gripping Amber's fingers. "Okay."

"Good." After kissing her one last time, this time on the cheek, Amber slipped out of bed. "Just using the bathroom."

"But then you're coming back to bed, right?"

"Do I have a choice?" A cheeky something flared in Amber's eyes.

"No." Rosie flicked up one eyebrow, some of her old cockiness returning.

It seemed to have an excellent effect on Amber because, as she got to the door, she threw a wink over her shoulder.

Rosie held in a squeal, allowing her toes to curl and her fingers to sink into the sheets. Amber was here in her bed with her. They were dating and Amber had slept over. Things moved in the correct direction. She just needed to make a good impression with her friends now.

Nico ran after his ball, kicking up sand under the pier. Rosie was disappointed she couldn't reach down to throw his ball for him—her belly was too big and the manoeuvre too awkward. *Later, matey. Once I'm no longer with child, I shall play fetch with you until your heart is content.*

Two men walked towards them. One had dark curly hair; the other was blonde with striking blue eyes. Curly-Locks appeared older, more her own age than Amber's. He shook her hand and gave her a big smile.

Matthew was slightly more reserved in his welcome, as Amber had predicted. But he still gave her a little wave and a polite nod.

Once they'd managed to clamber out of each other's arms and Rosie's lovely warm bed, Amber had driven them both back to Amber's to collect a plastic bag which contained something flat and oblong and, of course, Nico.

Amber held the oblong out to Harry. "I made you something."

Harry let out a noise like an owl. "What could this be?"

"Late Christmas present. Or it could be an early birthday present."

"Can I see too?" Matthew stuck his head over Harry's shoulder.

Ripping ensued until Harry pulled out a canvas. A photograph of him and Matthew, their lips millimetres apart, perhaps postkiss. The sun caressed their cheeks, the wooden slats of a fence a blur between them. A black-and-white horse stood in the distance.

The look of absolute dumbfoundedness was comical. Harry held the thing at arm's length and just stared at it. "You sneaky little thing. When on earth did you take this?"

"Few weeks ago. That day I took pictures of Florence."

"No way." It was Matthew's turn to gawp. "That's literally going up on the wall the minute we get home."

Harry snorted. "You own picture hanging paraphernalia, do you?"

A *pfft* noise. "I can supervise. You can hammer."

Harry stepped into Amber's arms. "You," he kissed the top of her head, "are the photography queen." He moved back, thumbed her cheek, and grinned. "It's beautiful. Thank you."

"You're welcome." Amber's expression was all sunshine. She pushed her shoulders towards her ears and stooped to grab Nico's ball. He yapped at her feet until she threw it.

Harry inched the canvas back into the plastic bag, still shaking his head in wonder. "One day you'll be one of these professional artists with galleries all over the place."

Amber waved him away. "I just like to do it for my friends."

Matthew tripped up beside Rosie and nodded towards Amber. "You should do a shoot with Rosie. Get some excellent pregnancy photos."

"Now, come on. Rosie's not into things like that." Hope sparkled in Amber's eyes though.

Something to consider. Especially in the next couple of weeks, when I'm as big as I'll get.

They continued along the sand, under the steel skeleton of the pier, where much of the debris and driftwood collected after a high tide. A smile tugged Rosie's cheeks as Amber appeared at her side, hand fitting snugly into her own. They kept a good pace and Rosie was determined to keep up.

After a while though, she was defeated. "Guys, can we slow down a bit? I've got extra baggage."

"Sorry, lovely." Harry dropped back and held a hand out, as if to cradle her at her back. He didn't touch her though, and Rosie got the impression it had been a gesture of chivalry.

They made their way to the Marine Lake, encountering the first few people with children playing on the sand. It wasn't yet the Easter holidays, so these were simply locals out for some fresh air.

A little boy ran past them with a football, his small sister hot on his heels. "If you can catch me, I'll let you score a goal."

"Simon, no fair! Your legs are bigger than mine!"

Chuckling, Rosie swung Amber's hand as they scuffed the sand. "All that to look forward to."

Harry followed her gaze. "Do you want just the one child? Or do you have plans for more?"

It was a personal question, intimate for a first meeting, but he seemed genuinely curious. "Just one at the moment. But I've not ruled out having two. I think I'd stop there though. Keep up with the family tradition."

"I'm an only child." Matthew flinched as the football sailed a metre away from his ear. "I always wanted a sibling."

"Me too," Amber said. "Although, who knows? I might have hated a brother or sister."

"I suppose you never know, do you?" Harry's curls bounced as he jogged up to the forgotten football and tapped it with the inside of his foot.

The ball skidded across the sand, and the little girl grabbed it with a triumphant hoot.

Amber squeezed Rosie's hand and sent her a smile.

The walk back along the beach, under the pier, and up the slope onto the promenade was filled with chatter and jokes. Rosie enjoyed Harry's more mature humour but was enamoured by Matthew's willingness to be silly and play around. She could see why they were such a good match—they complimented one another, being near-opposites. It made Rosie hopeful she and Amber would continue to grow together as a couple.

She got a hug from both boys when they parted, and a thumbs-up towards her bump from Harry. He clutched his canvas and gave Amber the most excited grin before they walked towards their car.

With her fingers slotted between Amber's, Rosie led them along the prom towards Jilly's little white car. The comfortable companionship that flowed between them made Rosie's heart skip. It was so easy to imagine them as parents together with two children, bio-mum to each, maybe. Amber was so beautiful, and any child she produced would be an absolute stunner.

Rosie could think about these things, of course, but there was no way she'd voice them yet. *Slow and steady, that's what we're doing.* It didn't help that the sun was out, the noises of kids playing on all sides hinting at such a future.

Amber's smile lasted until she pulled the car up to Rosie's house. Nico's tongue was out, his paws on the passenger-window ledge. "Thanks for having him on your lap." Amber curled her fingers into his harness and pulled him to her own side of the car.

Leaving Amber without a proper kiss was not in Rosie's plan. She ignored the doggy tongue that poked at her hand as she gathered Amber up and locked their lips together.

Amber gave as good as she got, small sounds of enjoyment vibrating through her. She was the one to break away. “Nico’s foot is in my groin.”

“How rude.” Rosie gave the dog a pat, then shuffled to open the door. “Oh, it’s our usual day to meet up tomorrow.”

“You should have an evening off.” Amber kept hold of Nico as he struggled, clearly wanting to follow Rosie out of the car.

“Sure?”

“We can do something next weekend.”

“Okay. Text me, yeah?”

“I will.”

Rosie closed the door.

Amber secured Nico to the seatbelt in the passenger’s seat and waved at Rosie before turning the car back on.

As she drove off, Rosie touched her lips, and a sudden rush of affection passed through her. And there was that arousal again. *I’m going to have to do something about that tonight. Perhaps next weekend, we can sleep together again and…*

Imagination now at full-throttle, Rosie made her way through her front door. *An early night is definitely in order.*

Chapter 30

That Friday, Rosie waited for Amber by the AA meeting room door.

Amber went straight up to her and kissed her full on the lips. Rosie clutched the small of her back, so Amber tilted her head and smoothed her hands around Rosie's neck.

Needing eye contact, Amber broke the kiss but remained close, breathing Rosie's air. "Hi."

Rosie swallowed but apparently gathered enough self-control to smile at her.

A group of people exited, and one nudged Rosie's back as they brushed past, causing her to stumble.

"I've got you." Amber dropped her hands to her waist. She pouted, sending whoever had pushed Rosie irritated thoughts.

A look of appreciation from Rosie. "Sorry. I'm all off-balance."

"Fall into my arms any time you like." Amber winked, and they walked down the short corridor. "How're you?"

"Massive. K.B.'s really slowed down too. I was a bit worried for a while, but turns out it's just because she's all smooched up in there." Rosie took Amber's hand and led it to her belly.

Standing at Rosie's side, with no one in the corridor to see them, Amber closed her eyes. Under her fingers, something popped up: perhaps an elbow, perhaps a foot. It trundled around an inch or so before smoothing out.

"I think she knows you now. She knows when you're there."

"Do you think she recognises my voice? In her little watery cave?"

Rosie's cheeks pinked. "Maybe she notices when my heart speeds up."

"You're such a romantic."

A wide shrug, hands out. "What can I say? I'm a stud."

Stud, my arse. But Amber didn't tease her.

"This is my last rehearsal until post-baby."

Amber's heart fell, but she collected all the positive thoughts she could muster. "That's okay. Are you going to make the concert in ten weeks?"

Another shrug. "I want to but…" Rosie made a nasally sound. "Unless Enid doesn't mind me singing whilst breastfeeding…"

"Way to make an artistic statement." Amber smirked. "Get your best singer to play the part of the mother, actually on stage."

"I don't think the Colston Hall is quite ready for my tits."

I'm ready for them. Amber thanked the universe Rosie couldn't hear her thoughts. She took Rosie's hand and led her into the hall. "Let me get your chairs."

"Amb…"

But Rosie wasn't going to lift a finger. *Not if I can help it.* She'd pamper Rosie during the evening too, after rehearsal. Even if Rosie didn't want her to.

"I was going to say Lorna could do that, but thank you."

Amber bowed, shiny shoes squeaking on the dusty floor. "I have some massage oils in my bag. For later, you know?" She pulled her mouth to one side and looked at Rosie from under lowered lashes.

Rosie's entire face reddened. "Trying to get me into bed, Miss Kingsley?"

"Only if you're comfortable." She made sure her smile was caring, gentle. "I want to give your muscles some relief." *So many of her texts this week have been about how stiff she feels. I want to help.*

Rosie nodded, sat, and got out her folder. "Seems kind of pointless being here, if I might not be at the concert."

"You're part of what makes this choir great though, aren't you?" Amber perched beside her. "You're here for moral support."

"I'll get tickets. Even if I am attached boobily to a baby."

Amber snorted and glanced at the place she and Hayley usually sat. "I'll um…" She motioned towards it and stood to collect two more chairs.

The choir was now quite sure of all six movements of *Lullaby of the Ocean.* Amber had listened carefully over the last few weeks, when she hadn't been dealing with the drama between her and Rosie, and had practised at home. She'd even taken her music to Fiona's and pleaded for some clarity on a few sections. Fiona, a musician herself, was able to hum the tune to the bits Amber wasn't sure about. *Such great luck my sponsor used to play the French horn.*

Section one, "Leaving Home", was a sad piece, in something Fiona explained was a minor key, but finished on a happier set of notes. It made Amber think of sacrifice, and the words pointed to a mother deciding between her parents, siblings, family, and her partner, a long way away. It was slow and had lots of long notes where the choir needed to do "staggered breathing"—where individual members would breathe at different points of a note to make it carry on longer.

"Casting Off", in contrast, was joyful, bouncy. It sounded as if the inhabitants of the island were holding a farewell party. The tempo continued into the third part, "Stormy Waves", but here they encountered a minor key again, and there were parts of the song the choir were meant to wail. It was a strange thing to do when Enid usually encouraged them to sing with good tone.

A long pause after that part. Then, a soprano voice sang alone. *This would have been Rosie's part. I wonder who will take it for the concert.* For now, the front row of sopranos sang the tune and the back two rows pitched in with the hummed accompaniment.

Amber struggled to hear the original words; Rosie's plea for her forgiveness was louder in her mind than that of the entire choir. When she looked over, Rosie and she shared a smile.

Part five was quicker, livelier, and full of hope. "Sight of Land", with its tenor solo, taken by Gareth, Amber's old water-cooler buddy, spoke of the mother and her baby seeing their new home for the first time, a speck on the horizon. It rose in a crescendo until it burst to life, her new family taking her within their arms.

"Home With My Love" did not specify the gender of the mother's partner, the baby's other parent. Amber hadn't noticed this before, and as they sang the gentle and loving section, she wondered at Enid's choice. *Did she pick it especially for the LGBT community? Did she want to provide the choir with something inclusive, something to show the audience everyone is welcome in the world?* As she gazed at Enid, her gnarled fingers covered in rings, she wondered about her life.

Once they'd gone through the whole thing, it was past time for a break. "I do need volunteers for the soprano solo though." Enid cast her gaze around the sopranos. "If no one comes forward, I will have to choose for you."

Hayley's hand shook as she filled her bottle at the cooler. "What do you…?" She cleared her throat. "Um…what do you think about maybe… maybe me saying I could do it?" Her eyes flicked back and forth, unable to settle.

"Absolutely." There was no point in responding with hesitancy. Hayley would need a confidence boost if she was serious.

"Are…are you sure?"

"Do you really want to do it?" *She does sing very nicely. I can picture her on stage, doing the solo.*

Hayley gulped. "I…I don't know. Yes. Maybe." She eyed the warblers on the other side of the room.

Amber gave Hayley an encouraging expression. "Then you should definitely go offer your services."

"Shall I go now?"

Amber nodded.

Off Hayley hopped, her bottle clutched in both hands.

"What's that about?" Rosie snuck up to Amber's side.

"Hayley's going to volunteer for the solo."

The breath that whooshed out of Rosie ruffled Amber's hair. "Thank goodness."

"Yes, I did think that myself." They grinned at one another. "It'd be good for her anyway. Let alone the service she's doing to the community."

"Stopping Linda from warbling her way through it? She deserves a medal."

They leaned against a table. Amber inched her hand across Rosie's, traced her knuckles with feather-light touches.

All too soon, it was time to go through the parts they weren't sure of.

During a break between pieces, Hayley whispered, "She said yes." She had developed a new energy. She sat up taller, opened her mouth more widely, and looked at the music less frequently.

"Let's try 'Lullaby'." Enid motioned for Hayley to stand by her. "And, sopranos, please sing the parts not taken by the soloist."

Hayley fidgeted next to Enid but remained in her place. She held her music so only her eyes were visible.

Enid counted her in.

Her soft voice grew surer as the first verse and chorus finished.

The choir came in underneath her, swelled, and needed to be dampened by Enid's conducting. Hayley wasn't a strong singer, but Enid didn't seem fazed. When the song ended, everyone clapped. Hayley went beetroot and sped to sit back next to Amber.

A few more bits needed going over, then rehearsal was done.

Amber followed Rosie to her car, and then tried not to look at her too much on the drive to Rosie's house.

Spring had sprung on Rosie's street. Pots of spring flowers littered the front gardens like splatters of paint in an artist's studio. All pastel and smooth and elegant. Amber wondered why Rosie didn't have any. Would Rosie want some? Jilly had far too many for their garden.

Rosie made them cups of tea. Her eyes drooped and her shoulders sagged despite her gentle grin. "We can watch some TV for a bit, if you like?"

"Just for a while." Amber took her tea into the living room, Rosie close behind. "Then we're going up to bed."

"Yes, ma'am." Rosie saluted her before she sunk onto her sofa.

Amber pulled a beanbag over, piled it high with cushions, and shoved it under Rosie's feet.

"I love you." It was almost a groan.

Amber giggled and settled on the sofa next to her.

Comedy programmes, something mindless and mellow. The tea filled Amber with a warm haze, her body dipping into the cushions. She put her arm along the back of the sofa and allowed Rosie to lean into her.

It was domestic and docile, with no real agenda. And that was such a change from the women Amber usually dated. She'd had some one-night-stands, usually whilst intoxicated, but they'd been unfulfilling and boring. Now here she was with someone she loved, cuddling her with no intention of doing anything that didn't seem like a natural continuation of this tranquillity.

They finished their teas just as the comedy show ended. Rosie switched the TV off without preamble, and they put their cups away before heading up. As before, Rosie used the bathroom first.

Amber got dressed in Rosie's bedroom, then sat on the bed to wait.

When Rosie re-entered, she had the shyest look on her face. "I, um… go for it." She gestured towards the bathroom.

"You okay?"

Rosie smoothed the large T-shirt over her bump. "Yeah. Got a grumpy cat on this T-shirt."

Amber regarded her with amusement. "I like the dinosaur one better, but that one will do." *Is she nervous? Doesn't she know I'm not going to force her into anything she doesn't want?*

But it seemed presumptuous to bring it up yet again, so Amber went to brush her teeth and take off her make-up.

As on the week previous, Rosie had covered her bump with the duvet and looked ready to lie down when Amber came back in. She gave Amber a little one-fingered wave.

"How's your back?" Amber went to her handbag to put her wipes away but waited by it.

A huge sigh. "I worry."

"You worry? About your back?"

Rosie snorted. "A massage sounds amazing. But I'm not sure I…" Her lip went between her teeth. "Amber, I don't want you to feel like you need to…"

Amber went over to the bed, the bottle of oil in her hand. "Are you… Do you think I'd feel obliged to have sex with you if you got horny whilst I was giving you a massage?"

One shoulder pushed up. "Kind of."

Amber smoothed Rosie's shoulder until Rosie relaxed. "You have the power in this: you've got the body that's big and uncomfortable and feels awkward."

"Hardly fair."

"Completely fair. You're growing a fricking baby inside you. And I'm grown-up enough to know what I want, so don't deny yourself something I want to give you."

"You—you *want* to have sex with me?"

"Have I not made that clear enough to you?"

Rosie stared at her feet.

Amber gave her some time. *It must be so weird in a body you don't recognise. And all her worries about how she'll look if she takes her clothes off, all the stress she feels about it all, it must be so difficult for her.*

"I love you." Rosie turned towards her and caught her chin. "I don't want you to feel like you have to touch me yet if..." A shrug. A nervous laugh.

"Trust me. I do."

Finally, Rosie's lips tugged into a smile. "You know what? Let's just trust each other. You'll tell me if you don't want to do something, right?"

Amber smacked a palm against the bed. "My thoughts exactly." She twirled a finger in the air. "Now, come on. Can you lie on your front?"

"Sort of." Rosie shuffled down the bed, her pregnancy pillow under one arm. She turned half onto her side, one knee bent.

All businesslike, Amber rolled the large T-shirt up as far as it would go. Smooth thighs came into view, as well as a thin backside. The top of Rosie's underpants were those elastic ones with the letters on. It made her smile to know Rosie continued to wear boxer briefs even with her belly as huge as it was.

She started at the base of Rosie's spine. "I've only done this a few times. Tell me if it's nice, okay?"

"I will." Rosie's voice was thread-like, as if she were ready for sleep.

The oil made patterns in the downy hair on the small of Rosie's back. The bumps and valleys of her spine were fun to trace, sweep in and out of, circumnavigate. Areas of tension were easy to spot; Amber had nothing else to focus on apart from the hitches in Rosie's breath and the feel of her skin. When she concentrated on the knots, Rosie made happy noises.

Farther up, larger muscles, a few more places to rub the tautness away. Rosie wiggled a few times, then quietened with a sigh. Each moment of release made her back softer, her muscles less bunched.

When Amber reached her shoulder blades, she found the back strap of a white, heavy-duty bra. She lingered for a moment before tucking a fingertip underneath. "Okay if I undo this?"

A nod into the pillow. Rosie didn't even open her eyes.

With an attempt to be careful, and even though it was wide and had three hooks, Amber managed to unclasp the strap. That gave her more skin to touch, more muscles to ease. She smoothed a few more drops of oil across Rosie's upper back. She dipped under the bunched-up T-shirt and rounded Rosie's shoulders.

A stretch, then a deep inhale. Rosie blinked at Amber.

"Is um…" Amber smoothed her hands over Rosie's shoulder blades. "Was that okay?"

"Do you want to stop?"

"The massage?" Amber smiled down at her. "I can carry on for a while, if you like."

Another stretch, another sigh. "Feels nice. K.B. likes it too."

The large expanse of her belly had disappeared partially against the pregnancy pillow. Amber took a chance and shifted her hands around Rosie's waist. "Hey, little one. You want a massage too?" She dropped her gaze to Rosie's. "That okay?"

A nod.

Amber made gentle circles across Rosie's belly, marvelling at the stretched skin, wondering at how round she was compared to the shape of the baby inside.

Rosie pulled the pillow more securely under her thigh.

Wanting to be closer, to hold Rosie, Amber snuck up to her back and bent her knees under Rosie's.

It was slow and silent. Rosie was warm and heavy against Amber's front. Amber made sure to keep her hand from wandering, just stuck to the skin above Rosie's navel and as far away from her still-in-situ bra as she could. Rosie's ribs expanded and fell. Her arm curled around her pregnancy pillow.

After several minutes, all of which Amber spent burying herself in the combined scent of the oils and Rosie's shampoo, Rosie shuddered.

Amber stilled her hand. "Sorry."

"Were you serious?"

"About what?"

"About…wanting me?"

Amber kissed the back of Rosie's head. "Of course."

Another few minutes of silence, punctuated by a few wiggles. "Goodness, I…"

"Rosie." Amber breathed the name against Rosie's ear. "Do you want me to touch you?"

A tiny, wobbly gasp. Then a nod.

"Where?"

"Seriously?"

"No, I mean…" Amber rose onto an elbow, head in her hand, to look down at Rosie. "I know that—that some women…when they're pregnant they—they don't like to be touched on their breasts."

"Think I'm going to squirt you or something?"

They both laughed.

"I don't know. Will you?"

"My colostrum hasn't come in yet. Thank goodness."

"Well on the off-chance this causes it to, are you okay with that?"

"Are you?"

"I guess so."

Rosie turned more onto her back and pursed her lips. She tucked some of Amber's hair behind her ear. "In that case, I think we should see what happens." A note of unease still sat in her eyes, but her jaw was set and she continued to smile. "But I would like to see you, to be able to touch you as well."

"How can I say no?" Amber wiggled out of her pyjama bottoms, then flicked her eyebrows up. "Ready?"

There was something about the nod Rosie gave her that made Amber relax. *Here we are, then, getting naked. Suppose I'd better put all that time I prepared with internet research to good use.*

Amber inched her T-shirt over her head, making a bit of an inelegant show of it. Figuring she'd want to reclaim the garment later, she shoved it under the pillow. Now only in her briefs, she rolled over to resettle against Rosie's back. "This seemed to work before. Comfortable?"

"Yeah."

"Want help getting your clothes off?"

Rosie swung her heavy body into a sitting position before she lifted her arms. Once Amber had tugged the T-shirt over her head, the bra fell away and Rosie threw it over the side of the bed. She flopped onto her back.

Not wanting to stare, Amber turned her head, lying down to rest on one elbow again.

But Rosie's fingers were at her cheek, allowing her gaze.

Amber had to swallow. Rosie's belly button stood out like the tip of a balloon, which wasn't an inappropriate simile for the rest of her tummy. Her breasts were small in comparison but swollen, nipples dark red, veins just visible under her skin. She was flushed right from her forehead to her cleavage.

"Still fancy me?" Rosie's joke held a hint of worry.

Dropping down and sliding her hand under Rosie's head, Amber took Rosie's lips with her own. As they kissed, she lay against her side, skin against skin. How wonderful it felt. Amber moved her hand back to Rosie's belly, the same circles occupying her whilst they kissed.

This time, Rosie didn't seek sleep. She shivered, and the hairs under Amber's fingertips rose. The residual oil made Rosie's skin silky, as if each touch flowed like a stream. When she slid her fingers up towards Rosie's breast, Rosie undulated and moaned against Amber's lips.

After breaking the kiss, Amber snuggled down, her nose against Rosie's ear. "Talk to me. I don't want to do anything you don't like."

Rosie took a few slow breaths, as if she tried to calm herself.

This seemed like a sensible idea, so Amber made her caresses more leisurely, softened her whole hand. She lingered over the patch of skin below the crease under Rosie's breast. This meant when she moved upwards, she touched the swell, Rosie only reacted with a peaceful sigh. "That's good."

Amber painted lines with the oil, back and forth, then slipped up and around Rosie's nipple. "You feel nice." She kissed below Rosie's ear.

Rosie turned her head and smiled. "The oil is lovely."

"Lavender. I checked—it's okay when you're pregnant."

"I might…I might borrow it, if that's okay? For when I'm in labour. Or I could give you some money to get me some—"

Amber placed a finger over Rosie's lips, then traced the edge of her areola.

It puckered at her touch and Rosie's breath rushed from her.

"You okay there? You want to lie on your side again?"

With a nod, Rosie rolled away from her and draped a thigh over the pillow again. Amber's hand got squashed between the pillow and Rosie's breast, causing her palm to touch Rosie's nipple with pressure.

Rosie moaned and arched her back.

Figuring that was a good sign, Amber rubbed Rosie's nipple in circles. She couldn't tell whether she'd caused anything to happen, assumed she hadn't. She wasn't sure what it would feel like anyway. Wasn't sure if this was the kind of thing that *would* cause it.

"Keep doing that." Rosie rocked her body back and forth in encouragement.

Amber rolled and rubbed, her lips brushing Rosie's shoulder. The moan that fell from her own lips was genuine and unintentional. Until now, Amber hadn't registered her own arousal. Pressing her front against Rosie's back, she pushed her knee between Rosie's legs.

After pulling her hand out so she could sweep Rosie's hair from her face, Amber pressed a series of kisses against her neck. "So sexy." Her tongue came out to tease the skin where Rosie's neck met her shoulder.

Rosie surged in her arms.

"Sorry." Amber chuckled and went back to Rosie's breast. She cupped the weight of it and pressed her palm against her nipple again.

Rosie's breath became deeper, faster. Her hips rolled, the muscles in her arms tensing.

Amber trailed the back of her hand down Rosie's side, which made her twitch. "It's okay. I'm just taking things slowly."

"Maybe too slowly."

"Is that right?"

"Mm."

Amber smoothed her palm around Rosie's bump and cuddled her close.

This was not the time to become stressed out about how her body would respond when Amber finally put her hand where Rosie wanted it.

Rosie had discovered during the last week or so that her body still desired in the same way it always had. Unease had crept in about her body changing its preferences when it came to sex. All the books mentioned perhaps a difference, one that might not right itself after baby came. The relief she'd remained unaffected meant she didn't need to be anxious. *But what if sex with another person is different? What if my body doesn't do what it usually does?*

There was only one thing she could do—utilise her new breathing techniques and coax herself to relax. It wasn't difficult either; Amber had stilled for the moment, as if she waited for the go-ahead. *She's so sweet. It's as if she knows I need time, whatever I say to her.* Amber's body against her back made her feel safe.

A big breath in was needed. Rosie let it out and, with it, her worries. The feeling of being comforted intensified. *Amber will make sure I'm okay. I trust her to do that.*

Rosie looked over her shoulder and nodded. "I love you." It seemed the perfect time to say it again, not in the throes of passion, or sated among sweaty sheets. Right now, with an understanding between them and the promise of intimacy on the horizon.

"I love you too."

Have we ever exchanged the words in that way?

Millimetre by millimetre, Amber slid her hand south. Tickling patterns made Rosie's skin goosebump. By the time Amber got to the waistband of her underpants, Rosie started to wish she'd already taken them off. But it looked as if Amber wanted to do that herself. Deft fingers tugged, so Rosie pushed her hips in the air as best she could. Amber sat up to pull them down her legs.

She wasn't sure where they ended up. It didn't matter because in the next heartbeat they kissed again, thoroughly, deeply, their tongues just coming out to touch. Rosie couldn't decide which way to go: knee up against the bed, or that leg down and her other foot on the bed.

Amber made the decision for her by hooking her fingers around Rosie's knee and tugging, which meant her foot ended up against the mattress. "Okay?"

"Yes."

"Just lean your weight on me."

"I'll crush you."

"Don't worry about that."

Rosie rolled backwards, her other knee bending too. She was a little exposed, but that worry was a tiny dot, far away.

Amber combed her fingers through Rosie's hair, cupped her whole sex. She was motionless for a while, her kisses insistent but deliciously slow. A gentle dip, a tentative brush against Rosie's inner lips.

Rosie groaned, arched her back.

A breathy giggle from Amber. "So sexy."

I doubt that, but who am I to argue? Rosie curled her toes into the mattress before wiggling calmness back into her body.

As if coaxing a tiny flower to open, fluttery touches started up against Rosie's sex. A rolling caress, back and forth, in and out, like a serious of sighs.

It was exquisite, and had it been nine months previous, Rosie would have begged her to get on with it. But the andante movements made her insides quiver in a new, trickling way she hadn't experienced before. Sparkling pleasure erupted in tiny pings across her sex, like popping candy.

"That's amazing." Rosie needed to move, so she rolled her hips with Amber's rhythm. Forth and back, forth and back; the tips of Amber's fingers pressed against her entrance but didn't go inside.

"Amazing." Amber's dark eyes were wide. Her teeth glinted in a smile that could only be described as beautiful.

Rosie's insides quivered, making her groan.

"More?"

She nodded, allowing her eyes to close and accepting the pleasure without letting it tense her up. The pressure between her legs increased as Amber sped up the fluttering movements. Rosie opened her thighs wider and tilted her hips to meet Amber's fingers. Amber moved her hand forwards, fingertips circling her clit in an agonisingly slow cadence.

It was as if Amber touched every nerve in that brilliant, white-hot bundle. She swept her fingers in different patterns, keeping Rosie at such a height. Rosie wanted to touch her too, to hold her somehow, but she was limited due to being the little spoon. She held Amber's forearm, the one that disappeared between her legs, with sweaty fingers.

The pleasure intensified, her whole sex juddering and quaking in a mass and a mess of sexual desire. She moaned, her hips rolling faster now, wanting and wanting. Amber's breath was against her ear, fast too, the occasional murmur of delight brushing Rosie's skin.

A gush of wetness panicked Rosie for a moment. By Amber's gasp of enjoyment, she figured she was just about to come, that was all.

And her orgasm hit her, colours and emotions and music fizzing through her bloodstream. She arched right back into Amber's arms, her clit on fire and her thighs trembling with the force.

She had to catch her breath. Pelvis still thrusting, she pushed Amber's hand away, too much now, too sensitive. Second by second, her body sank into the bed. Each muscle relaxed in turn.

With a hissed curse, she turned onto her other side so she faced Amber. She touched Amber's chin and gazed into her eyes.

Amber soothed her still oil-slick bump, massaging sweeping circles. "Still reckon I think you're an unattractive bowling ball?"

"Doubtful."

"Good." Amber trailed a free hand down her cheek. "Are…are you okay?"

"What d'you mean?"

"I, um, I didn't hurt you or anything?"

"No." Rosie wanted to joke, to scoff at Amber's care for her. *But how can I when she looks at me like that?*

A moment more of breathing, relaxing, and allowing the sweat on Rosie's skin to evaporate. In fact, after some time, goosebumps rose for a different reason. "Time for some duvetage."

"Bit Baltic." Amber helped Rosie shuffle up the bed and climb beneath the covers. She lay behind her again and snuffled her shoulder. "You smell so good."

"It's the oils."

"Not just the oils." Amber's voice was so soft, as if she wanted to sing Rosie to sleep.

Rosie struggled to get onto her back, then faced Amber. One arm went about Amber's hips; the other fitted itself under her head. "Mind being my pregnancy pillow?"

"Oh, not at all. If you think you'll be comfortable."

"Mm. Definitely comfortable."

Amber heaved a sigh and closed her eyes.

Does she want to go to sleep? Maybe I'm not the only one who's knackered after a long week of work. Maybe that's all she wants to do tonight.

Rosie remembered her promise to trust Amber to say if she didn't want to do something. Because Rosie very much wanted to touch Amber, to make her feel as Rosie had just felt.

So, with a pace a snail would be proud of, she tickled a few circles into Amber's hip. The lace she'd noticed when Amber had doffed her pyjamas was silky under her fingertips. Apart from another deep sigh, Amber didn't react.

With more than a little mischief, Rosie continued the too-gentle caresses across Amber's waist, up to her ribs, down to her navel. Up and down, over and over, until Amber squirmed.

She kept her eyes closed though, the tiniest of smiles pulling her lips.

Rosie took that as acceptance. It was a lazy evening anyway; why increase the speed of things? Slow and steady, even when it came to sex.

Creativity sparked her. She used each part of her fingers, each side and surface, changing the way her touch felt. She varied the pressure too, extra soft, then a firm sweep. Still up and down, up and down, lengthening her sweeps each time.

When she brushed the underside of Amber's breast, she was sure Amber moaned. But Amber was motionless except for the rise and fall of her ribs.

Rosie had been a tease in her time, had held a woman on the brink of orgasm, had become quite good at it with regular lovers. She didn't want to do that with Amber but, again, trusted Amber to complain if it got uncomfortable. Touching Amber like this, with such unhurried experimentation, almost coaxed her own arousal skyward again.

Unable to resist, Rosie pressed her lips to Amber's shoulder, then peppered kisses everywhere she could. She hooked her bent leg over Amber's, trailing her hand higher. Amber's small but soft breast fit perfectly in her hand. The nipple poked her palm.

At last, a long hum that sang of bliss. Amber turned towards her on the pillow, her lashes lowered.

"Not quite ready to go to sleep yet." Rosie didn't want to break the quiet spell.

Another hum, this time of agreement.

Rosie moulded Amber's flesh, marvelling at the curve and at the way Amber continued to make small noises at each new feeling. She honed in on her nipple, brushing it up and down with a fingertip.

A real half-giggling moan.

She kept doing it and Amber's smile widened. Her hair fanned against the pillows, her neck arched just a tad each time Rosie touched her.

"Would it be weird if I kissed you there?"

"'Course not." Amber inched up the bed and cupped Rosie's cheek. She rolled onto her side so Rosie could remain on her side too.

The minute Rosie took Amber's nipple into her mouth, Amber sank her fingers into Rosie's hair. Rosie tried to copy the caresses she'd done with her fingers, the rapid flicking, using just the tip of her tongue.

"Yes." Amber shivered and pushed her chest against Rosie.

Rosie moved to her other breast, giving it the same attention. An idea sprang into her head, something she hadn't even considered.

She shuffled farther downwards on her side. Amber's knees brushed the top of her bump. Her lips trailed with her, down Amber's sternum, down her midline.

Amber pulled for her to come back up.

It's too hot. Rosie pushed the duvet away, intent on her goal now that she had it in sight.

"Rosie." A breathy plea, along with another tug to Rosie's head. "You don't have to…"

"Want to. Unless it's not something you're into?" Rosie smiled up at her, her chin level with Amber's navel.

"Oh, I am. I just don't want you to be uncomfortable."

"Trust me?" And with that, Rosie curled her fingers into Amber's underwear and slid them down her legs.

At the precise level to do so, Rosie moved forward to kiss Amber's belly button and lower. She cupped the back of Amber's knee, and somehow they got into a position where Amber could tilt her hips forwards and Rosie could lift her chin.

Waiting any longer was far too much of a trial, so Rosie wrapped Amber's top leg around her shoulder before resting her cheek against Amber's other inner thigh. One hand cupped her mons, fingers sliding through, urged on by the squeaky moan that hit her ears.

My goodness, she's so wet. She'd hoped for it, but the reality—*she really does fancy me, she really does think I'm sexy*—was like angel song. Rosie touched her for a while, getting her bearings, drawing a mental map of the places Amber liked. She found Amber's entrance and slid a finger inside her.

Amber surged with a gasp. The hand at the back of Rosie's head squeezed.

Two fingers had an even more powerful result—a moan this time, throaty and alto. Rosie started to slide in and out, a lazy rhythm, with the occasional curl on the withdrawal.

Amber rocked her pelvis in circles and her whole body stirred. The black line of hair that ran down the centre of Amber's pubic bone brushed Rosie's nose as she moved in.

At the first touch of Rosie's tongue to Amber's clit, Amber groaned, her hips pressing forward. And she tasted so good, of a million different exotic things but of something so familiar. Rosie flicked her tongue as she had on Amber's nipple, her fingers pumping in and out, in and out. She tried to keep up with Amber's hips, wanted to give her the pleasure she requested.

Soon, they moved as one, Amber's moans bouncing off the walls, the duvet long forgotten. *She's crushing my ears with her thighs, but I don't care. She's the sexiest thing I've ever seen, heard, tasted, smelt. Touching her is like a dream, one I don't want to wake from.*

"Oh gosh, Rosie. Just…" A few gasps, a pant or two.

Rosie pressed, making sure she was inside Amber as far as she could go. She curled and uncurled her fingers, matching the rhythm of Amber's hips. Her tongue flew, no rhythm at all there, flickering like a light bulb on an overdose of electricity.

Amber bent forwards and spread her thighs wide. She moaned on every breath. She clutched Rosie's hair.

And Rosie felt it, wrapped around her fingers like a hundred butterflies, then tugging, pulling her in.

Stillness. The whole of Amber's body was taut except her sex, which quivered and quaked against Rosie's mouth.

A long, held breath. Then a rush as Amber exhaled, low moans now.

Rosie continued to lap at her, easing the pleasure from her, each last drop.

Eventually, they both quietened to rest. Amber soothed gentle lines across Rosie's scalp. Once she lifted her top thigh, Rosie struggled back up the bed, her bump getting in the way.

Their chuckles mixed in the quiet room. The silliness made Rosie tingle in all the right places. Remaining on her side, she opened her arms to Amber.

Amber curled up in Rosie's arms, her breathing still laboured but a great smile creasing her face. Amber settled one of her hands on the side of Rosie's belly, more circles in the half-absorbed oil. "Now we definitely need to sleep."

Rosie pushed away a yawn. "I could go another round."

"Fuck off." There was no malice behind Amber's words. Her hair had taken on that bird's nest quality once more.

"I do need to get up and wash though." Nothing had ever disappointed Rosie more. "It's important."

Amber was immediately out of her arms. "Of course it is."

Rosie touched Amber's cheek. "Doesn't mean I want to. Just need to."

The twinkling smile followed her as she waddled naked out of the bedroom.

Rosie stepped into the shower and made sure all her bits and pieces were clean. Guilt pulled her as she washed away the oil—it smelled so good and felt even better, but it was more important she didn't get an infection anywhere, and she wasn't sure where the oil had ended up.

She made sure everything was dry too before she padded back into the bedroom.

Amber was already out of bed, her pyjamas over her arm. She gave Rosie a blushing smile before leaving to use the bathroom too.

Rosie didn't fancy putting her pyjamas back on but grabbed some clean underpants. The risk of spotting or even sneezing and causing her bladder to embarrass her lingered. Time for the pregnancy pillow. Her bed was especially warm and comfortable. *That'll be the blindingly amazing orgasm. I expect the massage helped too.*

Not long after she'd settled down, a warm body joined her. A kiss to her shoulder, a few wiggles of the bed. The *thuck* of a bottle hitting her bedside table. Underneath the duvet, Amber moved her hand around Rosie's waist. Slick, oiled fingers swept circles into her skin.

How did she know I'd like that? Rosie's eyes started to droop.

Amber's lips tickled her ear. "Just something for K.B. as she's been so good this evening."

The next moment, Rosie fell asleep.

Chapter 31

A TEXT ARRIVED FROM HARRY, wishing her luck. Not that Amber needed it. Rosie's family were under strict instruction to be nice to her.

Since Rosie had gone on maternity leave at thirty-seven weeks, Amber had received a lot more texts from her. They'd spoken on the phone each night, which always left Amber with a massive smile. They'd agreed seeing one another every night was just too much, especially as it was a good half an hour drive between their homes. Weekly was, perhaps, more sensible and in line with their plan to take things slowly.

Rosie wasn't leaving home unless she needed to. It seemed simultaneously strange and prudent to Amber; she hadn't considered Rosie might go into labour whilst out at the shops or visiting a friend. She'd need her hospital bag and the pink file she took to her midwifery appointments. She'd need Charlie to drive her to Ashcombe Ward, where she intended to give birth.

Dates consisted of Amber hanging out at Rosie's house. Rosie assured her that once K.B. was old enough to be left with Grandma, they could go to restaurants and the cinema. Not that Amber minded—this way of getting to know each other was comfortable. They exchanged romance in other ways—a touch to Amber's cheek, a cup of tea Rosie didn't need to get off the sofa for. And Amber massaged some oil into Rosie's bump and shoulders before bed.

Jilly was using her car, so Amber got the train to Yatton Station and walked to Rosie's house. Rosie had assured her she could manage the walk to Charlie's—it wasn't quite a mile away.

They held hands as they stepped onto the pavement and Rosie's garden gate swung closed behind them. "Janet and Olivia—you know, the gay couple I met at antenatal?"

Amber nodded.

"They had their baby. A little boy called Edmond. I think he's named after the character from the Narnia books."

"Oh, that's cute." Amber relished the sunshine. The bulk of her camera, secured and inconspicuous in her handbag, bumped her leg as she walked. The plastic bag with the heavy gift inside sat next to the camera. "I like old-fashioned names."

"I teach an Iris and a girl called Darcy. I think those names are coming back."

Amber nudged her hip. "Have you chosen an old-fashioned name for K.B.?"

A snort. "You *still* don't get to know."

Good job she knows I'm teasing. "Whilst you were in the bath last weekend, I got one of your baby books down, gave it a read."

"Did you?"

With a one-shouldered shrug, Amber made a little skip along the concrete. "Well, figured it would be handy to know a few things. In case I'm so good in bed you drop K.B. on the bedroom floor."

"What did you learn?"

"The LGBT book was interesting. I didn't know you could breastfeed even if you've never given birth."

"Yeah. The human body, eh?"

"Magic."

A pause and a sideways glance from Rosie. "You, um, you don't want to try, do you?"

Amber put up her free hand. "Oh, no. That's definitely your job. But if you ever express and want me to…you know, if I'm round yours and you need a nap…"

I hope she doesn't think I'm stepping on anyone's toes. I'm well aware her sister and mum—and dad, if I'm honest—get first dibs on feeding the baby if she needs a break.

Rosie led them up the front path of a bungalow lined with sturdy wooden arches bursting with deep purple clematis.

A woman who looked nothing like Rosie but exactly like the picture of Charlie on Rosie's phone opened the door. "Pleb!"

"Dipstick!" Letting go of Amber's hand, Rosie stepped into Charlie's arms.

"And this must be…Amy? Anna? Adam?"

Amber shrunk in her shiny shoes.

"Just kidding. Nice to meet you, Amber."

"Oh." Amber let out a bark of a laugh. "Um, hi."

"Well, come in, come in. Welcome." Charlie's golden ponytail flicked high as she ushered them inside.

The hallway was cream with a dark dresser to one side and a coat stand on the other. Amber followed Rosie's example and hung her jacket up, cringing at how cheap the fake velvet looked against the varnished mahogany. At least Rosie's coat was real leather.

The scents of roasting meat, an array of vegetables, and some kind of fruit pudding drifted through. Amber's mouth watered—she loved a roast, especially when it was cooked with skill. Her grandma cooked a great roast—used to anyhow. The kitchen was around the same size as Jilly's and contained a man in a flowery apron.

"My husband, Tom. He's the chef in this house." Charlie plucked at his shirt with beautifully manicured fingers.

He smiled at Amber, gave his wife a kiss. He clapped his oven mitts at Charlie. "Mind the kitchen shark."

Charlie rolled her eyes but her smile was bright.

An older gentleman entered, a bottle of wine in his hands. "Did you get a new corkscrew, Char?" He startled but smiled as he caught sight of the new arrivals. "Rosie!"

"Hi, Dad." They exchanged a hug.

Nick Tanner had a vicar's dog collar through his pale blue shirt collar. He had a warm demeanour as if everything was a delight. When his gaze moved to Amber, she was no exception. "This must be the lovely Amber."

"Amber, Dad. Dad, Amber." Rosie went to the fridge.

With his beige dress shoes clopping on the tiles, Nick approached Amber, his hand out. "Lovely to meet you, finally. Heard a lot about you."

As was British custom, or maybe a cliché, Amber laughed. "Nothing bad, I hope." She shook his hand.

"Of course not. Never!" His hand was as warm as his expression. He had almost-white hair and hazel eyes just like Rosie's. "Kath will be through in a moment. She's just choosing some Sunday lunch music."

"Oh, um, I brought you a gift." Amber handed over the plastic bag containing a brightly coloured pot with long leaves sticking out. "They're tulips. Jilly says they'll flower in June."

Charlie's face broke into a brilliant smile. "Thank you, hon. How pretty."

"We, um, I mean Jilly, had some left over from a client. She said they'd be pretty anywhere. I don't know what your garden is like, so...I just thought..."

Charlie placed a hand on Amber's shoulder. "You can stop talking now. I love tulips and the gift is much appreciated."

After a few deep swallows, Amber allowed her shoulders to drop. Some of the twitchy feelings remained though and would linger until the bulbs blossomed in a couple of months. *I hope they like them. I hope they match the garden. I hope they don't think I'm stupid for giving them something originally intended for someone else.*

Rosie poured both her and Amber a glass of sparkling water. They took them through the house and out of some French doors into the small garden. Grass ran down both sides of a path which ended at a shed with a little window. Against the shed stood a large hutch with a small blonde girl halfway inside it.

"Ginger, you ninny. Come here. I want you to meet Auntie Rosie's new girlfriend."

A chuckle bubbled out of Rosie. She went over and knelt on the path beside Chelsea, placing her glass on the top of the hutch. "Is Ginger being a ninny, monkey?"

"Oh!" Chelsea threw her small arms around Rosie but seemed to catch herself and gentled her embrace. She turned back to the guinea pigs. "You see? She's here, and you're not ready to see guests yet. Naughty piggies." Again, she startled and jumped to her feet. "Amber!"

"Wow." Amber stood still, waiting for Chelsea to come to her if she wished. "I thought I was coming to meet a kid, but you're very obviously a grown-up if you've got your own guinea pigs."

Chelsea hopped over to her. "Well, not really. I'm very nearly nine. I suppose that means I am a bit grown-up." She became very solemn and held out a hand. A pink, plastic, star-shaped ring sat on her third finger. "Good afternoon, Amber. Welcome to the garden."

"Thank you." Amber giggled. "It's very nice to meet you, Chelsea."

"Oh, you too." Clear manners there under all the excitement. Amber was surprised—having new guinea pigs *and* meeting your aunt's girlfriend for the first time might have caused Chelsea to forget.

Rosie stood with a huff, brandishing not one but two guinea pigs on top of her bump.

"Auntie Rosie's a guinea pig whisperer!" Chelsea raced in circles for a minute before she lost her breath. She took the orange pig from Rosie. "This one is Tallulah, and the white one you have is Ginger."

Rosie cocked an eyebrow. "Um. The *white* one is called Ginger?"

"Yes." Chelsea didn't seem to catch the irony. She grinned and raced inside with Tallulah clutched to her chest.

Rosie looked down at the white guinea pig, then carefully took her hands away from it. The pig rested quite happily on top of her sizeable bump, its pink feet splayed and its whiskers waving as it took in this new human.

"Guinea pig whisperer *and* hands-free carrying facility." Amber was at her side, and she stroked the pig's ears with one hand. "Well, she's cute."

"Why hasn't she called the *ginger* one Ginger?"

"Creative licence?" Amber pulled out her camera. "This I've got to get a snap of."

Rosie stood awkwardly. A smile tugged her expression when Amber lifted the camera.

Amber took their drinks inside and found Chelsea jabbering to her grandmother about Rosie's newly revealed abilities.

Stylish and with dark blond locks—dyed but done so with great care—Kath Tanner stood by a case of CDs. She had a few in one hand; the other was firmly on Tallulah's backside as it slid down Chelsea's front. "Both hands, cherub. Otherwise the dear thing will fall."

No need for verbal pleasantries. The minute Kath caught sight of Rosie she strode over, the pig forgotten. The CDs ended up on the armchair, and Kath used both hands to cup Rosie's belly. "Look at you!"

"Yeah, go ahead. Look at me." Subservient but affectionate, Rosie allowed her mother to feel, look, and make all the usual noises a grandmother would make to her unborn grandchild.

"I do apologise. Bump comes first, I'm afraid." Kath straightened to take Amber in.

The scrutiny made Amber want to be small again. "Hi."

"Aren't you a pretty thing?" Kath clasped her hands. "And where on earth did you get that blouse?"

"Um…" Amber was sure it had been one of her charity shop purchases but wasn't comfortable admitting it. "I don't remember."

"I love it. So cutesy and chic."

Not words Amber had expected to come out of the mouth of a woman in her sixties. "Thank you."

"Rosie tells me you're an admin assistant?" Kath guided Amber back into the kitchen.

"Yes. At a dental surgery."

Rosie followed with Ginger still atop her bump. She caught her drink from Amber as she went to the breakfast bar to perch on one of the stools, eager to make friends with the guinea pig whilst keeping an ear on their conversation.

"I bet you see all sorts." Kath stroked Nick's spine and received a kiss in return.

"All walks of life." Amber took a sip of her drink.

She looks as if she's keeping everything in check. I hope she relaxes soon. My family really isn't that scary. But then, Amber had had such a tough time with her own family, meeting someone else's was a big thing for her. Amber hadn't admitted her nerves, but her back was so straight and she sipped delicately from her glass.

Unable to really go to her with Ginger occupying one of her hands and her drink the other, Rosie stayed at the breakfast bar and allowed Amber to chat with her mum.

"Do you help them pull out teeth?" Chelsea bounced from one side to the other. Tallulah's eyes were round and Rosie imagined she felt rather green.

"No. I just do the paperwork, ring people to remind them of their appointments, and make sure everything's in the right place."

Chelsea pouted for the briefest of minutes, then smiled again. "I like writing poems. Do you write poems?"

"I don't, but I'd love to hear one you've written."

"After we've eaten, Chels, okay?" Charlie sped past with hands full of cutlery. "And pop the pigs away, hmm? Wash your hands."

"Aw, I just got them out."

"Well, it's fifteen minutes until dinner, so they need to go back in." Charlie gave Chelsea a look, chucking her head towards the garden.

After Charlie exited the kitchen, Chelsea rolled her eyes. "Parents!" She beckoned to Rosie's guinea pig. "Come on, then."

Rosie transferred Ginger to Chelsea, who carried both guinea pigs out. Finally free from pig-cuddling duties, she washed her hands, then sidestepped her father to get to Amber.

"There are six of us in reception; we each have our own dentist. The nurses sometimes switch who they work with but not often. And there are hygienists too—they work in another building. I've been there just over a year and the surgery has expanded so much. We have three more dentists, a load more buildings, and a whole new training department for dental students."

"Business is going well, then." Tom placed a tray onto the counter. It contained a leg of lamb, juicy and punctured here and there with sprigs of rosemary. Potatoes surrounded it, crisp at the edges.

Good food and family. Rosie wanted to show Amber how wonderful having a meal with her family could be. K.B. rolled a little, probably from Rosie's mouth watering.

A twinge at her middle. She placed a hand onto her bump and grimaced.

Eyes wide, Amber stepped closer. She didn't verbalise her concern, simply rubbed Rosie's lower back.

That helped. Rosie smiled, hoping to reassure her. *Just Braxton Hicks, no need for concern.*

Amber let out a breath before smiling too. Her hand lingered.

"It's the biggest surgery in Weston. There are smaller ones around but nothing as big as Gerard and White."

"Aptly named." Tom winked.

Amber dropped her head a bit. "Jilly thought I was kidding when I let on what they were called."

"And Jilly's your landlady?" Kath returned and collected condiments.

A nod from Amber. "She's awesome. Like a kind of auntie-slash-mate. She keeps me sane."

"And is she in AA as well?"

A moment of apparent panic; Amber's gaze flicked to the floor then out of the window. She sucked her bottom lip for a second before inhaling. Her gaze returned to Kath. "Yes. She was the one who first took me to a meeting."

She's so brave. Rosie wasn't sure she'd manage a stranger knowing such an intimate detail of her own life. Amber took it in her stride.

"Sounds like a very good friend." Once Kath had all the pepper mills and mustard jars she needed, she breezed into the dining room.

The next moment, lilting piano notes drifted through. Mozart, of course. Rosie took the moment to lean into Amber's side and slide a hand around her waist.

Tom was still dealing with the lamb, which slipped from the bone like butter. He hummed along to the music and definitely ignored them on purpose.

A slight shudder went through Amber before she pressed her cheek to Rosie's shoulder for a snuggle too.

Rosie kissed the top of her head. "Great first impression."

Amber lifted her head to catch Rosie's eye.

It was too much to refrain from kissing her, even just a short peck in her sister's kitchen.

Footsteps caused Amber to move away. Her cheeks had gone pink.

Kath gave them both a knowing look but went about her business, collecting more things for the table.

"Oh, can I help?" Amber held out both hands, which Kath filled with serving spoons and a small glass of water containing sticks of carrot.

"For Nick. He refuses to eat cooked vegetables. Just pop them on the table at the head." Kath chuckled. "Even in Charlie and Tom's house, he has to be master."

Nick swept in to grab a couple of dishes. "If only at the table."

Once everyone was seated—Nick at one end and Charlie at the other—they bowed their heads and clasped their hands. As usual, Rosie waited whilst her father said Grace.

Amber worked a hand into Rosie's, so Rosie squeezed her fingers and dropped her voice to a whisper. "It's not mandatory."

"Oh, no." Nick lifted his head and that generous smile was back. "Do sit out the spiritual stuff if you wish." He'd finished anyway.

Charlie dished out meat, but otherwise, everyone was encouraged to help themselves. There were arguments between Chelsea and her mother, mostly focusing on the dietary benefits of broccoli and why its presence was required on Chelsea's plate. A similar discussion took place regarding Nick's fondness for gravy and a large quantity of potatoes.

Tom kept the adults topped up with wine. And because everyone knew Amber didn't drink—apart from Chelsea who, frankly, didn't give a hoot about who drank what—the atmosphere was no different to usual.

Rosie enjoyed watching Amber integrate herself. For a while, discussion centred around Ginger and Tallulah and guinea pig care in general. Rosie wasn't sure whether Amber knew nothing on the subject or was humouring Chelsea by feigning ignorance. Either way, Chelsea chattered away as if she'd done a degree in it.

The peach crumble topped off the main meal nicely. Nick and Amber fought over the custard. Chelsea stole one of her grandfather's carrot sticks and munched cheekily. And there was action once more as everyone pitched in to clear away. As Charlie and Tom had cooked, and Rosie was retired from duties due to her bowling-ball status, Amber, Kath, and Nick washed up, with Chelsea overseeing proceedings.

The sofa was incredibly comfortable when Rosie lowered her stuffed body into it. "Yet another amazing dinner, guys."

"You're welcome." Tom flopped onto the sofa at the opposite end; Charlie took her place in the middle.

Chelsea gave directions: "No, Granddad, it goes in the special-glasses cupboard. Not the boring-glasses cupboard."

Rosie snorted. "You have different cupboards for different glasses?"

"We wouldn't need them if your mother hadn't left us three thousand glasses when we inherited the house." Charlie directed her comment at Tom.

He shrugged and lined the back of the sofa with his arm.

"So," Charlie nudged Rosie's leg, "everything's ready for the great arrival?"

"Yup." Rosie stroked her bump. "Biologically, she's in the right position. And my bag has been packed for weeks now, so don't worry."

"And you still want me there?"

"Yeah." Rosie blinked. "If that's still okay?"

"No, I thought I'd bail on you three weeks before your due date."

Rosie smacked Charlie on the shoulder. "Don't, okay? I'm freaked enough as it is."

The quiet moment stretched, during which Charlie clasped Rosie's hand. "It'll be fine."

A nod just to convince herself Charlie was right calmed Rosie's heart. "And you'll tell me if you need to go, won't you? You've got your own stuff here—Chelsea and Tom and the guinea pigs and…and laundry and stuff."

"Oh shush, you pleb. Tom can deal with stuff here until you're finished your cow noises."

"I will *not* be doing cow noises."

Charlie stared at her, one eyebrow up.

"And, *no*, Granddad. The gravy boat does *not* go in that cupboard."

"Go Chelsea, putting Dad in his place." Charlie sunk back under Tom's arm. "Maybe you should have a back-up though in case I get mowed down by a charging rhino or something."

Rosie's knee wiggled. She pulled at the elastic of her jeans where they tugged over her bump. The movement was a fidgety betrayal of her emotions.

Who else can I call on? Mum would be willing, but I'm sure I'd want to kill her. Claire would be a complete nightmare in a stressful situation, and there's no way I'm letting Vincent anywhere near my nether regions.

Her gaze drifted out the door and into the kitchen.

"Auntie Amber, it's okay. We can put the wet tea towels on the radiator."

More organising from her niece. Then the name Chelsea had used brushed Rosie's face like a summer breeze. *Auntie.* Is that how Chelsea saw Amber already? After only one meeting?

Perhaps it had been a slip of Chelsea's tongue. Maybe she called everyone Auntie: her mother's friends, family acquaintances. *Has Chelsea misinterpreted our relationship as more formal and sealed than it actually is?*

"I've got a poem!" Chelsea bustled in, a piece of paper in her small fist. "Can I read it to everyone?"

"'Course, go for it." Charlie shifted to the edge of the sofa.

Tom sat up straighter too.

"Okay." Chelsea cleared her throat.

The adults returned from their pot washing. Amber cast her gaze around for a beat, then settled on the floor by Rosie's feet. Rosie passed her a cushion to sit on.

Another clearing of her throat meant everyone's attention was on Chelsea. "There was a guinea pig called Tallulah…"

"It's a limerick?" Rosie was on her feet in a very pregnant instant. "We've got to sing it, monkey."

"Okay!"

Rosie went to the piano and sat. She started the marching tune they always played for silly limericks. A lift of her head and Chelsea began.

"Oh, there was a guinea pig called Tallulah,
Who liked to eat chicken bhuna,
One day she saw a whale
And she ate some curly kale
And she wanted to be a beluga!"

Everyone clapped. Rosie continued to play the march.

"There's another verse." Chelsea bopped with her poem held out.

"Oh, there was a guinea pig called Ginge,
Who one day ended up getting singed,
She fell over an iron
And met a bloke called Brian
And it really, really made her whinge."

More applause erupted, along with a bucketload of laughter. Rosie exchanged a relieved look with Amber. There were worse words one could rhyme with 'Ginge' than Chelsea had chosen.

The walk home under the mid-April evening sun was just the ticket. Rosie's hand was in Amber's again, just the noises of the street between them. Another Braxton Hicks contraction forced them to stop for a while and Amber returned her hand to the small of Rosie's back.

"Take your time." Amber sounded like one of Rosie's relaxation videos but nowhere near as cringeworthy.

"Just takes my breath away a bit." A convenient garden wall was a step away, so Rosie rested her backside against it for the duration. "Like someone pulling a big elastic band around my uterus."

Sympathy shone from Amber's eyes. "Your niece is going to grow up to be an amazing comedian."

"I know; she really has talent in that department."

"And you guys have obviously been singing limericks for a while."

"My granddad used to do it. He made up songs for all his grandkids."

"You'll have to sing me the one he wrote about you one day." The circles against Rosie's back slowed. "Is…is this helping in anyway?"

"Yes. Loads." Rosie beamed at her. "I put the oil you gave me in my bag, ready."

"Nice to know I can help a bit when the day finally comes."

The perfect opening. *What happened to not asking her? What happened to it being too intimate a thing? What happened to taking things slowly?* Rosie shook her head to rid herself of these thoughts.

"Charlie seems to have her head screwed on. She'll be an excellent birthing partner." Amber's fingers still circled and it spurred Rosie on.

"But, I mean, what do I do if she has to go, or I get sick of her and, you know, want to kill her? Like, in an emergency?"

Amber's eyes shone. "I don't know."

Everything inside Rosie fell about a foot south. "I'm sure I'll muddle through."

"I mean…" Amber held up a hand. "I'd be no good as a cheerleader for your uterus."

Cramps eased for now, Rosie pushed from the wall to take Amber's chin in her hand. "Hey." Once Amber looked her way, Rosie tilted her head. "None of that."

A chuckle sprang from Amber's lips before they curled upwards. "I just have no experience at all with babies or…hospitals."

"Doesn't mean you wouldn't be good at keeping me company whilst I'm waiting for this one here," she patted her bump, "to get her arse in gear."

Amber winced through a smile. "Just don't expect me to bring my own pompoms."

She really isn't keen. Best to just drop it. "Gotcha." Rosie clicked her fingers and pointed back at Amber.

The whole walk home, Rosie wondered where she could get labour pompoms from and, if she did find them, what colour they should be.

Chapter 32

WEEK FORTY-ONE, FOR FUCK'S SAKE. More Braxton Hicks, but nothing else that indicated K.B. was on her way. Pressure on her pelvis, the constant need to use the facilities, and a desperate longing to be free of her sizeable belly were just some of the delightful side effects of being a near mother-to-be.

Janet and Olivia had been round with their little one, and they'd fawned over Rosie's baby's bedroom. In the master bedroom, Olivia had helped Rosie position the bedside cot where she would find it most accessible. They'd shared a host of important tips and baby hacks which she'd immediately forgotten. *Bloody baby-brain. If only I had the baby to show for it.*

Watching Janet breastfeed had been an eye-opener. And Rosie had looked once Janet had brushed off Rosie's blush and encouraged her wholeheartedly. Janet had even put her free arm around Rosie, pointed out where her nipple was in comparison to the baby's chin, how she got a good latch. *She's only had the baby a few weeks. How has she learned all this so quickly?*

It seemed like degree-level academia. When Rosie thought about it, her chest squeezed and her heart pattered. She was under no preconception she would just fall into breastfeeding like some hippie mum with flowers in her hair.

Regular phone calls to Amber reminded her of the outside world and the fact that she was in a new and exciting relationship. It was an odd feeling, dating someone but also being on the cliff edge of another life chapter. It all rushed towards her, shells and sand and pebbles in between her toes, not quite knocking her onto her arse but certainly fucking with her balance.

Now it was 3 a.m. and all she could think about was how uncomfortable she was. K.B. squirmed against all her vital organs, and whichever way she lay wasn't comfortable. Tossing and turning commenced until she seriously considered a good masturbation session to get things moving.

I'm not even in the mood for that. She tried to think about Amber, how beautiful and sexy her body was, how amazing it had been to touch her and make her come. But her imagination failed her—birth-related images swarmed like bees after an assailant to their hive. Episiotomy scars, sore nipples, and baby's first turd.

A twinge, like Braxton Hicks but more intense, squished her middle, vice-like. She gripped the sheets, waited for it to subside. It did.

With a whoosh of air, she relaxed.

It started again, gripped her until she had to remember to breathe.

Then nothing.

Lying as still as she could, she put her hand down her pyjama trousers and investigated. Nothing out of the ordinary. *I really hope this is it.*

She rolled onto her side, hugged her pregnancy pillow, and drifted off.

She was woken again by the gripping, squishing sensation. A thin hum crept from her a second before the pain went away.

No more sleep, I guess. She rolled out of bed, her swollen feet aching as she padded around the bedroom.

The next pain was definitely not a simple twinge, and it stopped her in her tracks, made her whine like an injured animal.

Time to phone Charlie. It was a few seconds before she picked up. Charlie's voice was muffled, probably by one of Tom's limbs. "Morning, pleb."

"Dipstick, I think I might be in labour." Fear constricted her ribs, and Rosie had to lean against the foot of the bed. "Aw, man. I don't like it."

"No worries." The noises of someone dashing out of bed. "I'll be ten minutes, okay?"

"Thanks, Char."

After a few choice swear words, Charlie rang off.

Rosie's bedroom was too dark, so she turned on the main light, squinting as her eyes adjusted. It was the middle of the night, and she was more wide awake than she'd ever been. Perhaps her brain had known it would all start soon and had kept her up so she wouldn't miss it. She was under no misconceptions her labour would be quick—first baby and all—but she hoped she'd be awarded some sleep once everything was confirmed.

What if it's false labour?

She collected the few things she hadn't been able to pack, stuffing them into her holdall. She donned a pair of jogging bottoms and a baggy T-shirt, then sat on her bed to wait for her sister.

She trailed her hand along the edge of the three-sided cot. That was where K.B. would sleep from now on. She studied her own hands—the hands that would hold K.B. safe and close. The stuffed rabbit Rosie would wiggle in front of K.B.'s face once she was old enough to appreciate a silly voice and a pair of button eyes. The crocheted blanket her cousin had made, grey and yellow and white, was folded over the side of the cot.

A contraction—for that was definitely what it was—arrived the minute Charlie bustled through the bedroom door, her keys still in her hand. "Pleb."

"Bugger off." Rosie growled, knuckles white where she gripped the mattress. "Ow."

"'Ow' is new."

"Tell me about it."

Charlie sat beside her and soothed her shoulder. "Hey, I'm here now. What do you want to do?"

"Sleep."

Charlie's laugh rattled Rosie's cage. "Hmm. Might be an issue with that."

Rosie huffed and stared at her feet—what she could see of them.

"What have they said? Can we go straight in or…?"

"Got to wait until they're three in ten minutes."

"Are they?"

Pouting seemed childish but Rosie did it anyway.

"Let's settle down, then. You got a story tape you want to listen to, or some TV?"

Rosie padded to her side of the bed. The last person to sleep in her bed with her had been Amber. Her presence seemed to linger.

Moving to the other side, Charlie pushed off her shoes and got in. She leant up on one elbow, patted the bed beside her, and reached for the remote. "There's always something good on *Dave* at this time, isn't there?"

"How would you know?"

"The occasional bout of insomnia."

They curled up in bed facing one another. Charlie stroked Rosie's hair a couple of times before closing her eyes.

Might as well take a leaf from Charlie's book. Maybe sleep will come. And it did, or at least rest did. Rosie remembered to breathe, remembered to try to relax, to just experience each strengthening of her muscles as it came. Looked forward, as much as she could, to her baby being born.

By eight in the morning, the contractions were more frequent and *Dave* wasn't showing anything funny anymore, so Rosie changed the channel. She sat up in bed, her focus on the morning news.

Charlie, her eyes bleary, stretched and sat up too. "How we doing?"

A look at her watch and Rosie grimaced. "The last three were in twelve minutes." She squirmed and rolled her neck, rocking her spine one way, then the other. Her middle stiffened, and the pain shot like a tight band around her. "Oh, bloody hell."

"How's the pain?"

"Shitty."

Charlie stroked Rosie's hair. "Maybe it's time?" She nodded towards the door.

Rosie held up a finger until the contraction finished. She got to her feet. She pushed away Charlie's proffered arm but gripped it when her knees buckled.

"Don't be a martyr. I'm not here for my dazzling good looks."

"No comment."

"Excellent. Still got a sense of humour." Charlie grinned and wrapped an arm around her waist.

With both their bags over her other arm, Charlie led Rosie downstairs, then out to the car. Once Rosie was in the passenger's seat, Charlie rounded the vehicle and slid in too.

"To the hospital," Charlie said as if they were setting out on a quest.

Rosie smiled back despite the nerves swishing in her belly.

Rosie's midwife had the sleekest black hair of anyone she'd ever seen. Rosie wanted to skim her hands down it to make it shimmer even more. *Get a grip, Tanner.* She pressed a fist into her leg to cope with the contraction that took her body.

The badge pinned to the midwife's grey uniform read *Martha.*

"That's a nice name," Rosie said as she waddled into the room she'd been allocated. It had a computer in one corner, a large window with blue curtains, and a hospital bed. There were also a bathroom and an exercise ball similar to the one Rosie had at home.

"Thanks." Martha skimmed through Rosie's notes whilst Rosie settled on the bed.

"Old-fashioned." Rosie pushed her trainers off and slid on her thick bed-socks. *So comfortable.* "I like old-fashioned names."

"Me too. My little sister is called Veronica. Think my parents had a plan."

"Ronnie was one of the names I had in my list. For this one." Rosie patted her bump. "I'm going for gender-neutral."

"Excellent." Martha tapped at the small computer in the corner of the room. Mid-twenties but held herself with quiet confidence. "I'm going to do all the usual checks: BP, blood sugars, and an internal exam, if that's okay?"

Past caring about the midwife, or Charlie even, seeing her underwear, Rosie took off the outfit she'd come in and pulled on the long nightshirt from her bag. Until she was in the pool, something loose and cotton was required. A sweat-absorbent article of clothing.

The BP cuff squeezed her arm, the tiny pin pricked her finger, and Martha's gloved fingers dipped between her legs. A contraction hit Rosie just as she was going in, so they waited until it passed before Martha had another go. "You're a little dilated. Maybe four centimetres. Nothing to write home about just yet, but you can stay."

"I was kind of worried you'd send me home." Rosie smoothed the nightshirt back over her knees. "I've only been contracting since three."

"How's the pain?"

Rosie smiled, noting Martha's avoidance of the issue of pain relief. Just like she'd requested in her birth plan. "I'd say it was manageable."

"Good. You want to have a walk up and down the corridor whilst I record your obs?"

Charlie stood from the chair next to the bed and offered a gentle arm.

With a roll of her eyes, Rosie placed her hand inside Charlie's elbow before tugging them both out of the room. There were a few staff members at the nurse's station. Busyness was the state of play, with notes being written and things being hole-punched left, right, and centre.

The corridor was just long enough for Rosie to accomplish some sort of exercise but not so long she ended up out of breath. Rosie kept her appreciation of Charlie's arm to herself, figuring she should maintain an air of control whilst she had the chance.

Four centimetres isn't bad considering only a few hours ago I was lying in bed wondering whether I should have a wank. Things didn't need to be chivvied along at any rate: that was good. K.B. was ready and waiting. All Rosie had to do was be ready and wait.

It's been hours. Why isn't she here yet? Rosie made it her mission to stomp the hallways, up and down, up and down, always on Charlie's arm, like some sort of old pensioner on a stroll. Her legs ached and her back hurt and she was *bored.* The discomfort was more like being run over by a train than a little niggle now.

Relaxation tapes helped halfway. They meant she focused on her breathing between contractions, was able to come down from the groaning agony each time. Tears came to her eyes now, and the bouts of pain were getting more intense and much closer together.

Lunchtime passed in a blur of tuna sandwiches and crisps. Rosie was offered a granola bar at around 3 p.m. which she nibbled, her stomach lurching a little. She wasn't sure whether it disliked the thought of upcoming events or the healthy combination of oats and dried fruit.

"The gas and air is right there." Charlie's hand was tight in Rosie's.

"I don't want it." Rosie wiped her eyes and sipped from the cool glass of water Martha poured for her. "I'm good without meds."

The look in Charlie's eyes indicated she didn't believe her. She'd left the room twice for the toilet and once to call their parents. True to her word, Charlie was the rock Rosie hadn't realised she'd need. *Thank goodness I have a sister I can rely on.*

The ball Rosie sat on was smaller than the one she had at home, and for some reason this made her skin itch. "Don't you have a bigger one?"

"No, lovely, sorry. That's your allocated ball."

"Well, it sucks." Rosie pouted but couldn't give a toss. The ball didn't squish as much as hers, and she was lower down on it. She wanted to bounce and rock the way she had practised.

Martha put a hand on her back. "I'm sorry. You're doing really well though."

"Am I?" Tears rolled down Rosie's cheeks. "I don't feel as if I am."

"Last time I checked, we had three more centimetres. So that's..."

"Three more to go."

"When you get to eight, you can go in the pool."

Rosie relinquished Charlie's hand and used both of hers to clap. "Yippee."

Martha laughed. "That's the spirit." She went back to her computer.

Scepticism still flowed from Charlie in abundance.

The next contraction had Rosie making the noise she'd been adamant she wouldn't. She clawed at the rubber surface of the ball, the pain excessive and, in her opinion, far beyond what was legal. Her fists pummelled her thighs, and expletives fell from her lips in wild abandon. "Bugger, Charlie, why did I think this was a good idea?"

"You'll feel differently when it's all over." Charlie's tone suggested she was trying to keep up the bravado they always relished, but it faltered.

"Oh, what would you know?"

"Shall we watch something?" Charlie waved one of the DVD box sets she'd brought.

"Oh, I don't know, Charlie." Rosie wanted to be positive, she really did. But Charlie was getting annoying, always suggesting things to keep Rosie's mind off what was happening. It was difficult to think when the pain was so extreme.

Martha came over to her other side and smoothed Rosie's arm. "Sometimes when you're in labour, it's difficult to focus on anything else. Sometimes women like to be in the dark, with less distractions, nice music."

Relief caused Rosie's bottom lip to quiver.

"Is that something you think you'd benefit from?" Martha's voice was matter-of-fact.

"Possibly."

Martha tucked Rosie's hair behind her ear. "Okay. Let's make this room nice and low stimulus for you." Her head came up, a smile for Charlie crinkling her features. "Want to give me a hand, big sis?"

The room became very mellow and dark, the blue curtains hiding much of the sun. Rosie found her labour playlist on her phone and turned the volume to a level that was almost too quiet. Martha sat quietly at the computer, her hands in her lap.

Charlie sat at her side again.

With nothing but the music touching her ears, small pieces of Rosie's irritation fell away. Each of her senses faded. She could focus on the pain of each contraction, focus on her breathing, grip Charlie's hand when she chose to.

Not too long later, Rosie moved onto all fours on the bed, and everything was black around her. All she could feel were the cotton sheets, the hoarseness of her throat, and the pain that seemed to reach the back of her neck, the soles of her feet, and every cell in between. She batted away Charlie's hands as they soothed her lower back, her cheek, her thigh. *Don't touch me. I can't have anyone touching me.*

Still, pain relief was not an option. She wanted to stay with it during labour, and there was always a chance K.B. would be affected by the medications. Charlie broke her vow of silence to beg her, hated seeing her as she was, and cried too on the periphery of Rosie's consciousness. And then she was gone, and Martha was by her side, holding her hand. Charlie had needed to make a call, but that was lost on the wave of another contraction.

Harry and Matthew's house, or at least the house they wished to buy, had been everything Amber could have imagined. Big but not so big they'd feel lost in it, prettily decorated but plain enough to be a blank canvas. She'd left them in a haze of having made an offer already.

Things had moved for them. Gladness rolled inside her, a happy puppy in a field. Harry's eyes shone with love each time he looked at Matthew, and the light was reflected when Matthew looked back. Amber couldn't be in their presence without feeling it.

After lunch out and an extensive afternoon at their flat chatting and watching TV, they dropped her back home. Nico yapped at her heels as she got through the door. She had her jacket off and her bag on its hook when her phone rang. Using one hand, the other pulling off her shoe as she wavered on one foot, she answered it. "Hey, Rosie."

"It's Charlie."

"Oh." Amber checked her phone: it definitely said Rosie's number. "Everything okay?"

"Rosie's in labour."

"Oh." *She didn't tell me. Not that we'd agreed she would. I suppose I would be the last thing on her mind.* "She okay?"

"I don't think I'm cut out for this." A sniff. Was Charlie crying? "She's all…she's in a lot of pain and…"

"Well, I…" Amber didn't want to step on any toes. "What about your mum, or…"

"I think she needs you."

Amber ran a hand through her hair. "But, I mean, we did discuss it and we decided…"

"Whatever you decided, Amber, I think that's pretty null and void right now. She won't let me near her and she won't let the midwife give her any pain relief."

"She's stubborn." Amber could imagine Rosie just suffering through.

"No shit. She told me about how good you were when she had that… whatever it was called. When she was bleeding."

"It was nothing." *It's difficult not to be hard on myself.* "I did what anyone would."

"If you've nothing on for the next few hours, I think she'd really appreciate you being here."

She won't; at least she won't admit it. Amber's heart grated against her ribs. If Rosie was in pain and she could do something to help, should she? Wasn't it her duty as girlfriend, lover, friend even, to ease Rosie's agony?

But was it her *place* to get involved? It wasn't her pregnancy, her labour, or her baby. Was it too soon to be that one person Rosie relied on?

"Okay. She can always send me away again, I suppose."

"That's true. She's seven centimetres dilated, so I guess it won't be long."

Amber pushed her shoe back on whilst trying to stop Nico jumping up at her. "Give me like thirty minutes. Need to sort a few things, then I'll walk on over."

It was bordering on 8 p.m. as Amber popped a few cereal bars and packets of crisps in her bag, then let the dog out. As he did his business, she sent Jilly a text, explaining where she was going. Once Nico was back inside, she locked up, grabbing her phone charger on the way out. *No good running out of battery in the middle of things.*

After hesitating, she placed her camera into her bag too. On the off-chance Rosie might want some snaps of her new baby, Amber figured her high resolution camera was better than her crappy phone one.

She was panting by the time she got to the hospital, having hurried along at quite a speed.

Charlie leant against the wall by the entrance to the maternity ward, leg jumping. A weight appeared to fall from her as she took in Amber. "You are such a sight for sore eyes."

"I'm not making any promises, but let's see what I can do."

They used alcohol gel to clean their hands before being buzzed in.

"She's allowed two people in there, but we've made it all quiet and dark for her. We're not supposed to talk as it can distract her from the contractions."

A young woman in a uniform came out as they arrived at Rosie's room.

"This is Rosie's girlfriend, Amber." Charlie made a sorrowful gesture as if relinquishing the gauntlet.

"I need to just ask Rosie if it's okay you're here, all right?" The midwife went back into the room and closed the door.

"What if she says no?" Amber fiddled with the strap of her bag.

Charlie shrugged, her eyes wet.

Amber wanted to go to her, hug her, make her feel better, but they'd met only once. So she sat next to Charlie on the plastic chairs by the door and waited.

It wasn't long before the midwife—her badge said *Martha*—returned and gave Amber a thumbs-up. "She almost smiled when I said you were here."

"She did?"

"Almost. Just try to be quiet. If you have any questions, just point outside and we'll come out here to talk."

Martha waited outside whilst Amber went in.

Once the door closed, Amber looked around. The curtains were closed, the only light shone from the computer screen off to the left. Soft music came from Rosie's phone on the bedside cabinet.

Rosie lay on her side on the bed, her breathing audible but her eyes open. Her hair was slick and messy and she wore a nightshirt down to her knees. "Hi."

"Hi." Amber made sure to whisper. "How are you?"

"Excellent."

Unable to hold in a chuckle, Amber stowed her bag under the chair before lowering herself into it. "You should have texted me."

"Didn't want to bother you." Rosie's face scrunched up and her mouth opened.

I don't know what to do. Why did I not think about this? Amber put her hand on the bed, palm up. Rosie's hand was sweaty when she put it into Amber's. Her grip was like concrete.

Amber wanted to encourage her, tell her it was okay, soothe her in some way, but was aware of the need to keep quiet. *Let Rosie deal with the contraction.* She sent her positive thoughts, not that she believed they worked, but something was better than nothing.

Rosie blew out a breath and closed her eyes. She tugged Amber's hand, made a noise like a sorrowful child.

There wasn't room for her to sit on the bed properly, so Amber perched and helped Rosie to sit up.

With eyes still closed, Rosie leant against Amber's shoulder, wrapping her arms around Amber's back.

Rosie's hair was straggly between her fingers. Amber stroked Rosie's head. When another contraction built, Amber started to rise, but was restricted from doing so by Rosie's vice-like grip.

"No." A groan rumbled from Rosie.

There was nothing more to do than hold Rosie, to support her physically and, she hoped, emotionally. *I can't do it for her, but I can be here.*

Martha returned during Rosie's third contraction. She winked at Amber and lifted her eyebrows a touch as Rosie growled out various choice words. All in a day's work, Amber supposed. Martha came over, a fresh pair of gloves donned, and tapped Rosie's knee. "Am I okay to check you?"

Rosie nodded. She lay back, one hand gripping Amber's, the other pulling up her nightshirt.

Her cheeks hot, Amber looked to one side. She'd seen Rosie have this done before, back when they weren't together, in A&E but it still made her toes curl.

A noise of discomfort from Rosie and Martha was done. "Eight. Well done, you."

"Pool now?" Rosie whined.

"Yes, pool now. I'll go get it set up for you."

"Can Amber come?"

"Of course."

"Not Charlie." Rosie had her bottom lip out.

"You're the boss." Martha winked before going out.

Rosie snuggled against Amber's shoulder. "I feel better now you're here."

"Good. Charlie said you were being a pain in the arse about the gas and air."

A scowl wrinkled Rosie's brow. "She was trying to push me into having it. I don't want it."

"Okay." *I'm not going to try to convince her. It's her body.* "What d'you want me to do?"

Rosie squeezed her. "For some reason, you holding me isn't annoying."

"I'm glad of that."

Rosie let out a small sob, then tensed up.

"It's okay. Just breathe." The no-talking rule seemed to have flown out of the window.

With pursed lips, Rosie panted out the pain. Amber kissed her forehead as it receded.

"This..." Rosie rubbed her belly in large circles. "This is what I need."

Martha and another midwife arrived with a wheelchair, which Amber helped Rosie into. They managed to get her down the corridor and into the room with the birthing pool without another contraction forcing them to stop.

Rosie was able to stand from the wheelchair and seemed to want to stay that way. She began to undo her shirt. "Hey, um, could you help me?" Rosie rolled her eyes. "I'm feeling a bit cack-handed."

With one of Rosie's hands on Amber's shoulder for balance, Amber unbuttoned the shirt all the way down for her.

"I've got underwear on, don't worry."

"Like I haven't seen you in your altogether." Amber threw the folded shirt over a chair, then took Rosie's waist.

Rosie inched her pants down, leaving her only in her black bra. "This is different though." The look Rosie gave her next was apologetic.

Amber shook her head. "You're just as beautiful."

A still moment. Gazes locked and realisation dawned. *She's for me. I'm here for the long haul and not just for today.* Amber kissed right next to Rosie's nose, slowly and gently.

A real smile flickered onto Rosie's face before her eyes squeezed closed.

"You want to sit?" Amber looked around for a place to put her, on the edge of panicking as nowhere seemed suitable.

Luckily, Martha and her colleague were there in a flash.

Rosie looped her arms around Amber's neck and gave over some of her weight.

"Gravity is your friend, lovely." Martha rubbed Rosie's bare back. "If you're more comfortable staying on your feet, feel free."

"Bloody bastard contraction," Rosie said through gritted teeth.

The three of them got Rosie into the pool. It was lined with a plastic sheet and was a couple of metres wide. The sides were soft, just perfect for leaning against, which was exactly what Rosie did. The water was warm, but not like a hot bath—more like the baby pool at the leisure centre.

Martha brought Amber a towel to kneel on.

Rosie rested her cheek on her arms, her breathing steady. She let out a hum of contentment.

Wanting to give her space, Amber kept her distance but didn't take her gaze off Rosie. There were a few minutes of quiet—just the occasional lap of water and the midwives sorting out whatever they needed to in the background. *I'm not sure I* could *go anywhere right now. Here seems right.*

Martha waggled a wand connected to a small unit. "Shall we have another listen?"

"Okay." Rosie's voice was a sigh.

"You stay where you are, lovely. I'll reach under."

Rosie remained in her sleepy state whilst Martha turned on the device and poked the wand under the water to press against Rosie's belly.

A thrum, not unlike footsteps, echoed through the room. *Baby's heartbeat.* The reality of it made Amber's insides lurch. *Wow, this is really happening. She's going to have a baby.*

"All tickety-boo."

"Excellent." Rosie's words were slurred and muffled by her arms. She took a big breath, then lifted her head. Her face was unlined, eyes accepting as they settled on Amber. "This wasn't the plan, was it?"

"Not really." Amber traced designs across Rosie's wet forearm. "How's the pool?"

A puff of air escaped Rosie. "Nice and warm." She shot a derisive look at the machine over to one side. "No need for any of *that* stuff."

Amber followed her gaze. "The gas and air?"

"I know, I know, I'm being an arsehole about it. But I want to do this myself." A smile tugged at her lips. "I dislocated my shoulder when I was in my twenties. The gas and air made me really silly. I don't want to feel like that now, not when I'm about to meet my daughter." The mini-smile became a fully-fledged grin, complete with sparkling eyes.

"You're going to meet her today."

Rosie's gaze flicked to the clock on the wall. "Maybe. Maybe tomorrow." She knelt up and took Amber's hands. "Could do with moving around a bit. Mind helping me have a swim?"

"Do some laps, right?" Amber turned to Martha and her colleague—the badge on her uniform said *Louise*. "Can we get Rosie some armbands?"

A couple of gentle giggles drifted over. "Move around in there as much as you like, lovely." Martha waved at her. "Your birth plan says you don't want us hovering around you, so if you need us, you know where we are. I'll keep coming over to stick this in your ear," she held up a thermometer, "and to do your pulse."

"Thank you." Rosie splashed a little before gliding around the pool in a suspended seated position with the water over her breasts. "Another positive of the pool—I'm a lot lighter in here." Rosie stopped drifting when her face scrunched up. "Oh, okay, wow." Rosie slipped her hands back into Amber's.

Amber stayed close and waited with her until the contraction ended.

"I hope they don't slow down." Rosie wrinkled her nose. "I've heard being in the pool might make that happen."

"I'll keep my metaphorical fingers crossed."

That was how it continued: Amber assisted Rosie to drift about, change position, get comfortable between contractions; and she held her hands during one. They chatted about silly things, aimless things. Rosie seemed more like herself, less like the caged animal Amber had encountered on her arrival. Her muscles were softer, her limbs looser, and she smiled more. *This pool is a miracle worker. If I ever give birth, I'm definitely demanding one.*

At every one of Amber's caresses, Rosie made a happy noise and moved into her hand. Just like Nico when he wanted a belly rub or an ear-fuss. Amber experimented with touches, swept her fingertips across Rosie's arms and shoulders, across her cheeks, across her neck, and down her back. She stroked her hair, which was as wet as the rest of her, making sure it was out of her eyes.

"That oil you gave me is in my bag."

"Want me to get it?" Amber opened the backpack and—after rifling through various packs of nappies, beauty products, and clothes—located the bottle. "We can use this in the pool, right?"

Martha looked up. "I mean, don't dump the lot in there, but yeah."

"A sexy massage." Rosie winked at Amber.

Amber rolled her eyes. "Really?"

Rosie snorted and closed her eyes as another contraction hit.

Waiting until it ended seemed prudent. Amber put a little oil into each hand, then pressed her palms over Rosie's shoulders and down her back.

Rosie had taken up her original position, leaning forwards against the pool edge. A huge sigh softened her shoulders. "Nice."

Amber continued, touching not only her muscles but also her bones and the areas of tissue between. She made circles, traced letters into Rosie's skin, and sent her more happy thoughts.

As each contraction arrived, peaked, and washed away, Amber stayed where she was, kneeling on the towel. Martha and Louise came over every now and again to do their tests but were so quick Amber barely noticed them.

Rosie slipped into a near-sleep state, punctuated by groaning and panting, the moments of which seemed to last longer and longer. By 11 p.m., they spanned at least a full minute.

Footsteps close by signalled that Martha and Louise had drawn near. "How we doing?"

The last contraction had made Rosie's voice hoarse. "Feels weird. Different than before. Like there's pressure."

"Like you need a poo?"

Rosie winced. "A bit. Oh!" She looked down into the water. "Something popped."

"That might have been your waters. Want me to do an exam and check?"

Rosie's shoulders lifted and tightened her grip on Amber. "Um, would it be okay if you didn't?"

"We could see whether you're ten centimetres, then." There was no hassle in Martha's voice.

"No, thank you."

"Okay, lovely. I don't do anything you don't want me to do, okay?"

Rosie put her own hand down. "The water's warmer down there. Either I peed myself or…yeah. Waters. Amniotic fluid. Etcetera."

"Nice one," Louise said.

"K.B.'s still shifting around. Obviously isn't that bothered about being squeezed like a sausage." Rosie let out a strangled giggle.

Amber frowned. "So, do waters breaking mean baby's going to be here in a minute…or…?" *My lack of knowledge on the subject is embarrassing. I should have read more of Rosie's books.*

"Not necessarily." Louise donned a pair of gloves and sat on the floor next to the pool. "It just means if baby doesn't arrive in twenty-four hours, we need to give her a helping hand."

"Oh." Amber stared at her lap.

"Amber's a new addition to my life. She's not had time to research everything." Rosie smiled at her, her thumbs rubbing back and forth against the backs of Amber's hands.

Amber wanted to hide her face. Were her cheeks as red as they felt?

"Hey, I've had mums-to-be that think waters break the same as they do in the movies. You know, in a big gush every time." Louisa laughed. "I actually kind of like those guys. The ones who have disregarded all the prenatal information in favour of what happened in *Bridget Jones's Baby*."

Conversation halted for a while amid groaning and contracting.

Amber held Rosie through it, then kissed her knuckles as it subsided. "Did you get up and dance when your pregnancy test was positive? Like Ellen and Sharon in that film?"

"No, I sat in stunned silence, then phoned Charlie." She gave the door a lingering look.

"She's still out there if you need her," Martha said.

Rosie swallowed, then wiggled around in the water. She knelt up and started to pant. Another contraction contorted her face and flushed her skin. "Oh, ow, crap, that hurts."

"How do you feel?" Louise had moved closer.

"Like I…" Rosie squeezed her eyes shut. Water dripped from her bra, sparkled against the skin of her round belly. "Need to push." Her plea came out through gritted teeth.

Martha came to sit by them too, at Amber's other side. "No problem. That pressure is baby's head on your birth canal." Calm tone and soft words were accompanied by the lapping of the water as Rosie rocked her hips back and forth.

"I don't like it. It really hurts."

"I know it does, lovely." Martha rubbed Rosie's arm.

"Can…" Rosie gripped Amber's hand. "Can you please go get Charlie?"

"Sure. I can wait outside."

"Don't you bloody dare!" Rosie growled low in her throat. "I want you *both* here."

"Oh." Relief flooded Amber. "Okay, then."

With soggy knees, Amber scampered down the corridor.

Charlie was in the same plastic chairs they'd sat in initially. Her mascara had run but she wasn't crying anymore. She looked up when Amber approached.

"Rosie wants us both with her. Her waters broke. I don't think it'll be too long now."

One of Charlie's eyebrows rose but she nodded. Their strides were speedy down the corridor.

The minute they entered, Rosie reached out both hands, slipping forwards into the water, which splashed over the side of the pool.

Amber took her left hand, Charlie her right, and Martha knelt next to Charlie in a plastic apron.

"Hey, pleb, did I miss anything?" Fake bravado tinged Charlie's voice.

"I did a shit in the pool." Rosie's eyes were wide as if no one anywhere had ever done such a thing.

Martha smiled. "I told you; it happens all the time."

"Yeah, but…sheesh." With a shake of her head, Rosie doubled up. "Ow, bloody hell."

"All right now, dude. You just breathe, yeah?" Charlie knew the words, knew what to say. She breathed with her as if blowing out a candle, and Rosie shuddered and copied her.

That's good. I don't seem to be able to help verbally. Guess my job is hand-holder and hair-stroker. Amber used her other hand to trail up and down Rosie's arm again.

"Just try to relax." Charlie nearly toppled forward when Rosie put a load of her weight on her. "Yikes, you pleb. I don't want a bath."

"Sor-ry."

Amber used her free hand to reach around and rub Rosie's back. *She liked that before. That can be another area of employment for me.* Circles were good, as well as figures of eight. Amber caught Rosie's gaze at one point and they exchanged a tiny smile.

A few more contractions. The minute hand hit twelve, along with the hour hand, and Amber kissed Rosie's cheek. "It's tomorrow."

"Dad won't be pleased. Day of rest and all that." Charlie had a wet front and even wetter jeans.

"Yeah. Oh!" Rosie bent over again, hands slipping from theirs and to the side of the pool. She swore and grunted and bore down.

Amber sat back to take it in.

The strength of Rosie was awe-inspiring. She was flushed from her brow to her bra, her huge belly half in the water, her skin stretched so tightly. The muscles in her arms were prominent, her tendons distended as she hung onto the pool side. Her knees were parted, hips wide where she held herself up.

"Amber, bra off." It was a bark but one of strain and discomfort.

Amber fumbled for a moment but got the sodden clasp undone. It stuck to Rosie's skin before Amber peeled it from her.

Rosie moved up close to Amber, cheek against her neck.

With one arm around her back, Amber kissed Rosie's forehead and started to hum nonsense tunes. Another contraction hit, along with some serious pushing which Rosie didn't seem to be able to control. Amber lowered her lips to Rosie's ear.

"Rock, rock, go to sleep,
Baby mine,
Oh, so sweet,
Baby mine."

She didn't even know where it came from. The "Lullaby" section of the songs they would perform at the choir concert seemed the perfect thing. *Something we've shared as well as something she's sung to me.*

Rosie snuggled against Amber's neck as her contraction faded. A few seconds later, she tensed once more.

"Bear down, lovely. Time to get some work done."

"Am…am I okay like this?" Rosie indicated her position on her knees.

"Whatever is comfortable. Do what your body asks."

"Right now…my body is asking for a holiday in the Bahamas."

Amber squeezed her fingers. "Want me to go online and order you some palm trees?"

Rosie's chuckle was strangled. A whine, then a groan rumbled through the water like a steamship.

Pushing commenced in earnest, with barely any rest between contractions. Rosie was a soldier, and Amber couldn't take her gaze off her. *I'm the body she clings to and the lullaby singer. She's the hero in this movie.*

"Ow, ow, ow, fucker."

Both midwives chuckled. Two pairs of hands reached towards Rosie, touching her and ready to hold her if she needed it. "Don't forget to breathe, lovely."

And Rosie pushed and pushed, water splashing around her, eyes squeezed shut, and face in a grimace.

Charlie held her elbow as well as Rosie's other hand, her eyes rounder than dinner plates.

Rosie cried out. "It's…it's…" She let go of Amber's hand to reach down. "I've…" Her wild gaze moved to Martha.

Martha sunk one hand beneath the water. She grinned. "I can just feel the top of baby's head. What a trouper."

"Tell me this is nearly over." Rosie sniffed and bore down once more.

"Nearly." Martha smoothed her shoulder.

With a sense of wonder stilling her brain, Amber could only hold on to Rosie and sing "Lullaby".

A long, low moan sounded.

Louise peered downwards. "Okay, slow breaths now and little pushes, okay?"

Rosie panted through pursed lips. Her whole body shook.

Something was visible below Rosie's round belly.

"Head's out. Well done, Rosie." Louise tucked some of Rosie's hair behind her ear.

Rosie clutched Amber and pressed her lips against Amber's neck sloppily. "Oh my God. This is insane."

Amber wasn't sure what to say. The feelings spinning around inside her made her giddy.

And she wanted to be the rock Rosie could lean against; feeling giddy was not in her job description.

"I love you." Rosie touched Amber's cheek.

"I love you too." They exchanged a quick glance before Rosie shifted to look at Charlie.

"And I love the shit out of you."

"Yeah, love you too, pleb." Despite her mocking tone, Charlie's eyes were wet. She looked about as light-headed as Amber felt.

Three more contractions, three more massive pushes from Rosie.

In fantastic warrior style, she reached down before the midwives could get there and caught up the pink bundle of curled-up perfection.

The baby was wrinkly and covered in strings of bloody sinew. Her eyes were closed, her little fists up to her chest.

Rosie reclined backwards and rested against the rim of the pool with a sigh. The water was misty, orangey brown. She held the baby against her chest, both hands protecting her with gentle strength.

There were a few heartbeats where no one spoke. Charlie crawled around the tub to kneel behind her. "I'm promoting you from pleb to knight of the round table; you're aware of that, right?"

Rosie swore, her voice like a breeze. She looked down at her silent baby girl before lifting one hand to wipe some of the crap from her tiny cheek. "Hey. Welcome K.B."

"Really?" Charlie lifted an eyebrow.

"I guess I get to tell people now. Her name is Sidney Michaela Tanner. Sid, this is your Auntie Charlie."

"Hey, kid."

"That's a beautiful name," Amber whispered.

Rosie's head shot up. Had she forgotten Amber was there? She beckoned Amber over. "Come meet each other."

Amber settled at Rosie's other side, one hand hanging over the pool edge. "Hi, Sidney."

"We're doing delayed cord cutting, aren't we, lovely?" Martha had a pack on a table with shiny circular scissors and a kidney-shaped basin.

"Yeah. Do I need to get out?"

"In a moment. I'll get some towels down for you."

Amber looked down at the miniature being in Rosie's arms. Sidney was cleaner than she had expected—she supposed the water from the pool meant babies came out less covered in gunk than they would if she'd been land-born. Sidney squirmed a bit but didn't cry. *I always thought babies cried when they were first in the world.* "Is she okay? She's very quiet."

"She's fine. She's still nice and warm in the water," Martha replied. "It's normal for newborns to not cry in a pool."

Another thing I've learned today.

"Cramps again." Rosie pushed her lips forward.

"All right. Wait for it to pass, then out we come."

Amber and Charlie helped Rosie stand, Sidney cuddled close to her chest, and they manoeuvred her onto the towels.

"Need to deliver the placenta outside the pool. Just in case something happens and we need you out quickly."

Amber was learning something new every nanosecond.

Lying back against a couple of waterproof pillows, Rosie smiled down at Sidney. She ran her fingers all over the pink body: legs, toes, back, arms, and head. A dark crop of hair dusted Sidney's crown.

Martha covered Sidney's lower body with a small towel.

Baby Sidney nestled between Rosie's distended breasts. She moved her head back and forward a little.

Rosie took both hands away, and there was bated breath as Sidney wriggled with clear determination. Several minutes passed. Rosie cupped a hand under Sidney's bottom and slid her towards a dark nipple. "Breast crawl going on right here."

Martha smiled. "Go, Sidney."

Amber gave her a confused look.

"Newborns crawl up to a nipple by themselves, if you give them time." Rosie's expression was all pride. She tensed, her face showing a series of strains, and something dark was in the kidney dish between her legs.

"Still pulsating, so we'll wait. No rush."

Amber guessed Martha meant the placenta. She tried not to think about it, which wasn't difficult when Sidney squirmed closer and closer to her goal. *Come on, perfect one, nearly there.* She held her breath.

Sidney finally inched close enough so when she turned her open mouth, Rosie's nipple touched her tongue. A lot more wriggling and searching, and she settled with her mouth closed around a large portion of Rosie's breast.

"Magic." There were a million other words to be used, but they wouldn't come to mind. Amber stroked Rosie's shoulder, wanting to touch her somewhere that wasn't too close to the baby. It was Rosie's first few moments with her daughter, and she shouldn't get in the way.

Charlie passed her palm over Sidney's back, then brushed her thin hair with a fingertip. "She's adorable, Rosie."

"Thanks." A few guttural sobs and a tear trickled down Rosie's face.

"Happy tears?" There was a note of jest in Charlie's tone.

"Definitely." She fake-smacked her sister. "I saw you crying too, so don't take the mickey."

"I'm not." Charlie wiped her mascara-smeared eyes. "I just can't believe my baby sister now has a baby too."

"The massive bump didn't give it away?" Rosie placed a hand over Amber's against her shoulder. "Hey. You can touch her too, if you like."

The overwhelming fear she would hurt Sidney made Amber hesitate. But she set her jaw, lifted a hand, and stroked Sidney's cheek.

Sidney turned towards her and let out a tiny squeak. Rosie's breast popped from between her lips.

"Rooting reflex," Rosie said. "She likes you."

"Good job."

Rosie's glittery gaze caught Amber's, and she slid her hand into Amber's too. "Thank you."

"For what?"

"For being here. You made a massive difference."

She wanted to say she hadn't done anything, that Rosie had been the hero of the hour. But her throat closed around a lump, and it was all she could do to contain her emotions.

"You're welcome." If Rosie thought she'd helped, then she had.

Chapter 33

Rosie woke from a snooze of unmeasured length. The sun had risen through the blinds next to her bed. *A date I will always remember—13th May.* Her right hand rested next to the bedside cot, similar to the one she had at home. She spent some time gazing at her daughter, marvelling at the pointy nose, the dark hair, both just like her own.

The space between her legs felt battered. After the initial wonder of lying on the floor with Sid, the placenta had been checked and she'd been helped into the wheelchair. All her stuff had been carried by various members of her posse to the maternity ward. Sid remained in her arms: precious cargo.

It was a bay of six, her bed right next to the window and away from the corridor beyond. There was one other mother in the far corner. They'd exchanged waves when they'd arrived.

Charlie had stayed an hour, then gone home for some sleep. She'd promised to bring Chelsea and Tom to visit when Rosie was ready.

Rosie's heart had been so full; she hoped the hug she'd given her sister conveyed at least some of her appreciation.

The curled-up form in the chair next to her slept soundly, although Rosie couldn't imagine she was comfortable. Rosie's heart overflowed almost as Amber's ribs expanded and fell, her dark eyelashes brushing her pale cheek. She'd kicked off her shiny shoes, and the black cotton that covered her legs was still darker in patches where she'd been splashed.

I had such a good birth experience. Some of that was due to Amber being there—she was my rock yet again. Little things stuck in Rosie's mind: the way

Amber had held her when she'd pushed, the way she'd rubbed oil into her skin, the way she'd stayed close. Amber had just *been* there.

Attention back on Sid, Rosie passed her hand over the onesie, too big so far but she'd grow into it. Sid weighed seven pounds exactly. Six days late and a twenty-two hour labour, at least from her first real contraction. No complications. Baby was fine. Her initial latch had been like a dream; Sid had made her own way. An hour later, at around three, she'd had her first proper feed.

A glance at her phone told Rosie it was nearly six. She struggled to sit before leaning over to gather Sid to her.

Sid's face scrunched for a minute before she let out a long cry.

Rosie's belly ached. She bopped Sid on her arm until she quietened, then poked her pinkie near Sid's mouth. "Shh. S'okay, baby."

Amber sat up with a jolt and rubbed her eyes. The minute she focused on Rosie, she smiled. "You're awake."

"We both are." Rosie removed her finger and stroked Sid's cheek, giggling when Sid turned towards her, lips parted. "Oh, okay. I'm just going to try feeding her."

"Want me to go?"

"No." No point beating around the bush, especially when she was about to get her boob out. Rosie pulled the front of her robe down and held Sid as she'd been shown in the breastfeeding class. She and Janet had mucked around, using the plastic baby dolls to act out scenes in a restaurant—what was one supposed to do during a lull in conversation?—but she'd taken a lot away from it. "Right then, Sid, my girl. Let's do this." *Tummy to tummy.* She pulled her robe out of the way bit more, wanting Sid to feel her skin.

Sid gazed up at Rosie.

"It looks really complicated." Amber pressed her cheek to the back of the chair.

"I've been told it'll start to feel more natural at some point. But yeah." Rosie repositioned so her nipple was closer to Sid's top lip. "I can see why some mums don't carry on." She poked Sid's lip a few times with her nipple. "Come on, then."

"How long do you intend to do it?"

Sid lifted her chin. She caught hold of Rosie's breast with her mouth and did a little sigh. Her jaw went up and down a few times, then she closed her eyes.

Result. That was so much easier than the first two times. "As long as I want to. Six months is recommended, but the World Health Organisation says two years. I'm just going to see how it goes."

"Does…" Amber pushed her mouth to one side. "Does it hurt?"

"No. Feels weird though." Rosie slowly took her hand from her breast to thread her fingers with Amber's. "Especially when all I've done with them so far is, you know, adult stuff."

Amber giggled, her gaze locked on Sid. "She's so cute."

"Take a picture, it'll last longer."

The joke made Amber chuckle again. "I actually could. I have my camera."

"You do? Well get it out!" Rosie bit her bottom lip as Sid decided the loud noise was not compatible with breakfast. Her hand splayed against Rosie's breast, and an indignant look seeped into her eyes.

"Really?"

"Really." Rosie relatched Sid before smiling up at Amber. "Got to get some of this documented. Rosie with her tits out in public. Definitely not a first, but a first sober."

Amber cocked an eyebrow. "See, who needs alcohol to have fun?"

"Neither of us, apparently." Rosie dropped the tease. *I want to thank her for being here, for what she's done for me, but I don't know which words to use.*

Amber grabbed her handbag. Once her camera was out, she glanced down the bay. "Hope this is okay."

"You have my consent. Just don't point it at any of the midwives."

"I won't." A whirr sounded as Amber turned the thing on, then she twiddled a few things. After lifting it to her eye, she took a couple of quick shots. "I'll call that one *Mum and Daughter: Breakfast*."

"Make sure to mention my boobs in your speech when you win all those awards."

"Will do." Amber moved in, took a few close-ups of Sid. "She's *just* so cute."

"As you keep saying." The tugging to Rosie's breast lessened. It faded. She manoeuvred Sid to the other breast. "How are *you* feeling?"

"Me?" The camera away now, Amber sat back on the chair. She pushed her hands between her knees, shoulders up to her ears. "I'm good." A wide yawn suggested otherwise.

"I mean, like..." Rosie's mind was fuzzy, as if her thoughts moved through treacle. "You're the girlfriend of a single mum now."

"Is...is that all?"

"All? That's a very important job."

Amber stared at her feet. "I guess I thought, maybe, you'd want me to step up. Which would be absolutely terrifying, if I'm honest."

Rosie placed her hand on Amber's. "Just because Sid's here now doesn't mean things between us have to change." She caressed Amber's knuckles. "I did wonder whether I'd get this sudden urge to merge, want to get married or move in together or something." She shrugged. "But I don't feel any different about you. I still love you and I want to do the dating thing and build a relationship with you. Not cobble together something massive neither of us is ready for."

"That makes sense." Amber nodded once. "Good plan."

"Not the original one, but, hey, I'm adaptable."

Amber shifted close, then stroked Sid's back, her hip, her shoulder.

Sid relaxed from feeding, her mouth closed now.

Amber ran her fingertip over Sid's fine hair. "Me too."

"Want a cuddle? With Sid, I mean?"

A tentative nod, followed by a shy smile.

Rosie pushed her feet out of bed before sitting sideways with them on the floor. She relinquished her precious load into Amber's arms.

A single tear slipped down Amber's cheek as she held the baby.

After swiping it away, Rosie pressed her lips to Amber's forehead. "We're a weird one, but I reckon we could be classed as a family."

Amber's eyelashes sparkled as she caught Rosie's gaze. "And Charlie and Chelsea and Tom and your parents..."

"And Jilly and Harry and Matthew and Nico and...what's her name, the horse?"

"Florence."

"That's her. One big family."

Amber's nose wrinkled. "You're a proper loon."

"I am *your* loon though."

Sid squirmed, and a hand star-fished in the air.

Amber tucked her fingertip into Sid's palm and Sid closed her fingers around it.

"See, you're Sid's loon too. She's made it official."

Amber let out a humungous sigh, then kissed Rosie's cheek.

Rosie leant down to kiss her, and, even though it was chaste, it meant more than any words could convey.

Chapter 34

In the end, Rosie chose to just listen at the concert rather than perform. Sid was a good baby—that was what her mum and Charlie told her; Rosie knew no different—but her arms felt empty without the tiny weight in them, and she didn't feel like relinquishing responsibility to her mum whilst she sang with the choir. *Plenty of time for that in years to come.*

She sat right at the back, with easy access to the exit if Sid decided today was the day she'd be not so good. Her mum and dad sat on either side, Charlie farther on with Tom and Chelsea.

The last four weeks had been lazy. She'd been looked after by Charlie and her mum, deliveries of cake, prepared meals and flavoured hot chocolate in abundance. She'd eaten a brie sandwich. She'd had a small glass of wine. Most of her day was spent on the sofa, cuddling her precious Sid with some TV, some music, some silence.

Amber had popped round most evenings. She'd turned up on Tuesday evening and proclaimed it hadn't been a problem to get time off. They'd chilled out, chatted, snoozed. Amber had stayed overnight a few times.

Rosie had been worried; she didn't want Amber to have broken sleep. When Sid had woken them both, Amber's sleepy smile had settled Rosie's nerves. The way she gazed at them both when Sid fed, the half darkness seeping grey over them all made the experience all the more special.

The Colston Hall was packed. The lights on the audience dimmed. First, the orchestra took their seats. Rosie recognised a few of the players from her earlier years—being in orchestras and string groups meant she knew a lot of the professional musicians as well as the instrumental teachers.

She caught sight of someone she'd sat next to in an orchestra in university and felt a burst of warmth and familiarity when she noticed she still played the same violin.

Tuning commenced: oboe, the rest.

Sid stirred, thwacked out a hand which hit Rosie's sternum. *Don't worry, baby. It's going to get noisy but if you fuss, I'll take you out, okay?* Rosie made her usual shushing noises and bounced Sid in her sling.

The choir entered in a practised way, and Amber blinked out into the audience. Hayley stood beside her, looking pale but determined. Gareth puffed his chest, his apple cheeks red.

Next, Enid clopped in, her black and red outfit immaculate. She stood before the orchestra and nodded to the leader, who nodded back. She held up the baton, reserved for important performances. Rosie imagined her smiling at the choir as always.

It was odd being on the other side of it all. Rosie was so used to being the one Enid relied upon. Soloist, veteran choir attendee, and occasional accompanist stand-in if their regular was off. But tonight she was simply there to enjoy the music.

She watched individual singers throughout the pieces. Hayley gave it her all during the fourth section, as did Gareth during the fifth. The look on Amber's face during the whole thing was enraptured and enrapturing.

Rosie sang along to "Lullaby" so only Sid could hear. It had been their song, the three of them, for weeks now.

It was over far too soon. Applause rang through the hall, bigger and bolder than at any concert they had ever done before. Rosie struggled to clap, the sling getting in the way. She tapped her foot on the floor instead.

Sid slept on, unaware of anything other than the sound of Rosie's heartbeat against her cheek. *You're getting a pony* and *your own piano when you're old enough.*

After waiting for the majority of the patrons to leave, Rosie stood, one hand supporting Sid's back. She followed her parents into the foyer.

People milled around but gave her a wide berth when they saw the sling. Sid did her usual "I want milk" wiggle. Rosie sank into a comfy chair by the bar and pointed to the rest. "Take a pew. I'm just going to give this one her dinner."

It wasn't difficult to whip out a boob underneath the sling—that was what it was designed for. If anyone noticed, they didn't give her any odd looks. Not that Rosie gave a crap—people were strange creatures who cared more about their own comfort than her child's nutrition. She'd had a go at two people in Waitrose already; she would happily rip a hole in a third.

Nick got some drinks, and Chelsea entertained them with the voices she had allocated for Ginger and Tallulah. They, apparently, had conversations all the time, usually about boy guinea pigs, sometimes about girl ones.

A clattering of people made Rosie look up. Red-and-black-clad choir members milled around. Linda's hair was even taller than it had been at Christmas. There was a glance filled with derision from her, which was swiftly shielded by Kath's body as she moved out of the way of someone.

Rosie stayed seated with Sid suckling steadily until Amber stepped out from hugging Hayley and sidled over.

Red coated her lips and her lashes were especially black. She slid a hand around Rosie's shoulders and pressed a kiss to her forehead. "So, what did you think?"

She's way more confident these days. "I thought it was exemplary." Rosie wrapped an arm around Amber's back. "You were all brilliant."

"I agree." Jilly's voice filtered through until she joined them physically, flanked by Matthew and Harry. Nico, of course, was having a night in with his tennis ball.

Warmth shone from Harry. "Our little superstar."

Amber swirled little circles against Rosie's neck. She knelt down to Sid's level and pulled back the edge of the sling. "Hey, Siddy. Did you enjoy the concert?"

"She slept the whole time. Which means that, yes, she did enjoy it."

"No crying? Praise indeed!" Amber kissed Sid's head before leaving her to her meal. "And what a good girl."

"Such a good girl," Kath said.

An older woman came over, long hair streaked with grey. She wore a beautiful handmade cardigan covered in flowers. "Great show, Amber."

"Thanks." Amber held out a hand. "Fiona, everyone. Everyone, Fiona."

They all said hi. Fiona beamed down at the baby.

A tall man in an evening suit arrived in the vicinity with a glamorous woman on his arm. "Amber, my dear. How fabulous was that?"

"Oh, thank you. Um…" Amber's cheeks pinked. "This is Mr Harrison, the dentist I work for."

"Please, call me Pete. Lovely to meet you all." He winked at her, a grandfatherly air surrounding him. "See? I told you I'd get tickets."

"You did."

"And this is my gorgeous wife, Sally."

More handshakes, bows, and general small talk. Claire and Vincent arrived too, followed by yet more introductions.

Sid wriggled inside her sling and one pudgy hand popped out.

Chelsea, who had crouched down on Rosie's other side, stroked Sid's fingers. "Hello, Siddy. Cousin Chelsea is here; no need to fret."

"Fret? Where do you get these words from, monkey?" Rosie smothered a giggle.

Amber leaned against her, backside perched on the arm of the chair.

"Ginger says them. She's very posh."

"And Tallulah isn't?"

"Not so much."

Rosie undid a couple of the poppers on the sling and surreptitiously covered her modesty.

A coo rumbled through Chelsea. She couldn't resist a look into Sid's eyes—still baby-blue but bound to change at some point to Rosie's hazel—and chattering to her. In fact, most of the group seemed enthralled by the baby. Mr Harrison even made a pouty face at her.

She's such a charmer.

"Just like her mother." Amber nudged her.

Rosie hadn't realised she'd spoken. "Charmed *you*, didn't I?"

"After several months and at least two bumps in the road."

"Hmm." Rosie pulled Sid out of the sling and onto her shoulder, muslin already in place, and patted her back. "Don't you dare throw up on the nice chair, otherwise we shall demote you from 'little charmer' to 'baby who embarrasses herself in public.'"

"Like you did at Waitrose last week." Amber stroked Sid's cheek though, clearly in no rush to blame Sid for anything, ever.

Amber's friends said their goodbyes, although Jilly indicated she'd wait outside for Amber to give her a lift home. Claire and Vincent left too, with school in the morning. Then Charlie, Tom, and Chelsea.

"Oh, I must say before I forget." Kath leaned forward, hands clasped. "Amber, you're invited to Nick's birthday next week."

"Oh." Amber's smile was bright. "That's so kind. I'd love to come."

"We'll get your favourite drink in," Nick said with a wink. "And there'll be extra custard."

"Fantastic." Amber flushed but continued to smile.

"Dinner at five as usual."

Sid burped.

Rosie wiped her mouth. "Good girl."

"Good girl," Kath echoed.

Rosie held her upright, and Sid's feet brushed her knees. "All right, babe?"

With an expression softer than clouds, Amber knelt next to the chair and held Sid's hand. "Did you recognise your song? Did you like 'Lullaby'?"

Sid gurgled and spat a bubble of milk.

Quick as a whistle, Amber swiped it away with the muslin. "Good." She smiled at Rosie's parents. "I sing it to her when I stay over. She seems to like it."

"It's because *you* like it." Rosie bopped Sid on her lap. "She can tell, I think."

"Well, it was the first song you ever wrote for me."

"Kind of." Rosie lifted a shoulder. "Sort of."

"Definitely." Amber's thumb smoothed back and forth on Rosie's knee. They moved closer for a kiss.

Sid squealed at not being the centre of attention.

Laughing, Rosie cradled her close. "Drama queen, aren't you?"

"Nothing like her mother."

Rosie glared, with a wide mouth, at her dad. "Excuse me?"

"Grade One exam, she stomped in with her quarter-sized violin and pigtails and demanded to know whether the examiner had their Grade One as well. How old were you, Rosie?"

"Six." Rosie's cheeks burned. "I think I scarred the woman for life."

Nick gestured as if to say "You see? " and went back to his whisky.

Amber giggled, but she was all eyes for Sid.

They're best mates already. Sid sleeps better when Amber stays over. Maybe it's the potential for double cuddles. Maybe it's the fact I'm happier when I'm with Amber. There's certainly more laughter in my house.

For now, things were just right. A little family unit tucked safely inside a larger extended family group. Rosie understood now what people meant when they said it took a village to raise a child. She was no longer on her own, and although it was far from her original plan, the place they had ended up, she didn't want it any other way.

She'd sailed across the waters and had reached the place she wanted to be. Becoming a mother had been the most storm-filled journey she'd ever travelled, but now she was on dry land. Life was good.

Amber had brought something into their lives Rosie hadn't bargained on. Nothing more would do. Amber was just right exactly as she was.

Other Books from Ylva Publishing

www.ylva-publishing.com

Hooked on You

Jenn Matthews

ISBN: 978-3-96324-133-8
Length: 281 pages (98,000 words)

Anna has it all – great kids, boyfriend, good teaching job. Except she's so bored. Perhaps a new hobby's in order? Something…crafty?

Divorced mother and veteran Ollie has been through the wars. To relax, she runs a quirky crochet class in her English craft shop. Enter one attractive, feisty new student. A shame she's straight.

A quirky lesbian romance about love never being quite where you expect.

Popcorn Love

KL Hughes

ISBN: 978-3-95533-265-5
Length: 347 pages (113,000 words)

Her love life lacking, wealthy fashion exec Elena Vega agrees to a string of blind dates set up by her best friend Vivian in exchange for Vivian finding a suitable babysitter for her son, Lucas. Free-spirited college student Allison Sawyer fits the bill perfectly.

Contract for Love
Alison Grey

ISBN: 978-3-96324-086-7
Length: 301 pages (97,000 words)

Sherry lives in a trailer park with her son, trying to make ends meet.

Madison's life couldn't be more different. Her only goals are partying and bedding women.

When her grandmother threatens to disinherit her, Madison has to find a way to prove that she's cleaned up her act.

After a chance encounter with Sherry, Madison comes up with a crazy idea: she wants Sherry to play her fake girlfriend.

Falling Hard
Jae

ISBN: 978-3-95533-829-9
Length: 346 pages (122,000 words)

Dr. Jordan Williams devotes her life to saving patients in the OR and pleasuring women in the bedroom.

Jordan's new neighbor, single mom Emma, is the polar opposite. Family and fidelity mean everything to her.

When Emma helps Jordan recover after a bad fall, they quickly grow closer.

But neither counted on falling hard—for each other.

About Jenn Matthews

Jenn Matthews lives in England's South West with her wife, dog, and cat. When not working full-time as a health-care assistant at a mental health rehab unit, she can be found avidly gardening, crocheting, writing, or visiting National Trust properties.

Inspired by life's lessons and experiences, Jenn is a passionate advocate of people on the fringe of society. She hopes to explore and represent other "invisible people" with her upcoming novels.

CONNECT WITH JENN MATTHEWS

Website: www.jennmatthews.com

E-Mail: jenn@jennmatthews.com

Sing for My Baby

ISBN: 978-3-96324-469-8

Available in e-book and paperback formats.

Published by Ylva Publishing, legal entity of Ylva Verlag, e.Kfr.

Ylva Verlag, e.Kfr.
Owner: Astrid Ohletz
Am Kirschgarten 2
65830 Kriftel
Germany

www.ylva-publishing.com

First edition: 2021

Credits
Edited by Miranda Miller and Sheena Billet
Cover Design and Print Layout by Streetlight Graphics

www.ingramcontent.com/pod-product-compliance
Ingram Content Group UK Ltd.
Pitfield, Milton Keynes, MK11 3LW, UK
UKHW041858190726
13854UKWH00002B/960